NO ACCIDENT

DAN WEBB

1

Howard Cummings looked in his rearview mirror and saw the black coupe pressing forward through a staggered caravan of drivers. The coupe was catching up.

What kind of jackass buys a sports car with an automatic transmission? Howard asked himself.

Now the coupe stood beside him at the traffic light.

The same kind of jackass who revs his engine at a stoplight.

It was a warm December day, and both drivers had their windows down. The coupe's churning motor was impossible to ignore, but Howard wouldn't be baited into a drag race. Howard wouldn't turn his head. After all, the driver had to know that Howard's car was faster. Probably just caught up to get a closer look.

The light turned green, and the coupe sped away. The driver's shaggy blond head emerged from the open window to shout at Howard, "See ya, pops."

The coupe roared off toward the traffic ahead. Its transmission did the driver's thinking for him, shifting too smoothly and too soon. Howard knew that chasing after the car would be immature, but Howard was only forty.

Up ahead, the coupe jumped from lane to lane like an injured beetle flinging itself across the dirt. Howard accelerated in pursuit.

Howard's ex-wife had complained ever since their first date that he was a dangerous driver. He was not. Behind the wheel, he was like a skier carving a path down a backcountry slope. His driving was just the opposite of the vengeful lurching in traffic that coarsened life in L.A. His driving was beautiful.

Howard hoped the driver of the coupe was getting a good look in his rearview mirror as Howard's low red roadster traced a smooth path forward through the scattered traffic. Howard drew closer until three cars in three lanes all driving the same speed blocked the way. Then, for one impossible moment, he crossed the double yellow line and faced the charge of oncoming traffic. Right there, on the coupe's left, Howard showed the kid how to downshift to pass someone.

Howard darted back to the right side of the street, only a foot or two ahead of the coupe's front bumper. An angry clamor of car horns rose up and then faded behind him.

In his rearview mirror, Howard spotted the coupe caught in a throng of cars whose timid drivers all reacted to Howard's progress by slowing to a crawl. Howard let his eyes linger there.

I hope you crash into an ice cream truck, he thought.

When his eyes returned to the road, there was no time to stop. The truck in front of him—a battered pickup carrying overfull bags of lawn cuttings—strained against its squealing brakes. Momentum carried the truck's rear wheels up and off the ground. From the perspective of Howard's low-slung sports car, the heaving back end of the truck was the mouth of a monster gaping wide to swallow him.

2

Alex Fogarty did the math in his head again. *Five first mortgages, five seconds. One house vacant* . . . Why did his mind turn this way when he was driving, or when he was bored or trying to fall asleep? *Five property tax bills due in February* . . . But he wouldn't be paying any insurance bills—screw that, he was upside down.

"Alex? Hello?"

Alex had forgotten about Zeke Andrews. "Sorry, daydreaming," Alex said. He glanced away from the freeway to give the reporter a sheepish smile. He'd been driving Zeke around all day, and they'd touched virtually every freeway in L.A. County, and Alex had run out of things to talk about.

At least his pickup truck was comfortable to drive. The truck was like his houses, Alex thought, an alluring, wasteful indulgence whose market value was now less than the debt he owed on it. Zeke didn't know all that; Alex kept his truck clean.

"Fraud," Zeke said emphatically. "This morning you told me it's everywhere."

"Insurance fraud *is* everywhere in L.A., if you know where to look," Alex said. "Most people don't."

"So I'm guessing you don't either," Zeke said with a mischievous twinkle in his eye. "After sitting in this pickup truck all day, all I've learned is that the life of an insurance investigator is pretty boring."

Alex thought that was ironic, because it was Zeke who proposed this ride-along, after Alex, one night over beers, retold stories of some of his more colorful investigations. Zeke was always looking for something interesting to write about for *The Los Angeles Chronicle.* Alex kept putting Zeke off—not every day as an investigator was interesting, and in truth maybe the beers had led Alex to exaggerate his past cases a little bit—but Zeke wouldn't hear it. Finally, Zeke went over Alex's head and pitched the idea to Alex's boss at Rampart Insurance, who loved it—"Free publicity," he told Alex, "and the story'll make us look good because Zeke's your friend, right?"

Right—the kind of friend who sells you out to your boss when you don't give him the answer he wants.

"You asked for this, remember?" It was too late in the afternoon, and the glare from the winter sun too bright, for Alex to try to hide his annoyance. "The best way to get war stories from an accident investigator is to *talk* to an accident investigator, not follow him around. Much as I love your company, Zeke." Zeke didn't react, so Alex pushed him a little more. "So you'll go halves-ies with me on gas for today, right?"

Zeke lifted his little notepad with metal rings around the top and threw it to his feet. "This isn't a joke for me, Alex. I should be off investigating corporate corruption. But *no, The Chronicle* can't afford shoe-leather journalism anymore, we can't piss off our advertisers. So you'd think it should be easy enough to find some two-bit insurance scam artists and write about them."

Zeke's small, wiry body was now crouched over his knees in despair. The sunlight coming through the windshield twinkled in the premature flecks of gray in Zeke's short, dark hair.

"I've told you plenty about the insurance business," Alex said. "You can make a story out of that, can't you?"

Zeke didn't respond. After an awkward period of silence, Alex said, "Got an interesting case this week. Remember that big accident right before Christmas? The one where a guy plowed into a gardening truck and van?" Alex knew he shouldn't talk to a reporter about an open case—even when the reporter was a friend, sort of—but he couldn't help himself. He felt somehow responsible for Zeke's melodramatic disappointment.

Zeke's eyes brightened. "An impromptu drag race, right?"

Alex nodded. "Eight dead."

"And let me guess, your company insured the guy who was driving like an idiot."

Again Alex nodded. Zeke took a handheld recorder from his jacket pocket and held it an inch in front of Alex's nose.

Alex recoiled. "Put that thing away."

Zeke cradled the recorder in his lap like an injured doll. "I just want to get the quotes right."

"I can't go on record about a pending case. This is background."

Zeke groaned as if physically pained. "The first hint of excitement all day, and you just tease me with it. Are you *trying* to make me miserable?"

"I'll go on the record when I can," Alex said.

"I really can't afford many days without a good story, you know?" Zeke's expression drooped a little, then he added, "Things are tough at *The Chronicle*."

Alex rolled his eyes. "I remember what it's like. Remember how much we complained as rookie reporters?"

"And we didn't know how good we had it," Zeke said. "Any job stinks when you're coming out of college. But believe me, the paper's not like it was when you were there." Then in a hushed voice he said, "The paper's losing money."

"I know it," Alex said. Everyone knew it. Alex felt even worse now that he had gotten Zeke excited again for nothing.

Their voices fell silent, and a rhythmic hum from the road took their place. This was a good stretch of freeway. There were grooves in the road and grooves in the tires, and the soothing sensation was like someone had amplified the sound of fingernails running sideways along corduroy. On bright afternoons like this, a good road made you sleepy.

"So what do you think caused that Christmas accident?" Zeke said.

It took Alex a moment to remember what they were talking about. When he did, he smirked and gave Zeke a long, sarcastic look before responding.

"You mean besides stupidity?"

Alex expected the little car in front of him to keep up with traffic. Instead, while Alex looked at Zeke, the car stopped short.

Zeke gasped, Alex hit the brakes, and they both braced for collision.

For an instant the face of Alex's last girlfriend flashed clearly in his mind. *Pamela*. Then his brother's face did. *Del*.

The next instant the crash came, with a loud clap and then a crumple. It sounded worse than it was—the airbags didn't even deploy in Alex's truck—and both vehicles pulled off to the shoulder under their own power. Once there, Alex and Zeke nodded to each other to confirm they weren't injured, then stepped out of the truck and onto the concrete shoulder of the freeway. Alex saw that his pickup, the larger vehicle, had done better in the contest, suffering just a shallow crease in the bumper with some damage to the chrome finish.

The other car was a domestic two-door hatchback, older than most models still on the road. It hadn't had much left to lose even before Alex's bumper collapsed its trunk space and turned the rear window into a mosaic of tiny glass gems. Zeke stood by the truck while Alex walked up toward the car. Dust and grit from the road swirled around his feet. The draft from five lanes of vehicles speeding by rocked the little car on its tires. When Alex reached the driver's door, the glare off the window made it hard to see inside. He saw only his own distorted reflection in the window—his image short instead of tall, wide instead of lean, with a hand cupped over his brow to help him see.

The occupants weren't making a move to exit the car—a bad sign. There were five of them inside, two in front and three in the back. Alex lifted the handle and opened the door.

"Are you all right?" Alex said. He spoke slowly and clearly to the driver, who responded with only a dazed look and then pulled himself up and out of the car. The front seat passenger also got out and ambled toward the back of the car, favoring one foot. A rolling chorus of pained groans came from the three in back.

"This guy looks hurt," Zeke called out, talking about the limping passenger.

Meanwhile, the driver leaned on his elbows against the roof of the car, with his head in his hands and his back to Alex.

"I don't think he speaks English," Zeke said. They were all young Hispanic men, and the driver was muttering something in Spanish.

Alex leaned over and asked the driver in fluent but accented Spanish if he was hurt. The driver looked back with some surprise, and replied that he didn't know. He asked to see Alex's insurance card. Alex nodded and walked back toward the truck.

"What did he say?" Zeke said.

Alex didn't reply. Instead he approached the passenger with the limp. The passenger had reached the back of the car, where he leaned against its crumpled rear end, holding his ailing right foot a few inches off the ground. Alex squatted by the man's feet. The man wore jeans and old sneakers. The driver came around to watch.

Alex asked the man if Alex could touch his ankle. The man nodded, and as Zeke and the driver looked on, Alex lifted the cuff of the man's jeans and put a thumb and forefinger on either side of the ankle. The man winced. "Let me help you," Alex told him in Spanish.

The man smiled weakly, and Alex lifted him under the shoulder and hoisted him upright so that he was standing on one foot. Alex was taller than the man and was able to lift him without straining. "Just a moment, I have something that will help you," Alex said, and the man thanked him.

At that point, Alex turned as if to walk toward his truck. Under his breath, he said to Zeke, "You ready for a little excitement?" Zeke's expression showed confusion. *No matter.* Alex spun back around toward the man with the limp and with both hands pushed him squarely in the chest.

"What the hell are you doing!" Zeke said.

The man was as shocked as Zeke. He backpedaled with both feet until he regained his balance, then crouched like a wrestler, ready to defend himself.

"How's the foot?" Alex said quietly.

The man shot a glance toward his feet, then lifted one of them off the ground.

"See that, Zeke? My touch can heal the sick."

Zeke laughed. Alex turned toward the driver of the car. "Who do you work for?" Alex said, and proposed a few names.

The driver shifted his attention to Zeke and pointed toward the three men in the back seat. "The guys in there are really hurt," he said in English.

"I doubt that," Alex said. "I'm an insurance investigator."

The driver looked at Alex and then at Zeke, who now stood with his arms folded over his chest. In a flash, the driver covered the distance back to his car, hopped into the driver's seat, shut the door and drove away. A muffler knocked loose by the accident scraped and bounced on the concrete like a can trailing from a car of newlyweds.

The man left behind, the limper, shook his fist at the receding car and called out, "José! Hijo de puta!"

"How'd you know?" Zeke asked Alex. "I thought we were screwed."

"People don't often sprain an ankle in a fender bender," Alex said. "And when they do, the sprain doesn't travel from one leg to the other like I saw it do with this guy." Alex then turned to the man who was left behind. "What's your name?" Alex asked him in Spanish.

"Juan," he said.

"I'm Alex. You're new at this, aren't you?"

"First day."

"How much is he paying you?"

"He said he would pay me fifty dollars, but there's no chance I'll get that now."

"What is he saying?" Zeke asked.

"Fifty dollars," Alex said to Zeke. "This guy's playing stunt driver for fifty bucks."

"You mean this was all planned?" Zeke said.

"Look," Alex said to Juan, "we'll give you a ride home, and if you tell me some more about your friend José, I'll give you your fifty dollars."

Juan agreed, and they filed into the cabin of Alex's truck, with Juan in the middle. The wide bench seat now felt like a tight fit—the air was cool outside, but they had all been sweating.

"Seatbelts, everyone," Alex said.

3

Walking into a law office often made Luke Hubbard wonder why he had never practiced law. The lobby at the offices of Powers, Torres & Schwartz LLP, the fashionable Century City address, the commanding views of Los Angeles and the Pacific Ocean, the plush furniture that had outlasted multiple recessions—on visits to lawyers, perks like these made Luke wonder why he hadn't chosen a more stable life, a life swaddled in the comfort of regularly tallied fees and steady progress, instead of one driven by risk and consequences.

Then he remembered why: the people in a law office. Exhibit A was the secretary in the conservative suit who escorted him to the office of Leon Schwartz. She looked like somebody's least favorite aunt—stout and middle aged with joyless eyes.

Watching the woman's slouched walk, Luke straightened his own posture in reaction, as if he could will her to do the same. *Projecting success leads to success*, Luke thought. He was a tall, trim man in a fashionable, well tailored suit. His thick dark hair was sprinkled with gray at the temples. The image of success. And the reality.

Leon Schwartz's corner office was large, cool and dark. The blinds were raised, but even with windows along two sides of the room, there was no direct sunlight at this time of day. Schwartz was a small man with a lined face and gray hair that had once been dark.

Luke found his host curled over papers strewn across his desk, scratching at them with a dull pencil. Half of Schwartz's face was illuminated by an incandescent desk lamp that shone down on him and his work. *Just shoot me if I'm still working at his age*, Luke thought. The lawyer might have continued that way all morning had his secretary not quietly cleared her throat and reminded him that it was time for Mr. Hubbard's initial consultation.

Schwartz smiled amiably. "Mr. Hubbard . . . of course." The diminutive lawyer hopped off his chair and stepped around to the side of his large desk, where Luke met him to shake hands. Schwartz's charcoal pinstripe suit with matching vest fit the sober reputation of the firm he helped found, a firm whose lobby Luke had found nearly bare of holiday decorations even though it was late in December.

Luke accepted his host's invitation to sit, but then Schwartz proceeded to deliver hushed instructions to his secretary about a pending deadline and an unnamed client. That annoyed Luke, so he stood up again and inspected the diplomas on the wall.

"Hey, a fellow lion," Luke said once they were alone. "I see you got your J.D. from Columbia."

"My LL.B.," Schwartz said. "You went to college there?"

"Law school," Luke said. "Never practiced. You a Columbia boy all the way through?"

The lawyer looked at Luke with warm brown eyes that didn't match his formidable reputation. "City College in those days."

They sat down in matching black leather chairs across a coffee table made of dark wood.

"So, a lion in winter," Schwartz said. He smiled at his own pun. "What brings you to my den?"

"I'm getting a divorce," Luke said. His announcement came without the customary level of distress.

"Go on." The lawyer's patient enunciation and even tone gave Luke the impression that his utterances, even when simple, were the product of judicious consideration. *Either that, or supreme boredom*, Luke thought. *Well, I'll get your attention, Schwartzie.*

Luke leaned deeply into the cushioned back of the chair and steepled his fingertips together. His blue eyes drifted toward the ceiling as he began his tale.

"Well, let's see . . . I'm the CEO of a Fortune 500 company—but you knew that," Luke said with a sideward glance. "And, after spending the past ten years pursuing discreet affairs, I've finally lost patience with the charade of marriage and started taking vacations with my mistress."

Luke paused, but the lawyer didn't offer any comment.

"And . . . I have vulnerabilities," Luke said. "I've built my career on what might appear to be—*appear* to be, Leon—questionable business practices. Oh, and I've cheated on my taxes more than those wacko separatists in Texas who print their own passports, but nobody knows about that."

Schwartz still offered no reaction.

"Not even my wife," Luke said. Schwartz remained stone-faced.

"Except now for you, of course," Luke said quietly.

Finally the lawyer spoke. "That's a memorable litany of horrors."

Luke nodded. His shoulders drooped. "It's been a burden for a while."

"It sounds like you've recited it before," Schwartz said, and Luke shrugged his shoulders half-heartedly.

Schwartz wheezed quietly and then chortled into his vest as if snickering at a private joke. Luke leaned forward with earnest anticipation.

"Consultation, my ass," Schwartz said finally. "Stop wasting my time."

Luke sat up straight. "I'm not here to be insulted."

"Neither am I, and I see exactly what you're doing," Schwartz said. He spoke now in a tone of indifferent observation. He rose and returned unhurriedly to his desk.

"Don't tell me you actually plan to hire me," Schwartz said. "It's clear that you've come here only to unload your secrets on me and disqualify me from representing your wife, so that she'll be forced to hire a less able lawyer. Yes?"

Luke stuttered a little but couldn't spit out any intelligible words.

"Fortunately for me," Schwartz continued, "I'm too old and too rich to care about sucking up to you, or about chasing this shitty piece of business, so let's just stop wasting each other's time. You can show yourself out."

With that, Schwartz calmly sat down and returned his attention to his papers.

After a moment, Luke stood up sharply and clapped his palms together. "All right, you got me," he said. Then he sat down sideways on the lawyer's sturdy desk, interrupting his work.

"You're smart, all right," Luke said, languidly wagging a finger at his host. Luke picked up a desktop family portrait and looked at it. "You know, you're the first lawyer I've seen today who didn't decorate his office with pictures of celebrities—golfing with Dan Aykroyd, that kind of crap."

Schwartz angled his head up and gazed patiently at Luke, perturbed but not distressed by his visitor's continued musky closeness.

"What you're doing here is despicable and childish," Schwartz said, "but unless you plan to go through this routine with every good divorce lawyer in Los Angeles, this game of yours won't do you any good."

Luke spread his lips across his teeth in a gesture that wasn't quite a smile. "It's funny," he said, "everyone said you were the best, but I didn't believe it because I never see you on TV."

"The two facts are intimately connected," Schwartz said.

"How's that?"

Schwartz led his guest to the door with a light touch on his jacket sleeve. "When you finally choose a lawyer," he said, "choose one who understands his role."

"Good advice. How much will it cost me?"

"It's common sense. And I don't charge people who aren't my clients."

A moment later, Luke found a long hallway ahead of him and Schwartz's office door shut behind him. This was not how people treated Luke Hubbard. Luke pivoted and jutted a grinning face back inside Schwartz's office. "Almost forgot," he said with perky glee, "Merry Christmas."

Luke reached the elevator as the doors were closing on a descending car. Another man who was leaving at the same time held the doors open, assuming that Luke meant to go down, but Luke dismissed him with a smile and a wave. Once the doors closed again, Luke pressed the button to go up.

He got a warmer reception than Schwartz had given him three floors up at Hanson Stackhouse & Hanson. The receptionist, a babe in a Santa hat, immediately greeted him as Mr. Hubbard, and Luke gamely accepted the miniature candy cane she offered. He soon learned that she was separated from her husband and that Joe Hanson could see him right away, even though Luke was a few minutes early for his initial consultation.

4

Some marketing manager years ago, undoubtedly one whose spouse was still living, had convinced the president of Rampart Insurance that his investigators should bring flowers to widows to improve customer relations. If the company ever studied the effect of this practice on policy renewals by widows, Alex wasn't aware of it.

Today, Alex would be bestowing Rampart's hospitality on Roberta Cummings, widow of Howard, the middle-aged drag racer.

Alex disliked interviewing widows. They never were happy to see him, they never had any useful information, and there was nothing for him to say to cheer them up. Plus, visiting a policyholder meant Alex had to put on a jacket and slacks, rather than the blue jeans he typically wore when he was on investigations away from the office. But Alex didn't write the corporate policies, and the people who did write them didn't like being told that they were wrong. Alex would think about that every time he felt the urge to sound off about pointless procedures in the employee handbook. Then he would think about how he might manage unemployment. Those thoughts always managed to propel him to the next widow's front door.

In any event, the drive west from Rampart's downtown offices to the Cummings home gave Alex an opportunity to check in on a couple of his properties and mow the lawns. Alex liked that about his job, the freedom away from the office. Some days he carried a surfboard in his truck, just in case.

Alex mowed the lawns weekly to keep his renters happy and to keep his one vacant house attractive to potential renters, but five lawns were too many to mow. And five houses were too many to own, at least for Alex. His idea had been to sell the houses quickly, double his investment and find something more fun to do with his life. Why not? Everyone was doing it at the time, and the prospect of easy money had been tantalizing enough for Alex to follow the crowd.

Alex now admitted to himself that "everyone" didn't take house-flipping to the extreme that he had. Now, four years later, Alex's key chains still had five times as many keys as they should have, and his inheritance from his father was almost gone. The banks didn't care; they wouldn't even let a live person talk to Alex on the phone. As far as Alex could tell, the banks reserved all their human beings—if that was the right term—for trips around town trying to track down disfavored clients like Alex and collect money that the clients didn't have. That was a reason Alex welcomed assignments like this that took him away from the office—he liked being hard to find.

The Cummings residence was a small stucco house on L.A.'s west side. The grass in the little front yard was shabby and overgrown, and a strand of Christmas lights still framed the doorway. The property had been let go—probably since before Howard's death, from the look of the lawn. The widow herself was an overweight woman in her late thirties. She looked like she hadn't brushed her hair, and her face was red and swollen.

She took without comment the flowers Alex offered and distractedly invited him in. A young boy about two or three years old peeked tentatively at the stranger from behind his mother's legs.

The cramped living room housed a plush sofa that Alex was afraid he might sink into. Alex sat on the front edge of it, while Mrs. Cummings sat across from him on a tattered couch. The loquacious Cummings toddler was indifferent to the grown-ups' concerns and sat on the floor, running a toy car in figure eights around Alex's feet.

"I received this." Mrs. Cummings handed a paper to Alex. It was a summons for a lawsuit filed by the widows of the gardeners who died in the crash.

"We're aware of this lawsuit," Alex said. "Don't worry about this. As your insurance company, Rampart will defend the suit on your behalf and pay any judgment, up to the coverage limit."

She looked skeptical, and Alex added, "Usually the insurance money is all the plaintiffs want." Alex then explained that he had to ask her some questions, and she nodded her assent.

The interview started off as a monologue, with Alex reciting from memory an introduction that came from Rampart's handbook for investigators. The introduction was designed by industrial psychologists specifically to convey empathy, so the handbook forbid any deviations from it. Alex moved smoothly onto a set of scripted preliminary questions for the file, to which Mrs. Cummings simply nodded. Howard Cummings was indeed a forty-year-old engineer, he did have a five-year-old Dodge Viper. Alex didn't ask how she felt about him drag racing the car like a thrill-seeking teenager.

The air in the room was warm and close, and Alex sped up the pace. His mind drifted to the coming freeway rush hour. A sharp reply from Mrs. Cummings brought his attention back to room.

"No, I didn't know Howard to drive erratically. What are you getting at? You have his driving record, don't you?"

"I have to ask these questions for the file, I know they seem ridiculous. The police report said your husband was responsible for the accident. The report said he was weaving in and out of traffic."

"Yeah, he did drive fast," she said with a weary sigh. "He got in little drag races all the time. Drove me crazy. But drive erratically? No. He was always in control. No accidents. Why did he finally get in an accident after all these years?"

"Maybe he ran out of luck," Alex said. He thought it was a lame response, but the conversation was way off Rampart's script now anyway.

Mrs. Cummings shook her head emphatically. "But Howard was as careful as a surgeon with his car—I know that sounds like a contradiction. What I mean is, he checked the fluids and tire pressure before he drove to work each morning. He rotated and balanced his own tires."

"Really?"

She nodded. "He was an engineer. He loved that stuff. I think he loved that damn car more than us." She laughed through a cough. "Isn't it typical? Turn forty . . . dump your wife . . . buy a sports car?"

"I'm sorry. I didn't know."

Mrs. Cummings stared at her toddler playing on the floor. "He hadn't paid child support in three months, and here he is pouring money into that stupid car of his. So typical."

Alex couldn't tell whether she was waiting for him to respond, but the silence was awkward. Alex knew there were two sides to every story, but he had heard enough to decide that he didn't like the late Howard Cummings very much.

"My dad left when I was young, too," he said quietly. That wasn't in Rampart's script either.

"Howard didn't leave—I kicked his cheating ass out last spring," Mrs. Cummings said with a flash of anger, and Alex decided that he really didn't like Howard Cummings. He couldn't say that, though, and he saw that Mrs. Cummings had grown self-conscious after her outburst. At that point there was little more to say.

Back in his truck, Alex caught a glimpse of himself in the rearview mirror. His brown eyes were rimmed with red. He looked away from the mirror, and thought about Mrs. Cummings, left high and dry. He thought about Mrs. Cummings' son, who would never get to know his deadbeat dad.

He trotted back to house and knocked on the door. Mrs. Cummings was surprised to see him again and even more surprised by his offer, but assented to his request. Alex pulled the lawnmower down from his truck, wheeled it over to her lawn and pulled the cord to start the motor.

＊

Alex thought about her on the drive downtown—about Roberta Cummings. Alex knew what it felt like to have your lover rip your heart out. Pamela had seen to that, after accepting an engagement ring from Alex, after sending out friggin' wedding invitations to every second cousin and anyone they ever rode the school bus with.

Alex also knew what it was like to have your father leave you, to have your father die too soon. Alex hoped Mrs. Cummings' little boy was too young to remember as an adult all that he'd lost in the past year. The boy seemed well adjusted—little kids were amazing—but Mrs. Cummings looked like she was at her wits' end. She had to bear the burden of a painful past as well as an uncertain future.

Alex wondered if he could help Mrs. Cummings somehow. He thought about what she said about her ex-husband, *as careful as a surgeon with his car*. Maybe he could help her, Alex decided. If he could prove that Howard in fact wasn't responsible for the accident, then Mrs. Cummings might be able to get some money in legal damages from the insurance company of one of the other drivers. That would also save Rampart Insurance some money—a bonus for Alex's career. Most important, the blame for the accident would fall wherever it really belonged, and Alex could help make life for Mrs. Cummings and her boy a little less unfair. A win-win-win, in Alex's view.

Back at Rampart's offices that evening, Alex searched his cubicle for his file on the Cummings case. His "filing system" consisted of setting papers on his desk when he was temporarily finished with them. That made finding papers again difficult—especially difficult when he was really excited about a case. A bobblehead doll with a photo of his boss's face taped to it nodded mockingly at him. *Yes, Chip, I see you*, Alex thought.

When he finally found the Cummings file, he pushed the Chip bobblehead into a drawer and read through the file's scant contents—the police report, his own handwritten notes and some police photos.

The file was not encouraging. Alex didn't have the original photos of the accident scene. He had low-resolution color printouts of digital photographs taken by the detective who wrote the police report. Up close, the images dissolved into small, grainy squares of color—up close, they didn't look like anything. All Alex could make out was his imagined happy ending drifting away.

Alex had older cases still open that Chip Odom really wanted him to finish. Chip would not react positively to Alex making a priority of the Cummings case. Alex stood and rubbed his eyes. He imagined his supervisor chiding him in his slightly nasal voice. *Alex, I'd really like to clear your backlog. You think we could do that?*

"No, Chip, we can't."

"Excuse me?" The words came from the man in the next cubicle, a visitor from another office, who stood up to peer over the low wall. Alex realized with chagrin that he must have spoken aloud.

"I was . . . talking to someone else," Alex said. Alex's neighbor scanned the otherwise empty office, nodded suspiciously and sat back down.

Alex was prepared to give up on the Cummings case if the facts ultimately showed Howard was responsible, but he wouldn't give up on the case just to make Chip Odom's cushy life a little bit easier. He took the blurry photo printouts from his desk and taped them to the wall of his cubicle. If Howard Cummings was a "surgeon" with his ninety-thousand dollar sports car, then the car needed a better E.R. nurse, because the photos showed the hood of the car flattened nearly to two dimensions.

Still staring at the photos, Alex took three long steps backward into the hallway. He forced himself to relax and just look at them. Then he remembered something from the police report and raced back to his desk. He flipped through the report, scanning for a passage he had read minutes before. He found it, read it again, then looked again at one of the photos.

"Stupid bastard," he exclaimed.

"I *beg* your pardon." It was the man from the next cubicle again. He was standing again. Alex just gave him a sheepish shrug. Then Alex collected the contents of his file and picked up his car keys and jacket.

* * *

The police substation was a low, wide structure in the southwestern part of the city, in a mixed industrial and residential neighborhood close to the airport. Overhead electrical wires loped from tower to tower like wet yarn strung between assemblies from an erector set. It was a neighborhood that Alex, like most residents of the city, usually drove through on the way to someplace else.

Alex had driven all the way out here only because he wasn't a former cop. Without that connection, no policeman had a reason to do Alex any favors, and it was no surprise to Alex that his calls to Detective Albert Lutz had gone unreturned. An in-person appeal to Lutz was Alex's only choice.

From reading Lutz's report, Alex didn't start out with a favorable impression of the man. The report was scrupulously detailed in the maddening way with which Alex was well familiar. Time, place, the names of victims and witnesses, license plate numbers—who, what and when were all carefully recorded. But Lutz's answer to the one question that really mattered—*how* the crash happened—appeared anticlimactically, draped over a frame of classic bureau-cratic weasel words: "Evidence is consistent with rear-end chain collision of three cars initiated by Dodge Viper."

In other words, Lutz had no idea. And because Rampart had insured Howard Cummings, Lutz's lazy conclusion was going to cost Rampart money. It might cost Roberta Cummings money too. Hadn't Lutz looked at his own photographs?

Inside the police station, Alex approached a raised counter and spoke to the station desk officer with a carefully cultivated attitude of undemanding neediness.

"I'm an investigator with Rampart Insurance reviewing a recent collision in this precinct . . . I'm hoping you can direct me to the right person to talk to," Alex said. The desk officer, a large, balding man in his early forties, watched Alex impassively, his chin resting in his meaty palm. Sucking up to guys like this always left Alex feeling like he'd gone swimming in sewage.

"You may remember the accident—three cars, eight dead, right before Christmas? All over the news?"

The officer grunted quietly in assent. From the way the flesh of his neck overflowed his collar, Alex guessed he'd been behind a desk for a while. In exchange for boredom and gentle mockery from officers working in the field, guys like this got eight hours a day of petty authority—authority over who got prompt help, over who got their calls returned, over who got taken seri-ously. In conversations with dozens of desk officers, Alex had only rarely met a solicitous one. This one watched him as indifferently as the Emperor Nero at a Roman circus that had gone on too long.

"Anyway, I have a few quick questions on the investigation and—"

"What's the detective's name?"

"Lutz."

"Then he's the guy."

"Great. Would it be possible to—"

"He's out on a case."

"I see. Do you know when Detective Lutz's shift ends?"

The officer shrugged his shoulders. "Depends."

"Oh, I understand. I'll just wait for him here."

Alex waited a long time.

Finally seeing Lutz did little to improve Alex's opinion of him. He was a little guy, short and wide, with big, over-muscled shoulders, narrow, suspicious eyes and a dark mustache starting to go gray. Even in slacks and a blazer he looked more like a beat cop than a detective. Alex guessed he hadn't been a detective for long.

He caught Lutz on his way out the front door. Lutz agreed to talk but didn't disguise his eagerness to leave, which he expressed by continuing his brisk walk out of the station. Alex followed close at his heels on the way out, trying to get as many answers as he could before Lutz reached his car.

"It's all in the report," Lutz said. He looked straight ahead and stepped with short quick paces into the station parking lot.

"Yes, it's very comprehensive. I was just wondering—"

"Where are you from again?" Lutz stopped and scrutinized Alex's face in the orange light cast by the mercury streetlamps.

"Rampart Insurance."

"Let me guess, you insured the poor sucker in the sports car who slammed into those lawn guys."

"That's right, and I'm just trying to follow up on a few details."

"What details? You want to know what the asshole had for breakfast?"

"I was trying to figure out which car was the first to explode."

"What difference does it make? They're all dead."

"Well, it may make a difference in legal liability. Like if one of the cars exploded because it was designed poorly, or maybe it was carrying flammable materials or—"

"Look, we had no witnesses worth a shit and the guy in the sports car was driving like an ass. Just like a million other accidents in L.A." Lutz threw his hands up in exasperation. "There are limits to human knowledge," he said. Alex thought that was an oddly mannered phrase to come from the mouth of this modern-day Neanderthal, and reasoned that it must have started as one officer's witticism that got picked up as a tag line by the rest of the precinct. But the way Lutz said it, it wasn't so witty.

"With all that media attention, you didn't do any forensics?"

"Didn't you read the report? We ID'd the bodies and performed autopsies, we followed all the procedures." With that, Lutz stiffly strutted off, bouncing on his short legs. *Procedures are made for guys like this*, Alex thought. He overtook Lutz at a jog.

"Yes, of course, but there was one thing that didn't make sense for me," Alex said. He took a copy of one of the police photographs out of his back pocket and unfolded it for the detective.

"This photo is from your report. It shows the front end of the Viper after it was removed from the crash scene."

"If you say so," Lutz said.

"Here's where Viper collided with the gardening truck," Alex said. He pointed out a deep, ugly gash across the width of the Viper's hood, near the windshield.

"Yeah, so?"

"So it looks like the gardening truck landed on top of the Viper, like the force went downward. The whole front end of the Viper is flattened, like an empty box after someone sits on it."

"Fine, so maybe the truck lands on the Viper after it explodes."

"But if the Viper ran into the gardening truck to start the whole collision off, like your report said, you'd expect the front end of the Viper to be crumpled inward, like an accordion."

"So?"

"So, the only way this photo makes sense is if, first, the gardening truck hits the van ahead of it; second, the back end of the gardening truck flies up, maybe from the explosion, maybe from the driver slamming on the brakes. Finally, the Viper slides in under the truck, which lands on top of it, crushing the hood—like you see in the picture."

Alex heard the excitement growing in his voice as he explained his theory, but he couldn't help himself. Saying it out loud, Alex felt even more sure of his theory. He looked at Lutz and held his breath, waiting for the detective's reaction. Lutz knitted his brow as he thought about what Alex had said. He sputtered out the beginning of a response, then cut himself off and yelled at Alex. "Look, you want to depose me, go ahead and fucking depose me. Now get out of my face."

That was about the last response Alex expected. Lutz hurried away before Alex could follow up with another question. Lutz didn't look back.

Alex watched Lutz fumble with his keys trying to get into his car. Alex noted that the detective hadn't denied what Alex showed him—that it was physically impossible for Howard Cummings to have initiated the collision.

Was Lutz flustered because he knew he was incompetent? No one liked to be proved a fool. For a moment, Alex fantasized about a deposition of Lutz, about the little man sitting in an even littler chair and squirming under a lawyer's questions. If Rampart's lawyers walked through the evidence the way Alex just had, Alex knew that the truth would become obvious, and that Rampart would be collecting money from the insurers of the other cars, rather than having to pay money out to them. It wasn't often as an investigator that you were able to disprove a police report so decisively.

Then Alex asked himself who he was kidding. With Chip Odom in charge, the truth didn't matter. All that mattered was that litigation was expensive—a crapshoot, to use one of Chip's favorite words. Rampart would rush to pay a quick and easy settlement for the Cummings case, just like it always did.

Unless . . . Unless Alex could find evidence so clear that Chip would have to fight the case. And then Alex remembered another detail from the police report.

Back in his truck, Alex reread the report by the cabin light. His fuzzy recollection was correct: he found a familiar name among the victims—Jorge Ramirez. Alex once helped put away an insurance scam artist with the same name. Then Alex checked his sudden excitement. *Now I'm just grasping at straws,* he thought. There must be a thousand people in L.A. with that name. It had to be a coincidence.

Didn't it?

5

Alex left the police station and drove home. He still lived in the first house he had bought and, as long as he could, he would keep on living there. It was small, and the kitchen appliances hadn't been updated since the 1950s, but Alex didn't cook much anyway and the house was two short blocks from the shore, close enough to tote a surfboard.

Alex didn't pull into his driveway, though. He drove past his house, saw that his street looked quiet, then turned the corner and parked on the other side of the block. Exiting the truck with a file folder pinched under his arm, Alex approached the front gate to the house immediately behind his own. There Alex saw the owner of that house coming toward him along the sidewalk, with a little dog on a leash. So Alex waited at the gate and opened it for the man when he arrived.

"Evening, Scott," Alex said.

"After you," the man said.

Alex reached down to scratch the dog's head, and the dog licked Alex's hand. Alex passed through and held the gate open for Scott, who entered his home without looking back. For an uptight yuppie, Alex thought, Scott wasn't so bad.

Alex went around the side of Scott's house to the wooden fence at the rear of the back yard. There he peeked through a crack between the planks, looking for any sign of movement on his property.

Alex's house was dark. His yard was dark.

Alex hoisted himself onto a low, thick branch of his neighbor's lemon tree and, taking care not to drop his file, climbed over the fence and dropped down onto his own patch of dirt.

This was Alex's new routine, morning and night—all to ensure that his coming, his going and his staying in his house were as invisible as possible. Maybe his precautions were extreme, but if the bill collectors didn't know when Alex was home, they couldn't bother him there.

Alex entered his house through the back door. The curtains were drawn, and the inside was darker than the outside. Navigating by touch, Alex made his way to the front room. Alex's furniture looked better in the dark, as its various blemishes, including scratches in the upholstery left by a former owner's cat, weren't visible. "This house has the potential to be great," his fiancée used to say when trying to convince him to buy new furniture. *No, this house is great.*

Alex stood for a moment by his front door, straining to identify a sound he heard from the street outside. A kid skateboarding, he decided. Or just the rumble of the ocean.

Alex dropped into a chair, felt around a table top for his flashlight and opened the file folder he had brought from his truck. He pulled out the police report on the Cummings accident and read it by the focused, eye-watering glow of his flashlight. A man named Jorge Ramirez had died in the crash, the report said. Jorge had been a passenger in the van that was at the front of the collision. Alex assumed that meant Jorge was employed by the company that owned the van, an oil company called Liberty Industries.

The Jorge Ramirez that Alex used to know was a low-level insurance scam artist. The last time Alex saw him was several years before in a courtroom where Alex gave testimony that led to his conviction. Alex tried to imagine whether that Jorge Ramirez would have ever settled for a straight job at Liberty Industries. Maybe—after all, Jorge wasn't very successful as a criminal.

Alex's musings were interrupted by a sharp knock at his front door, five feet away from where he sat. The sound froze Alex in his chair. It wasn't the hesitating, respectful knock of a neighbor or a salesman. It was the assertive knock of someone who expected a response. Only a very determined bill collector would knock at a darkened house. The visitor knocked again.

"Dude, Alex, it's Del," a voice shouted. "Lemme in, bro."

Hearing his brother's voice filled Alex with both relief and annoyance. The two rarely spoke, due more to inertia than bad feelings. Del didn't pick up the phone unless he needed something, usually money, and for him to come all the way to Alex's house unannounced—well, Alex figured Del needed a lot this time. This time, Alex didn't have any money, and he knew he was about to get the full court press from baby brother.

Alex rushed to the door and opened it as wide as he dared.

"Come in," Alex said in a hoarse whisper.

"Dude, your porch light's burned out."

Alex grabbed a handful of Del's T-shirt and pulled him into the house. Del could be so dense—when he wanted to be.

"Whoa," Del said as Alex shut the door. Del set a skateboard against the wall and cast a look around the darkened interior. "Dude, it must be your circuit breaker," he said. "Where's your fuse box? I can fix it."

"*Dude*," Alex said, "the reason it's dark is because I keep the lights off." Alex tried not to sound impatient with his brother, but, to be fair, sitting at home in the dark wasn't something that people normally did by choice.

"Why'd you wanna do a thing like that?" Del said.

Alex ignored the question and instead asked, "How'd you know I was home?"

"I didn't think you were," Del said. "House is dark, truck's not here . . ." Del made his way to the kitchen where, as Alex could have predicted, he immediately opened the refrigerator and took out a beer. He left the refrigerator door open for some light, while he continued rambling. "But I'd skated all the way down here, y'know?, and it's too late to skate back, so I was gonna ask you for a ride when you got home, whenever *that* was, so I figured, what the hell, I'll just give a knock on the off chance you're in here napping on the couch."

Del wrapped a fist around the top of the beer bottle and wrenched off the cap, which wasn't designed to be screwed off, and then grinned at Alex. "So, it turns out I'm in luck. Sorry to wake you."

Alex joined his brother in the kitchen, where they gave each other an initial wary look. Del was the first to smile, a warm smile from childhood, and then Alex felt his own face light up. The two hugged each other tightly and then separated.

"I wasn't asleep," Alex said. "Why did you come all the way here if you didn't know I'd be home?"

Del stood up straight and took a swig from the bottle. "Maybe because you don't return my calls."

Alex hadn't returned Del's calls because he was afraid to hear what trouble Del had gotten himself into now—that, and Alex resented always being asked to bail out his brother and, of course, to do him a favor and not tell Mom.

Del kept his hair short, like Alex, and had a pronounced Adam's apple, like their father had. Del was the taller brother now, and looked even taller than that because he was thin. To Alex, it looked like Del had lost some weight—another sign he was gambling again.

When Alex didn't respond, Del said, "You got a jacket or something I can put on?"

"Check the closet," Alex said, and gestured toward the coat closet in his small living room. Del was wearing jeans and a T-shirt, despite the damp evening onshore breeze. He left the kitchen for the living room. There he picked up Alex's flashlight and began rummaging through the coat closet. He emerged holding a woman's jacket.

"That won't fit you," Alex said.

"Um, dude," Del said, "why do you still have her shit in your house?"

Alex shrugged. It was almost a year after their break up, and "her" still only meant Pamela. It was an unwelcome reminder that he hadn't had a relationship since her. Del's reproof was like having a neighbor rest his forearms on the back fence and casually ask when you were planning to do something with the growing pile of refuse in your yard. "I just haven't gotten around to cleaning out that closet," Alex said.

"Pro'bly 'cause it's too dark . . ." Del said. He replaced Pamela's jacket and put on an old jacket of Alex's, then returned to the kitchen and took another gulp from the beer bottle.

"Very funny," Alex said. He wished Del would get to the point instead of poking a stick at Alex's problems. Alex's problems weren't in the same league as Del's, no way. Not on the same planet. "Are we going to do this all night?"

"Do what?"

"Play 'who's on first' while I try to guess why you came here." Alex took a beer from the fridge and uncapped it with a bottle opener. The brothers stood an arm's length apart, leaning against opposite walls in the small kitchen.

Del smiled coyly, daring Alex not to care. "Why don't you just ask me?"

Alex shook his head. "Why did you come here, Del?"

Del smiled again, this time more self-consciously. "I guess you could say I've got trouble with some bill collectors," he said.

Del's words didn't come as a surprise, but they still hit Alex in his gut. "Jesus. Again?"

"Don't start with me, Alex. You think this is easy for me?"

"Apparently it's easy enough for you to do every year or so."

Del gave Alex a doe-eyed look full of genuine hurt. To his own private embarrassment, Alex found himself wondering cynically whether this was the same routine Del gave to his bookies. "That's not fair," Del said. "This time it actually isn't my fault."

"Wow. Where in the world do you get the money?"

"Look, I'm a good customer, so some people fronted me the cash. I had a system this time, but the NCAA has been a roller coaster this year, and even when the favorites win it's like they refuse to cover the spread—I mean, Stanford playing its second-stringers for almost the entire second half last week—that's not sportsmanship against a weaker opponent, it's like giving the middle finger to sports fans nationwide. So like, so much for my system—you still follow basketball, right?"

Alex ignored the question. "It's not a system, it's gambling."

"It's a fucking system, Alex"—he stopped himself and lowered his voice. The doe-eyed look was gone. Now Del's eyes showed the glassy intensity of a starved dog's. "It's a system, a proven system that I got from a guy who has made millions betting on sports. Millions, Alex. You don't chase the sexy long shot, you look for a lot of little inefficiencies and exploit them. See, you can use math to model basketball scores: there's a mean, and a variance. It's like a bell curve, right?" Del made the shape of a bell curve with his palms. "And the idea is you stay right in the hump of that bell curve, and the odds will work *for* you."

"But you didn't," Alex said.

Del swallowed a large mouthful of beer. "But I did, Alex. I did. But like I said, this season has just been crazy. Outside the mean."

Alex didn't want to hear any more. It was the same story Del had been telling for the past seven years, but with different words. It was like the Bach etudes Del used to play on the piano before he gave up music for basketball—Del's crises were all variations on a theme. "Del, I don't have any money."

Del narrowed his eyes in suspicion. "Bullshit. Since when?"

"Since the real estate market went south and one of my renters moved out. I'm just trying to keep my own head above water."

"Yeah, that's convenient."

Alex rolled his eyes. A secret part of Alex was relieved that poverty meant he didn't have to feel guilty about not helping Del—or, for that matter, feel guilty about *helping* him. "Sure, Del, I engineered a global recession just to spite you."

"You know what I mean," Del said, but Alex really didn't. As kids they could almost have passed for twins; Del was always tall for his age. In sports with the neighborhood boys it was like they could read each other's minds—Del always knew where to pass the ball, and Alex always knew Del would be right behind him. But their tacit bond had come apart over the years. Nowadays, Del seemed to hold Alex responsible for betrayals that Alex wasn't even aware of. Del took another mouthful of beer and swished it around in his cheeks like mouthwash as he looked up at the ceiling, thinking. Alex waited as Del swallowed the beer and continued.

"OK, so you're cash constrained right now. I get it. So here's what I'm thinking, bro: I invested with you on your last house, right? So all I want is to take my money out of it. I get my money back, and I sign over my interest in the house to you. The house'll be all yours."

Alex finally took a drink from his own bottle, a small sip. "That's a cool idea, *bro*," Alex said, "but it doesn't address the fact that I have no cash to buy you out with."

Del didn't seem to hear him. He just kept on repeating the rationale that he must have told himself a thousand times. "It's statistics, Alex. Reversion to the mean. College basketball scores have been out of whack all season, they've got to snap back into the pattern. All the math says so. All *logic* says so—"

"I don't have the cash, Del."

"I'll cut you in on the upside."

"Jesus, Del, I don't want to *invest* with you."

"Don't say it like I'm contagious. You could go back to the bank—"

Alex laughed loudly.

"—or ask Mom, or Uncle Hugh, or—"

Alex raised his voice. "I made a bad investment, Del, and it's hurting me as much as it is you, but that's something we both have to live with."

"Yeah, we do. But the bottom line is, I gave you money, I need it back now, and you say you can't give it to me. That seems like a problem."

Del gave Alex a hard look. Alex wasn't intimidated—just insulted that his own brother would try this *Godfather* crap on him. He reached out and grabbed Del's T-shirt. "Don't come in here and talk to me like one of the knee-cappers who you say are—"

Del slapped Alex's hand away. "You don't believe me?"

It took a lot of effort for Alex not to react in kind. "I never doubt your ability to get into trouble."

Alex had been a decent older brother, he thought, not unusually mean to Del when they were kids. Their mom blamed Del's troubles on their father, but Alex saw them as an overgrowth of Del's strengths. Del was always heedless and bold, willing to take great risks for a chance at a great reward, for a chance to distinguish himself among Alex and his older, stronger friends. As his older brother, Alex had encouraged Del's fire. On the basketball court, Del would always try to take the ball to the hoop, even when the result was slapstick failure. By the time Del reached college, his athletic skill was no laughing matter, and Alex was so proud of the little brother who had exceeded his own success in sports. But Del flamed out after a year and a half—he couldn't focus his energy. He had to be number one at everything—on the court, with girls, with money, which of course he didn't have, with drinking—and he wasn't number one. And then he wasn't on the team, and then he wasn't in school and then . . .

Del finished the beer in one long draught and set the bottle on the counter. He looked at Alex and shrugged.

"That's fair, I guess," Del said. "But I thought being family still meant something."

"I'm not Mom. So spare me the guilt trip."

Del's fingernails worked the label off his beer bottle, working inward from the edges. "Do you hate me that much?" he asked without looking up. "I mean, not returning my calls—fine, you're a busy guy, I can accept that. But all this cloak-and-dagger shit, pretending not to be home? It's like you're obsessed with giving me the room to fail."

No, Alex wanted to yell, *you're obsessed with yourself.* Instead, Alex took the bottle from Del and put it in the sink. "The so-called cloak-and-dagger shit has nothing to do with you."

Del cocked his head. "What, then?"

Alex sighed. "If you must know, I've got bill collectors of my own to worry about."

"You think bill collectors can't find you in the dark?"

"They can't find me if they don't know where I am, Del," Alex said. "I keep the house dark, and you didn't see my truck in the driveway because I park on another street."

"But the mailman still comes, right? What about your mail?" Del seemed genuinely interested in the logistical details.

"P.O. box," Alex said. He didn't enjoy being on the other end of an interrogation. "Nothing but junk mail comes to the house."

"And they never catch you coming out the door?" Del said.

Alex sighed again. "I come and go through the back yard."

"What do your neighbors think?"

"My neighbor is a very sensible young man who understands the effect that a foreclosure on *my* house would have on *his* property value." Alex took a beer from the fridge. "Plus, I walk his dog every morning."

Del laughed. "Dude, you're extreme," he said. Then he added, "But you've got good technique." *Great,* thought Alex. *Maybe next we can trade pointers on blackjack strategy.*

"How long you been doin' this?" Del asked.

"Too long."

"Does Mom know?"

Alex said nothing.

Alex thought he saw the hint of a smile on his brother's face. "I know—it's embarrassing," Del said.

This time Alex didn't try to hide his anger. "Don't patronize me, little brother. I've got my own problems, but y'see, I make sure they stay *my* problems."

"So not repaying my investment, that's keeping it all *your* problem?"

Alex answered him with a look.

"Aren't you even going to ask me how much I need?" Del said.

"Aren't you listening? It wouldn't make a difference."

"You know, your bill collectors go home at night, but the bill collectors I've got aren't going to go away."

"You'd know that better than I would."

Alex's voice was tired and flat. Del recognized the finality in it and clapped Alex on the shoulder and pretended to smile. "You know, the trip down here wasn't a total waste." He took another beer from the fridge and shoved it into the jacket pocket, then started walking toward the front door. Alex followed him. "Because I learned something," Del said.

"What's that?"

"That there's no difference between us. Till now I always thought it was that you're more responsible, more stable. But that's just what Mom and the others tell themselves, so they don't have to admit our generation is a total flop." Del opened the door. "Here you are sitting in the dark hoping your mistakes don't catch up to you." Del stomped a foot deftly on the back end of his skateboard, and it flew straight up to where his hand waited to catch the front axle. "You're just like me, Alex, you're just a little luckier, that's all."

"Is that right?"

"Just a little luckier. Thanks for the beer, by the way."

Del closed the front door behind him and, seconds later, Alex heard the chime of a bottle cap bouncing on the street, then the gritty treble buzz of skateboard wheels rolling over asphalt. Other people had trouble seeing past Del's bravado, but Alex could tell that Del was more desperate than other times he had gotten behind with his bookies. This time Del seemed . . . scared.

Alex took his nearly full bottle of beer back to his chair, where the Cummings file waited for him. He tried to read the police report again, but his heart wasn't in it. He kept thinking about what Del said, that they were both failures. If his little brother was trying to get a rise out of him, it was working. Alex was in denial. He knew that. About everything. It wasn't just the five houses and the bill collectors looking to bleed him dry. It was his priorities. Here he was, chasing foolish ideas about the Cummings crash, just like he'd chased the idea of easy riches in real estate. Both led to the same place. Anyway, who was he to think he could rescue Roberta Cummings from the damage her ex-husband's reckless driving had caused? She had never even asked him for help. What could he do for her? Let her live in his vacant house? That house was close to foreclosure—and if Roberta Cummings couldn't afford her own mortgage payments, she couldn't afford to pay rent to Alex.

Alex knew he needed to focus on keeping his boss happy and keeping his job, not wasting time in a cockeyed quest to save Roberta-freaking-Cummings. Shit, he couldn't even save his own brother.

6

No, the worst thing about riding the bus wasn't the delay, Brad Pitcher decided. The bus schedule in L.A. was an optimistic fiction, and whenever you really needed to be on time, that was the day it seemed a wheelchair boarded at every other stop. That was bad enough. So was the dirt, the noise, not finding a seat and, for that matter, actually finding a seat, especially when the seat was next to, say, a brooding homeless guy, or a teenage mother with a colicky baby, an active sex life and unlimited minutes on her cell phone.

No, for Brad the worst thing about riding the bus was the time he wasted on the bus. It was dead time. The bus was too crowded for paperwork, so riding the bus left Brad with lots of time and no distractions. That forced him to think, and today his thoughts turned to how his career had gone wrong.

He saw with clarity just *when* he had gone wrong. That would be last week, when the cantankerous federal judge downtown granted a motion that effectively killed Brad's biggest case, a nationwide class-action lawsuit that he brought alleging gender discrimination by a chain of home improvement stores. If the judge had ruled in his favor and certified the class of plaintiffs, the case—even if it settled—would have made Brad rich.

That would also be a year ago, when Brad decided this case had so much promise that he would work full time on it and let his busy criminal defense practice dwindle.

Oh, and that would also be a few months before that, when Cindy, sweet Cindy, came into his office almost in tears, humiliated by the way that a tool salesman talked down to her and then sold her a more expensive power drill than she needed, and had asked Brad, looking at him with big round eyes the color of milk chocolate, "Shouldn't the law put a stop to that?"

And today Brad remembered an even earlier step in his downward path—the day Walt Peters showed off his new 7 series BMW to everyone in the office. That was the day Brad decided that if Walt, who graduated from a law school that advertised on TV, could afford a 7 series, then Brad should be able to afford one as well. That was the day that Brad's entry-level 3 series ceased to be good enough.

In a sense, Brad mused, that last problem had solved itself—his 3 series had been repossessed a month ago.

Brad looked up to the front of the bus to see a very elderly woman searching her purse for change to pay the fare. Searching very slowly. And her hands shook.

He didn't have *time* for this. The bus was still a block away from his stop, but Brad exited anyway. Now, he was sure, the bus officially had no more Harvard Law graduates on board. With his BMW gone, it was like he was fifteen again, taking the bus and bumming rides from friends. The only thing that tempered Brad's humiliation at taking public transit was the fact that no one on the bus knew he was a lawyer. Lawyers didn't ride the bus. Nobody rode the bus in L.A.

Brad's office was in a small commercial building on the outskirts of downtown whose principal virtue was being within walking distance of the courts. Brad shared the space with Walt Peters and two other lawyers. They split the rent and Cindy's salary.

Brad entered the building lobby and ascended the central staircase to the second floor. Before opening the door marked "Law Office," he ran his fingers over his head to smooth down his curly red hair. Behind the door he found Cindy at her desk in the foyer, holding the telephone to her ear and patiently listening to a client vent his frustrations. Cindy was great at screening calls.

Brad picked up his mail from a tray on the other side of Cindy's desk. Cindy promised the person on the phone that she would pass along his message, then she hung up the phone. Before Brad could even say good morning, Walt swept out from his office and called out to Brad in his booming baritone.

"You look like you've been out jogging, Pitcher. Was your bus late again?"

Brad smiled playfully at Cindy as he responded. "If you're wearing a suit, they make you get out and push."

Brad hoped his little joke would make Cindy smile, but instead she gave him a reassuring look and said, "You'll get your car back." Pity—she viewed him as pitiful now. Brad had liked it better when Cindy smiled at him, bantered with him, batted her eyelashes at him once in a while, way back a month ago when he had a car.

"Save those nickels, Brad," Walt said loudly. "Rent's due in a week."

Brad smiled at Cindy—smiling now required exertion—then passed into his private office and closed the door. He had to be in court in an hour—a crappy drunk driving case, but it was a start on rebuilding his practice. Brad draped his jacket over the back of his ancient leather desk chair and rolled up his sleeves. He sat and tried to read the documents for the drunk driving case, but he couldn't concentrate.

Instead he thought about his father, smiling in a photograph that hung on the wall. He thought about the new Cadillac his father bought his mother for Christmas—*Jesus, I need a car*, he thought. His father, the firefighter, who never read past the sports page, who had a pension after twenty years. Not to mention the great benefits, his mother repeated like a mantra, the great benefits for firefighters.

He thought about the seedy indignity of criminal defense work—mostly the opposite of the lofty fantasies that led him from Harvard Law School to his first job in the public defender's office. Instead of freeing the innocent, he continually found himself shoulder-to-shoulder with swaggering, unashamed criminals, pounding the table to win them a few months of freedom out of a longer sentence. Was he too old to become a firefighter? No—but he was too smart.

He was also too smart to fall for the allure of the one big sexy case that would make him rich and famous. At least, he was too smart to fall for that a second time.

Cindy entered without knocking. This time, smiling at her felt like lifting a bucket of rocks with his cheek muscles . . . but he did it.

"A Miss Hubbard?" Cindy said. "She has a 10:30 consultation, remember?"

Brad had forgotten. "I'm preparing for court. Make an excuse and reschedule, OK?"

Cindy stole a backward glance toward the door and then leaned in toward Brad. "I think you should see her," she said in a hushed but urgent voice. "Walt is out there chatting her up right now, and it looks like she can pay her bills."

Brad heard that loud and clear. He quickly rolled down his sleeves and buttoned his cuffs. He pressed a palm along each sleeve to flatten out the wrinkles and noticed new stains on his tie—where had those come from? Better no tie at all than one that made him look like a slob. Brad groaned and tugged the tie out of its knot and off his neck with two strong pulls. He let it fall carelessly under his desk.

With great effort he imagined he was not at all worried about paying his rent, and then put on an open, confident smile in anticipation of his visitor.

* * *

"Let's not start off lying to each other," the woman said. The words set off a nervous twinge in Brad's chest. Her name was Sheila Hubbard, and her husband was divorcing her.

"I only meant that my experience includes a few divorce cases," Brad said. Based on thirty seconds' acquaintance, Brad couldn't see why any man would let her go. She was intense and haughty, but undeniably very pretty.

"Look, if you were any good I wouldn't be here," she said calmly. "My husband is cunning, and he's managed to get all the good divorce lawyers in the city conflicted out of representing me, so now I'm left with—"

"Our profession's emerging talents," Brad said.

"Yes," she said, surprised but not angry at the interruption. She was well dressed, in an expensive-looking dark jacket worn over a lighter sweater, and she sat up as straight in her chair as if she had been standing. A thin gold chain around her neck drew out the color in her blonde hair. Cindy was right—Sheila Hubbard looked like she could pay her bills.

"My dispiriting search led me to a lawyer who claims that you are 'pretty good'—those were his words. Are you 'pretty good,' Mr. Pitcher?"

"I'm better than that, trust me." Brad made a note to look at her shoes. Plenty of women owned one decent suit, but their shoes showed whether they were just playing dress up.

"Funny, your partner—Walt, I think his name is—suggested you were not the best choice."

"He's not my partner," Brad said. "We just share office space. He's not as bad as all that, though . . ." Brad spoke without really planning to, rambling. He knew he must sound like an idiot. Brad had danced over bullets from some of the toughest judges around, but for some reason this woman's intensity unsettled him.

Her blue eyes narrowed and she looked at him in silence for an increasingly uncomfortable few seconds. "Where did you go to law school?"

"Harvard?" Out of habit the name came out with an upward intonation, like it was a question.

She chuckled without embarrassment. "Are you sure?"

"The diploma's right there," he said quickly, and flung a hand toward the wall behind her. She grasped the arms of her chair and twisted her head around, trying in vain to make sense of the Latin lettering partially obscured by the coat rack. Brad carried on talking while she did so and leaned forward to try to catch a glimpse of her shoes. He couldn't see them, but her handbag looked like the real thing. His mind scrambled trying to come up with what to say.

"I have a pretty general practice—family law, criminal, tax—which actually is an advantage in a case of any complexity given the various . . . complexities that can arise, and I don't know if there are children involved, but I have experience in—"

She whipped her head back around. "The only child involved is Luke Hubbard, my husband of twenty years." She smiled when she said it. She had straight white teeth. She was distractingly pretty. Married twenty years—she didn't look that old.

"You mean, Luke Hubbard, the CEO of Liberty Industries?" Brad asked.

She ignored his question. "Mr. Pitcher, I'm not interested in your experience. As I said, the lawyers in this town with the experience to help me are not available. So as a threshold matter, what I'm looking for is someone who shows up on time and takes instruction well."

"Yes, ma'am."

"And who projects an acceptable image. Stand up."

He did, and she looked him over. She scanned his fleshy face like she would the cover of a magazine. He didn't smile. Her gaze fell to his open collar and then to his wrinkled white shirt. The shirt billowed from his hunched shoulders down to his belt, which collected the fabric in untidy pleats. Her eyes lingered for a moment at his pudgy belly, which had no jacket to hide behind. Her eyes went no farther. She didn't smile or nod or sigh.

"Put on your jacket," she said.

Eager to finish with the inspection, Brad took the jacket from the seat back, swept it like a cape over his shoulders and pushed both arms through the sleeves in one ungainly, improbable motion.

"What size is it?"

Brad's hasty move had bunched up his shirt sleeves inside the jacket, making it feel a size too small. He felt more ridiculous than ever. "Thirty-eight regular," he said loudly.

She gave him another quick, appraising glance. "You're a short, not a regular," she said. "Buy a new suit."

Brad ignored her criticism. Instead, he bit his cheek to stop his mouth from twitching into a smile. People didn't bark orders at lawyers they didn't plan to hire. *Call me short, call me fat, just pay my rate*, he thought.

"Clear your schedule for Thursday morning," she said. "I'm giving a press interview then and I'll want you there. I'll call you. Cut your hair and be sure to comb it."

She took her purse from the floor and turned as if to leave.

"Mrs. Hubbard, there's the matter of my retainer?" Brad said, again like it was a question.

"I'm going to pay you on contingency—ten percent of every dollar you get for me above my husband's initial offer."

"That's, um, a creative idea, but unfortunately contingency fees aren't allowed in divorce cases."

She sighed, clearly annoyed. "All right, boy scout, what's your retainer?"

Brad felt a rush of adrenaline. *Five thousand*, he thought. *No, ten—or twenty, or—remember the handbag!*

"Fifty thousand for a case of this magnitude," he said. For the first time, he spoke as evenly as if he was reading off a menu.

"That's ridiculous."

Brad put on a look of piteous disappointment. "Look, Mrs. Hubbard, I'd like to help you, but I'm very busy and—"

"Fine," she said. "You'll bill that much for me soon enough, anyway."

Brad smiled coolly back at her and said nothing.

"You want it today?" she asked with surprise.

"It's . . . customary at the beginning of an engagement," Brad said, then, thinking that too brusque, quickly added, "but you can pay when we meet on Thursday, too—really, it's no problem." He thought he saw her face redden, but if so, the moment passed as fast as it had come.

"What kind of car do you drive?" she asked.

Brad sputtered something about his car being in the shop again. She cut him off when he started bemoaning the general unreliability of British cars.

"Will it be in the shop on Thursday?"

"Yes," he said.

She opened her purse and pushed a hand forcefully into it. "Let it not be said that I omit the customary gestures of goodwill." She spoke more to the purse than to Brad. Finally she pulled out a car key, which she placed in his hand.

"Your, um . . . retainer . . . is parked in the filthy lot across the street. It's the black 7 series. You'll see it, there's only one."

She interrupted his expressions of gratitude. "Don't thank me. Thank my husband. He paid for it. And with your help he'll be paying for a lot more."

Brad closed his fingers around the key and felt better than he had in weeks.

7

A couple of days after Alex's visit to Detective Lutz, Zeke called Alex at work with some questions about the accident that he and Alex had gotten into together.

"So these guys we ran into," Zeke said, "you're saying they actually wanted to get hit?"

"That's the basic idea," Alex said. "They call it 'swoop and squat.' The crooks swoop in front of your car, then they squat and wait for you to hit them."

"When I cut somebody off, I want to make them mad. I don't want a broken neck."

"Neither do they. What they want is a minor fender bender—pull over to the side of the freeway, then everybody gets out and pretends to have whiplash. And usually a fender bender is what they get. Then, with the help of some crooked doctors and lawyers, they sue and try to score a quick settlement."

"So why don't you insurance people shut them down?"

Alex rolled his eyes. Zeke might as well have asked why Alex hadn't found a cure for cancer. "Man, we'd like to," Alex said. "And when we catch them cold we don't pay. Truth is, it's usually cheaper to settle than to defend a suit, even a bogus one."

"Doesn't that piss you off?"

"You have no idea."

"So it must be lucrative for the guys who do this," Zeke said.

Alex shook his head, though he knew Zeke couldn't see him. "It can be for those at the top, the ones who organize it. The poor schmucks we met—the ones who ride around in cars and pretend to get hurt—probably make less per accident than you spend each week on cigarettes."

"That doesn't sound like a great deal."

"No health insurance, either," Alex said dryly. "People get really hurt pulling these scams. Some die, even."

"I had no idea this sort of thing went on."

"Oh, yeah. It's a whole little industry."

Zeke was silent for a few moments. Alex's attention drifted back to the paperwork on his desk. When Zeke spoke again, it startled him.

"That accident over Christmas—the one you're investigating—you think it could have been one of these swoop and squat deals gone bad?"

Alex immediately became cautious. Sometimes Zeke wanted a story so bad, he would mistake his own conjectures for sourced facts. Alex didn't want Zeke to start printing his fantasies in the paper—especially if it came to light that Alex was his main source. And especially since Zeke's latest fantasy wasn't too different from Alex's evolving suspicion about the case—Alex still suspected that one of the employees who died in the van, Jorge Ramirez, might be an insurance scam artist that Alex once encountered. But until Alex could confirm his suspicion, he had to discourage Zeke from pursuing the fraud angle and mucking up Alex's own efforts. "No way," Alex said. "I've read the police report. The facts in the Christmas accident are much different."

"How's that? You had people loaded in a van, the van was at the front of the collision, just like the car full of guys in our accident. The difference from our accident is that people died."

Alex had to admit that he had noticed the same similarities after finding Jorge Ramirez among the names of the victims. But he wouldn't tell Zeke that. He would use this conversation to test his own speculation, as well as to throw Zeke off the scent.

"Zeke, you're letting your imagination run away from you. First of all, the van belonged to Liberty Industries, a big oil company—and the people who do these scams don't use company cars to do it, they buy or steal the cheapest piece of junk they can find."

"OK then, how about the other cars in the accident? Wasn't one of them a beat-up old pickup truck?"

"Sure," Alex said, "driven by some gardeners who had some equipment in the back—if they planned to fake an accident, why would they risk destroying their tools?" This was good, Alex thought. Talking through the fraud hypothesis made Alex see just how many problems it had, which was disappointing in a way, but definitely productive.

"Maybe it was a spur of the moment thing," Zeke said. "Maybe they saw the sports car racing around and decided to try to make a quick buck."

"Trust me, Zeke. I do this for a living."

"I'm not telling you how to do your job. I'm just saying there's a lot at stake here. What is it, eight people dead?"

"That's right." Alex knew what was at stake. He thought about Mrs. Cummings and the lawsuit she was facing from the families of the others who died.

"And the police report said the driver of the sports car was at fault," Zeke said. *Right again*, Alex thought. Remembering Detective Lutz's stubborn incuriosity made Alex angry. Zeke continued. "So this accident is a big liability for Rampart Insurance. But . . . if the accident was really caused by the van or the gardening truck, Rampart wouldn't have to pay, right?"

"Sure . . ." Alex said cautiously. *Damn straight*, he thought.

"So maybe the accident deserves a closer look."

Alex sighed. This is what Zeke always did—push and push until you got tired and gave in. But the facts—the police report, Howard Cummings' speeding—were against Mrs. Cummings. The fraud hypothesis was intriguing, but Alex was due back on Planet Earth. "Look, if I assumed that every single accident was fraud, my backlog of cases would be even longer than it already is. Speaking of which . . ."

Zeke took the hint and said a gruff goodbye, but Alex, despite his full inbox, kept thinking about their conversation. In a perfect world, Alex wouldn't need to prove fraud in order to help Mrs. Cummings and prove that Howard wasn't at fault in the accident. After all, the evidence from the accident scene photos contradicted the police report. But Rampart Insurance would have to go to court in order to prove that, and Alex's boss didn't have an appetite for the legal fees or uncertainty that would require. Add evidence of fraud, though, and even lazy Chip Odom would have to greenlight a legal fight.

Alex thought again about the name Jorge Ramirez. Alex had tried to forget about the coincidence, mostly because Alex had convinced himself he was a fool for imagining—for hoping—that the accident had ulterior causes. But that hope had been revived by Alex's conversation with Zeke.

Alex knew he was obsessing. He needed to stop. Jorge Ramirez was a common name. Alex needed to get back to the harder work of figuring out how to prove—to Chip Odom and then to a court—that Howard's Dodge Viper didn't cause the accident. Yet Alex knew he wouldn't be able to let go until he had proved that it was just a coincidence, and he knew a quick way to do so—a phone call to Liberty Industries and a little play acting.

Alex recalled that the Jorge Ramirez he knew was tight friends with another guy; they had staged accidents together, perjured themselves together and gone to prison together. They were an inseparable team—Jorge provided muscle, while the friend was small but wily. Neither had the talent to succeed on his own, and Alex knew they would likely stick together after prison. The Jorge Ramirez who died in the crash was an employee of Liberty Industries. If it was the same Jorge that Alex had known, then Jorge's friend probably worked at Liberty, too. Alex would put the coincidence to rest by calling Liberty. Liberty would confirm that the friend wasn't an employee, and that would be that.

Alex phoned the company and asked for the human resources department. He didn't expect H.R. to just tell him whether Jorge's friend worked there. Alex needed a cover story. While the receptionist connected his call, Alex conjured an image in his mind of his whiny, overweight ninth-grade science teacher and channeled the man's voice, a nasal drone that was at once grating and pathetic.

"Mm, good morning, my name is Don Pringle," Alex said to the woman who answered in H.R. "I'm a parole officer with the county and I'm calling to confirm your employment of one of my parolees."

"What's the name, sir?" The woman on the other end spoke too loudly, and Alex pulled the telephone back from his ear.

"Rigoberto Capablanca."

After a short interval in which Alex heard the woman humming to herself, she said flatly, "We have no employees by that name, sir."

Just as Alex expected. He couldn't help feeling disappointed, though. One little follow-up question couldn't hurt. "You got anyone at all by the name of Capablanca?"

Alex heard the tapping of keys on the other end of the phone. Then the woman said, "All we have is a Beto Capablanca."

Rigoberto had often gone by "Beto." Alex's heart leapt. "Um . . . yeah, that'll be him. And what was his job title?"

"Motor pool technician."

Alex ended the call and paced down the hallway with excitement. This could not be a coincidence. As anyone who had met the man would agree, there was only one Beto Capablanca.

* * *

Beto Capablanca rattled the dice between his palms in a quick, steady beat and threw them with a shout. The dice bounced off the soft wall of the craps table and tumbled to a stop with seven dots on top. Beto shouted in delight, and the gamblers around the table echoed his shout with cries of their own. Beto smiled at the congratulations they offered and took up the dice again.

His heart always beat faster in a new gambling club. It was more than just the money at stake. Would he get cheated? Robbed? Beat up? Would he win big? Beto never smoked marijuana when he went to a new club.

He liked this club. Everyone was classy and well dressed. It was a plush room in a basement under a Russian restaurant on a side street in West Hollywood. From the outside, you never would have guessed it was there, which was the point. He'd had some language difficulties with the big Russian who answered the door, and had wondered if he'd come to the right place.

He'd come to the right place. After some ups and downs, he was up. He was up big, and that was changing people's attitudes. The snooty Russian girl with the big boyfriend, the pretty one with the boob job at the other end of the long oval table—now she was smiling at him. He put an arm around the girl he had brought, Juanita was her name, and kissed her on the mouth. He told her to get him a drink.

His usual clubs were too crowded—too many people he knew. His bookie, his ex-girlfriend—they didn't know about his recent windfall from Jorge, and Beto aimed to keep it that way. But he couldn't just stay home, not when luck was running his way. His good luck had started when he got drunk and over-slept, and missed the job that Jorge had set up for them. If he had been more responsible and arrived on time that day, he would have been blown to bits with Jorge and the others in that accident. That's how Beto's luck ran. He was lucky when others weren't. Jorge and the other guys had been paid in advance—what a rookie operation—and, being dead, hadn't objected when Beto removed their fees from their lockers at work.

Now, with his winnings, Beto was sitting on a pile of chips worth thousands, and most of the gamblers were betting with him rather than against him. They put more money on the table as he kept hitting his numbers. It was a random crowd. Mostly Russians, a few Latinos and others. But they were all friends now. They were all winning with Papa Beto. He flashed a smile of straight white teeth at the pretty girl and rolled another seven. Beto pictured the girl without her tight dress on, with her long black hair draped over her shoulders. She looked beautiful.

It was his third winning seven in a row, and now the table was electric. Action at the other tables had slowed down as people stopped to watch. Two of the bulky gangsters who ran the place approached and peered sullenly over the shoulder of the croupier, a skinny young guy with bad teeth who was sweating at the temples. Beto smiled at the gangsters and winked at the pretty girl. The chatter around the table picked up as people debated strategy and directed the croupier to place their wagers. The girl's oafish boyfriend ostentatiously placed a large bet against Beto on the Don't Pass Line. Beto leaned over the table and wagged his finger like his mother used to do. "Don't do that," he said in Spanish. A couple of the Latinos laughed. The girl looked up at the boyfriend, but he stood in grim silence, ignoring her, glaring at Beto. Beto shook the dice and flamboyantly tossed them directly toward where the girl and her boyfriend stood at the other end of the table.

The dice bounced off the wall and came up showing four. The gamblers gasped. To keep the dice, and his winnings, Beto would have to roll a four again before he rolled a seven. He'd drunk too much whiskey to do the math, but he knew the odds were against him. Some gamblers placed hedging bets, and the dice were returned to Beto. His mind raced with the possibilities, and the stress knotted his stomach. He wished he had smoked some marijuana. He felt Juanita's hand at his elbow and he shook it away.

The next roll was a six. He was still alive. He pressed his hand against his shirt until he felt his medal of San Martín beneath it. Beto needed his help now. Beto cast the dice with gusto and with a shout.

A three and a four. The gamblers who had wagered for Beto to win cried out as if in pain. Beto didn't say anything, but his shoulders slumped.

The big guy at the other end of the table didn't say anything either. He didn't even smile. He took his chips, grabbed the girl by the arm and filed out of the club with a couple of his big friends. At the door, he looked back at Beto with undisguised hatred. When the man to Beto's left took the dice and cast them, it was a much quieter table that cheered him on.

Beto took a long swig of whiskey and fingered his meager stack of chips. All his winnings were gone. A couple hundred dollars was all he had left. But Juanita was still there. He pulled her by the waist up to the edge of the table and told her to watch his drink while he went to the can.

The bathroom was opposite the entrance to the club. Beto locked the door behind him and, without lifting the toilet seat, wearily emptied his bladder. There was a little window above the toilet that let out onto an alley, and Beto noted with dismay that it was getting light out. On top of this miserable night, now he had to go into work. Liberty Industries would fire him if he missed another day, which would have been fine if he'd kept all his winnings . . .

He thought again about the girl he'd been flirting with and this time felt nothing. She'd get a slap, maybe a broken tooth. And what the big boy held back from her, he and his friends would unload on Beto, whenever Beto finally stepped out of the club.

Beto zipped up his pants and stood with his hands on his hips. After gauging how far up the window was, he sighed, knocked the toilet lid down with one foot, stepped up onto the back of the toilet and lifted the sash. It would be tight, and his clothes would be ruined, but he would save himself some broken bones. Beto prayed for a little more luck as he hoisted his head and shoulders through the narrow window frame. He pulled his body through by wiggling from side to side on his belly like a salamander. The alley into which he emerged was blessedly empty. Beto stood up, looked left, then right, and ran.

Juanita would be all right. She could make a new friend. She was bad luck anyway.

8

Luke Hubbard hated earnings calls. As far as he was concerned, investors and analysts were ignorant sheep, and he would have preferred to ignore them. Let them read the annual report if they wanted to know how the company was doing.

But Luke's vision for Liberty Industries included quick growth. That meant continual capital infusions from investors. That meant that he had to pretend to care about what they wanted. And if what they wanted was a quarterly call to summarize results they could read for themselves, read from a script that the lawyers drafted as tightly as a church liturgy; and if his chief financial officer did most of the talking; and if follow-up questions from investors were strictly limited, then fine, he'd indulge them. It took an hour four times a year, and Luke could spend much of that time sending emails from his smartphone.

Luke took his smartphone and, with great effort, ignored the flashing red light that announced new email messages waiting for him. Instead, he opened an application called "Bird's Eye," and looked at a silent video feed of the interior of his wife's office at Liberty Industries. Crash Bailey had installed it overnight; Luke wouldn't have trusted anyone else for the job. The camera was working beautifully. Sheila wasn't there right now. That was annoying. Luke wanted to spy on her, to see her act out the frustration he was causing her. Maybe she was out at a long lunch, maybe a job interview—he could hope, anyway. Here they were, getting divorced, and she was still working away in Liberty's human resources department, with her soon-to-be ex-husband as her boss. Was she just a glutton for punishment? *Or does she stick around to keep an eye on me?* Luke wondered. That would be ironic, because here he was watching her, or at least watching her empty office.

"Welcome to the Liberty Industries Q4 earnings call . . ."

A woman's voice made Luke remember where he was. It was the call moderator delivering her dreary introduction. Her voice emerged from a speakerphone in the conference room where Luke sat with his CFO. Her voice was *un*sexy. Why weren't women sexy anymore? Luke thought about Petra, his mistress. He thought about her fishnet stockings and her long, strong legs. Then he felt a physical response and forced himself to stop thinking about that. He thought about revenue recognition instead.

His CFO waved at him to get his attention; Luke was up. Luke listlessly took a sheet of paper that had his lines and began reading in a sonorant baritone.

"This was a strong quarter to end a milestone year. Our alternative energy products are really starting to see traction, and we have a lot of exciting new clean tech ideas that we hope to bring to market within the next year. Meanwhile, our legacy fossil fuels segment led us to record revenues this year and continues to provide funds for further research and judicious acquisitions. Now I'll turn the call over to our CFO, Jim Branford, for a more detailed discussion of this quarter's financial results. Jim?"

God, Luke thought, *this call is so dull I'm even boring myself.* He couldn't help thinking of all the real work he could be doing if he weren't wasting time on this conference call. Another peek at the Sheila-cam showed she was still not at her desk. If Luke didn't already have other plans to make her life miserable, he would have fired her for that. He wanted to see her squirm. He wanted another misery fix, like when he'd had a secret microphone installed in her office—*thanks again, Crash*—and listened to the desperation in Sheila's voice as she called lawyer after lawyer all across Los Angeles, trying to find someone to represent her in the divorce. "What do you mean, you have a conflict?" she asked again and again, as curt and indignant as if she were snapping at a bellhop. Then the lawyer on the other end would say something like, "I can't give more details than that," and would offer his regrets and a recommendation for another lawyer she might try. But guess what? Luke had already visited the next lawyer, too, told the lawyer all his dirty laundry, and created yet another conflict. Luke loved remembering that. He couldn't wait to do battle with Sheila in court. He would bring the biggest guns of the L.A. bar, and she would bring . . . well, who knew what the hell she would bring, but it wouldn't be a fair fight.

Jim had finished his spiel for investors, and the moderator started into the queue of questions from analysts. For Jim's benefit, Luke pointed to his smartphone to indicate that he would be paying attention to his email rather than the questions. Jim nodded energetically: he would answer the investors' questions and not bother Luke unless necessary. Jim was in his forties, but still as enthusiastic and as eager to please as a puppy.

Luke turned to his email. The past ten years, it had felt like sending emails took up most of Luke's waking hours, and too many of the hours he should have been sleeping. And just when he finished answering one email, another two or three came in.

Luke thought of his smartphone like the world's tiniest newborn baby. Instead of crying it flashed a little red light, and it needed his hands on it constantly to give it peace. Sheila had never borne him a child, and now they were splitting up, so Luke's life basically consisted of his job, more of his job, his mistress and his smartphone. They would have to stand in for the nuclear family he was supposed to have at this stage of his life. Today, each email was more exasperating than the last: . . . *Blix needs our answer on the Corcola investment . . . an accounting clerk we fired in Peru called the compliance hotline, said the manager there is taking kickbacks . . . the supplier says the drill parts won't be ready . . .* He paid his people a lot of money. Couldn't they figure out some of this stuff on their own?

The first few questions from investors were anodyne requests for clarification about accounting details, asked by research analysts who all sounded about twenty-one years old. Right up Jim's alley.

"The next question is from Ray McLean at Vertigo Capital," the moderator announced in a robotic monotone. Luke's shoulders tensed, and he saw Jim waving to get his attention. Luke instantly forgot about his email inbox. Vertigo Capital was a notorious activist hedge fund. If they were nosing around on his earnings calls, the next step could be an approach to his board of directors. That could lead to meddling with his strategic plans or worse. *These cowboys just love to replace management teams*, Luke thought. He wondered what their play would be.

"Luke, can you provide some color around the impact on revenue of the insurance proceeds that Jim mentioned?"

"Well, they increased revenue, *Ray*," Luke said. Stupid question. And Luke resented that some asshole he had never met would address him by his first name, but such was the custom.

"Thanks," Ray said. "Just one follow-up."

Luke made a throat-slashing sign at Jim, but the questioner continued before Jim could react to cut off the questions.

"Can you tell us how recent distractions in the news have affected management's focus?"

What bullshit, Luke thought. "Management is *not* distracted."

With that, Luke stood up and walked out, leaving Jim to handle the rest of the call. He headed to the basement gym to burn off some steam.

Recent distractions—everyone on the call knew it was an oblique reference to Luke and Sheila's pending divorce. The couple was active on the philanthropic scene, and because of their wealth and glamour the local tabloids had decided that their personal problems were interesting. Luke didn't know this little shit Ray McLean, but he knew the type, all right—young, arrogant and richer than he deserved to be. Luke imagined Ray sitting in an office in Manhattan somewhere, grinning as he toyed with Luke on the earnings call, asking questions that seemed innocent but that were meant to send Luke a threatening message. *Two can play that little game*, Luke thought. He decided he would send Crash Bailey on a trip to New York with a message for Mr. Ray McLean. Crash was good at delivering messages.

In the gym, Luke looked again at his video feed of Sheila's office. Still gone. Luke wished she would stay gone. He started jogging on a treadmill. He imagined how good it would feel to fire her; he wouldn't even do it in person, she'd just show up to work one day and her electronic passcard wouldn't work anymore and an intern would meet her with a box full of her personal effects— but only half of them. *I'd love to get a video feed of that*, he thought.

Then he let go of his little fantasy—as if he could fire her in the middle of divorce proceedings without sparking a legal firestorm. *What will it take to get rid of that harpy?* Luke wondered.

He nearly stumbled off the treadmill when he saw his wife on television. She was standing among a swarm of bald children. Their drab scalps bobbed about her waist like a cluster of grounded party balloons. When Luke turned up the volume he heard her telling a reporter what a shame it was that her husband cancelled a grant he had pledged in their name to a local children's hospital.

You bitch, he thought. *We both agreed to rescind the gift, and now you throw the fucking cancer kids at me?*

The sensors on the treadmill handles showed his heart rate spiking. Luke forced himself to calm down. Sheila had some sort of scheme in mind. But what?

* * *

"No one here deserves to be here. No one deserves cancer."

The pretty young television reporter nodded attentively as Sheila Hubbard answered the question: where does your passion come from?

"Every time I look at these kids, I realize how blessed I am." Sheila said.

"How blessed we all are," the reporter said.

"Yes. That's why I got involved and joined the board."

The two women were walking side-by-side down a bright, tiled hall at the Children's Oncology Institute. The walls were adorned with large framed pieces of colorful juvenile art. In front of them a cameraman walked backward, filming them.

Sheila led the reporter down a side hall and pulled back a heavy sheet of plastic draping to reveal a large, unfinished chamber. Before entering they each pulled their hair back and donned orange plastic hardhats. Sheila's voice echoed off the concrete floor as she described the features that would be built there.

"The genomic diagnostic lab will go here," she said. She stretched her arms toward a dusty corner of the room partially enclosed by a drywall barrier. She moved on immediately. The heels of her shoes clicked loudly on the concrete floor and the reporter and the cameraman hustled to keep up. Sheila stopped in front of an array of upright wooden beams that framed a series of planned interior walls.

"These will be the private rooms," she said, and stepped through a future wall into a future room. She looked around and inhaled deeply, notwithstanding the dust. "We'll be done with crowding. There will be room for family. There will be privacy. We'll even have facilities for pets to stay overnight."

"Pets are very therapeutic," the reporter said.

Back in the children's playroom, the two women continued their conversation. Sheila's thick blonde hair showed no hint of having been matted under a hardhat minutes before. Children played on the floor at their feet.

"For children for whom life itself is . . . precarious," Sheila said, "this new wing will be something solid, something permanent."

"But it takes money," the reporter said.

"All worthwhile things do."

"Let's talk about that for a minute," the reporter said. "There's been some controversy around the fundraising for this new wing." Sheila nodded ruefully, and the reporter continued. "At the beginning of the fundraising campaign, you and your husband, a business executive who also sits on the hospital's board, made what the hospital called a 'signature gift,' and it was substantial—five million dollars. All to great fanfare. Then, a month ago, you quietly withdrew the gift. Why?"

Sheila wore a subdued smile as she listened to the reporter's long question, and she responded with pleasant equanimity. "My name was on the gift, Carla, but it wasn't my money, or my decision."

The reporter hurried in with a follow-up question. "People have speculated that the gift was announced simply to draw in other gifts, then withdrawn when the money wasn't needed. 'Priming the pump,' they've called it." The reporter stared intently at Sheila.

"I guess gossip wouldn't be gossip if it wasn't hurtful," Sheila said. "And besides, it's untrue the gift was withdrawn because it was no longer needed. We still need money to finish this project. People withdraw gifts all the time for reasons no more mysterious than simple selfishness."

"Is that why your husband withdrew the gift—selfishness?"

"As you know, my husband and I are separated, and I'm not going to speculate on his state of mind," Sheila said. Then she added, "but I think the facts speak for themselves."

Sheila looked out over the sunlit room with a knitted brow. "I came to this room a year ago. The room was full of children, just like it is now. Some of those children aren't here anymore." Sheila stared at something beyond the wall in front of her. "I told the children then that we would build a new wing so that Children's Oncology would be the leading center in the country for the research and treatment of cancers affecting children." Sheila turned and looked straight into the camera. "I have a long memory, and I'm going to keep my promise."

9

So Jorge Ramirez and Beto Capablanca had worked together at Liberty Industries. Alex didn't know exactly what scam Jorge Ramirez had been trying to pull, but he was certain that Jorge and Beto had not learned any lessons in prison. With Jorge dead, Alex wanted to speak to Beto, but Alex remembered that Beto was hard to find when he didn't want to be found. Alex also knew that Chip Odom, his boss, wouldn't be eager to devote resources to track Beto down solely on the basis of Alex's hunch.

Alex decided there was an easier way. He needed to speak with the auto insurer for Liberty Industries. If Alex could convince them that the gardening truck really caused the accident, or that Jorge Ramirez somehow caused it with a scam gone awry, they would have the right financial motivation to gather evidence to prove it. And if they did, Chip Odom would agree to a deeper investigation, and odds were that Rampart Insurance would avoid liability for the accident and Roberta Cummings would get a well needed financial benefit out of it.

Alex called his company's own claims department. Curiously, Liberty's insurer had not yet contacted Rampart about being reimbursed for the destruction of Liberty's van in the crash. Rampart's claims department didn't even know yet who Liberty's insurer was. When would they know, Alex asked. Hard to say, they said.

Hard to wait, Alex thought. He wouldn't wait. He would call Liberty Industries and bluff them into telling him the name of their auto insurer. The call where Alex bluffed Liberty's H.R. department had gone fine, so why not try the same thing with a different department? He didn't know the name of the insurer, so he figured he would just say he was calling from "the insurance company." For the bluff to work, he needed to call someone who wouldn't ask too many questions, so he called Liberty and asked for the accounts receivable department, hoping to reach a gullible, low-level bookkeeper.

The receptionist connected Alex to a woman with a hard-to-place foreign accent. She spoke loudly, but it didn't make her accent any clearer.

"Hi," Alex said. "I'm calling from the insurance company to confirm the status of the insurance payment for the accident on December 23rd. You remember, the big one?"

"Oh, I remember. Everybody remembers. You want to talk to the finance department?"

No, Alex didn't. Finance types were more inquisitive than accounting clerks, but he had no choice.

"Yes. And tell them I'm from the insurance company."

Alex held his breath as he waited on hold. What was the worst that could happen if his ruse was discovered? Just that the person on the other end of the phone would note Alex's phone number and track the call back to Rampart. Then Alex would be fired and very quickly go bankrupt. Which was distinctly worse than Alex's current trajectory of slowly going bankrupt. Alex was wishing that he'd thought this plan through a little better when a male voice greeted him on the other end of the line.

"Finance. Daugherty."

"Yes, I'm calling about the December 23rd accident?"

"You with Peninsula Life?"

Alex paused. That wasn't a name he was expecting. Peninsula was a life insurer, not an automobile insurer. Finally, he said, "Uh . . . that's right."

"You work with Susan, uh, Susan what's-her-name?"

"Yes I do, and she asked me to apologize for the delay in getting back to you." Alex apologized for the delay in order to ingratiate himself with this guy Daugherty. Alex figured he was taking only a small risk—even if Daugherty had spoken with Susan ten minutes ago, any delay was too long in the client's eyes.

"Yeah, fine," Daugherty said. "So I hope you're calling to tell me we're all set for payment."

Alex paused, then said, "I wish I were." He gritted his teeth. There was no telling where the conversation would go next.

"Not what I wanted to hear—what did you say your name was?"

"Um, Alex."

"No offense, Alex, but let's get Susan on the line."

"Actually, she's in a meeting right now, and—"

"Oh, the hell she is. Look, Alex, I just want to know when you folks are going to pay us. Susan said you were all set with the paperwork, and now you call . . ."

So the paperwork was done. That gave Alex an idea.

"Well, we *were* done with the paperwork, Mr. Daugherty."

"Were? What kind of run-around is this? You tell Susan that—"

"Have you ever dealt with OSHA, Mr. Daugherty?"

"The workplace safety agency? Sure, but what has that got to do—"

"Well, we're dealing with them right now on our end. Seems some government bean counter spotted rat feces in our document warehouse and got all excited about it, and they've decided that now is a great time to close off the entire warehouse and test it for the hanta virus."

"You're kidding me."

"I wish I were. Anyway, unfortunately the paperwork for your case, along with a thousand others, is quarantined for the rest of the week."

"So you're not paying us till next week? All five policies? Ah, crap. We've already booked the proceeds to revenue. My CFO is *not* going to be happy about this, Alex."

"Well, hold on, I was calling with a solution. If you could just fax the paperwork again, we can pay you on the basis of a fax signature. I know it's an imposition, but—"

Daugherty sighed. "What's the number?"

Alex gave Daugherty Rampart's fax number and told him to make out the cover sheet to Alex F.

"You tell Susan she owes me lunch," Daugherty said.

After hanging up, Alex paced the halls. His heart was pounding and he felt as if he had been surfing among sharks. He couldn't believe his luck.

The Cummings case had just gone from intriguing to disturbing. Daugherty only mentioned policies from Peninsula, which wrote life insurance, not auto insurance. It looked like Liberty didn't have insurance for its van at all. Daugherty also talked about five policies—Alex guessed that meant one policy for each of the dead employees in the van. He raced to the fax room. He couldn't wait to find out if his guess was right.

* * *

The faxes from Daugherty confirmed Alex's suspicion: Liberty had taken out insurance policies on the lives of the five employees who died in the van. As a result of their deaths, Liberty was entitled to two million dollars in insurance proceeds from Peninsula Life.

Now that he knew that Jorge and Beto worked at Liberty together and that Liberty had insured the lives of its dead employees, Alex thought he had enough information to convince Chip Odom that the case deserved Alex's full attention. Chip had a mercurial temper, just like his father, who happened to be the founder and president of Rampart Insurance. People in the office said Chip was in a disagreeable mood today. Alex resolved to speak with Chip tomorrow.

The next morning, when Alex got to his cubicle, he found that all his files had been removed. When he turned to go find out where they were, he ran right into Chip Odom, who wore a malevolent grin.

"Alex Fogarty," Chip said loudly, in a needlessly musical tone. He took a slow look at Alex's loose interpretation of business casual wear, and said, "Looks like you left your tuxedo at the cleaners."

Chip's distinctive cackle followed, a high-pitched staccato alarm that let everyone nearby know he had made a joke. Laughing at his own bad jokes was Chip's prerogative as the founder's son. Chip always wore a suit but, within that constraint, still found ways to surprise. Today he paired a blue pinstripe suit with a light orange shirt and a paisley necktie of the same shade. Add to that his curly hair, and he looked like a well-tailored clown.

"Good morning, Chip. I've actually been meaning to speak with you."

"I'll bet."

"Um, do you know where my files are?"

"They're in my office now." Chip grabbed Alex by the arm. "Walk with me," Chip said, and they walked.

Chip was chubby and had the droopy features of an aging babyface. Some of the more irreverent secretaries would tell stories of Chip as a mama's boy on his childhood visits to the office—expansive and demanding when accompanying his mother, sullen and withdrawn with his father.

"Where are we going?" Alex said. Chip didn't answer.

They marched around the perimeter of the floor like Chip was trying to catch up to someone. As Chip walked, his loose curls bounced over his ears and forehead. A warren of cubicles lay on one side of the hall and an outer ring of private offices and conference rooms on the other. Chip pulled Alex into one of the conference rooms, where someone from H.R. sat waiting. She was a dour older woman in a dark suit who didn't rise when they entered. Chip sat. Alex looked at them both. "What the hell's going on?" he said.

"I assume you've seen *this*," Chip said. He picked up a folded newspaper and tossed it onto the table so that it faced Alex.

It was the Metro section of that morning's *Chronicle*. One of the lead articles was entitled "Maverick Investigator Bucks Trend Toward Compromise," by none other than Alex's old acquaintance Zeke Andrews.

"No, I hadn't seen this," Alex said. He picked it up. Starting with the headline, it didn't look good.

"It's . . . engendered some discussions around here," Chip said. "There are some real gems in here—let's see," he said, and he picked up another copy. "'Fogarty opines that tranquility rather than curiosity is what succeeds in the new corporate environment.' Oh, and, 'Fogarty admits that it is often cheaper for an insurance company to settle a fraudulent claim than to litigate and prove that it is unjustified.' Why don't you just write the crooks an instruction manual, huh?"

Alex vaguely remembered saying something like that, but how could Zeke put that stuff in the paper? And why did Zeke let Alex get blindsided by the story? Alex grew hot with anger at the betrayal.

The H.R. woman spoke for the first time. "The article also contains a troubling account of an accident that you and the reporter were involved in, where you assaulted one of the accident victims and then fled the scene."

"Shit, Chip," Alex said. "I didn't assault anyone. I didn't *flee* from anything."

Chip didn't answer. He was reading the article again. "Oh, and here's the worst one." Chip poked a finger into the flimsy newsprint. "'A lot of these insurance scammers are undocumented,' says Fogarty. 'The ringleaders like them because they work cheap and won't go to the police.'"

"But it's true," Alex said.

"Jesus . . ." Chip sighed.

Alex looked at them both. The H.R. woman was looking at her hands, which lay folded on the table in front of her. "Will you excuse us for a minute?" Alex said to her. She looked at Chip. Chip nodded, and she left.

"You can't fire me, Chip. I'm your best investigator. Zeke twisted my words around so he could write what he wanted to write."

Chip studied Alex's face, looking for a tell. Finally he shrugged. "You're probably right, Alex, but it's too late for that."

"Chip, I'm begging you. Besides, you need me. Remember the Cummings case? Well, the police report doesn't make sense. There are discrepancies that favor us, and you'll never guess who one of the victims is. Remember Jorge Ramirez?"

"Mmm, no."

"Remember his skinny little buddy Rigoberto Capablanca?"

Chip chuckled. "I'll never forget that guy."

"Well, Capablanca also works at Liberty Industries, and Liberty took out life insurance on the employees who died. There's something funny here, I just know it."

Chip raised his palm to end the discussion. "Alex, stop. The Cummings case has been closed."

"Closed? Since when?"

"Since my dad read this story," Chip said, gesturing toward the newspaper. "The story says the dead Cummings guy had been kicked out by his wife. Dad read that and insisted we check the address of record in the policy. Turns out Howard Cummings didn't update his address when he added on insurance for the sports car, and the big guy demanded we deny coverage for false representation."

"That's bullshit! It's a harmless mistake. He left a wife and son, y'know."

"Look, Dad gets angry and he lashes out. The dead Mr. Cummings was an easy target for him."

Alex remembered how bereft Roberta Cummings looked when Alex visited her. "And the person it hurts is *Mrs.* Cummings. You know that, right?"

"I'm not saying it's fair, Alex."

React without thinking—classic Rampart Insurance, Alex thought. "Mrs. Cummings was an easy target for your father, and I was an easy target for you," he said.

"No, Alex. Firing you was Dad's choice, too."

"You're a big boy, now, Chip. Quit hiding behind Daddy's skirt."

Chip frowned. "All right, Alex, I tried to make this easy for you, but you asked for it. You want to know why you were never going to succeed here?"

"I'm not getting paid to listen to you anymore. Goodbye." Alex turned to leave.

Chip grasped Alex by the arm. "No, you'll listen." His voice became raspy. "It's because you never saw the big picture." He stabbed a chunky finger into Alex's chest. "You never accepted that fraud is a cost of doing business. You thought your job was all about solving cases, and being clever and unique and oh-so-special Alex."

This was rich, coming from a man with the work ethic of a hung-over college kid. "Silly me," Alex said, "I thought my job was to be thorough and save the company money."

"Yeah, silly *you.* For every random fraud case you uncovered, your thoroughness delayed payment to a hundred honest policyholders. Those hundred policyholders cancel their insurance with us and then they tell their family and friends. And then they complain to the insurance commission. You *cost* the company money."

"There's your cost of doing business, champ," Alex said, but Chip kept going.

"That's why an investigator is all you were ever going to be. This company's growing, Alex. I'm going to grow it even more than my dad did. And in the big picture, customer relations matters more than a few two-bit scam artists."

Alex noticed that a spot of foam had appeared at each corner of Chip's mouth. Chip was full of crap, but it felt good to push his buttons.

"You know, you're smarter than people give you credit for," Alex said.

The corners of Chip's mouth twisted upward into a tentative smile, and his features softened. A baby seal looking up at a falling club.

"But no matter how smart you are," Alex said, gently straightening Chip's tie and giving the knot one neat pat, "people will always know you as 'junior.'"

* * *

Alex walked past the main reception desk as casually as he could while toting a box with a bobblehead toy and the other personal leftovers from his years at Rampart. He was staring straight ahead, ruing his outburst at Chip, when a woman he hadn't seen coming slapped him across the face.

"You came to my house with flowers. I confided in you. And now you send me this!"

The woman pushed a crumpled page into Alex's chest. Alex cracked it open to find a printout of an email from Rampart denying insurance coverage. Alex looked at the addressee line in the email and then looked up at the woman's face. Roberta Cummings had been crying.

"I wasn't responsible," Alex said.

"And now with the lawsuit from the accident and no liability coverage . . . we'll probably lose the house." Her shoulders buckled and she gave in to sobbing. Alex touched his fingertips gently to her shoulder—he didn't know what else to do; he didn't need a sexual harassment suit on top of everything else—but she jerked upright and slapped his arm away.

"Don't touch me, you creep," she shrieked. She turned and fled to the elevator. There she stood, awkwardly waiting for the elevator doors to open. Under the rapt watch of those in the reception area, Alex carefully approached her from behind. The brushed steel of the elevator doors reflected a distorted image of her clenched jaw and downcast eyes.

"Mrs. Cummings," he said, but she didn't look up or respond. He wanted to tell her everything, pour out the details of his theory of the case and all the work he'd done on it right there in front of everyone. He couldn't possibly look more foolish than he already did. But he knew she wouldn't hear it. She had been wronged and was in pain. His response had to be as simple as that. "Listen," he said, "I . . . wasn't . . . responsible. Rampart did this to you."

She faced him and spoke so softly that Alex had to lean in to hear her.

"But Rampart used you to help them, right?" Alex didn't deny it. The elevator doors opened and she stepped inside. "That's just as bad as doing it yourself."

NO ACCIDENT

The elevator doors closed, leaving Alex to face his own distorted reflection. Feeling angry and embarrassed and foolish, Alex squared his shoulders and marched back to Chip's office. He wasn't leaving without a fight, and he fantasized about Chip squealing for someone to call security.

Chip was away from his office, which made Alex even angrier, but then Alex got another idea. He looked out into the hall to make sure Chip wasn't on his way back, then he opened a drawer—and removed the Cummings file.

10

The conference room at Liberty Industries' headquarters could hold up to twenty around its long, polished wood table. Today only two were seated there, together at one end of the grand chamber. Two lawyers: an older one and a younger one, waiting.

The older one, Alan Mathews, was about sixty. He had a deeply lined face, but he was tall and gave an impression of physical vigor. His starched white shirt matched his full head of wavy white hair, which was combed back and fixed with mousse so that it looked like it had been carved from marble. The other lawyer, a young associate, had loose brown hair that fell almost to his eyes and was combed to look like a tuft of wind-blown grass.

They heard the door open and Alan immediately stood to greet his client. Instead, a man he didn't know entered and said that Luke Hubbard would be with them shortly. The man was taller than Alan, powerfully built, and wore a suit that was almost as impressive as Alan's. His close-cropped hair was strikingly pale—silver—even though the man was not old.

The door opened again and Luke Hubbard entered. Alan instantly forgot the other man existed and approached Luke with genial greetings.

"You've met Crash Bailey, I see," Luke said.

Alan distractedly looked back. "Um, yes, we were just introducing ourselves."

"Crash here is going to be my emissary to Ray McLean, aren't you, Crash?"

Alan smiled at Crash with genuine warmth. "I'm sorry, I didn't realize you were a lawyer."

Crash was impassive, but Luke had a good laugh. "Crash isn't a lawyer," he said. "But you don't need a law degree to be persuasive."

Alan's face lit up. "Well, Ray McLean's hedge fund is well known for hostile takeovers, which are just a corporate law minefield. We'd be more than happy to help you on the legal side with all of that."

"As always, Alan, if there's a way you can help," Luke said wryly, "I'll find a role for you. Now, let's get down to business."

Crash left, and Luke and Alan sat at the table with Alan's young colleague, who didn't introduce himself to Luke and wasn't introduced.

"I've seen the TV news, and I know what the problem is," Alan said. "Sheila's trying to pressure you into an expensive divorce settlement by bad-mouthing you to the press."

"By *lying* about me to the press," Luke said firmly. "Not to mention all our philanthropic friends. Making me look like some sort of charity deadbeat. It was *her* idea to cancel the gift to the cancer center."

"I know," Alan said softly.

"And now I don't know if they'll keep me on the board. Same with the board of trustees for the museum. Once one domino falls, they all fall. And she knows that." Luke's shoulders drooped a little, and his voice became emotional for the first time. "Tell me, Alan, what kind of screwed-up world do we live in where *I* have to pay *her* to stop messing up my life? She doesn't have any kids to raise. She has a degree, she can work. Why does she get to sponge off my success?"

Alan gave a resigned shrug. "Our matrimonial law was designed for a different time. The law is always slow to catch up with social developments. But what matters is you've got the right team on your side." He patted Luke on the arm.

"I'm glad for that," Luke said, more composed. "There was no one else I considered for the job."

"We were just glad we could build on the close relationship between Boswell & Baker and Liberty Industries," Alan said.

"So has she got a lawyer yet?" Luke said.

"It's no one we've heard of before." Alan tapped the table in front of his associate. "What's his name again?"

"Bradley D. Pitcher," the associate said crisply.

Alan shrugged dismissively. "A nobody. That's good for us. Only a handful of divorce lawyers in town are worth worrying about, and they're all hell on wheels. God knows why she didn't pick one of them."

Luke smiled to himself and chuffed a little laugh. "God knows," he said. "Anyway, it's not her lawyer we need to worry about. It's her. She's smart, Alan, cunning. All she needs is a mouthpiece to do her bidding."

The associate busily scratched out notes on a thick legal pad.

"That's right, kid," Luke said to him. "Write that down, get it tattooed." He turned to Alan. "Now we need to pressure her. I'll tell you a secret, Alan: she's vain."

Alan laughed despite himself, and Luke laughed with him.

"Oh, you're not surprised?" Luke said. "She's vain, and she spends a lot of money. She can't stand not to keep up appearances."

"Keep going," Alan said.

"So what I want you to do," Luke said, "is to find a dozen young lawyers like this guy here, and put them to work drafting every motion they can think of."

Alan nodded. "The longer we delay a settlement, the more she'll spend and the more desperate she'll get."

"Right," Luke said. "Resist everything, assist on nothing and delay, delay, delay."

"Luke, it's great to have a client who gets it," Alan said. He thought of all the billable hours this strategy would mean. "You're a dream come true."

"I know. So, delaying is part one of the Luke Hubbard strategy."

"And part two is?"

"That's what I want *you* to tell *me*. Part two is: find me a way to shut her up."

"But the First Amendment—" the young associate started, but Alan tapped the table at him again.

Alan nodded thoughtfully, then said. "Luke, it's impossible to stop people from gossiping. But let's consider the tactical opportunity here."

"I'm listening . . ."

"We simply let her talk. We give her enough rope to hang herself with. She'll pay the price when we get in front of a judge. Remember—the judge has a lot of discretion."

Luke considered the proposal. "That's . . . creative, but I want her to stop now. I can't just stand by while she makes me look like an ass."

"We could ask for a restraining order," the associate said. The partner turned and glared at him. Luke seemed not to hear; he was pondering.

"God, it's so simple," he said finally. "I'll just fire her."

"I'm not sure that's such a good idea."

"Thanks, Alan. I didn't ask. I'm going to do it."

"It's going to look terrible to the judge," Alan said.

"You don't understand, that's where part one of my plan works its magic. Without a job, she'll be hurting for money even more. She'll beg me to settle with her."

"Firing her will invite a sexual harassment claim against you and the company."

"That's crap," Luke said airily. "I'm not firing her because she's a woman, I'm firing her because she's a heartless medusa."

"Now, Luke, I'm guessing that up till now, your wife has had good performance reviews, has been well respected in the company?"

"Sure, I've protected her," Luke said. "I mean, she does fine." Alan regarded Luke skeptically, and Luke laughed. "Come on, she does H.R. How hard can it be? It's not like she's got revenue projections she needs to hit."

Alan nodded sagely. "I thought that might be the case." More profound nodding followed, and Luke realized that a lawyerly shift in course was coming. "Firing your wife under the current circumstances would expose the company to a serious risk of liability under employment law."

"Fine, Alan, I get it. That's a risk I'm willing to take."

The lawyer shifted on his seat, but his voice was reassuring when he spoke again. "The problem is that your interests diverge from the company's here. We think the better approach is to let the board of directors decide whether to fire her."

"I've listened to people like you say 'no' my whole career," Luke said. "And if I had followed that advice, Liberty Industries would still be a sleepy little family company. No, worse—it would be bankrupt by now."

"Mr. Hubbard, a conflict like this is explicitly covered by the board's policies," the young associate piped up. He was pointing to a document that he had pulled from a folder.

"Nobody asked you, junior," Luke said.

Alan jumped in. "Given our representation of you in the divorce and the company in other matters, if you fire Sheila we'll have a conflict of interest under the bar's ethics rules. We'll have to get a waiver from the board of directors."

"Last time, Alan: not gonna happen."

The young associate looked at Alan, who looked at Luke.

"Then we may not be able to continue representing you in your divorce," Alan said.

Luke clapped his hands together. "Ah, so *that's* it. You're worried about covering your own asses."

"It's not a situation we want to be in, but there are ways to resolve it for everyone's benefit."

"I'm sure there are," Luke said mockingly. "Look, Alan, we've known each other a long time, so don't try to sweet talk me, OK? You're worried about a conflict? I'll make it real easy for you. You withdraw from my divorce, and I'll make sure you lose every piece of business you have with Liberty Industries. Every deal, every litigation, every last one."

Alan's voice remained even. "The Boswell firm has had a long and productive relationship with—"

"It should be called the 'Hubbard firm' after all I've done for you," Luke countered. "When you first started working for me, you guys could barely afford to hire associates. You didn't know how to do a merger. You didn't know how to do a stock offering. I made you. And I can un-make you."

Alan looked impassively at Luke. Luke stared back without blinking. Only the young associate showed frenzy in his eyes. It was Luke who finally rendered the verdict.

"All I'm asking you to do is your job. You give the advice. I'll make the decisions."

* * *

Brad was trapped. His office door was closed, and between him and the door stood Sheila. Brad had never seen Sheila this way. She had started out calm like always, serious but calm, until she delivered the news.

"He fired me."

She repeated the phrase every minute or so in between creatively profane bursts of vitriol that made the veins in her forehead stand out. Each time the vitriol ran out, she said the phrase again, and saying it stoked her anger anew.

"The son of a bitch fired me!"

Her pale skin reddened as her rant wore on. The color came in blotches that grew larger till her entire face, from neck to scalp, was an unnatural shade of red, beyond a sunburn, beyond heat stroke. The contrast with her golden blonde hair was unsettling. She looked like a figure from a lurid Andy Warhol portrait.

"He would be nowhere without me! Nowhere!"

Cindy, her eyes wide with concern, cracked opened the office door to see what the commotion was about. As Sheila cast a glance toward the ceiling to implore unnamed gods for aid, Brad discreetly shook his head at Cindy, and she vamoosed.

"His ingratitude is astounding. I should be the one firing him. I put my career in the back seat to help him get to the top. But who does he pull up with him? That cheap whore of his, that mail-order bitch!"

As she carried on, Brad stopped being frightened and even began to feel calm. He knew how to handle clients like this. Many of Brad's criminal defendants succumbed to fits of anger when they finally realized they were going to prison. For Sheila, being fired came with the same shock and disappointment. And for once she had reacted like anybody would react, not like the inscrutable blonde cyborg who first walked into his office.

"Sheila, we can deal with this," Brad said gently. "You've let Luke get you maybe a little overexcited about this? That's what he wants."

"Overexcited" didn't begin to describe his client's tantrum, but "hysterical" was a word Brad didn't feel bold enough to utter. Brad got the sense that all her yelling and cursing kept her from crying. From his perspective, crying would be even worse. Anger was always unpleasant, but it was never awkward.

"Oh yeah?" Sheila said. "What's your plan to *deal* with this? Read some cases? Scratch your ass?"

Brad kept his poise. Clients often lashed out at their lawyers. And when they did, their lawyers calmed them down. It was what lawyers got paid for. He kept telling himself that.

"Sheila, this will only harm him in the long run. It'll only harm him in front of the judge."

"Oh, thanks for the tip. Well, right now it's harming *me*. He wants to take everything away from me, Brad. And the only reason he has any power is because I helped him get it."

Sheila leaned over the desk and jabbed a finger toward Brad's chest with each sentence, and Brad leaned back in his chair to avoid contact. His words hadn't calmed her down. If anything, she was getting angrier.

"He couldn't have built Liberty Industries on his own. We were supposed to be a team." She rose to her full height, pushing back the hair on her forehand in one firm sweep. "Oh, the times I covered for him, the times I had his back. The stories I could tell you."

"Why don't you sit down and tell me?" Brad's chair was tilted as far back as it would go. His voice didn't reveal the alarm he felt, but his face couldn't hide it.

"Why don't *you* find a way to fix this?" Sheila said.

"Fix this?"

"Yes, you idiot. Fix this. Find a way to make Luke give up."

"Give up?"

"Are you lawyer or a parrot?"

Yeah, litigants love to "give up," Brad thought. *Wake up every morning wondering how quickly they can "give up."* Two weeks earlier, it was "show up and take instructions." Now it was "make him give up." He shouldn't be surprised. He was going to have to earn his fee, after all. Fine, then—it was time for some tough love.

"Sheila. Number one: control yourself." She came out of her snit and looked at him in surprise. "Good. Number two: Luke is not going to give up. Surprised? No. You're not. Number three: Luke has the money and the power, so he has the leverage and . . . he . . . is trying . . . to make *you* give up. Yes." She started to look defiant again. "Number four: I won't let him, but—Number five: I need you with me."

Sheila nodded with religious fervor.

"Do I need to count higher?" Brad said.

Sheila shook her head and collapsed into the chair. Then she started crying.

Oh, great, Brad thought, *why didn't I just let her keep screaming?* Her sobs were soft and tentative. *Because I'm her lawyer,* he thought. Brad came around to the front of his desk and put an arm around her shoulder. That comforted her.

Brad knew he wasn't a handsome man, and he was fine with that. Here for once he had his arm around a beautiful woman, and to his surprise he wasn't thinking about a beautiful woman, or the smell of her hair or how she filled out her skirt. He was thinking about his adversary and about how to stop him.

He was thinking like a lawyer.

The paper for this case had started coming in, a lot more of it than he had expected. Eighty hours this week—eighty *billable* hours—just to get through the first set of motions and other worthless bundles couriered to his office door once or twice a day by Luke's lawyers. He'd already billed beyond the amount of the retainer, and he'd meant to speak with Sheila today about arranging payment of his first month's bill, but now obviously wasn't the right time for that. Sheila's getting fired opened a whole new legal front on which Brad could attack Luke. But Brad's priority had to be getting Sheila some interim alimony, and fast—for both of their sakes.

The bright side was that the divorce saga appeared in the local tabloids almost every day. Even ugly guys were photographed for the paper now and then; with any luck, that would start happening soon for him. Some free publicity about his winning a great settlement for Sheila would certainly help revive his legal practice. In fact, this case was so high profile that it could do what Brad had hoped his hardware-store class action would do—bring him to a point where new clients looked for him rather than the other way around. This case could be his salvation yet, if he could find a way to save Sheila.

11

The night after he was fired, Alex drank to fall asleep. But he didn't drink enough to stop from dreaming. He had the Pamela dream, the one he'd had off and on for a year, even since before she left him. Each time the dream moved a little further along. In the dream, Pamela had warned him not to buy any more houses and then left when he did so anyway. This time Alex dreamed that he negotiated a miraculous deal with the banks in which they forgave all the mortgage debt and gave Alex an option to purchase a mansion in Bel Air. Alex raced around town to find Pamela, to show her that he had repaired his finances and to beg her forgiveness. He finally found her on Rodeo Drive, where he spotted her through the picture window of an expensive boutique. He approached the window and tapped on it with a fingernail to draw her attention from her shopping. She didn't look up. Then he rapped the window with his knuckles. Then he called her name and pounded his fists on the window, over and over until the glass undulated like a sheet being unfurled onto a newly made bed. But she didn't hear him. No one heard him.

Alex woke up sweating. These dreams weren't fair—he was always the bad guy. Alex remembered the indelicate way Del had broken the news that Pamela was cheating on him: "Dude, your fiancée's sleeping with this dude I know."

She didn't deny it when he confronted her. In fact, she was almost eager to confirm her infidelity. What a contrast to the modest, almost shy girl he fell in love with.

He first fell for her light brown hair and nerdy glasses. She didn't realize how pretty she was, which was refreshing, and though she could talk all day to a class of second-graders, she sometimes got tongue-tied around people her own age. She was tongue-tied around Alex at first. It was endearing, and Alex felt like a hero for making her comfortable around others and giving her confidence.

After two months, he introduced her to his family, and she got along with them as if she'd known them her whole life. Mom loved her and was delighted they had so much in common. They were both schoolteachers, they both liked sappy movies. *Less in common than you think, Mom*, Alex thought, looking back.

After a year, they weren't yet talking about marriage, but it was clear they were moving in that direction. Everything got more serious. Pamela wanted Alex to be more financially secure. Alex wanted that, too. By then he had quit *The Chronicle*, in part because he hoped he could eventually make more money in the insurance industry, maybe move into management. Alex was aware that part of his motivation for making money was recovering some of the status his family lost when his father was convicted of fraud.

But Pamela didn't have Alex's adventurous nature—or foolhardiness—when it came to his real estate investments. She thought it was cool when Alex bought his first investment property—she was dating a sexy wheeler-dealer. The second investment was less popular—shouldn't they pay down the mortgages on the first investment property and the house by the beach a little first? She was vocally nervous about the next investment property, but Alex explained his rationale over and over until she acquiesced.

Before they got engaged, Pamela made Alex promise not to buy any more houses. But three months later, the market was still red hot, and Alex got a call from a broker about an opportunity that looked great on paper and would be gone in a day if Alex didn't take it. So Alex took it.

Pamela felt betrayed, of course, but Alex sat with her for four hours that night, talking about their future together, and Alex explained how all his investments were meant to jump-start their nest egg so that he could provide her with the financial stability that she needed. There was a lot of soft crying on her part—she was never a screamer—but by the end of the evening, she wasn't upset anymore, and she said that she loved and trusted him. That was what Alex needed to hear. He believed it, and he'd learned his lesson—no more houses, he promised himself. Alex's aggressive investing had been the source of a lingering quiet conflict between them, and Alex felt like bringing the issue out into the open had strengthened their relationship as they prepared for marriage. He was wrong about that.

A month later, Del saw Pamela leaving the house of one of his low-life gambling buddies. It turned out he had chatted her up when she and Alex and some friends had gone to one of Del's parties early on in their relationship and Alex had left early. After Alex's final house investment, this dude saw her out with her girlfriends one night and tried to re-make her acquaintance. And she was willing. And now Alex felt like his insides had been crushed.

Del told Alex at the time that it was for the best, that he'd never really liked Pamela anyway, and that in a year Alex would look back and laugh about the whole thing. Well, it had been a year, and Alex still didn't get the joke.

His five houses were still a constant reminder of two big mistakes—foolish investing and corrupting his relationship with Pamela. Some days he blamed Pamela, some days he blamed himself. But his thoughts went in a circle, not forward.

Outside the sky was still dark, but Alex got out of bed and shuffled to the kitchen to brew some coffee. He wanted to clear his boozy head. At some point last night, he'd figured out what to do. Once he found out the truth of the Cummings accident, he would present Chip Odom with a simple choice—either Chip would hire Alex back and restore coverage for Roberta Cummings, or else Alex would take his evidence to a lawyer who would sue Rampart Insurance and embarrass them.

If Chip took the first alternative, Alex would also have his job back. If Chip refused to hire Alex back, then Alex would . . . what? After a couple sips of coffee he remembered—he would go out on his own as a private insurance investigator. The more coffee he drank, the more the plan actually made sense. Alex had enough experience and contacts now to make it as an independent investigator, and once Alex figured out what Beto's scam was, he could get some splashy publicity out of the story, which would help him in starting his business.

The sky was just starting to lighten outside, a bird was chirping . . . and something else was making a sound. Alex opened the kitchen window, and heard a persistent metallic scratch echoing in the quiet street outside. He poked his head outside the window and saw a large boxy shadow, which was his truck parked askew in his driveway—*Christ*, he wondered, *did I actually drive myself home last night?*—and he saw the shadow of a hunching man pressed against the driver's side door.

Alex dropped his coffee mug. It rattled in the sink as Alex ran into the front hall. A machine gun-fire narrative of self-reproach ran through his brain: *This is what I get for getting drunk and parking in my own driveway instead of the side street, and I shouldn't have driven home anyway; God, I'm an idiot.* Alex grabbed the keys to his truck from a side table and opened his front door. Then he turned back and threw open the door to the darkened coat closet, which he explored by touch like a blind speed reader. Inside, he found Pamela's jacket. Inside a pocket of that jacket, he found her canister of mace. *Fucking repo man*, Alex thought.

Alex bounded out of his house on the balls of his bare feet, surprised the repo man with a hand to the shoulder, sprayed mace in his eyes from an inch away, then tugged the hunched, wailing man by the shoulders away from the truck and hurled him onto the small patch of grass that counted as Alex's lawn.

Alex pulled the repo man's slim jim out of the truck door, inserted his own key into the lock and opened the door. He hopped into the driver's seat and turned on the engine. Before Alex could close the truck door, a hairy forearm reached in right in front of Alex's face and grabbed hold of the steering wheel. Without considering the consequences, Alex dropped his jaw open and bit down on the arm. A man shouted in pain, the arm withdrew, and Alex put the truck in reverse and hit the gas. The truck lurched out of the driveway at the same awkward angle it had been driven in on the night before, the tires making a serrated track across the lawn and bouncing over the curb onto the street.

In his rearview mirror, Alex saw two men—Mr. Forearm and Mr. Mace—get up from his lawn and run to their own car. *These guys are relentless*, Alex thought.

Given the light traffic at this hour, the pair caught up easily despite Alex's head start. Alex saw a streetlight ahead and timed it so that he entered the intersection just as the light was turning red. The pursuing car barreled through the intersection a full second later. Alex started to worry. *How bloodthirsty are these guys?*

A block ahead was another intersection, this time crossing a major artery. The light had just turned yellow, and Alex saw that, even at this early hour, cars were waiting to cross as soon as the opposing lights turned green. Alex gunned the engine and flew through the intersection, again just as the light was turn-ing red. This time his pursuers had cross traffic to slow them down. He heard screeching tires and car horns—no crashes, thank God—and in his mirror saw his pursuers weaving slowly through the intersection around cars whose drivers had dared to assume that at 5:00 a.m. they could proceed safely on a green light.

That little delay was all Alex needed. Many of the side streets down by the beach were narrow one-way alleys that gave access to garages and carports. Alex turned the truck the wrong way down one of them, and then turned into the first empty carport he saw. Standing next to him in the humble carport was a nearly new Mercedes, which he knew cost close to a hundred grand. It was people like the owner of the Mercedes who drove up property values. *God, I love gentrification*, he thought. A few seconds later, he saw his pursuers speed past the alley, not looking in his direction.

Alex would wait here a while and then move the truck somewhere else for the day. He obviously couldn't leave the truck in his driveway anymore. The bill collectors were watching him like ghouls. The encounter had shaken Alex, but in a strange way he felt satisfied. The morning's excitement proved that Alex's obsessive rituals to avoid his bill collectors were actually justified. He would just have to be more careful to follow them consistently.

Alex remembered something his brother said the other day, that the two of them were alike. Now that Alex had been chased from his home before dawn by people who wanted money from him, that comparison no longer seemed so crazy. Alex knew the repo men would be back. *Maybe Del can give me some tips on making my way as a deadbeat*, Alex mused.

Alex heard a beep come from the car seat next to him. His cell phone, which he didn't remember leaving there, was telling him he had a message. He didn't remember leaving his phone here. *How drunk was I?* Alex took the phone and listened to the voicemail. The message was from the night before. His uncle Hugh was returning his call—*that's right, I called Hugh from the bathroom at the bar*—and Hugh said that in fact he and Aunt Melinda were hosting Del for din-ner tomorrow—which was now today—and they'd love for Alex to join them.

All Alex had really wanted was a quick, five-minute conversation with Uncle Hugh about the life insurance policies from Liberty Industries, but he couldn't back out now. He waited a few more minutes, then drove off to find someplace where he could get a cheap greasy breakfast to settle his roiling stomach.

12

Del was already making merry at Uncle Hugh and Aunt Melinda's house when Alex arrived, playing rock n' roll songs on the piano. Their mother was there, too. *As if things couldn't get more awkward,* Alex thought. He quickly accepted Hugh's offer of a glass of wine.

On her way to the dinner table, Alex's mother stopped him and whispered, "I think Del may be in trouble again." Del only played the piano when he wanted to ingratiate himself with his mother; Alex of course already knew that Del was broke. Before moving on to the table, his mother shook her head with pity and whispered, "Things are always so hard for him."

Alex responded with a sympathetic smile, but thought, *yeah, like things are easy for me.* Del's downward spiral over the years had drained their mother's spirit, and Alex's relative success was a boon for her. He could tell that his mother, worried again about Del, was even now barely keeping her composure. If she found out how precarious Alex's own financial situation was, it would be another disappointment. He couldn't let that happen.

Melinda served dinner at a long, sturdy oak table that she had set with her good china. Their house was big enough to have a formal dining room that only got used on occasions like this. The house was spacious and tastefully, if conservatively, furnished, thanks to Hugh's successful accounting practice and Melinda's attention to homemaking.

The family had a reassuringly familiar conversation during the salad course. Melinda was overbearing and bossy, Mom was scatterbrained and ditzy from half a glass of Chardonnay, Del, still in entertainer mode, related a rambling story full of mildly off-color anecdotes, and Hugh occasionally tossed in little hand grenades of sarcasm. It was the usual, comfortable pattern. Alex's immediate family had felt smaller after his father died, even though his father had earlier moved out, and even though Hugh had sort of taken his sister and her two teenaged sons under his wing. Ever since then, they had get-togethers like this every few months. But as Alex saw it, the family members were all so different in personality that mutual aggravation was slowly wearing down the bonds of love and tradition. *Like grains of sand in a gearbox*, Alex thought.

As usual, Alex tried his best to keep anyone from getting too annoyed with anyone else. He was now annoyed with them all, but that was a cost he could bear to keep the peace.

Then Aunt Melinda said, "Alex, I called your office this morning to ask what time you would be coming, and the woman who answered the phone said you don't work there anymore. I'm sure she just made some sort of mistake?"

Nosy Aunt Melinda. Thanks a lot. Alex noticed the look of surprise on Del's face, and replied quietly, "It's not a mistake." Then, into his wine glass, he added, "It was a . . . politics . . . thing."

His mother said, "I'm sorry to hear that," and her expression of concern and surprise confirmed it. Just what Alex didn't want. "Especially in this economy," she added.

"There's always demand for accountants," Aunt Melinda said.

His mother nodded. "I know accounting isn't the most exciting profession, but it pays well," she said gently. Alex rolled his eyes a little. Every time they were all together, his mom prodded him into join Hugh's accounting firm. She had liked his being a reporter, because it seemed like an upstanding profession, and didn't like his becoming an insurance investigator, mostly because the job was unfamiliar to her and, Alex surmised, struck her—incorrectly—as routinely dangerous. She didn't understand anything about accounting either, but knew from her brother's experience that it was safe, respectable and stable—as aspirations went, stability was a greased turkey that the Fogarty family had been fumbling for years now.

"Accounting pays well enough," Melinda said. "By the way, Hugh, Alex wants to speak with you after dinner."

"I'm glad to hear that," his mother said. *Great*, Alex thought, *she thinks I'm finally going to hit Hugh up for a job*. But her mistake seemed to ease her anxiety, and Alex didn't speak up to correct her misunderstanding.

Alex caught Del giving him a dirty look, and Alex immediately deduced why. Del must have come here to ask Hugh for money himself and so he assumed that Alex had done the same. Alex was angry that Del would dare think that. *We're not* that *alike*, Alex thought.

"Mom, you don't know the half of it," Del chortled. "Alex has bill collectors crawling around his house like cockroaches. I was there—he keeps the lights turned off to fool them into thinking he's not home."

Del smirked triumphantly at Alex. So this stink bomb was Del's revenge—proving to the whole family that Alex had spoiled his own life just as much as Del had. Alex smiled back at Del and lifted his glass ironically, which was a more sober response than reaching across the table and dousing his brother's head with the contents of the wine glass.

Their mother turned very sad. The muscles in her face went slack, and she suddenly looked older. "Oh, Alex, I didn't think it would be like this for you," she said.

"What about me?" Del said. "I've got bill collectors, too."

He's even jealous of the attention I get when he rats me out, Alex noted. Del was on his third glass of wine, and Alex assumed Del had warmed up with a couple more drinks before coming.

Mom patted Del's hand. "If only your father had set a better example," she said.

"Mom, please don't make this about Dad," Alex said in annoyance. Whenever her sons needed a gut-check, they always heard it was Dad's fault—for leaving, for getting caught up in the insider-trading scandal that sent him to prison, for dying there, for getting cancer. Alex was tired of the Ghost of Christmas Past haunting every important family conversation. Del was ever ready to accept Mom's little fairy tale, but Alex found it insulting to his intelligence.

"All I mean is, you're almost thirty," his mother said.

"What about me?" Del said again. "I'm twenty-six."

Their mother sighed and spoke solely to Alex. "I just hoped you would be more settled by now."

"Me too, Mom," said Alex.

"By the way," Del said, still pleading for attention, "my car got repossessed weeks ago, not that anyone cares—you're never this disappointed when I screw up."

"Don't be silly," their mother said with exasperation. "I'm disappointed in you both." Then she realized what she had said, and excused herself from the table before anyone could see her tears.

* * *

Dessert wasn't so much served as it was foraged, with Del and the two women taking their bread pudding to the living room where they started a game of rummy in front of the television. Alex and Hugh retreated to Hugh's study, where they sat in two oversized leather chairs, accompanied by the soft rhythm of an antique wall clock counting off the seconds.

"So you didn't really come here to ask me for a job, right?" Hugh said.

Alex shook his head.

"Or ask me for money?" The tone of his voice told Alex that Hugh was ninety percent sure Alex hadn't come to ask for money. That was reassuring.

"Of course not," Alex said. "I wanted to ask you about this." He handed Hugh the faxed life insurance policies from Liberty Industries and explained that they related to a case he was working on.

"Looks like janitor's insurance," Hugh said after scanning the first few pages of the fax.

"These guys weren't janitors, they were mechanics," Alex said.

"That's just a little accounting humor," Hugh said with a playful smile. He was in his fifties, balding, soft. He hadn't let himself go so much as he had never been in shape in the first place. Aunt Melinda was quite good looking in her day, and Alex had always wondered how exactly their odd pairing originated.

"The formal term is corporate-owned life insurance," Hugh said. "It started off with companies buying insurance on their top executives—if the CEO dies from a heart attack, the company gets a payout to help it with the transition. When the policies are on low-level employees, like these are, people sometimes call it janitor's insurance. You're probably more used to seeing a company buy life insurance *for* its employees, for the employees' benefit. This is a company buying life insurance *on* its employees, for its own benefit."

That confirmed what Alex had guessed. "So the employee dies, and the company gets paid."

"Exactly. Guaranteed payment when the employee dies."

"What does the employee's family get?"

"Nothing. Not under these policies, at least. But if the widows and kids are beneficiaries under another policy, they'd get paid under that."

Hugh handed the faxed sheets back to Alex. Alex took them hesitantly. "It all sounds a little creepy," Alex said. "I wouldn't want my boss to have an incentive to off me."

Hugh chuckled. "Used to be illegal for just that reason. To get insurance on somebody, you need to have what they call an 'insurable interest' in the person—you have to suffer some sort of economic loss if the person dies. That way people won't buy insurance on random strangers and, as you say, 'off' them."

Alex leaned back into the leather cushions and pondered his uncle's explanation. "I can see the economic loss if your spouse dies. I can even see it with a company and its CEO. But if your motor pool guy dies, you just go hire another mechanic. It doesn't make sense to call that a loss for the company."

"That's logical, but it's not the law. Not anymore, at least."

"So what purpose does it serve?"

"Companies basically buy janitor's insurance to get a tax benefit."

Alex's eyes flashed with excitement. "Uncle Hugh, I knew you'd be all over this."

"When the employee dies, the money the company gets from the insurance company is tax free, just like most insurance proceeds are. That's better than the alternative. The alternative is for the company not to buy the janitor's insurance, and to take the premiums it would have paid the insurance company and go invest them in something else. Under that alternative scenario, the company has to pay tax on the gains from its investment."

Alex's excitement faded just as quickly as it had arisen. "So it's just a tax game."

"The point is definitely *not* for the employees to die, which is where I think you were going with this."

Alex shook his head in protest. "Hold on. Killing the employees might not be the *motivation* for these policies, but even so, the company still makes out better when the employees die young, doesn't it?"

"That's true . . ." Hugh said. "The company gets its money sooner, and in the meantime it's paid less in premiums to the insurance company." Hugh shook his head vigorously as if trying to cast Alex's suspicions from his mind. "No, you're chasing shadows. These policies may be a little weird, but they're just an innocent tax-planning technique."

Alex eyed his uncle skeptically. "Innocent tax planning—so you're telling me that my employer could go behind my back, insure my life for a million bucks, and that would be innocent tax planning."

His uncle considered the suggestion. "A million seems high. No offense, Alex."

Alex abruptly straightened up in his chair as a new thought occurred to him. "Holy cow. Maybe Rampart has a policy out on me right now."

"It's not like putting a hit out on you, Alex. They changed the law, and now a company has to tell an employee when it buys a policy on him."

"That doesn't really ease my mind. When I started working at Rampart, I signed a bunch of papers I didn't really look at."

"You and everybody else."

Alex idly skimmed the fax again. "What smells funny to me about this is that it's a lot of money. Look at these, Hugh." He pulled out the front page to each of the five policies and handed them back to his uncle. "Five mechanics. Probably each make fifty thousand a year, tops. But Liberty insures each of them for four hundred grand. Two million, total. I'll bet these guys never saw that much money in their lives."

Hugh nodded in agreement. "The numbers are on the high side. But it doesn't strike me as suspicious."

"Really? Two million dollars is a lot of money," Alex said.

Hugh responded more brusquely than before. "Two million is a rounding error to a company like Liberty Industries. Their revenue is in the billions." Hugh passed the papers back to his nephew. "Sorry, Alex, I'm sure you're a good sleuth, but I don't think you've uncovered a diabolical corporate plot."

Alex's face showed his disappointment.

"Is it because Liberty Industries is an oil company?" Hugh asked, as if he already knew the answer.

"No," Alex said indignantly. "No," he said again, more evenly. Alex didn't love oil companies; prior family dinner conversations had made that clear. As far as Alex was concerned, the oil industry was more culpable than any other industry for fouling the air he breathed and soiling the ocean that he surfed and swam in. And he thought it entirely possible that the industry's callousness could extend to murder.

"Good," Hugh said. "I was afraid I might hear about the Venice Boulevard trolley again."

Touché, Alex thought. He had told that story more than once, he admitted, usually after too much wine, about how the oil and car companies bought up Los Angeles' electric trolley network after World War II in order to shut the trolleys down and replace them with gasoline buses. Hugh was no environmentalist, but apparently he'd been paying attention after all.

Alex didn't share Hugh's blithe confidence that the insurance policies were pure and innocent. If the insurance policies were simply tax-planning techniques, like Hugh said, then it was unlikely that someone at Liberty Industries had orchestrated the accident to kill the employees in the van. And that was a setback to Alex's quest to prove that Howard Cummings wasn't responsible for the accident that killed him.

Alex's doubt must have shown on his face, because Hugh asked, "Why so skeptical?"

Alex gave Hugh a quick run-down of how Rampart Insurance had dropped coverage for Roberta Cummings.

"Wow," Hugh said. "That stinks. If that's how old Chester Odom runs his insurance company, maybe you're better off not working there."

"Exactly. I thought, if the accident was deliberately caused by someone at Liberty to cash out these life insurance policies, then Howard Cummings could no longer be at fault for the accident and his widow might get some compensation."

"Can I ask you a question, Alex?"

Alex nodded.

"If you don't work at Rampart anymore, why are you still working on this case?"

"It just got to me, I guess—the unfairness of it. I want to help my client."

"You mean, Rampart's client."

Hugh gave Alex the kind of benign, condescending smile that middle-aged men give to children who announce that their Christmas wish is for world peace. *Sand in the gearbox*, Alex thought again.

"You can't help everybody," Hugh said. He looked like he wanted to say something more, but didn't.

"You were going to tell me I should start by helping myself," Alex said.

"I wasn't." A moment passed, and Hugh said, "Have you ever thought about just giving up your houses?"

"You mean defaulting on the mortgages?"

"Mortgages are non-recourse in California, so if you defaulted, the banks couldn't come after you for their losses. You wouldn't be the first person to make that choice."

Alex wasn't cheered by this suggestion. "*Purchase money* mortgages are non-recourse, but refinancings aren't. And I've refinanced the houses several times."

"You really did put your foot into it, didn't you?" Hugh said.

"I try hard not to think about how deep."

Hugh's eyes filled with a new light, and he moved on to another topic. "Listen, your brother asked me before dinner whether I would let him borrow a car."

That was a new approach for Del. To date, Del had just straight up asked his family and friends for cash. "He's been getting around by bus," Alex said.

"And skateboard, I take it. Does Del have a job?"

"It's hard for me to get a straight answer on that," Alex said.

"Me too. I've got this pickup truck. It's old and I don't use it very much, but before I let Del use it, I wanted to get your opinion on whether he's responsible enough these days for me to trust him with it."

No pressure or anything, Alex thought, *just tell me what you really think of your brother*. Alex was still the older brother. He wouldn't rat Del out, no matter the circumstances. He wouldn't return the little disfavor Del had done him at the dinner table. As Alex stalled, an odd idea popped into his mind. In an instant it morphed into a great idea.

"Alex? You don't have to tell me if you don't want to."

"No, it's fine," Alex said slowly, letting the idea come to shape in his mind. "How about this? I talk with Del more regularly than you do. I'll let him use *my* truck so he doesn't have to skateboard around like a teenager. And you let me borrow your truck in the meantime—if you're comfortable with that, I mean."

Hugh looked very pleased. "I think that's a fine idea—a great idea. And you're OK with lending Del your truck?"

Alex wasn't really, but this convoluted plan would keep Alex's truck away from the repo men while giving both Alex and Del their own transportation. "I think it's a win-win," Alex said.

Hugh reached out and squeezed Alex's shoulder. "You're a good brother to Del."

13

They found Beto at the pool hall. Beto knew they would find him somewhere, so he figured, why not have a good time while they tracked him
down? If he went into hiding every time someone wanted to take his money
from him, he would never have a chance to spend any of it.

The bad thing about bookies was that they never forgot. The good thing
about them was that they remembered who kept them in business. Lenny had
never killed anybody that Beto had heard of. It would be like a farmer killing a
cow out of spite. But this time Lenny came with friends, which was a bad sign.

No reason to get all worked up about it, Beto thought.

Rather than acting like he had something to hide, Beto called Lenny over
to the pool table and bought him and his friends a beer.

"Good to see you," Beto said warmly. "Let's talk after I finish this game?"

Lenny silently assented and sipped his beer as Beto played the game out.
Lenny was a little guy who had never made peace with his size. His friends were
two big country kids who Beto didn't know. The skinny one had a mustache
and clearly had no sense of humor. The other had a sweet chubby face and
looked surprised to be inhabiting such a large, powerful body.

Beto's dreadful night at the craps table was ancient history. He had borrowed some money since then from a girl he knew. Five hundred dollars of it
lay on the side of the pool table, underneath another five hundred laid down

by Beto's opponent. Beto had spent all afternoon setting him up for this game. It was actually good that Lenny had come, Beto thought. Lenny could see Beto play this fool.

Beto's opponent wasn't very good. Even so, the opponent took the advantage early. He sank one striped ball on the break and had just sunk three more on three well-executed, but not very demanding, shots.

The man's next shot failed. Too many of Beto's solid colored balls blocked the way.

There were too many solid balls even for Beto, and he ambled around the table looking for a clean path to one of the holes. There wasn't one, and Beto studied the table until he saw an approach that could work.

With a tap from his pool cue, he nudged the cue ball down the middle of the table toward one corner. There the cue ball glanced a solid ball, which moved so slowly that every pockmark on its surface stood out as it turned. At the pocket, the first solid ball met a second solid ball in inaudible contact, transferring just enough energy for the second ball to wobble on the pocket rim until gravity reached up and gently drew it down.

"Nice shot," his opponent said, frowning.

No kidding, Beto thought. That shot was twice as hard as anything his opponent had even tried and was easily Beto's best of the day. He looked at Lenny and smiled. The bookie was watching him intently, his dark eyes expressionless.

Beto hit the next shot too hard. Another solid ball fell into a pocket, but the cue ball kept rolling, coming to a halt in the middle of a confused pack of stripes and solids.

Beto made slow circuits around the table, looking for a good line. He looked for a long time. A minute? Longer? He started to sweat when he became aware of how long he was taking.

A low, hoarse whistle sounded from nearby. Lenny's goon with the baby face had gotten bored and was blowing into his empty beer bottle. He set it down with embarrassment when everyone looked up at him.

Beto's next shot made his opponent smile. It didn't drop any solid balls into the pockets. Not even close. It just made the jumble of balls slightly less jumbled. The opponent quickly leaned over and sighted his cue behind what looked like a promising angled shot at a striped ball.

Beto winked at Lenny. The shot wasn't as easy as it looked, and the opponent misjudged the angle. The striped ball rolled toward a corner pocket but went awry and grazed the eight ball, which then rolled slowly, but certainly, into the hole. Beto's defeated opponent exhaled loudly in disgust. Beto extended his hand to the man.

"An ugly win, but I'll take it," Beto said in a respectful tone.

From off to the side, Lenny said quietly, "I sure will."

Beto looked over to see the bookie holding the thousand-dollar wager and silently counting the bills. The country boys had stationed themselves at either end of the table. Play was over; time for business.

"I'll buy you and your friends some more beer," Beto said cheerily to Lenny. Lenny continued counting without acknowledging Beto.

Beto walked purposefully to the bar, where he glanced over his shoulder and saw that Lenny and his goons were all focused on the cash in Lenny's hands. Beto took the opportunity to slip into the one-toilet bathroom down the hall.

Beto congratulated himself on his clever plan: when Lenny noticed Beto was missing, he and his goons would naturally assume that Beto had fled down the hall and out to the back alley—away to safety—rather than into the bathroom. Once the three of them passed the bathroom, Beto would sneak out and leave by the front door. Beto crouched so that he could watch through the crack at the bottom of the door for the men's feet running past.

Instead, he promptly saw three pairs of feet stop in front of the door. Then the door was pushed open with a force that would have been inexcusably rude under normal circumstances. The door knocked Beto onto his rear end.

"Hey, I'm trying to take a piss in here," Beto said.

"You always leave your pants on to take a piss?" Lenny said. He nodded to his two friends—Mustache and Babyface, as Beto thought of them—who picked Beto up by the arms and dropped him on the toilet. Lenny squatted on his heels to bring himself to eye level with Beto. Lenny's eyes seemed like they had X-ray power. Beto was almost afraid to lie. He remembered a story he once heard that Lenny had beaten a debtor unconscious with his own girlfriend's handbag.

"You've got a thousand bucks right there," Beto said, pointing to Lenny's pocket.

"You owe me more. I want all of it."

"I don't have it."

Lenny locked eyes with Beto and slowly shook his head.

"Right now," Beto said. "I don't have it right now—but I can get it."

"Tonight."

"I need a few days."

"You said that last time. Tonight."

"Lenny, come on, man, you saw me out there. A thousand bucks for fifteen minutes of work."

"You were lucky."

"I was good. I set him up for that last shot. I studied that fool all day. I knew he would go for the easy shot. I'm good, Lenny."

"Yes, you are," Lenny said. "But tonight means tonight."

Lenny cast a glance up at his friends. The two men approached Beto from either side. Beto could only imagine what was coming, and everything he imagined was dreadful. He whimpered as the two larger men pressed him down by the shoulders on the toilet seat. One of them wrapped a meaty paw around his wrist and pulled it forward. Beto wailed in protest while Lenny rested stoically on his haunches.

A closed-fisted pounding rocked the hollow door to the men's room. *Salvation*, Beto thought. The owner ran a family place; he would kick these thugs out.

Babyface stepped forward and jerked the door open half a foot. Beto looked with hope toward the narrow space. He couldn't see who was outside, but whoever it was looked just as big as Babyface. The two muttered quietly for a few seconds, then Babyface eased the door closed again and locked it. He nodded to Lenny, who had observed the conversation over his shoulder without standing up.

Babyface returned to his position at Beto's side and pulled his arm forward again. This time Beto resisted, but it was still no use. God hadn't built him for this sort of confrontation.

Lenny rose, pushing down on his knees to lever himself up. Without breaking his gaze, he pulled something from his back pocket.

Beto only recognized it when Lenny held it right in front of his nose— a nutcracker, two ornate metal rods hinged together, the kind people use at Christmas to open walnuts.

"Part of me actually enjoys listening to your bullshit, Beto." Lenny tapped the folded instrument lightly on one knuckle of each finger of Beto's outstretched hand. "But the time for words is over."

Beto realized with alarm what was coming. "Lenny, I shoot pool with this hand," Beto said between gasps for air. "How do you expect me to pay you back with broken fingers?"

"Good point," Lenny said to his henchmen. "Other hand."

Beto curled his body up in fright. The two men slammed him down hard onto the toilet seat, bruising his tailbone.

"Pinky," Lenny said. Beto tried to close his fingers into a fist, but Mr. Mustache unrolled the little finger and presented it to Lenny like he was offering his boss a cigar. The nutcracker wrapped around the finger in an instant, and just as quickly Beto heard the bone snap. He howled like a cat in heat. The goons held him down as he writhed on the toilet seat. Lenny leaned in toward Beto's ear so that he wouldn't have to raise his voice. "Next is your thumb."

"OK," Beto said. "OK, OK, OK . . ." Finally he looked up. "You win."

"I'm listening," Lenny said.

"I know where you can get a lot of money."

Lenny shook his head. "I'm not interested in a treasure hunt."

"I know a secret worth ten times what I owe you. Twenty times."

"Don't bullshit me, Beto. I'll break every goddamn finger you've got."

"It's a little blackmail scheme. No—a big blackmail scheme. I'll tell you the secret, and you can keep all the money for yourself."

Lenny looked at Mustache and Babyface, neither of whom offered an opinion. "Speak."

"It's this company I work for, Liberty Industries. The boss did something awful, and I have proof."

* * *

Some people golfed on Sundays, others went to church. Luke Hubbard used Sunday mornings to catch up on work. The office was quiet, the phone didn't ring, and he had time to think.

But first came Friday's mail. Luke's secretary knew to open the envelopes for him, and so a closed envelope in the stack of letters caught his eye. The envelope had been addressed to Luke by name, with the instructions "To be opened by Mr. Hubbard only." That wasn't so unusual, but in combination with no return address, it was a classic candidate for the circular file. The handwritten address on the envelope looked as if it had been drawn by an illiterate child using a tracing book.

How did this one make it past the asylum censors? Luke wondered.

The contents were even more strange than he imagined.

It was a single page, heavier than it should have been. Pasted onto it were letters cut from headlines in newspapers and magazines. It looked like a ransom note from a bad movie. Luke couldn't help chuckling.

But the letter brought bad news and promised much worse. Unless, of course, a hefty fee were paid, instructions to follow. Luke wondered whether they really had proof. He couldn't imagine what it might be. Calling the police wouldn't do in a case like this. They were too slow and they would bog the process down with inconvenient questions.

Like whether it's true, Luke thought.

Luke needed to make these blackmailers go away, but the only person he trusted to do the job was still in New York trying to make Ray McLean, the hedge fund investor, go away.

Luke dashed off an email to Crash Bailey to tell him to finish with Ray McLean and return to L.A. to attend to an urgent new matter. Then Luke reviewed the rest of his mail. When he was done with that, he checked his email again. Crash hadn't yet replied. That annoyed Luke. He typed another email: "Waiting . . ."

14

For a big guy, he can really move, Ray McLean thought. The man had occupied the center of the dance floor for three songs in a row, dancing with the woman in the red dress. The woman Ray wanted tonight. People gave them as much room as they needed.

Are they together? Ray watched them and decided they probably were not. She had been here since before the big guy arrived. They just happened to be two of the rare people in the club who could actually dance. They had found each other amid the masses whose dancing style amounted to bouncing inertly up and down or dry humping the drink in their hand.

Ray wouldn't debase himself like the rest of the men out there. He held court from a booth set back from the dance floor, an expensive booth consisting of a plush, wrap-around bench behind a long table, served by its own waitresses. Women came to him—they could just tell he was successful. Ray loved being rich and young enough to enjoy it.

The big man on the dance floor was the envy of every other man in the place. He had been dipping and twirling her, staring into her eyes, for ten long minutes now. What man there had the skills to cut in? For that matter, what man had the *cojones*? The dancer was about six-foot-five and looked to weigh a solid two-fifty.

The next song was a slow one. The pair smiled warmly at each other and separated. The man walked to the bar while the woman went the other direction, back to her girlfriends who waited for her at a table. The compliant crowd opened to let her pass. Ray scanned the club until he spotted the big guy. He was easy to find. He stood at the bar, sipping a drink. He seemed to be looking at nothing in particular. He was all alone. Ray got an idea and asked a waitress to fetch the man.

The man was even more physically impressive up close. He was nice looking, with a strong nose and jaw line, and blue eyes almost as light as water. His hair was closely cropped and had prematurely turned silver. Ray knew dye jobs and could tell it wasn't dyed that way.

He wore a suit and tie, of all things, and politely introduced himself to Ray's companions. Ray shooed the giddy crew out of the booth so that the man could sit in the middle next to Ray. Then they all piled back in. It was tight, but no one minded.

"People call me 'Crash,'" the man said when Ray asked his name.

"OK, good to meet you, Crash. Dom Perignon?"

Ray spoke loudly and exaggerated his pronunciation to make himself understood over the pounding music. He indicated a magnum of champagne resting in a silver ice bucket by the table. The man had brought his own drink from the bar—it looked like a gin and tonic—but Ray wanted to be a good host.

Crash shook his head and smiled politely. "I like to stay sharp," he said. His voice was effortlessly deep. Despite the din his words reached Ray's ears as clearly as if they had been spoken in an empty theater.

"You were on fire out there," Ray said, and smiled. People called Ray bold and brilliant rather than handsome. He had a weak chin and bags under his eyes that never went away, but when he smiled he looked happy. Ray and Crash watched the spectacle together for a moment. Then Ray stood up and exhorted the others in the booth.

"Looks like someone unloaded an Atlantic City tour bus out there," he said, gesturing toward a large, boisterous group that had taken over the center of the dance floor. Several of his companions laughed or howled in agreement. "Why don't you go out there and restore a little New York flavor?"

Ray's friends left for the dance floor, leaving Ray and Crash alone. "I'm Ray," he said, and extended his hand.

"I know," Crash said.

"Really?"

"Sure, you run Vertigo Capital, don't you? One of the 'thirty moguls under thirty-five'?"

Crash was referring to a profile of Ray and other young business figures in a recent issue of a New York style magazine.

"Not anymore, I turned thirty-five last month," Ray said with a grin. He was still getting used to people recognizing him. "Look, you and your friend down there were great, and I'd love to buy you both a drink. Do you think she'd like to join us?"

Crash smiled as if it were the most whimsical question he'd ever heard. "You mean Alicia?"

"Right, the woman you were dancing with."

"Oh, sure, I can have her come up here. Do you mind if her friends come, too? She really seems to look out for her friends."

Ray clasped his hands together in his lap. "That's fine, that's . . . great."

"No problem. I just have a favor to ask first."

"What is it?"

Crash leaned in toward Ray and dropped his voice to a hoarse, penetrating whisper. "Stay away from Liberty Industries."

Confused, Ray studied the man's face. "What are you talking about?"

"I know you want to destroy them."

Crash wrapped his large hand tightly around Ray's wrist. Ray recoiled and looked at Crash with alarm. Ray looked around for his friends, but they were out bouncing on the dance floor.

"I don't want to destroy Liberty," Ray said cautiously. "I want to help them, their shareholders. Their stock's been underperforming, I want to talk with them, I—ow!"

Crash twisted Ray's wrist sharply like he was revving a motorcycle, and Ray flinched at the feeling of a rug burn running under his skin, from his wrist to his shoulder. He flailed his legs under the table, but the table pinned him in and he didn't get anywhere. Crash's only reaction was to tighten his grip.

"You're wrong about Liberty, Ray. They give jobs to thousands of people, they're stewards of the environment. They do great things. Luke Hubbard is doing great things."

Ray had met plenty of weirdoes in clubs. This guy definitely made the top five. *Probably on drugs*, Ray thought. Ray decided his best bet was to try to calm him down.

"I can see you're passionate about the company," Ray said, "but I have to take the interests of my investors to heart."

"I'm trying to reason with you, Ray."

Ray's eyes narrowed. "If you don't let go of my wrist right now, I'll scream."

Crash released Ray's wrist, and Ray's body relaxed. But his relief was short-lived. Crash took Ray's little finger, pinching it hard between his meaty thumb and the knuckle of his index finger. Ray's finger felt like it was caught under the foot of a sofa. He kept his composure, but was growing concerned.

"I'm happy to have a discussion with you," Ray said, "but I think you're trying to intimidate me, and I won't be intimidated."

Crash flicked his wrist again, and Ray heard his finger snap out of joint. The pain took a moment to arrive and when it came, it came slowly, steadily rising in intensity like someone turning up the volume of a television. It kept rising, past the point when Ray was sure it could go no higher, until his hearing was dulled with the sensation of blood racing in circles inside his skull.

Crash's deep voice penetrated the swirl of pain in Ray's head. "I'm not trying to intimidate you. I'm correcting your behavior."

"Who told you to threaten me?" Ray asked, panting. "Was it Hubbard?"

"Luke doesn't tell me what to do, he doesn't need to. I know when he's in danger."

Ray now had a very bad feeling about this guy. His stock trader's instincts kicked in. *When you're in a bad trade, get out of it.*

"Fine," Ray said. "As of now I'm done with Liberty. Just like you said."

Ray's surrender didn't erase the cruelty in Crash's face. "That's good, but how do I know you're not lying?"

"You've been very, um, persuasive, Mr. Crash. You have my word."

"I'll tell you how I know. I've been watching you, Ray. And I've watched your trips to the motel with that young woman who works for you."

Ray came out of his fugue of pain to protest, "I-I don't know what you're talking about."

"I think you do. And your wife will know, too, if I find out you've lied to me."

"Look, I know how it looks, but those were business meetings and—"

Crash tugged Ray's finger half an inch. Tears flooded his eyes, and he felt like throwing up.

"See? You're lying to me right now."

Ray gasped in agony. "You win. Tell Hubbard he wins."

Crash didn't react.

"Please let me go," Ray said. He looked at Crash with brimming eyes. Crash looked into Ray's eyes, earnestly but not angrily. Finally Crash released his finger.

Ray fled from the booth, bruising his hip on the table edge as he scrambled to escape. His finger throbbed with pain as he ran to a security guard by the dance floor. He pointed frantically with his good hand back toward the booth.

But all that could be seen was the huge bottle of champagne.

15

"**S**o, Mr. Pitcher, what exactly *is* your point?"

The judge's stinging words still rang in Brad's ears as he blinked in the midday sun outside the courthouse. Sheila walked next to him, seething in silence. All Brad wanted to do was run away and hide somewhere. But the granite courthouse steps were too widely spaced to take quickly, so he and Sheila were forced to descend slowly, deliberately, as if they were part of a wedding procession.

The hearing hadn't gone well. The judge, a stooped, withered old bachelor, had given Luke and his lawyers virtually everything they asked for—Sheila would have to provide extensive information in the discovery process to Luke, and Luke would have to provide a laughably minimal level of disclosure.

Brad got tongue-tied every time he tried to speak. The judge was impatient and blunt, a cantankerous Boston transplant. Alan Matthews, Luke's lawyer, had responded to every barbed question from the judge with smoothness and calm, almost indifference, as if he had written down his often lengthy extemporaneous answers beforehand. Brad had been unsettled by the judge and by his adversary's reputation—Brad stammered, he forgot Matthews' name, he mixed up the holdings in two of the cases he discussed.

Brad didn't understand it. He spoke in front of judges all the time—he probably had twice the actual courtroom experience that Matthews had, even though Matthews was much older. And yet this boardroom backslapper had triumphed. Brad and Sheila were worse off than before, and they both knew it.

Off to the side, Brad spotted Grant Steele, the ambitious federal prosecutor, perched on the courthouse steps. Steele was surrounded by reporters and cameras. Brad couldn't make out Steele's words, but could hear his voice—fluid, rising and falling in a cadence that drew Brad's attention even from a distance. Steele was just finishing up, and one of the reporters spotted Luke coming down the steps with Matthews.

"Luke," he called out—not "Mr. Hubbard," Brad noticed. Did Hubbard know the reporter, or was he addressed by his first name because he was a celebrity now?

Luke smiled warmly at the reporter, who now had several reporters and cameramen trailing him. Luke's lawyer lifted his hand to them. "Nothing today, guys," he said.

Then Brad saw Luke's lawyer turn toward Brad and flash a smug smile as he stepped into a waiting car with Luke. That big-firm arrogance made Brad so angry. He had to do something. He called out to the reporters.

"Guys, I have an announcement in Luke Hubbard's case." A couple of reporters turned and looked at him quizzically. Sheila also looked at him quizzically. He started talking, and the clutch of cameras swung around toward him, their glossy lenses arrayed like the eyes of a giant spider.

"I'm Brad Pitcher. P-I-T-C-H-E-R. Mr. Pitcher. I represent Sheila Hubbard here in the divorce proceedings."

Brad extended a hand stiffly to his side to indicate Sheila. She looked desperately from side to side, wanting to make an inconspicuous exit but terrified to leave Brad alone with the press.

"As you know, we had a hearing today," he said. "We think the judge's decisions were wrong in, um, logic and in law, and we look forward to complete vindication when all the facts are presented to the court."

Sheila's eyes looked as wide and round as ping pong balls. She dug her fingers into Brad's forearm, but he kept going. He'd never given a press conference before, but this felt good, it felt just like speaking in court, and he did that all the time.

"Mr. Hubbard's attempt to smear the name of Mrs. Hubbard and deprive her of the protections of California law is just par for the course for rich men who are used to getting their way. Well, he won't get his way this time."

Just when Brad felt pleased with the gathering rhythm of his speech, he was interrupted by questions.

"Brad, what additional facts will you present?" one of the reporters said.

"Well, first of all, his affairs," Brad said.

"Petra P," called out one of the reporters. Another one made a wolf whistle, and many of them laughed. Sheila, her mortification complete, stood with her hands at her side now, her eyes directed somewhere far away.

"Old news—what else?" another reporter said.

Brad faced a dozen microphones now, and they pushed farther into Brad's personal space, creeping closer with each moment that he stayed silent. He'd look like a fool in front of the entire city if he didn't think of something to say. *I'll be a fool on TV*, Brad thought, and then the words were out of his mouth before he even realized what he was saying.

"That kid of Petra's—he's Luke's kid."

Gasps escaped from the group and cameras clicked. Brad shut his mouth and forced it into a smile.

"What's your evidence?" one of the reporters said.

"The boy looks nothing like Luke," said another.

"That's all for today," Brad said. He smiled desperately, then took Sheila's arm and led her through the boisterous crowd of journalists and down the steps.

* * *

Alex's conversation with his uncle Hugh only whetted his appetite to find out more about the accident. Alex was sure that Hugh was right—in *most* cases, these janitor's insurance policies were completely innocent. Corporate tax planning, just like Hugh said. But the coincidence with Beto Capablanca was too tempting to ignore. In fact, Alex was more convinced than ever that the accident with Howard Cummings was actually a crime, because now he knew for sure that Liberty Industries had profited by the deaths of the employees in the van.

First thing: Alex needed to find Beto, and he remembered that Beto was hard to find when he didn't want to be found. After that, Alex would have to get Beto to talk to him, and that could be even harder, since Alex had helped send Beto to prison years ago. And even if Alex succeeded, then what? Whoever at Liberty was ultimately behind the deaths was probably high up in the organization. Beto was a low-level mechanic and might not have any idea who was really pulling the strings.

Problem was, Alex himself also had no idea who pulled the strings at Liberty Industries. He needed help, from someone with the resources and motivation to take down Liberty Industries. That would definitely *not* be the police, since Detective Lutz had made it clear that he cared more about closing cases than finding the truth. But Alex knew who *could* help. He had caught a few minutes of the local television news, and it showed a young lawyer speaking from the courthouse steps—a funny-looking guy with red hair who was the divorce lawyer for the wife of Liberty's CEO. The divorce was messy and, to judge from the wife's facial expression on camera, Luke Hubbard had the upper hand.

The reporter helpfully repeated the name of the wife's lawyer—Brad Pitcher. To be that ugly and successful, Brad Pitcher must be smart, Alex reasoned. Pitcher would realize that he and Alex had a shared interest in finding out whether the auto accident was really a crime and whether Luke Hubbard was ultimately behind it. And with Hubbard's fortune at stake in the divorce, Alex hoped Pitcher would be willing to bankroll an investigation.

Alex found Pitcher's phone number on the internet and dialed it with excitement. The secretary was skeptical of Alex's claim that he had important business to discuss, but Alex was persistent, and she eventually patched him through to Brad Pitcher.

But Pitcher wouldn't even listen to Alex's theory, let alone meet with him to discuss it.

"Too much to do here," Pitcher said over the telephone in a garbled voice. It sounded as if he was eating lunch. "If you've got information, give me information. I'm not taking business proposals." *Munch, munch, click.*

Alex called back and left his number with Pitcher's secretary in case Pitcher changed his mind, but Alex wasn't hopeful.

Alex was disappointed, but he wasn't discouraged, because he got another idea. He hadn't forgotten about Zeke Andrews, his back-stabbing former colleague who penned the newspaper article that got Alex fired. Alex hadn't forgotten, and he hadn't forgiven. With all the damage Zeke had caused Alex, Zeke owed Alex a favor, and Alex had a favor that Zeke would actually *want* to do. When Zeke answered, Alex started the conversation in an annoyingly sing-song voice. "Zeke, it's your old friend, Alex Fogarty."

Zeke's tone immediately turned wary. "Uh, hi, Alex. Look, I'd love to catch up but my boss is stalking the halls looking for five more reporters to lay off by Friday, and now's really not a good time, OK?"

"Gosh, trouble at work? Me too. I've been fired!" Alex laughed loudly as if charmed by the coincidence. "No problem, though, bud, I'm calling on business."

"Oh. Alex, if you're calling about the Rampart story, I don't think a follow-up will be possible. The editor has lost interest."

A follow-up? Alex thought. *How about, "I'm sorry I got you fired, Alex"? What a selfish prick.*

"Zeke, Zeke. You forget how well I know you. I don't expect you to correct your mistakes, or even admit them." Alex waited a beat, then continued. "I'm calling with the story that's going to save your job. I'm sure you remember that big accident around Christmas? Eight dead?"

"Of course," Zeke said. "We talked about it."

"Well, I didn't tell you everything. You got a pen?" Alex told Zeke about Jorge Ramirez, the scam artist who had been killed in the accident. Coincidence number one, Alex called it. He summarized the "janitor's insurance." Coincidence number two. The third coincidence, that veteran scam artist Rigoberto Capablanca also worked for Liberty, was one that Alex decided to continue keeping to himself. If Beto's name showed up in the paper, Beto would make himself not just hard to find, but impossible to find.

"Add it up," Alex said, "and there's something rotten here, and chances are the rot goes deep into the organization."

"Intriguing . . . What are Liberty's annual revenues?"

"I have no idea," Alex said.

"What I mean is, two million's a lot to you and me, but it's nothing to a company like that," Zeke said.

Alex rolled his eyes. He felt like he was talking to Uncle Hugh again. "Look, Zeke, what would you say if you learned that your boss had taken out an insurance policy on your life?"

Zeke laughed. "I'd stop reporting on any stories involving wildfires, wild animals or wild women."

"And did I mention that Rampart also cancelled their liability policy on the poor sucker at the back of the crash?" Alex said. "Bullshit technicality, but they left his widow high and dry. She'll probably lose her house." Alex paused to let the information sink in. "Unless, of course, someone proves that her late husband didn't cause the crash. Think any of this could rekindle your editor's interest?"

Zeke said nothing. It sounded like he was sucking on a lozenge. Probably one of those nicotine substitutes, Alex thought.

"It'd be impossible," Zeke said eventually. "Liberty Industries is a huge advertiser with *The Chronicle*. Without their ad spending, the paper would be in trouble."

Alex groaned. "*The Chronicle* is already in trouble."

"Anyway," Zeke said, "even if my editor signed off, the C-Suite would go apeshit. He and I both would be fired."

"Zeke, Zeke, you're thinking too small," Alex said. "One of these days you're going to get fired from *The Chronicle*—"

"Thanks for the vote of confidence," Zeke said.

"—and the sooner, the better. It's a sinking ship, Zeke. You don't need to save your crappy job, you need to make a reputation that can get you into another, more solvent paper."

Zeke chortled. "If there are any."

That was as close to acquiescence as would ever pass from Zeke's lips.

"Anyway," Alex said. "You're a reporter. So go report."

Alex offered to fax the life insurance policies to Zeke, and Zeke gave a non-committal response about looking at them. Alex figured there was a fifty percent chance that Zeke would actually follow up on the story, but Alex didn't know who else to call. He turned the television back on and started flipping channels. He needed to relax for a while before he started looking for Beto.

Alex paused when he turned to a press conference given by a man in a suit. Alex quickly recognized the man as Grant Steele, a federal prosecutor who always seemed to be on television. Steele looked to be in his late thirties, was handsome and not fat, and wore his thick dark hair combed back from his forehead.

"It is . . . the most pernicious betrayal . . . of the public trust," Steele said.

The television camera showed a close-up of Steele's face. Even when he used the same clichés that everyone else in the media did, he filled them with drama. Alex couldn't turn away.

"They've placed money over country . . . self over community . . . lies over truth."

What is it already? Alex thought. *What's the crime?*

"The defendants will say that *they* are the victims—not you and I, they . . . are the victims . . . of their own poor record keeping. But I say that contracting with the government is a privilege, a sacred trust. I say . . . government contractors should be above suspicion."

Alex had trouble getting as excited about Steele's latest case—it sounded like a case of ordinary greed. Alex's own case was much more interesting— Alex's theory, at least, included greed *and* murder. In fact . . .

Alex picked up the telephone and looked up a number. The man who answered said, "Department of Justice, United States Attorney's Office."

"Hello," Alex said. "I'd like to speak with Grant Steele."

16

The air outside was in the high fifties, but Petra P's skirt stopped six inches above her knees. She inched one leg out the door of her small, well-kept house, and cautiously looked about.

Then she opened the door and with a catwalk sway stepped down the walk, her high-heeled shoes marking a confident beat. When she reached the morning paper, she folded smoothly at the waist to retrieve it.

The photographers were waiting, the same two as yesterday. They emerged from behind a car, tossed down their cigarettes and raised their cameras. Petra feigned surprise and turned away.

"Petra, baby, what does the 'P' stand for?" one of them said.

"The P stands on principle," she said in Russian-accented English. She tilted her head in a pose and smiled, displaying two rows of small, straight teeth. Her straight black hair flipped under her chin with the motion of her head, and her cobalt eyes flashed in the morning sun.

The cameras clicked like insects in heat.

A familiar rattle joined the cacophony, and within seconds Petra was showered from all angles with water from the lawn sprinklers. She screamed and reflexively put her hands to her hair. She twisted from side to side looking for safe passage back to the door, but in vain. Water spilled in streams from her dark, flattened tresses.

A young boy of four or five dashed out of the house. He jumped over the sprinklers and waved his arms with delight as the spray soaked his clothes.

"Dmitri! Nyet!" Petra said. She chased the child, who gleefully led her in a wide loop through the grass before disappearing back inside.

The cameras kept clicking.

* * *

Inside, Luke Hubbard crouched on a linoleum floor and shut the door to the bathroom to block out the noise of Petra yelling at Dmitri and Dmitri yelling at God knows what.

"How much do you want?" he said. Even though alone, he cupped his hand over his mouth as he spoke into the phone.

"Half a mil," said the voice on the other end, a man's voice, not particularly deep. Luke heard muffled but fervent words in the background. "No, one million," the voice said clearly.

Luke had no idea who he was talking to. Whoever had put together the amateurish blackmail letter had been sophisticated enough not to leave fingerprints on it.

"That's a lot of money," Luke said.

"Not for you, it's not. We seen you in the paper. You're rich."

Luke shrugged, though no one was there to see him do so. "It's not like I have that kind of cash in my wallet. I'll have to sell assets, move things around. It'll raise questions."

There was another muffled off-line colloquy.

"Just tell them you wanted to buy that pretty girlfriend of yours a new necklace," the voice said finally.

"It's especially a lot of money when I don't even know what it is you're offering." Luke spoke cryptically on purpose. If reporters could hide behind cars and bushes, there was no reason they couldn't pretend to be blackmailers and bluff him into revealing details of his personal life.

"Look, Mr. CEO, you bring the money, you see the proof. That's the deal. You don't like it, there's plenty of newspapers that'll be interested in what I got."

Luke looked up at a bird preening itself outside the bathroom window. Somewhere in the house, little Dmitri had started to cry.

"Hey, you still there?"

"I'm here," Luke said.

"One million. Today."

"Not possible. A hundred grand is all I can get today."

Luke waited for a reply. His blackmailers seemed to do everything by committee. It was as bad as trying to get a decision out of his board of directors. Finally the answer came back in the affirmative.

"Fine," the voice said. "We'll call again with the location. Come alone. You bring the cops, we go to the press."

"Don't worry," Luke said. "There won't be any cops."

Luke hung up the phone and left the bathroom. Petra's little house was quieter now, and when he entered the living room, he saw why. Crash had arrived to drive Luke to work, and now he was roughhousing with Dmitri, wrestling with him and tossing him in the air. Dmitri was giggling a little, but no longer screaming. Petra stood in front of the two of them, wearing a towel around her wet hair and a bathrobe that revealed as much of her thighs as her skirt had.

"Morning, Crash," Luke said.

Crash put Dmitri down and turned toward his boss, studiously ignoring Petra's damp skin inches in front of him. "Sir?"

Luke looked over at Petra. "What do you think, P? We should ask Crash to moonlight as a 'manny.' Save a little money on daycare."

Petra pulled her bathrobe more tightly around her body and smirked at Crash. "The sensitive men are so sexy," she said. "Maybe Crash could find a girlfriend and not be so lonely."

Luke gave Crash a playful wink. "Let's go, Crash. We've got business to discuss."

Outside, the photographers were gone. Luke leaned in toward Crash and spoke in a voice just above a whisper.

"I just spoke with the blackmailers. They want money today. I'd like you to take it to them."

* * *

In a conference room at the offices of Boswell & Baker, the two spouses and their lawyers started gathering at eight in the morning in business attire and varying states of wakefulness. They began early on the basis of the amicably agreed fiction that they would finish earlier that way.

Brad Pitcher chatted with Alan Matthews, his nemesis in these negotiations, about baseball and other banalities. Even Sheila was in a good mood this morning. Brad felt better than he expected to, given a nervous fit of vomiting around midnight. It had been a week since the disastrous discovery hearing and Brad's even more disastrous improvised press conference on the courthouse steps. The stakes for this meeting couldn't be higher for his client—and for him. But after plotting out the possible course of negotiations in a lengthy outline, after weeks of commutes spent visualizing his arguments and responses, this morning he felt the same calm confidence that he felt arguing before judges in the criminal courts. This was his house today, Matthews just didn't know it yet.

The bonhomie ended at twenty past the hour when Luke Hubbard arrived. He glided in, his head down as he tapped out an email on his smartphone. With a word to no one, he took a center seat on one side of an oblong conference table made of dark wood. After finishing his email, he looked up at Matthews impatiently.

Matthews gestured toward the table and smiled at the others. "Shall we?"

Luke's side of the table was more crowded than Sheila's. On Sheila's side, it was just her and Brad. They knew it would be that way—Brad didn't have a staff to help him like Alan Matthews did. On Luke's side, Luke and his lawyers took every spot. Arrayed beside Matthews were four more suit-clad lawyers, who appeared to be spaced by intervals of about five years of age: a junior partner, a senior associate, a mid-level associate and a junior associate—the last one a sleepy-looking young woman who tensely held a pen over a yellow note pad.

Something clicked in Brad's brain and he finally recognized the lawyer sitting to his far right. He was in Brad's class at Harvard Law. He had been an arrogant prick back then, a skinny little mole who talked to the professors as if his seat on the Law Review made him a peer of theirs. Brad recalled the disdainful way this classmate rejected Brad's offer to form a study group for their torts class. The haughty, cock-eyed expression on his face now was the same as back then, but Brad was sure that it was the names Boswell & Baker on his business card, rather than the Law Review, that now fueled his hauteur. It would always be something.

The mole looked back at Brad, unmoving and unsmiling. Clearly, the mole didn't recognize Brad. Brad noticed with satisfaction that the years had brought the mole's hairline and waistline into convergence with Brad's. Brad gave him a wide, thin-lipped smile and held it until he looked away.

A paralegal, an ungainly kid who looked fresh out of college, bustled in with a box full of files. He froze at the foot of the table with an expression of perplexed concern and stared hard at the empty chairs on Sheila and Brad's side as if trying levitate a chair over to Luke's side of the table by telekinesis.

"Looks like we have a few extra on that side, Robert," Matthews said. He shot Brad a malign grin.

Brad stood and pulled a chair out for the paralegal, which caused a renewed look of confusion on the boy's face. "I use what your firm would call 'thin staffing,' Alan," Brad said. "Your client will appreciate the difference when he pays Mrs. Hubbard's legal expenses."

All day, Matthews was the only lawyer from Luke's side who spoke, and Brad never figured out what the other lawyers were doing there.

The purpose of the paralegal became clear early on. He pulled files out of the box and replaced them, sorted papers and flipped through them in what seemed like a purposeless, repetitive chore. But every time Brad spoke, the paper flipping got much louder. Brad was sure that Matthews had instructed the paralegal to do that. Brad couldn't help admiring his opponent's diabolical attention to detail.

As the hours passed, the color of the sky outside the conference room windows deepened into the saturated blue of midday and then gradually faded again, until at last hints of brown and yellow near the horizon announced the start of the sun's slow retreat to the sea. Inside, time stood still, despite a messy accumulation of discarded scratch paper and empty coffee cups that made a misleading picture of progress.

With no children to divvy up, Sheila and Luke's disputes only related to how to split their property. The fact that the pot held more than enough for each of them only made the process more difficult. Which was the better asset, the Malibu house valued at ten million dollars or the one in Aspen worth nine million? How would they split the tax benefit from their charitable contributions? Should Sheila take her alimony over time or take a discounted sum up front?

That last question was the one that Brad had been trying to get the other side to focus on, but they stubbornly denied that Sheila would even get alimony.

"Your client has a degree and high-level executive experience. She could easily support herself—in fact, she could walk in as head of H.R. pretty much anywhere," Matthews said.

Brad's hands, resting on the table top, twitched in frustration. "Alan, you give new meaning to the word 'chutzpah.' The only reason Mrs. Hubbard doesn't have a job now is because your client fired her. He needs to correct his wrong."

Sheila huffed and then said under her breath, "Like I'd crawl back and work for him now." Brad laid a steady hand on her arm without breaking his stare at Matthews.

"Is she actively looking for a new job?" Alan said. He wore the same wry smile that he had when telling stories that morning before the meeting.

Brad and Sheila didn't have to answer because Luke looked up from his email to interject with a tardy response to an earlier part of the conversation.

"Wasn't me," he said. "Canning Sheila was approved by the board."

"Oh, and I'm sure the idea just came to them out of the blue," Sheila said. The two spouses shared a long, venomous look at each other. Brad smiled sympathetically at Sheila and then turned to Matthews.

"As good a time as any, I suppose—getting late," Brad said. Then he produced a folded sheaf of papers from inside his suit jacket and dropped them onto the table in front of Luke. "Mr. Hubbard, you're being served on behalf of Liberty Industries in a claim of sexual harassment and wrongful termination. Alan, I'm sure this doesn't come as a surprise." Matthews took the complaint off the table and looked through it.

Brad had been waiting for just the right time to play this card. Boswell & Baker was a corporate law firm—Liberty's law firm—and Liberty and Luke had conflicting interests regarding Sheila's termination. Brad was curious to see whether he could put some daylight between Matthews' two favorite clients— Liberty and Luke. If so, that would make it awkward for Boswell & Baker to keep representing both of them. Would Luke become more eager for a quick settlement? Would Alan?

"You'll understand if we don't take your client's word on the reasons for Mrs. Hubbard's dismissal," Brad said to Matthews. Then he added, as if an afterthought, "I mean, your client in the divorce case . . . not your client in the wrongful termination case, which is, of course, the company."

Matthews frowned. Brad knew he understood.

"That's why we'll be deposing all the members of Liberty's board of directors," Brad said. "As the group with ultimate legal responsibility for running the company, we need to know whether Mrs. Hubbard was fired in retaliation for reporting to Mr. Hubbard various . . . irregularities in the expense reimbursements by some of Mr. Hubbard's chief lieutenants. Anyway, I assume Mr. Hubbard *told* the board about those irregularities . . ."

Luke looked at Brad, then at Matthews. "Alan, we talked about this," Luke said. Matthews interrupted him simply by lifting his hand off the table. Matthews' wry smile was gone now.

Brad calmly rose, biting his tongue to suppress a grin. He brought Sheila up with him. He smiled condescendingly at Matthews. "Clearly, Mr. Hubbard has a lot of fight in him, so I doubt we'll be getting our quick settlement—in either the divorce case or the termination case. I'll call one of your associates to set up the depositions of your board members."

Brad nodded to Sheila, who peered with joyful triumph down at her husband. Luke's face had gone slack with disbelief.

Brad picked up his briefcase and turned to leave. Before he could do so, the door to the room jerked in its frame and discharged the old law school classmate who Brad had recognized that morning. He had left the conference room after lunch, and now rushed toward Matthews with the same urgent, hurried stride that carried him at the end of every law school class to the front of the classroom to brown-nose the professor. With his head slightly bowed, he solemnly delivered to Matthews a folded set of papers that could only be a summons that Matthews had ordered up for himself.

"Not so fast, Brad," Matthews said. He held the papers at the end of his outstretched arm like a carton of spoiled milk.

Fearing the worst, Brad tentatively reached out to take them.

17

Lenny took great care to choose a meeting spot where no one could sneak up on him, but with the sun now accelerating toward the horizon it was hard for him to spy any movement to the west. Lenny knew plenty of places in the city where people could hide in plain view. This industrial lot east of downtown was one of them. Lenny expected to see a car, and so by the time he first noticed the man approaching on foot, the man had come close enough for Lenny to see that he would be trouble. He was not Hubbard. He was tall and wide at the shoulders, with a long, even stride, and he and his briefcase cast a shadow visible from fifty yards.

Nearly everything did. It was the brilliant hour of the afternoon, and the sun's long, heavy rays illuminated the dusty air into a glittering fog.

The figure remained a tantalizing silhouette—the only visible source of movement—as he unhurriedly crossed the train tracks and the vacant concrete bridge toward where Lenny waited. Details emerged only at the very end—gray wool suit, white shirt, tie, dusty black shoes shaded by his legs. Up close, Lenny saw that the man's hair, which had looked a golden blond in the sun, was in fact silver, almost white. With the sun still behind him, the man's pale face was unreadable.

Lenny handed his briefcase to Rudy, a big man with a sweet face who had gone with Lenny to meet Beto at the pool hall. Rudy held the briefcase as daintily as if it were his mother's purse.

Lenny took a step forward to meet the stranger, who was almost a foot taller than Lenny, an imposing wall of gray and white. Only his necktie added a hint of color. It was a pale blue, scattered with tiny designs—little horses, maybe. A pair of handcuffs connected the briefcase to his left wrist.

"Where's Hubbard? We told Hubbard to come." Lenny had been looking forward to dealing with the CEO. On the phone the executive had sounded weak, always ready to give up something more to get rid of a blackmailer, just like Beto said he would be.

"I'm his representative," the man said.

Lenny slapped the man in the face, then bounced backward onto the balls of his feet, smiling ruthlessly. The man didn't react. Lenny turned to Rudy. "Frisk him."

Rudy set the briefcase down on the concrete and approached the man, who was taller even than Rudy. The man's face remained expressionless as he raised his arms away from his hips to give Rudy access to his torso.

Rudy looked slightly embarrassed when he found the shoulder holster, which held a dark gray revolver. Rudy made a move to tuck the gun between his belly and waistband but froze when Lenny grunted. Rudy handed Lenny the gun.

"You won't mind if we take this from you, *Mr. Representative*," Lenny said.

The man looked serenely into the distance. "That's OK," he said softly. "I don't need it."

Lenny ordered Rudy to search the man for a wire, and Rudy clumsily clapped his thick hands up and down the man's body again, but more firmly this time. The man stirred only when Rudy started to pick at the knot of his necktie. He gently wrapped his hands around Rudy's and put them aside, then deftly unknotted the tie.

"It was a gift," the man said. He loosely folded the tie and dropped it into an inside pocket of his suit jacket.

Rudy went in again, pulling open the top of the man's dress shirt and exposing nothing more threatening than a thin gold chain that surrounded the man's muscular neck and disappeared beneath a low-necked undershirt. Rudy stepped back and nodded soberly to Lenny.

"Did you bring the hundred K?" Lenny asked.

"It's in the briefcase."

"Open it."

"You'll see the money when I see the evidence you're selling."

Lenny frowned.

A black SUV pulled up to the men. It stopped sharply enough that its tidy wake of dust and gravel overshot the tires and peppered the men's shoes. The driver jumped out and ran to Lenny as if expecting an urgent order. Rudy and the stranger turned their heads toward Lenny as well.

Lenny spoke to the driver in rapid, hushed words that neither of the other men could hear. As he spoke, he waved the revolver around for emphasis the way some people wave a cigarette. Then Lenny turned his eyes and the gun on the stranger.

"Give him your tie," Lenny said. He snapped the tip of the barrel in Rudy's direction, a flourish that Rudy didn't seem to notice. The stranger did as he was told.

"Blindfold him with it," Lenny said to Rudy. Rudy did as he was told.

"Into the car," Lenny said.

The blindfolded stranger went compliantly into the car, moving carefully and steadily in spite of the rough shoves of Lenny's two henchmen. There he sat, holding his briefcase with both hands in his lap.

18

Alex hadn't heard again from Zeke Andrews or—no surprise—the super busy Brad Pitcher. Grant Steele's assistant had sounded noncommittal at first, but then perked up the more Alex told him. Alex hoped that either Zeke or Steele was looking into the accident and the life insurance policies.

In the meantime, Alex needed to find Beto. Alex had tried for a week now, but without success. Back when Alex was first investigating Beto for the fraud that sent him to prison, Beto seemed at any given moment to be avoiding a dozen different landlords, bosses, ex-partners, bookies and gangsters and an untold number of girlfriends and their male relations. Alex couldn't help but admire the man's cracked gift for deceit and evasion. Alex remembered that even while encircled by danger, Beto remained flamboyant—his silk shirts, all the girlfriends. Even his taste in food was ostentatious. The cops told Alex that during questioning they offered him a cold slice of the pepperoni pizza the detectives had been picking at all night—and he had insisted on a new pizza with anchovies and pineapple, and no cheese, before he would talk. And of course, Beto had almost escaped from the county jail with the help of a lonely, love-struck female guard.

Alex drove east to Beto's old street for the third day in a row. Alex's discreet visits to various of Beto's former associates had been fruitless, and at this point

Alex was just burning gas money and hoping to get lucky. He wasn't even sure if Beto still lived around here.

On a weekend morning five years ago, when Alex had surprised Beto coming out of his house, wrestled a knife from him and pummeled him into submission in the middle of the street, no one had come out of any of the houses to watch. No one had shouted or called the police. It was that kind of a neighborhood back then, and it had only gotten uglier since.

Another family seemed to have moved into Beto's old house. Like most of the other houses on the block, it was a small stucco cube with red tiles on the roof. What told Alex the occupants had changed was the set of plastic children's toys in the front yard—chairs and a table, a tricycle—all faded from their original primary colors to sun-bleached pastels. Alex couldn't imagine Beto having children—couldn't imagine him ever sharing a house with children, anyway.

The children were either gone or grown up, by the look of it. The toys clearly hadn't been moved for a long time, as weeds with brittle yellow stalks and serrated tufts on top had found time to grow in the spaces between them. Alex drove on.

He peeked into all the local pool halls and pawn shops—again—and wondered how long it would take before someone noticed that he had become a regular in the neighborhood. It was the middle of the afternoon, late enough for the more committed drinkers to appear at the local bars. Alex picked one to visit first. He parked and was about to enter when he saw a thin, shortish man in a silk shirt exit the front door with a pretty young woman about his height with long straight black hair. If they'd been drinking, they'd sure started early. Alex stopped and watched them walk away from him. From a distance, the man looked enough like Beto to pique Alex's interest. In any event, this was the closest hit Alex had had all week. He followed them on foot, giving them distance. They walked quickly but unsteadily, like they'd been drinking.

Two blocks away, Alex watched them enter an apartment building. The building was a two-story, U-shaped structure with apartments arranged around a central courtyard. Alex rushed forward to get a closer look. If they disappeared into one of the apartments, Alex wouldn't be able to confirm that the man was indeed Beto, and he might never find them again. There was a black steel gate at the front of the complex that slowly swung closed after the man and woman entered. Alex reached the gate just before the lock clicked shut again. He silently eased the gate ajar and slipped into the complex, where he hid in the shadows by the wall of mailboxes.

The front doors of the apartments let out onto the central courtyard, and concrete stairs led up to an open-air walkway with a metal railing that gave access to the second-floor units. Alex watched the man and woman climb the stairs, still oblivious to their follower. The woman unlocked the door to the first apartment by the staircase, and the couple entered.

Now what? Alex pretended to look at the mailboxes and, rather self-consciously, tried to look casual. There was no name on the mailbox for the apartment the couple had entered. The complex was quiet; people were at work or doing whatever they did during the day. Alex waited, playing out scenarios of what he might say if one of the residents confronted him and asked what he was doing here. If only he'd worn a suit he could have pretended to be a Mormon missionary.

After a few minutes, he heard a crash like the sound of breaking glass come from one of the apartments. He looked up toward the second floor but saw no activity there. A moment later, from within one of the ground floor apartments, a woman started shouting in a language he didn't recognize, there was a loud clap, and a child began wailing. But none of the doors opened.

Alex came out of the shadows and walked around the courtyard. A swimming pool in the middle of the courtyard that once held up to nine feet of water now held scattered scuffmarks from skateboard wheels, ornate graffiti in several styles and a lonely brown puddle at the bottom where the remnants of winter rains patiently awaited evaporation. Near the door to the room with the garbage cans, Alex noticed an empty pizza box lying haphazardly against a wall, and that gave him an idea.

With an empty pizza box balanced on one hand, Alex climbed the stairs and paused in front of the door that the man and woman had disappeared into.

To the left of the door, a ragged curtain made from a torn bed sheet billowed out of a large window that had been opened wide. Alex glimpsed only a tabletop and an ashtray before the curtain slumped back into the aperture. He heard the sound of an electric fan blowing inside, but no speech.

Alex knocked on the door, which he was careful to do not too sharply.

"I gotta pizza here?" he said. "Order for a large anchovy and pineapple, no cheese?" If it was Beto inside, Alex knew he would open up for his favorite pizza. Beto would assume the girl ordered it. Unless Beto asked her. And she said no. And Beto got suspicious.

The door swung open.

There stood the woman, even prettier up close. Her black hair fell over her shoulders. She wore a T-shirt and men's boxer shorts and nothing else and looked neither surprised, nor ashamed, nor distressed. Calm.

"Yes?"

"You order a pizza?" Alex did his best to sound like he was bored and tired from driving around all day, instead of jumpy and tired from driving around all day. The open door revealed an efficiency apartment, with a bed pulled out from a sleeper sofa and the sheets and pillows in disarray. Lying among them, languidly smoking a cigarette, was Beto.

It was him, all right. He looked the same as when Alex had seen him taken away in handcuffs, but a few years older and with his thin face relaxed in what Alex surmised was post-coital tranquility.

Alex took a large step forward into the apartment. The woman took three quick steps backward. Alex closed the door behind him. "Beto, we need to talk."

Beto seemed to take notice for the first time that he had a visitor. He bolted upright in bed. His unbuttoned silk shirt fell open and exposed his thin, hairless torso. He too was wearing boxer shorts.

"It's been a long time, Beto. You look good."

Beto's hand shot under the sheet and the sheet rose up, draped over something in his hand that he pointed at Alex. He looked at Alex with fury, and the cigarette bounced in his lips as he spoke.

"Take one more step and I blow you away."

19

When the men took off the necktie blindfold, Crash found himself sitting on a small wooden chair in a windowless room with unadorned steel walls—maybe a portable office or pre-fabricated storage shed. The leader, the one who liked to wave Crash's pistol around, sat on the other side of a flimsy card table. The leader's own briefcase lay in front of him on the table.

The light in the room came from an incandescent bulb hanging from the ceiling inside an upside-down pie dish. The man's two goons stood behind and to either side of Crash. The chubby one with the baby face had Crash's revolver wedged in his waistband.

"Don't look around, we're here for business. Open the briefcase."

Crash's hands weren't tied, and he still had his briefcase handcuffed to his left wrist. He placed the briefcase on the table but didn't open it.

"Are you deaf or something?" the leader said.

"Show me what you've got," Crash said.

"First you show me the money."

"I don't think so," Crash said.

The leader opened his briefcase and removed a pistol. To his left, Crash heard the chubby one gasp. The leader pointed the weapon at Crash's heart, wielding it with his arm rigid and straight this time, rather than casual and loose like before. The man sneered triumphantly at Crash.

"Looks like all I have for you is this," the man said.

"Oh . . . that's too bad," Crash said.

In one motion, Crash slid off the chair and kicked the near end of the card table up into the leader's face. The man's gun discharged into the ceiling—instantly a yellow beam of sunlight connected the ceiling to the floor at a lazy slant. Crash hammered his briefcase into the chubby one's knee. The chubby one's legs buckled, lowering his hips enough for Crash to reach the pistol tucked in his waistband. Crash pulled it out and from the ground let off three quick shots through the underside of the table to a spot where the leader's scrambling feet told Crash that his torso must be. The thump and rattle of a heavy weight landing against the back metal wall told Crash that he had hit his target. Still lying on the floor, Crash swung his arm to the right and fired three times into the chest of the thinner henchman, whose mouth was agape in surprise. Crash was out of bullets, and the chubby one was frantically wrestling with the doorknob.

Crash smoothly replaced the revolver in his shoulder holster, pulled one leg underneath his body and launched himself like a sprinter off the starting blocks into the man's back. The two fell hard against the door and the man let out a pained wheeze as the impact squeezed the breath out of his lungs. The walls of the little room shuddered around them, echoing the vibration of the door.

Crash rose to his feet, turned the kid around by the shoulders and slammed him against a side wall—the briefcase still attached to Crash's wrist danced wildly with the motion. The man's head snapped back and met sharply with the steel wall. His eyelids fluttered as if he was about to lose consciousness. Crash slapped him across the cheek, and the man regained his senses.

"Where's the evidence?" Crash shouted. "*What* is the evidence?" Crash slapped him again when he didn't answer right away.

"I-I don't know. Lenny never showed me."

"There's not much time. Tell me where it is." Crash was standing over the man, shaking him by the shoulders. "Who does it point to? Is it Hubbard?"

"I don't know . . . I just know that Lenny got it from Beto."

"Who's Beto?" Crash was panting from exertion and adrenaline.

"Capa . . . Beto Capabla . . ." The other man was fading—shock, probably. Crash slapped him one more time, more out of frustration than an expectation that the other man would regain his wits. The other man looked up, with pain and confusion, into Crash's eyes.

"Why . . . why do you kill for him?" he asked Crash.

"So that he doesn't have to."

The man's mouth rounded and his tear-stained eyes widened in fear. Crash spun the man around again so that the man faced away from him, and he hooked the chain of the handcuffs he wore under the man's chin. On one side of the man's head was Crash's thick wrist; on the other side, Crash's briefcase. Crash took hold of the chain with his free hand.

Crash pulled. The man surged his body back and up in resistance. He was a big man and he reached his arms backward over his head to try to pull Crash's hands down, but Crash was bigger still, and too strong.

Crash pulled harder. The other man's resistance was strong and steady and abated with dreadful slowness. This way was always an ordeal.

"Shh," Crash said to the man. "Shhhh . . ."

After what felt like a lifetime, the man faded to dead weight, and still Crash held him close, until his limbs convulsed in a wild spasm that marked the end.

Crash laid the man's body against the wall, legs out, head on his chest as if he were stealing a nap in the middle of a long train ride. Then Crash stepped nimbly to the door, placing each step carefully to avoid the vivid puddle of blood that steadily crept across the floor from the other two bodies.

Outside, Crash used a handkerchief from his jacket pocket to cover his hand before he pulled the door shut. He stepped out into what appeared to be an abandoned junkyard. In the departing daylight, piles of debris and hunks of metal cast large, lumpy shadows that looked like misshapen beasts. Crash walked over them in a straight line toward the bulging orange sun.

20

"You can go, Mrs. Hubbard," Alan Matthews said, but of course she stayed.

Brad wished she hadn't. She wasn't being sued, he was. Brad felt the eyes of everyone else in the conference room boring into his back.

Brad scanned the legal complaint that Alan had just served him with. Defamation, intentional infliction of emotional distress—a grab-bag of tort claims. They stemmed from Brad's statements to the television reporters that Luke was the father of Petra P's son. Brad felt his face redden. His amateur press conference had come back to haunt him.

This new lawsuit would make it difficult for him to remain on the divorce case—he now had a potential conflict with Sheila's interests. By suing Liberty and creating a potential conflict between Liberty and Luke, Brad had hoped to put pressure on Matthews. Matthews obviously knew that game, too, and now he had forced Brad into a similar dilemma: Brad could resign from representing Sheila and slink back to the criminal courts, away from the cameras forever, or else he could get Sheila's blessing to continue and then try to prove something that none of them believed to be true—that Luke was the father of the child.

Fired. Disbarred. Bankrupt. Shunned. Brad envisioned a bleak future, one that was supposed to be for other people, for dumber people.

"What does it say?" Sheila asked.

Brad unfastened his briefcase with a quivering hand and dropped the summons into it. "Bullshit," he said. "It's bullshit."

"An apt term," Matthews said. "Because 'bullshit' is just the word I would choose to describe your wanton assertions that Mr. Hubbard is the father of his friend's child."

"His friend," Sheila said disdainfully. "You mean his whore."

Luke sputtered a profane objection, and Sheila egged him on. "Go ahead and deny it. I hear the rumors, too, that you found her in a brothel and had Crash beat up the Russian gangsters who were holding her there."

The others gasped, but Luke actually laughed. Luke composed himself and stared at Sheila coldly. "And so I'm sitting here wasting a perfectly good workday because you slept with me for twenty years and now want some money for it. What's the difference, Sheila?"

Brad swung his briefcase up and slammed it on the table. It landed flat and hard, and the sharp smack resounded through the room. "That's enough," he said quietly.

Everyone froze, waiting for Brad to say something more, to offer a strong and gallant response. But Brad just stared at the table.

"My associate will call you to schedule your deposition," Matthews said finally.

Matthews was a prick. Brad knew that even if he quit the divorce case, Matthews and his gang would keep hounding him with this new suit out of spite. The suit would kill his career, less like a car crash than like pneumonia—if it stuck around long enough, it would do him in. Brad composed himself and looked up at Matthews. "Let me understand," he said. "Is it your position that Mr. Hubbard is *not* the father of that darling little sprinkler-hopper?"

Matthews laughed merrily, as if he had caught a neighbor's child in a charming lie. "How could he be? The child is five. He hasn't even known her that long."

"It's more complicated than that." It was Luke who spoke. He had remained sitting at the table.

"It's simple enough, Luke," Matthews said insistently. "Pitcher said something false about you, now he'll pay for it. Just like we discussed."

"Sit," Luke said. "I'll explain."

They took their seats, looking nervous and confused, Matthews more so than anyone else.

"The truth is, I've known Petra for quite some time. Off and on, I mean. We first met over five years ago, when I took a trip to Prague."

Sheila rose from her chair. "You bastard, that was when you took me to—"

"Maybe he's mine, maybe he isn't. That's just it, y'see. I don't know." After a leisurely pause Luke continued. "There are virtues to not knowing. But now I suppose I'll be finding out." He didn't seem to care. "Point is, I'm cool either way. I'm not the father, and I put your sorry ass on Skid Row," he said, flicking an index finger in Brad's direction. "If I am the father, then I've got the son I always wanted."

"Luke, you've got to stop," Matthews said.

"Who knows? Maybe I'll adopt him."

"Luke!" Matthews shouted.

"Maybe I will, Alan, maybe I will. Pitcher, you know what a poison pill is?"

Brad self-consciously cast a glance at the lawyers across the table. "Not by direct experience."

Luke chuckled. "No, you wouldn't. It's a cute technique corporate lawyers use to help people like me get rid of pests who want to take over our companies. It's a special kind of corporate stock that works so that if you start buying up a lot of shares in my company but don't get my blessing, your investment gets diluted to hell. You end up worse off than if you'd never invested at all."

"Charming. Now I know why Alan loves corporate law so much."

"Well, I'm bringing a little of the boardroom home for you two," Luke said to Sheila and Brad. "Think of this as my personal poison pill. If you push me too hard on the divorce settlement, I'll find myself a son. You know what that means, Sheila—child support, support for my special friend Petra, all coming off the top. You may get a bigger slice in the end, but it'll be from a smaller pie—much smaller." Luke trained his stare on Brad. "OK for you, though, Pitcher. My acknowledging paternity makes Alan's little defamation suit go away. So I guess you and I both get something."

Sheila's expression had grown morose. Brad wanted to reassure her but didn't know what to say. Alan, for once, looked like he didn't know what to say either, and his associates, as ever, didn't dare say a thing. Only Luke had a smile on his face.

21

Beto, stop playing games. I know that's not a gun." Alex knew Beto wouldn't really roll around in a bed with a loaded gun.

Beto leaned forward to study Alex's face, and his eyes widened with recognition. He cast an accusing glance at his lady friend.

"Don't look at her," Alex said. "She's as surprised as you are."

The woman had retreated to a corner, where she held a pillow tightly against her stomach and was crying softly. Alex felt bad about that. She seemed resigned, not shocked, as if she understood things like this were supposed to happen to bad girls.

Beto shrugged and pulled his hand out of the sheet to reveal an ashtray. He stubbed his cigarette out in it. "What the hell are *you* doing here?" he said venomously.

"I'm here for information. As soon as I get it, I'll leave."

"Why don't you just leave now?"

Alex laughed, then turned toward the girl. "Don't pick up that phone, miss. Stay right there, I'll be done here soon."

The woman froze against the wall. She replaced an old telephone on the nightstand from where she had removed it.

Alex leaned against a wide-screen television that rested on the floor across from the bed. He held the now-ridiculous pizza box in his lap with both hands. "Liberty Industries. You work there."

"I'm on disability—my finger." Beto raised a hand and showed Alex a splint on his pinky.

"Your old pal, Jorge Ramirez. He worked there, too."

"Used to."

"Up until he died. Help me understand something. Why is he dead while you're still alive?"

"Jorge was never very smart."

"Were you smart enough not to get in the van that day? Is that what you're saying?"

"Did Crash send you? I don't know nothing."

Who was Crash? Alex knew he wouldn't get anywhere with Beto by admitting ignorance. Better to push harder and scare some information out of him. "Did you know Liberty had an insurance policy on Jorge's life?" Alex said. "They got paid when he died. I think you did, too."

"It was all Jorge," Beto said. His voice had turned high pitched and hoarse. "He didn't tell me nothing, he set it all up."

"And he's dead! How did that happen, Beto?" Alex was standing over the bed now, his legs spread hip width as if for a fight, the frame of the pizza box crumpling in his clenched fists.

"I don't know, I don't know," Beto shouted. "I told Lenny already," he said.

"Who's Le—?"

Alex didn't finish the question. His eye caught the movement first—the woman's arm arcing in an awkward but energetic overhand heave—and then the knife was hurtling toward him. Reflexively, helplessly, he held the pizza box out as a shield in front of him, and the first inch of the serrated blade of an old steak knife greeted him on his side of the box. The sound was like a rusty saw stalling in damp wood. Alex danced a jig as two more knives skidded past his feet from the miniature kitchen at the far corner of the room.

The woman's aim was laughable, but too good to ignore. When she reached into a drawer for another knife, Alex took his turn. He hurled the pizza box end over end. A corner of the box hit the table, sending plastic cups and other kitchen gear flying. The woman fled with a curt shriek into the bathroom and locked the door behind her. She was no longer a danger, but she had played the part of the loyal girlfriend well. Alex turned his head to see Beto leap headfirst like a circus clown through the open window, holding a sofa cushion in front of him in lieu of a helmet. The makeshift curtain tagged along, and Beto was gone.

Alex threw open the door and spotted him—could have had him—and ran out of the apartment only to collide with another man climbing the stairs. Alex pardoned himself and took the stairs three at a time, while Beto—barefoot and wearing only boxers—dashed out the back of the apartment complex into an alley.

Alex was in a frenzy. He got lost running through streets and alleys looking for Beto. *Not good streets to get lost in*, Alex told himself.

He came to a convenience store and stepped in to catch his breath and get directions. A single copy of that morning's *Chronicle* lay askew in a rack by the counter. Alex placed it next to the register.

"They're selling like crazy today," the owner said with pleasure.

The front page headline was dynamite—*The Dead Pool: Petro Company Bets Against Employees' Lives.*

The story itself was riveting. It started with the sensational claim that Liberty Industries had been "betting that its employees would die." A sentence like that would never have left the editor's desk when Alex was at *The Chronicle*, but these were different times—even a Twitter addict couldn't put aside a newspaper article that began like that. Buried at the end of the article were several paragraphs of "balance," quotes from prominent accountants and lawyers saying that corporate-owned life insurance is a well-established and innocent financing practice, but only a news zealot like Alex would ever read that far.

Zeke had used the information Alex had given him, and found some of his own. The five Liberty employees who died in the accident all worked in job categories classified as risky by the state occupational safety agency. Zeke played that up as a suspicious coincidence. Playing devil's advocate, Alex noted that people in risky jobs would be more likely to die under any circumstances—not necessarily due to murder. But all the same, Alex knew the story would have an impact. And it raised enough open questions to put the rest of the city's journalists on the hunt. Alex was eager to see what prey they flushed from the undergrowth.

* * *

The reporters had waited for Luke outside, for hours some of them, littering the planters with cigarette butts and staring each other down, and when Luke finally emerged into the night from the office building they took revenge on an afternoon of boredom. They sprang up, toted gear, hustled toward him from all directions as if with a tacit understanding—trap the quarry first, then every man for himself.

They surrounded Luke. The cameras snapping made a frenzied racket like speeding tires on a gravel road. Their flashes combined to make a strobe light that put Luke at their mercy—a TV camera suddenly loomed by his head, a microphone came at his teeth from nowhere. With the crowd of reporters now thick around him, Luke's progress slowed.

Chin up. Smile.

They hurled questions like darts.

"Mr. Hubbard, how many insurance policies do you have on your employees?"

"Did the families get any of the money?"

The questions came too fast to respond to. Luke wouldn't reward this behavior anyway.

You've done nothing wrong. Keep moving. You won big today.

From one side a hand shoved a copy of *The Chronicle* under Luke's nose; from another side a hand snatched it away. He would be sure to read it tonight.

And tomorrow you'll kick all these dogs in the ribs.

22

Alex admitted to himself that he would probably never find Beto Capablanca again. He considered his options while lying on a surfboard. It was a winter morning at the beach, and Alex was the only one in the water or on the sand. Low cloud cover seemed to magnify the noise of the ocean.

Admitting Beto was gone also meant also admitting to himself that he would not help Roberta Cummings or embarrass Chip Odom and Rampart Insurance with his brilliant deductions about the case. Alex would also never get an answer from Beto on who Crash and Lenny were. So he'd failed as an investigator. No sugarcoating that. And he still needed a job.

Surfing helped Alex work the frustration out of his system. A couple hours in the water stayed with him all day—and better to be relaxed when he called around after job openings.

The water was cold and choppy. Decent waves came rarely. When a promising swell finally rolled his way, Alex paddled and rose. He sprang into a crouch and lifted his arms for balance, but the board started to slow almost right away. He slid onto his belly as the board sank back into the water. Alex watched the wave rumble on toward shore without him, led by a ragged lip of foam. *Story of my life*, he thought.

Disgusted, Alex left the water and lugged his surfboard across the empty beach to the parking lot, where the truck he'd borrowed from his uncle waited for him. There was nobody in the parking lot either. The morning fog was still thick overhead, and he quickly began to feel a chill. With no one else around, he propped his surfboard against the side of the pickup truck and shielded himself behind the open driver's side door, then began to undress.

He peeled the top half of his rubber bodysuit off his arms and torso and went to work drying himself with an ancient, threadbare towel whose once-blue dye had faded almost to pink. The empty rubber sleeves of his bodysuit hung away from his hips like vestigial limbs that shuddered when he moved. Once his top half was dry, he peeled the bodysuit down from his hips.

"Excuse me."

The woman's voice surprised him because it sounded so close and commanding. Alex reflexively took up the surfboard, and its sharp front tip hovered near the woman's chest.

"Hey, I'm unarmed," she said with a nervous laugh. Her gaze drifted below Alex's waist for longer than it should have, then she looked up at Alex's face again. She smiled, a little too familiarly, before making an exaggerated turn of her head to look away. Alex hiked the bodysuit back up over his hips.

She was dressed for the office rather than the beach, with unfastened blonde hair that she would have to brush again when she got inside. When, after an appropriate pause, she turned her head back toward Alex, the wind pulled a thin film of hair over her eyes. Her manicured fingers brushed away twenty strands out of a thousand. Then the breeze turned and, bit by bit, pulled back most of the others.

"Are you Alexander Fogarty?"

Alex remembered the repo men. "Are you a process server?"

"No."

"Then yes," he said. She was much better looking than the repo men, which was a good start.

"You're very cautious," she said. "I'm Sheila Holtz."

Alex found her tone suspiciously self-assured, like she'd come to sell something, rather than to ask for something. "Should I know you?"

"My married name is Hubbard."

Alex threw the towel around his shoulders. The cold had leached the color from the woman's cheeks and turned her small, pointy nose red. Still, Alex could tell she was pretty.

"I called your lawyer," Alex said, recognizing her name.

"That's why I'm here. I'd like to talk."

Each waited for the other to say something, and Sheila pulled her arms into her body for warmth.

"Not like this," she said. "It's cold."

"You noticed. Where's your lawyer's office?"

Sheila wrinkled her nose. "There's a public library down the street. Get dressed and meet me there."

Alex paused, considering his response. He wasn't used to being bossed around by women he'd just met.

"All right," he said. "Funny place for a talk."

"You'll come?"

"I said 'all right.'"

"I don't like to wait."

"So read a book," he said flatly.

Alex turned his back and rubbed the damp towel fervently against his scalp. The motion made the rubber sleeves hanging out from his hips bounce like needles in a dial. He didn't like being surprised with his pants down. He didn't like being cajoled into an unscheduled meeting. But, then, *he'd* called *her*. He should be happy. He looked over his shoulder, but she'd already started walking away.

* * *

In front of the library, Alex found Sheila standing alone in the damp, heavy air, her hair starting to curl. Alex had changed into dry clothes and a light jacket. It was warmer inside but empty, except for a few drowsy retirees in sweaters.

Sheila led the way toward a grid of tables with shaded lamps that filled the center of the room. Her bee line there was diverted only as she neared a homeless guy hunched over a book. There her path bellied out into a gentle arc before returning to its original course, as if she and the man were the ends of two magnets repelling each other.

Sheila and Alex sat at a table away from the other patrons. Alex leaned across, ready for a quiet conversation, but she held back, sitting erect, with her hips planted firmly in the uncomfortable wooden chair. Alex asked how she had found him, and felt foolish when she said his address was in the phone book. After no one answered at Alex's door, a barista in the coffee shop told her Alex could often be found surfing, and the barista was right. She preferred to speak with people in person rather than over the phone, she said, answering the question that Alex was about to ask.

"My lawyer says you have information that could help me. What is it?"

She faced him with a lifted chin and eyes that remained half shut, like two flower buds weighing whether to open on a cloudy day. *So much for small talk*, Alex thought.

"I think your husband may have killed some people," he whispered.

She laughed, too loudly for a library, and over her shoulder a shriveled man with white hair looked up at the noise and shot Alex a lively, mischievous smile. Out of the cold, with the color coming back to her cheeks, she was pretty. Beautiful, in fact.

"My husband's a prick, but he's not a killer," she said. "How'd you get such a crazy idea?"

"He took out insurance policies on five employees who died in . . . suspicious circumstances."

"You mean his company did."

"Yes."

"So you're just talking about the recent stories in the paper." Now she leaned in, pivoting on her elbows. "That's a question."

It didn't sound like a question, but Alex answered anyway. "Yes. But there's more to the story than what's in the papers."

"What, exactly?"

The truth was, Alex didn't know. He only had suspicions. And the coverage in the papers, all based on his leads, made his revelations old news. Yet Roberta Cummings still needed a way to save her house. And Alex still had five mortgages to pay.

"That's what I'd like your help to find out," Alex said.

"Fine. You have my benediction."

"I need more than that."

Her eyes narrowed again. Up close, Alex noticed mascara and pores and crow's feet. She was a bit older than him. None of that changed his opinion of her looks.

"I don't have time in my life for another greedy person," she said.

She started to rise. Still seated, Alex grabbed her wrist before she could turn away from the table. For someone who came off as highly strung, Sheila's reaction was less alarmed than Alex expected. She looked down at him, stern but patient, like he was a rescue dog from the pound who had just peed on her shoes.

"I'm the one who gave the story to the papers," Alex whispered. Sheila looked at him impassively for a moment, and then sat back down, resting her hands on the table in front of her.

Alex quickly delivered the heart of the story—how he had been an investigator for Rampart, how he had been assigned to investigate the accident, how the police report raised more questions than answers, how the cops couldn't be troubled to care. The early events tumbled out in an eager monologue that was just hushed enough not to draw the attention of the sleepy readers around them.

Alex mentioned with casual detachment that his bosses at Rampart had found a quick resolution more appealing than a drawn-out investigation. He skipped the Cummings widow, her toddler and their overgrown lawn. Alex explained that his interview with Zeke got him fired—she could verify the interview just by finding the newspaper article on-line, he pointed out. Zeke owed him one, that's why Zeke started reporting on the accident and Liberty Industries. And those insurance policies that Zeke used to stoke public outrage? Alex had supplied Zeke with the copies.

He supplied them to Sheila, too. He plucked a folded sheaf of photocopies from inside his jacket and passed it across the table as if it were a hit list.

"Just like I said, the time stamp on the fax is weeks before Zeke's story," Alex said. He gestured toward the fax header on the top edge of the page. Sheila didn't look down.

"So you just carry these pages around with you?" she said.

"I had them in my truck."

"OK," she said. She seemed to be considering all she had just heard. It didn't take long for her to speak again, and when she did she remained very composed.

"Suppose everything you just told me is true. What's your plan? Where will you get more evidence? After all, you just admitted the police botched the forensics."

"I know a guy."

She laughed amicably. "Figures."

"Have you ever met a man named Rigoberto Capablanca?"

She laughed again, almost a giggle. "I'd remember if I had."

"I just wondered, because I read you were the head of human resources for Liberty. Anyway, Capablanca works there. He knew the employees who died. If you can help me get into Liberty to find him, I can find out what your husband knew about all this."

She frowned and looked down at her hands, which lay solidly folded in front of her.

"I think we want the same thing," she said eventually.

"The truth."

One side of Sheila's mouth twitched upward in a half-hearted smile. "Just money."

Alex's wind-burnt lips cracked apart, as if he meant to say something, and then drifted shut again.

She spoke again more clearly, enunciating her words as if Alex had trouble with English. "What I'm saying is that I'd pay handsomely for evidence that my husband actually caused this accident."

Alex didn't respond. This was exactly the opportunity he'd hoped for, but now it had arrived suddenly, when he was ready to give up. It was disorienting.

"What's the problem?" Sheila leaned over the table again. "Let me guess: money disgusts you, but only when it's earned. You're one of those surfer, lifestyle types, aren't you?"

Alex shook his head. "No. I mean, I like surfing."

"You seem confused, Alex. I'm sorry we couldn't help each other." She stood for a second time. For a second time Alex grabbed her wrist. He'd meant to say he was pursuing the case for personal reasons, not for money. But this Sheila needed an uncluttered message.

"I mean I'm in," Alex said. "You get me access to Liberty and, if your husband really did it, I'll find the proof."

23

Alex spent the next day at home on the internet learning as much as he could about Luke Hubbard and Liberty Industries. The truth was, Alex didn't know whether the evidence pointed to Luke. Alex didn't even know if Luke was capable of murder. Sure, the cynic in him said that anyone was *capable* of murder. Yet agreeing with Sheila to investigate Luke made Alex curious about the man. Would Luke kill for an amount of money that Uncle Hugh said was just a rounding error for his company?

By all accounts Liberty Industries was big and growing fast. In fact, they were the darlings of Wall Street. In the last few months, several business magazines had run cover stories on the company. They all told the story of a rise from modest beginnings—for Liberty as well as for its celebrity CEO, Luke Hubbard.

It started with what was, by L.A. standards, some ancient history. Liberty Industries started life as Liberty Oil Company, a local outfit founded by a Dustbowl refugee who puttered around Los Angeles County in a rebuilt Model T during the Great Depression signing up mineral rights. He drilled holes across what was then farmland in search of oil.

He found it. By the 1950s, Jarvis "Mack" MacNeill was one of L.A.'s richest men. But by the late 1980s, when suburbia had swallowed up the farmland and the oil ran out, Liberty's business model was exhausted as well. During the recession of the early 1990s, its stock traded for pennies.

That was when Luke Hubbard entered the story. The more recent articles described him with terms like "visionary" and "ground breaking," but in 1994 people were using words like "naïve," "untested" and "foolish." The expansive clan of MacNeill children and grandchildren, more interested in spending money than reviving a dying business, thought Luke was a fool for offering to buy out their Liberty shares. So did every bank that he asked for financing. He ended up begging the MacNeill family to accept payment in installments out of the earnings of the business.

Hubbard brought a reputation to Liberty. The old timers there, cynical, hard-bitten engineers, were vocally skeptical of the young consultant with zero experience running an actual business. After all, his limited leadership opportunity had not endeared him to L.A. sports fans. In each of the two seasons in which the schoolteacher's son with movie star looks started as quarterback for USC, the Trojans lost more games than they won, including embarrassing losses to archrival UCLA.

On day one, Hubbard gave the old timers something else to complain about—pink slips. Luke brought in his beautiful young wife as head of human resources and a cadre of like-minded young executives, and they set about revamping the business model.

But first they needed cash. The MacNeill family had been milking ever-shrinking dividends from the company's dwindling oil reserves. Luke Hubbard's training as a lawyer helped him see a different opportunity. Every well came with a drilling easement from the landowner, a right to enter the property and dig an oil well. That had been a trivial matter for the landowners to sign away when Southern California was all farmland. But it was worth much more now that the land had been developed. Hubbard went back to every dry oil well and started digging, or threatening to dig—in the manicured front lawns of mansions, beneath new glass-and-steel office parks, anywhere an oil well would most be a nuisance.

At the airport he struck gold. He found a geologist to testify to a "substantial likelihood" of oil under the land slated for a new runway, and LAX paid millions to buy back the easement from him. "Hubbard versus the hub" was how the papers dubbed the showdown. People didn't talk about Luke Hubbard as the pretty boy quarterback anymore.

Five years later came a name change to Liberty Industries and a fresh stock exchange listing. With access to the capital markets, Liberty grew at a faster pace than ever before.

Under Hubbard's leadership, Liberty always seemed to be one step ahead of the rest of the energy industry. From Canadian tar sands to speculative solar panels, Liberty invested a year or two before everyone else piled in.

New technologies, new sources of energy. It was hard even for Alex, jaded environmentalist though he was, to resist feeling excited by the descriptions in the company's annual report. Politicians, academics and plenty of slick executives gave lip service to a green energy revolution. Liberty was actually making it happen—and tallying eye-popping profits along the way. The sleepy local company had become a global powerhouse to match Luke Hubbard's vision.

Luke and his wife also built up an impressive record of local philanthropy in a way that the MacNeill family never did. There was a Hubbard wing at the art museum, a Hubbard center of law and policy at USC, a Julius Hubbard Memorial Children's Medical Research Center, named after a stillborn child. When people thought of Liberty these days, they thought Hubbard, not MacNeill.

He was a workaholic, the articles said. He combined grand strategic vision with exacting attention to detail. Alex thought of the life insurance policies on the dead employees and found it hard to imagine anything of significance happening at Liberty Industries without Luke Hubbard's say-so.

Not all the press coverage was favorable. Rumors—never more than that—had surfaced of competitors being threatened. From time to time, lawsuits were brought against Liberty, then mysteriously dropped. And whenever a junior executive fell out of favor, look out. Luke's protégés didn't move on to leadership positions at other companies, as Alex would have expected. Instead, once they became too powerful, Luke forced them out of the company or sued them or did both.

Alex's thoughts turned to Sheila. He recalled their conversation in the library—the way her jaw set as she listened to him, the way she locked her fingers tightly together on the tabletop. Beneath her casual exterior, she was tense, like there was a glass vessel inside her and if she twisted the wrong way it would break. *That's what you get from life with Luke Hubbard*, Alex thought. Maybe Sheila wasn't as hard as she appeared to be. Maybe she was OK, for a vindictive, over the hill, still beautiful ice queen.

Alex looked again at one of the articles about Luke he'd found on the internet. It included a photo of Luke in a tuxedo. He and his wife posed with another couple at a charity dinner. The other three were beaming—deep in their cups, from the look of it. Luke's smile looked like it was pinned to his face. It was more formal, more reserved, almost withdrawn.

Was it the face of a killer?

Wealth, power, respect. These were all things people might kill for. Luke Hubbard already had them. Would he kill to add a few cents to his earnings per share figure? Would anyone?

Alex didn't know. Sheila's face appeared in his mind again. *What must it be like to lie down at night next to a killer?* Alex tried to read the other articles he'd collected, but his mind kept coming back to Sheila.

She seemed so different from other women he'd known—especially Pamela. Sheila's brusqueness raised his hackles, but maybe that was just because he didn't like feeling bossed around. But Sheila hadn't really been bossy at the library; she'd just been direct, clear about what she wanted, what she proposed and—what really annoyed Alex—effective at pulling out an equally direct response from him.

Being pulled out of your comfort zone was unsettling, but Pamela had lived safely within Alex's comfort zone, and how well had that gone? Alex got the sense that if Sheila was unhappy she'd waste no time in telling him, rather than keep her frustrations a secret and betray him. He knew it was silly to think of Sheila this way—they'd only just met, and she was all business anyway. But Sheila was the first woman he'd met since Pamela that he couldn't stop thinking about. Maybe, despite their differences in age and background, this was a woman he could relate to. A part of him hoped so.

24

Chip Odom walked next to Luke. Petra and Crash came behind. The symphony hall was crowded, and so they stayed close together.

It was slow going. Luke was stopped every few steps with greetings from one acquaintance or another, all of them interchangeable old men in tuxedos. The greetings mostly came with words of encouragement.

"Even for the newspapers, what they're doing to you is outrageous . . ."

"Let me know if I can help . . ."

"Give 'em hell, Luke . . ."

"We've pulled our ads from *The Chronicle*, just so you know . . ."

Whenever Luke had the chance he introduced Chip as well, as a friend and an up-and-comer at Rampart Insurance. By the time they reached Luke's box overlooking the stage, Chip was beaming from the attention. Petra was sulking from a lack of it. Luke and Chip took the two front chairs. Behind them, Crash and Petra headed for the two chairs in back. Crash unchivalrously barged ahead of Petra, but Petra took the initiative anyway, darting past Crash to take the further chair and giving Crash a quick pinch on the ass as she did so. She didn't bother looking back to acknowledge his glare.

"With all these friends, I'm surprised you use a bodyguard," Chip said to Luke.

Luke looked puzzled for a moment before he replied. "Oh, you mean Crash—he's an old friend. I don't bring him for protection, though that's within his repertoire. I bring him because he loves the music. You'll see."

The audience was reminded to turn off their mobile phones. Luke twisted around and smiled at Petra, touching her knee to draw her attention from a text message she was tapping out with red-lacquered thumbnails that fell like little hammers.

"Everything all right?" he said.

"I turn ringer off, darlink," she said without looking up. Luke turned back around.

The orchestra began to play, softly at first, with gentle strains that seemed to Chip to radiate from the walls, enveloping him in sound from all directions. Soon a sound coming from behind him stood out. Chip turned to find Crash, his head tilted back and his eyes closed, moaning softly and swaying with the music. Petra smirked contemptuously at him.

"You weren't kidding," Chip said to Luke. "He loves the music."

Luke chuckled. "He's full of surprises, and often misunderstood. But more than anyone I know, he understands the importance of what Liberty is doing for the environment."

Chip smiled weakly and cast another glance back at the enraptured giant.

"He's also my most loyal friend," Luke said. "With a divorce . . . well, you learn who your friends are. It makes you appreciate those who stick by you. Popularity's overrated, don't you think?"

Chip smiled at Luke in acknowledgment, then stifled a cough.

"You may have started to find this in your own career," Luke said, "but having responsibility sometimes means pissing people off."

Chip laughed loudly, and a bejeweled old woman whose eyes flashed with malice leaned out from the box to their right and ostentatiously shushed them. Unchastened, Luke smiled and waved.

"We can keep talking," Luke said quietly to Chip after the woman's wrinkled face had withdrawn into the box. "She thinks her seat on the board lets her shush anyone, but she'll be fast asleep by the end of the first movement. After that, nothing'll wake her but the tympani."

Chip tried to smile, but his eyes were watering and he coughed again. Now his face had flushed and he had begun to sweat. He tugged at the collar of his tuxedo shirt. "Ugh, this thing is killing me. You mind?"

Without waiting for an answer, Chip unclipped his bow tie and unfastened the top button on his shirt to release his fleshy neck from its torment. Luke patiently untied his own bow tie and popped his top button open with his thumb and forefinger.

"Reminds me of one of your father's contemporaries, Jamie Backman," Luke said. "Always took his tie off as soon as he sat down for a meeting. You ever meet him?"

Chip shook his head.

"Impressive guy," Luke said, and Chip nodded avidly.

"Thanks again for inviting me," Chip said. "I love it. I actually played piano when I was a kid."

Luke laughed amicably. "I have a hard time imagining your father at a piano recital."

"Yeah, more Mom's thing than Dad's. I was pretty good, but I didn't have the fingers for it." Chip fanned out his stubby digits in his lap to illustrate.

"I thought you'd enjoy this. There's something I wanted to talk to you about—and keep this under your hat—but a spot may be opening up soon on the symphony board."

"Oh, you mean—well, I guess our neighbor doesn't look very healthy." Chip cocked his head toward the next booth, where the shushing old woman sat.

"Oh, not her," Luke said. "That shriveled viper will live to a hundred. No, what I mean is my wife sits on the board too, as you probably know, and with the divorce, it looks like she'll be transitioning off."

"I'm sorry to hear that," Chip said, but he smiled discreetly.

"I've floated your name to some of the other members—hope you don't mind . . . I think it could be good exposure for you."

"Thanks for thinking of me. I'd be delighted."

"You know, you and I have more in common than a love of music," Luke said. "This accident last Christmas—the sports car, the gardening truck, one of my vans . . ."

"Right," Chip said, catching on. "The Cummings case. We insured the sports car. Man, the press just won't let it go."

"I know, can you believe it? These insurance policies on the employees were just a tax shelter put in place years ago by an old VP of Finance—Wharton M.B.A., by the way, smart as a whip. Anyway, I'd forgotten all about them, and now the press is acting like I personally *murdered* those people."

"Same thing for us," Chip said. "We had good grounds for rescission and so denied coverage on the sports car. But all the press cares about is how the widow was left without liability coverage. Dad was furious. Luckily I've been able to avoid the fallout."

Luke gave Chip a little wink. "It's good you could navigate that. You have a lot of rivals at Rampart?"

"In every cubicle."

"Tell you what I'd do," Luke said, finally getting around to his point. "If I were your old man? I'd give the squeaky wheel some oil."

Chip look confused, then said, "You mean pay off the Cummings widow?"

"Exactly—fighting that poor woman is a no-win situation. You've got to understand the public just sees guys like us as faceless corporations, always trying to screw the little guy, even when all we're trying to do is follow the rules."

"I don't know . . . settling seems risky."

Luke shook his head vigorously. "Chip, I've been through this sort of thing probably a dozen times. The only risk here is to Rampart's image—and you guys are getting killed in the press."

"True . . ."

"Actually, if it was me? I'd go even further. I'd pay off that plaintiffs' lawyer who's suing the widow and—"

"No way I'd pay that guy."

"Fine, but I'll tell you what—it'd vaporize your public relations problems. No helpless beleaguered widow, nothing for the reporters to sink their fangs into."

"Vaporize . . . I like the sound of that." Chip said with a lopsided smile. Then he shook his head emphatically. "But Dad would never go for it. He gets his teeth into something and he doesn't let go."

Luke nodded. "Founders are like that. You know, it takes a different mind-set to build something from nothing than it does to guide a larger company.

That's part of how Liberty Oil became Liberty Industries. Remember 'Mack' MacNeill?"

"Vaguely. Didn't he have that marble fountain on his estate that spouted oil instead of water?"

Luke smiled in reminiscence of the profligate MacNeill children. "No, that was one of his sons. I don't think old Mack ever spent a dime on luxury—he was still driving his old Model T in the Fifties. Classic 'founder,' just like your dad. Stubborn as hell, and I mean that in a good way."

Chip looked skeptically at Luke, who smoothly went on.

"I could never have done what Mack did, build something from scratch like that. But Liberty eventually got to a size where it needed a different skill set, and the second generation didn't have it."

The two sat in silence for a few moments while the music swelled toward a climax.

"It's interesting to think about how wealthy the MacNeills would be now if they'd been able to pass the helm to someone in the family," Luke said.

"I went to high school with one of the MacNeill grandkids." Chip shook his head. "Not an impressive guy."

Luke smiled. They turned their attention to the stage as the orchestra reached its finale in an ecstatic torrent of sound.

Then the music ended, the cheering began, and to Luke and Chip's right, the ancient lady awoke, jumped to her feet like a startled squirrel and launched immediately into speedy, percussive applause.

Chip nodded in the woman's direction. "She's energetic for a woman her age."

"It's hard for some people to let go," Luke said.

After a minute the applause died down, and people began to file out of the concert hall. Luke and Chip moved toward the exit, with Crash and Petra behind them.

"About the Cummings case," Chip said.

"Yes?" Luke said.

"I'll have a talk with my Dad, see if I can get him to see reason."

Luke clapped Chip on the shoulder. "I think that's the right move."

* * *

Working from a tip from a man whose attention was focused by the prospect of bodily harm, Crash found the apartment complex in which Beto's girlfriend was supposed to live. He parked his silver SUV across the street, where he had a good vantage of the complex and its entrance. The apartment building was fronted by a row of palm trees whose tops had been cut or had fallen off. But the trunks still stood, taller than the rooftop and solid and thick, like a row of columns in classical ruins that once supported a proud structure.

From the privacy of his SUV, Crash watched residents enter and leave the complex. As the day progressed, the thin shadows cast by the palm trees swiveled inch by inch around the trunks and swelled with the hastening afternoon.

People came home from work and found no reason to notice Crash. Crash waited until dark and watched as, one by one, the apartment windows lit up from inside—all of them but Beto's. Luke wanted Crash to trace the blackmail back to its root and then destroy the entire rotten weed. Beto couldn't hide forever.

25

Rampart restored Mrs. Cummings' insurance coverage. That's what the newspaper said, at least. Brad set the newspaper down on his desk and sighed. He had enjoyed reading articles day after day that dragged Luke and Liberty Industries through the mud, but this latest development, he thought, would take a lot of the heat out of the story. Plus, the papers had settled on a narrative that Liberty's insuring the lives of its employees was a macabre but entirely innocent practice.

Oh, well, Brad thought, *it was fun while it lasted.* Back to real life, which, Brad admitted, wasn't so great about now. These days Brad felt like he never left his office. Not that he had much to show for all his work—Sheila still wasn't getting any money from Luke, and Brad spent his days, nights and weekends doing paperwork for the case.

And what paperwork. Brad looked around his small office with dismay. It was a battlefield strewn with paper, each sheet a casualty in the grinding war of attrition being waged by Alan Matthews and the other lawyers from Boswell & Baker. There were tall piles of paper, rising in unstable stacks from his desk and floor, springing from crumpled manila folders stuffed desperately into open boxes. Brad had documents cataloging his documents, and still he couldn't keep track of them all.

Luke's lawyers had served him with interrogatories, questions that Sheila had to respond to in writing. Like everything Luke's lawyers did, the questions were over the top, asking for disclosure of all Sheila's assets, every job she had ever had, her college grades, details of every charity board she sat on—requests for a mountain of data that either didn't matter or that Luke already knew.

This was the kind of legal practice that Brad hated, and the reason he had stayed away from the big firms like Boswell & Baker that his law school classmates had eagerly flocked to—weeks of parrying back and forth with motions and countermotions, piling on pretexts for creative ways to embarrass and harass, a desk jockey's take on jiu-jitsu. No dramatic cross-examination, no definitive confrontation, just each side waiting for the other to lose heart. Brad knew that's just what Alan Matthews wanted. The longer Alan dragged this case out, the more financially hard up Sheila would become, and the more willing she would become to settle with Luke for a lower amount than she deserved.

But Sheila wouldn't do that. *I won't let her*, Brad thought. All this passive-aggressive paper pushing just made Brad angry. He wanted another chance to go toe to toe with Alan Matthews in open court, just one more chance. While Brad had spent hundreds of hours arguing before judges and juries, forest-razing cases like this one were the only kind that Alan did.

The office door swung open fast. Brad looked up to see Cindy.

"Another box from the copy shop," she said. She was frowning. Brad missed the fleeting smiles she used to share with him. She hadn't signed up for this much stress. She had also stopped wearing the little necklace Brad gave her for Christmas.

The box was a small one made from heavy cardboard that was built for stacking when the lid was on. But the lid wouldn't fit on this one, because its open top sprouted the long ends of legal-size papers like flowers from a vase. Brad took the box from Cindy, leaning his shoulders back to offset the weight.

"Careful with your back," she said.

"Got it." Brad's words emerged as two shallow grunts.

The new box didn't have an obvious place to go. The two chairs Brad kept for visitors already hosted boxes of their own. Brad sighed and, reluctantly, set the box down on his own chair. Now he didn't have anywhere to sit, either. He took that as a sign it was time for lunch.

"Sorry about all this," he said to Cindy, gesturing helplessly at the mess around him. "Let me make it up to you. Lunch at Chez Henri?"

Cindy's eyes widened on hearing the name of a pricey French restaurant, but her response was subdued.

"Brad, I couldn't. Thanks. I mean, after this case settles." She managed a smile. "Oh, I forgot to tell you, the guy at the copy shop asked about the outstanding balance again." Cindy offered Brad another sympathetic smile.

"Whoa, don't tell me you're packing up." It was Walt Peters, Brad's officemate, who had poked his head in Brad's open door. As usual, he was using his outdoor voice. "You're not calling it quits, are you?"

"No, Walt, just trying to get some work done," Brad said.

Walt whistled in mock awe. "It's like I tell the guys. This is what happens when cases don't settle soon enough. Anyway, I knew you wouldn't be packing up and leaving just like that. Not without paying your share of this month's rent." Walt winked at Brad, then turned to Cindy. "Ready for lunch?"

The phone rang on Brad's desk. Brad waved Cindy and Walt out of his office, picked up the phone, and wearily confirmed his identity.

The man on the other end said, "I'm calling from the office of Grant Steele, United States Attorney."

"And your name is?"

"I'd like to ask you some questions."

Brad rolled his eyes. He could tell this conversation was going to be more take than give. "What is it you'd like to know?"

"It's better that we speak in person."

A second question of mine ignored, Brad thought. "Tell me what it is you want to talk about."

"I'd like to have a conversation with you about Luke Hubbard."

"That's going to be a short conversation. Luke is on the opposite side of a divorce case that I'm involved in."

"I know. That's why I'm calling you." A pause. "It's better that we speak in person."

Mr. "In Person" insisted on coming at seven in the evening, when no one else would be around. He had a thin build and light brown hair and entered the office suite without knocking. The man took off his fedora, gave Brad a look that dared him to make a joke about the fedora, then tossed the fedora on a coat rack from a distance of half a foot.

"I'm Brad." Brad offered the man a business card. The man took it.

"Jeff Smiley," the man said. He showed Brad his business card, then took it away again when Brad reached out to take it. *He's just weird enough to actually wear a fedora*, Brad thought.

Inside Brad's private office, Smiley spoke without prompting. His voice was reedy and slightly nasal, which made it hard for Brad to take him seriously.

"What I am going to tell you is confidential, and disclosure of what I am going to tell you is a violation of federal law that my office will have no hesitation to prosecute." Smiley paused. When Brad didn't object, he continued. "My office is investigating Luke Hubbard and his company for a long list of federal crimes, and we'd like to confirm—"

"You can stop right there," Brad said. "The discovery materials in the Hubbard divorce are under court seal. I can't confirm anything that relates to the case."

"Can't you?" Smiley arched an eyebrow.

"Enough with the Jedi mind tricks, Mr. Fedora. It's late and I've got work to do. What do you want?"

Smiley was not amused. "I only want details on what you've already told the public. Tell me what you know about Luke's relationship with Petra P and her son. We believe both of them are in this country illegally."

Oh, brother. Brad was already in enough trouble over his spur of the moment claim that Luke was the boy's father. If Brad said any more about that to anyone, it would strengthen Luke's defamation case against him. "No," Brad said. "I won't discuss it."

"I'm sorry to hear that," Smiley said. "Because if that's your answer, we will have no choice but to open an investigation of you for being an accessory to immigration violations."

"That's ridiculous!" Brad stared hard at his visitor, who, for the first time, smiled.

"You know," Smiley continued, "the whole shebang—subpoenas, grand jury testimony, we interview all your clients and friends, take your computers in for analysis . . . I hear it's hard to run a business that way."

"I can't help you. Full stop."

Smiley looked around. "You've got a lot of paper around here. I can take care of this mess for you. I'll come tomorrow with a truck and some beefy FBI agents and cart it all away . . ." He was still smiling.

Brad wasn't. The little twerp had him beat. The little twerp sat politely while Brad slowly made peace with that fact.

"Look," Brad said finally, "I've got nothing on the mistress or her kid, but how about some details on Luke's personal finances?"

"That sounds . . . interesting. Yes. Yes, that would be helpful."

Brad went to one of his overflowing boxes of paper and pulled out a manila folder. "Take a look at this."

Smiley took the folder and looked through it. "*Very* interesting." Smiley closed the folder and got up as if to leave.

"No," Brad said, "you read it here."

Smiley sat down again and opened the folder. When Smiley saw Brad watching him, he glared at Brad. Brad turned away and looked awkwardly toward the ceiling.

Brad was sure he was breaking about half a dozen ethical rules. Jeff Smiley was breaking them, too, but that didn't make it any better. Brad thought of the library at law school, and the eight foot tall oil paintings of judgmental old Yankees on the wall. Langdell. Story. Holmes. *This isn't the sort of thing they teach you at Harvard Law*, Brad thought. This is the sort of thing you figure out on your own. What was it Holmes said? "The life of the law has been experience." Something like that. *Yeah, well, experience is what happens when no one's looking.*

* * *

In an empty conference room perched above the smog, Luke Hubbard and Jim Branford paced in tight, meandering patterns. Guests were expected.

The door swung open and four Arab businessmen in flowing white robes and headdresses entered. They were escorted by Crash, who stood a head taller than any of them. Luke and Jim eagerly approached them.

The initial pleasantries gave way to a morning of insistently friendly conversation into which candor made an occasional awkward intrusion. By a quarter to twelve, everyone was ready for lunch, and they all looked hopefully toward the door when it lurched open.

"My name is Grantham V. Steele, and I have a warrant to search these premises." Steele was accompanied by four FBI agents in dark gray suits who filed in and spread out around the room.

Steele pointed at the Arabs. "Search them," he said to the agents.

The agents pulled Luke's guests to their feet, and they glared at Luke with indignant betrayal. Then the agents frisked Luke and Jim, too. Crash quietly disappeared before anyone had a chance to frisk him. The visiting businessmen relaxed when it became clear that Luke and Jim were the ones being harassed, not them. After a tense minute or two, everyone sat down again.

Luke spoke softly and calmly to his guests, proposing that they move the meeting offsite until the unexpected misunderstanding with the authorities was cleared up.

Steele overheard and flung himself to the table where they sat. "No one is leaving this room until we've searched the entire building."

"This is ridiculous," Jim said.

Steele cocked his head. "You know what'd be even more ridiculous? You handcuffed to your chair. How about it?"

The door swung open again, this time thrust inward by the skinny backside of an attendant who struggled with a lunch cart. His elongated earlobes were pierced with round wooden plugs that bounced merrily with his clumsy efforts. He finally got the cart through without losing a plate, but flinched when he faced his audience.

"Whoa," he said. He turned his head to count the men, muttering the numbers to himself, and the jagged edge of a tattoo on his neck ventured skittishly from under his collared shirt. "I was told there would only be six?"

"Everyone heard how good your sandwiches are," Luke said drily.

"I don't make them, I just get them from the cafeteria."

"Why don't you go get a few more?"

"No," Steele said. "You people eat your lunch. One of my men will go out and buy sandwiches for my team." He scanned the faces of the agents, as if willing one of them to volunteer.

"I thought you said no one was leaving this room," Jim said wryly.

Steele's face turned red, all at once and all over, like someone fooling with the color on a television set. "No one likes a smart ass," Steele said finally, "especially one who's a suspect." Jim snatched the search warrant from the table and anxiously flipped the pages in search of his name.

Another cart came in, this one pushed by a woman. She looked annoyed when she saw the other cart already there. The two attendants began bickering about which cart was supposed to go where.

"Leave both carts here," Luke said. To the group he said, "Lunch is here. Apparently we'll all be here for a while, so we might as well eat."

The attendants then delivered to all, the invited and the uninvited, plates laden with salad, steamed chicken and some sort of chutney. The seated Arabs eyed the offering skeptically.

"This is good stuff," the tattooed attendant said encouragingly. "I had a little on my way up."

The FBI agents politely declined. One of them explained that they couldn't accept gifts.

"It's not a gift, it's lunch," Jim said.

"The rules," one of them said. "We have to pay market price."

Jim asked the female attendant, "What does this plate cost in the cafeteria?" She replied, and in unison the agents dug their wallets from their pockets. One of them offered a bill to the tattooed attendant, but he recoiled and eyed it disdainfully.

"Sorry, man, I don't have change. I just push the cart, y'know?"

The agent turned to the row of Arabs seated next to him. "Have any of you gentlemen got change for a twenty?"

26

Sheila's lead was a bust. His name was Raymond, but he introduced himself as Ray-bear, and over a year had passed since he quit Liberty Industries—quit or been fired, he never quite said—which he explained repeatedly was "on account of my medical situation." Since leaving, Ray-bear had let his hair grow out.

"Those insurance policies—man, I dunno what *those* were about."

He said that three separate times. His gaze kept drifting toward the view onto the street through the dirty living room window of his apartment.

Raymond didn't have anything of value to say about the insurance policies. He did have plenty to say about Sheila, all of it negative except praise for her figure, which he thought was especially fine "for a woman her age." He said that a couple of times, too. Alex guessed Ray-bear was not much younger than Sheila, but he looked older.

Alex dropped the courteous tone with which he had begun the conversation. "Let me ask you something—is it really possible to be a pot-head and get a cushy job in finance? 'Cause if it is, I've been busting my ass for nothing."

Ray-bear thought about the question, or at least paused before replying. "No, not really. That's sort of why I had to leave." He gestured to a small bag of marijuana on the coffee table in front of him that he hadn't bothered to hide. "It's on account of my—"

Alex finished his sentence for him and said a quick goodbye.

There was a breeze outside. Alex inhaled deeply. After the atmosphere of warm rot inside Ray-bear's apartment, he felt grateful for the cold day outside. Public pressure had forced Rampart insurance to restore Roberta Cummings' liability policy, but this case was still personal for Alex. He was certain that someone had murdered those people, and whoever would do something like that had to think that they were smarter than everyone. *No, you're not*, Alex thought. Luke sure thought he was smart. Alex was smart, too. But he was running out of time before he had to get a job.

So, forward, then—and so much for Sheila and her dead end with Ray-bear. Alex decided to go back to Liberty to look for Beto, and this time he wouldn't do it by telephone. He thought back a couple of weeks and recalled how he telephoned Liberty pretending to be Beto's parole officer. Alex decided it was time for another check-in by Beto's parole officer. This time, Alex would show up in person.

Alex went to his closet to choose the right clothes. The suit Alex had worn to his father's funeral, dark and now unfashionable, was perfect. And it was actually helpful that Alex's only white dress shirt needed to be pressed.

Alex tried to imagine his father's reaction if he could see Alex now. Probably vague disappointment, or maybe just confusion. His father had assumed that Alex and Del would both end up as respectable white collar professionals—businessmen, doctors, something like that. Alex had tried being a businessman in a way, with his housing investments, but obviously that wasn't a good fit. Dad had seemed like a nice guy, when he was around. Most nights or weekends he was travelling or at the office. It was Mom who raised them and, in some things, Alex and Del who had raised each other.

Alex's costume still lacked something—glasses. Alex didn't wear them, so on his way to Liberty he stopped at a drugstore and bought the ugliest pair with the mildest prescription he could find. Alex wanted whoever he met to remember his glasses, not his face.

At Liberty, they put him in a room and told him to wait. Then a pot-bellied supervisor entered, looking worn but surly. They shared an apathetic handshake, and Alex got right to the point.

"I got this guy—I'm from the county—his name's . . ." Alex flipped open a file folder he had brought in order to refresh his memory.

". . . Rigoberto Capablanca," Alex said, trailing off at the end of the first name as though he wasn't sure how to pronounce it. The last name he said clearly, in old white-guy fashion, saying the first syllable like the word "cap."

The supervisor said it the same way. "Capablanca's one of ours, that's right."

"I know, I called a while back on him. Anyways, they want me to show up on these guys, so I'm showing up. My sister lives out here and I need to see her for something, so . . . anyways, can I see him?"

"Nope," the supervisor said. "Out on worker's comp."

Alex tugged at his dark tie. The knot was so tight it looked like a plumbing joint.

"Workers' comp . . . He didn't tell me that. Oh, maybe he did." Alex made a show of shuffling through the papers in his folder as if looking for the answer, knowing he wouldn't find it there because the papers were a random grab from his glove compartment. He shuffled a little too hard, though, and the papers slipped out and to the floor, tumbling over one another like boisterous school-children fleeing the classroom.

The supervisor dropped gracelessly to one knee to help collect the papers. If the supervisor got a close look at the papers, he would discover Alex's deceit, so Alex moved faster. He hunched his body over the mess, rejecting the supervisor's courteous gesture, and pulled in the pages like they were twenty-dollar bills. The drugstore glasses made everything a little blurry.

When Alex was finished, they both stood up and pretended it hadn't happened.

"Great," Alex said. "Can I see his boss? Maybe that's you."

"That's me. And I'm his only boss now that we don't have a head of H.R. no more. Capablanca don't get along with me like he did with her—but then I ain't as pretty as she was."

Alex smiled at the joke. The supervisor was right—he wasn't as pretty as Sheila. "All right," Alex said. "Does he have a locker or something I can look at? They tell me if a guy's not there I gotta find 'objective corroboration he regularly attends the workplace.'" Alex tapped his folder definitively. "That's what it says."

"Sure," the supervisor said. "Hell if I care."

* * *

Five minutes later, Alex was back in his truck and driving fast.

So Beto and the former head of H.R. had got along . . . So Sheila *did* know Beto. The supervisor said so. Sheila had lied to him. After Alex had given her the benefit of the doubt, after he'd wasted time thinking she was different than other women—different than Pamela. After all that, she'd just been another liar.

His cell phone rang. "What?"

"Dude, why do you sound so pissed?" It was Del.

"Sorry. What is it?"

"Don't get angry, OK?"

"I already am angry, Del. So how much worse are you going to make my day?"

"Your truck got stolen," Del said.

So there was the other shoe dropping. He'd hoped Del might surprise him for once. Alex felt very sad and angry and didn't say anything.

"Alex?" Del said.

"Don't lie to me."

"What do you mean?"

"Lying to Mom is one thing, OK? I'm actually impressed you waited this long. I expected you to do it earlier."

"Do what?"

"Come on, Del. Sell the truck to pay down your debt and then call it in as stolen."

Alex knew his accusation was on the money when Del didn't respond immediately. Alex could almost hear the creaky gears turning in Del's head as his brother shifted his approach from lying to strategic honesty.

"On the bright side," Del said, "now you'll get a little sugar from the insurance money."

"No, Del. Now the insurance company will pay me the car's market value. But guess what? The truck is worth less than what I owe the bank on it. So now I owe the difference. That means the bill collectors will be coming back for me. So don't do me any more favors."

"Alex?"

Alex didn't respond. From the tone of Del's voice, he knew there was a third shoe about to drop.

"Alex? I need to ask a favor."

Of course, Alex thought. "What?"

"I need a place to stay tonight."

27

Of course Alex said yes. He even drove across town to pick Del up. He felt lousy the whole way there. Del had proposed staying in Alex's vacant house. Alex told him again that wouldn't work—Alex needed it empty while he tried to rent it and, besides, it had no furniture. Del would stay with Alex instead and sleep on the couch.

On the way home, Del said, "I can help find a renter for the vacant house while you look for a job. While you're out, I'll update the internet ad, I'll take calls."

"No internet poker," Alex said.

"No problemo, I only play strip poker now," Del said. When Alex frowned, Del said, "Kidding."

Del asked Alex what he'd been doing all these days if he hadn't been looking for a job, and Alex told Del basics of the accident and his investigation. And about Sheila, and her lie.

"Everything seemed so straightforward," Alex said. "I proposed to help her, and she agreed to help me do that. I don't understand why she'd lie to me."

"Well, start at the top. Why does she want to help to you in the first place?"

"Money."

"Whoa, don't say it like it's bad."

"She wants dirt on her husband to use in her divorce. She just doesn't want it bad enough to tell me the truth."

"What was the lie?"

"It was such a basic thing—I told her I was looking for this employee of Liberty, and she looked me in the eye and told me she'd never heard of anyone named Rigoberto Capablanca."

"Beto?" Del said. "I know that fool."

And he did. Del explained that they'd fallen into a casual camaraderie over the years as two generally unsuccessful gamblers. Del even had Beto's cell phone number. At Alex's request, Del called it.

"Beto! It's Del." There was a pause. "Del. Del Taco. Right, it's me, dude." Del glanced at Alex and shrugged. "Look," Del said, "I hear you're in some trouble . . . right, for a change. Listen, can we get together? I want you to meet someone who can help you . . . Actually, you already know him—Alex Fogarty. He's my brother."

Beto's exclamations were loud enough that Alex could hear them clearly. Beto included a few Spanish curses that Alex hadn't heard before. Alex grabbed the phone from Del.

"Beto, it's Alex. Listen. No, listen to me. I'm going to nail whoever set up the accident and got Jorge killed, and I don't think it was you. But either you put me on the right track, or I'll keep hounding you." Beto told Alex to put Del back on the line. Alex did, and Beto agreed to meet the two of them at his lawyer's office the next day to talk.

The lawyer's name was Stanley DeLay. His offices were in a small professional complex that housed doctors and other lawyers. He had a personal injury practice, and Alex cynically assumed that Beto knew the lawyer from running swoop-and-squat insurance scams back in the day. Scams like that required more than an old car and a willingness to risk serious injury. You also needed a crooked doctor and a crooked lawyer—it was a real team effort.

Alex and Del found DeLay waiting for them in the reception area. DeLay was middle-aged, with a pockmarked face and a comb-over.

"So you're Beto's lawyer," Alex said loudly.

At the mention of the name Beto, DeLay glanced nervously at the couple of clients sitting in the reception area. "I'm not the man's lawyer at this time," he said. "I'm merely acting as his agent in this meeting."

Alex found the nomenclature amusing. "I didn't know Beto had an agent," he said. "Have you booked him on Letterman yet?"

DeLay escorted Alex and Del to a small conference room where the blinds were shut. Beto was waiting there, pacing and looking nervous. The lawyer then excused himself. Beto continued to pace.

"Sit down, Beto," Alex said. Alex sat down himself. So did Del. "I'm not here to capture you this time."

Beto ignored Alex and wandered to the window, where he spread apart two slats in the blinds and peeked outside. "Can you protect me?"

Beto was pitiful, but Alex withheld a chuckle because he could see the man was scared. "That depends," Alex said. "Why don't you tell me what's going on, and then let's see if we can help each other. Tell me about how Jorge died."

Beto turned to Del with a fierce look. "I can't believe you're related to this *pendejo*."

"Me neither," said Del with a roll of his eyes. "Believe me."

Little brothers. Alex let Del's casual insult slide. Beto turned to Alex, with his eyes now starting to tear up. "I'm scared of Crash," he said.

"You're scared of a crash? I would be too if my friend died like that."

"No, man. *Crash*, the man."

"Who are you talking about?"

"Crash is the *enforcer*, man. You don't wanna mess with him."

"Whose enforcer?"

"Luke Hubbard's. Crash does all the dirty work. He'll slit your throat as easy as he shaves in the morning. He's *loco*. He killed Lenny."

"Who's Lenny?"

"My bookie."

Alex's head was spinning. He needed a list of characters to keep up. He shot a glance at Del, but Del's look said that he'd never heard of these people either. "Why did Crash kill Lenny?"

"Lenny was trying to blackmail Luke."

"For what?"

"For the crash."

"The crash at Christmas or Crash, the man?"

"The one at Christmas, man, the one at Christmas." Beto pulled a chair from the table and fell into it, exhausted. "You just gotta help me, man."

"And now you think Crash is looking for you."

"I don't think, I know. He's out there *right now*." Beto motioned toward the window, and Alex rose to see for himself.

"No, don't look!" Beto said.

Alex sat down again. "Why don't you go to the police?"

Beto spit out a puff of air and flipped his hands toward the ceiling. "They wouldn't help me, they would just arrest me for something. They always want the bigger fish, you know?"

"I never thought you were a big fish, Beto."

"Thanks," Beto said glumly. Then he thought about that a little more, and said, "You're a bastard, Alex, but at least you're honest."

"What does Lenny's blackmail scheme have to do with you?"

"I gave Lenny the evidence, and we were going to share whatever he got. I owed him money."

"I see . . . but Lenny couldn't pull the scheme off and got himself killed, and now this Crash person figured out you were involved and is coming to kill you. Is that about it?"

"Exactly, man."

"Why would Crash think you were involved?"

"Because I knew Jorge, and Jorge was in on the scam. Or maybe Lenny told Crash before he died. I don't know."

Alex wished somebody would just tell him what the hell had happened. "Exactly what was the scam?"

"For a smart guy, you ask some really stupid questions," Beto said. "It's the same scam as always—you load some poor losers in a car and go get yourself rear-ended."

Now we're getting somewhere, Alex thought. Maybe Zeke's crazy theory was right—but the details didn't quite add up. "I thought you and Jorge had moved up in the world. Why would he pull a stunt like that, and with a company van, no less? Did he miss prison?"

"Because they asked Jorge to do it."

"Who asked him to? Why?"

"It was some workers' comp thing. Jorge wasn't real clear about it."

Alex pretended to scoff. "He kept you in the dark? Some friend."

"He was a bastard. He didn't want me to steal his deal—like I gave a shit. He invited me to come along, but I was hung over that morning. I told him to cut me in, but he was only going to pay me the same measly share he paid those other losers in the van . . . Bastard . . ."

"And you're sure it was Luke who asked him to do it?"

"Luke or Crash, one of those two. Jorge never told me which because he wanted to cut me out. But he boasted over and over that it went all the way to the top. He thought he was *so* important. Anyway, Luke, Crash—same difference."

Alex looked skeptically at Beto. As much as Alex wanted to believe, now that he heard Beto's story, he wasn't sold yet. "And so the CEO of a Fortune 500 company asked Jorge to do a penny-ante car insurance scam for him?"

"No, it wasn't car insurance, that was the beauty of it. It was workers' comp. Jorge was supposed to go get hit by a car *without* insurance. That way someone like you"—Beto jabbed a bony finger at Alex—"wouldn't come snooping around and asking questions afterward."

That answered Alex's lingering question about why the driver of the van chose to get rear-ended by a beat-up old gardening truck—and if Howard Cummings' sports car hadn't hit them from behind, Alex would never have gotten involved and the scam would have actually worked. Maybe Beto wasn't lying, after all. Alex nodded as he thought it over. "And Liberty was self-insured on the van, so there was no outside insurer on that end to deal with. Nice little plan. So the idea was Luke or Crash or whoever would split the workers' comp payout with Jorge and the others?"

"Exactly, man."

Beto still hadn't answered the biggest question—why someone in Luke's position would commit murder. "You realize, don't you, that Luke is already rich? No offense, but why would he stick his neck out for a little scam like this?"

"That's what I told Jorge, but he wouldn't listen. He wanted to be a big shot with the bosses."

"And it all would have worked out fine if it wasn't for the explosion."

Beto sighed. "As soon as I heard about that, I knew it was a setup."

Alex's ears perked up. "Why did you think that?"

"Because vans don't just explode, man. They were *supposed* to die."

That might or might not make sense, Alex thought. "Why would Luke want to kill them?"

"Just Jorge—the others were unlucky. Jorge knew too much." Beto leaned in and whispered hoarsely, "Jorge used to get girls for Hubbard."

"That doesn't make sense, Beto. Luke Hubbard is rich and good looking, he can have any woman he wants."

"No, he likes them young."

Alex curled his lip in disgust.

"Not children," Beto said. "He's not some sort of . . . pervert. Just seventeen, eighteen years old. But a guy like him can't just go cruise around the high school in his Mercedes, you know?"

"Big difference between seventeen and eighteen," Alex said, even though he realized the remark was unproductive. He couldn't help it.

They were silent until Alex spoke again.

"So, do you have any evidence that the accident was a setup, or did that all get blown up, too?"

* * *

When Beto's black Camaro with the scratched fender pulled out of the lot at Stanley DeLay's office, a silver SUV parked across the street pulled out after it.

Crash was a patient man, but he was tired of trailing Beto. Pool hall, bar, girlfriends' houses—it was the same joyless cycle day after day. Crash had only contempt for Beto. Liberty had hired Beto, even though Beto was an ex-con. Beto should have been grateful, like Crash was grateful for all Luke and Liberty had done for him. Instead, Beto had helped Lenny blackmail Luke.

Sure, Crash thought, *I betrayed Luke, too.* But only once. Years ago, even though he was reminded of it almost every day. He didn't ask Petra to flash her ass in front of his face all the time. Anyway, Crash's betrayal was ancient history; Luke didn't know about it—and never would.

Crash kept a couple of cars between himself and the Camaro. He was pretty sure Beto had figured out he was being followed. It would be so easy for Crash just to make Beto go away. Crash wished he could. But he couldn't, yet. Luke wanted to know whether anyone other than Beto was involved in Lenny's blackmail scheme. So Crash was busy finding out.

The cars drove for a while down broad avenues that stretched for miles and intersected at right angles with other broad avenues. At the end of one of them, they drove deep into the hills on a narrow, winding street where Crash's large SUV was even more conspicuous. On the other side of the hills they drove out into the San Fernando Valley. There the grid of asphalt resumed, as persistent as if the streets followed lines etched in the earth's crust and the hills were just loose dirt piled on top. Beto had never come this way before, not as long as Crash had been following him. The Camaro stopped at a burger joint, and that made Crash happy. Beto was miles from his own neighborhood and so he wouldn't have the advantage of knowing the streets around here. This was as good a place as any to confront Beto—for information of course, with perhaps just a little physical persuasion.

Crash watched from his car as his quarry entered the restaurant and sat in a booth facing away from the parking lot. Crash walked in and, quickly but quietly, slipped into the booth across from his target. Crash found him grinning impishly.

It wasn't Beto.

"Damn it!"

Crash brought a fist down onto the table. He wanted to throttle the smirking young man in the booth, Beto's decoy. But he wouldn't. He would control his anger, just like Luke had taught him—*you don't suppress your anger, you just save it up for when you really need it.* Crash ran back to his car, gunned the engine and raced toward the on-ramp of a freeway that would take him back to where the real Beto had left long ago.

28

Beto's requests were conventional but heartfelt—money and shelter. The poor man was terrified of this Crash person, and couldn't safely return to the apartment where he had been staying. After a friend of Beto's drove away in Beto's car to mislead Crash, Alex and Del drove Beto across town and dropped him at a friend's place.

What Beto offered was evidence that Luke had been behind the accident.

For that, Alex decided he could oblige Beto with a house, temporarily. It was Del's idea, actually, to let Beto stay in Alex's vacant house. Del was pretty sharp sometimes.

Beto also wanted fifty thousand dollars. To Alex, it might as well have been fifty million.

"You're going to have to go back to Sheila," Del said after they dropped Beto off.

"The woman who lied to me? No way."

"It's worse than that. You're going to have to butter her up."

Del was right, of course. Alex was relieved that Del mentioned calling her. So now he had a reason to call her, and it would be all business. Fine. When they got back to Alex's house, that's what he did.

"Alex," she said. "I'd been hoping to hear from you."

Sure you have, Alex thought. "I found Beto."

"Beto?"

Alex couldn't stand her playing him for a fool. He ignored her question. "Beto confirmed there was a scam, he has evidence of who's behind it, and he wants to sell it. Pretty great, huh? I wanted to share the exciting news." Del was sitting across from Alex in Alex's living room, and he looked earnestly at Alex and made a motion with his hands like he was spreading butter on toast. *Butter her up.* Alex forced himself to calm down.

"I see," Sheila said. "Well, what is he offering and how much does he want?"

Sheila's tone was all business, like the first time they spoke, with no hint of chagrin at having lied to Alex. Alex gave her points for audacity. "Beto says he has a piece of paper from Luke—Luke or someone named Crash, he was never quite clear, I don't think he knows. He says if the trail leads to Crash, it'll also lead to Luke. Does that sound right to you?"

"Probably."

"I knew you'd know. Anyway, a piece of paper with the license plate number of the van and the date of the accident written on it by Luke or Crash. It supposedly has fingerprints from one of them on it."

"Is that so . . ."

"That's what Jorge Ramirez told Beto. Jorge was handed the paper when he was given his instructions on what van to use."

"How did Beto get this slip of paper?"

"Says he stole it from Jorge's locker at work after the accident."

"Charming. That seems like pretty flimsy evidence, though."

"That's what I thought at first, too," Alex said eagerly. Del gave him a thumbs up. "But if the paper is genuine, it's a good first step. The way I see it, we don't need to prove that Luke murdered Jorge and the others."

"We don't?" Sheila said.

Alex enjoyed hearing genuine curiosity in her voice. Once she heard his plan, she'd front the money Beto wanted—hopefully. "We just need evidence that Luke—or someone close to Luke, if it's Crash—sent them out to go get into an accident. That's conspiracy right there."

"Interesting . . . So what does he want for this so-called evidence?"

"Something that I can give him, and something I can't."

"But that *I* can give, right? So what is it?"

"Some money."

"How much, Alex?"

"Fifty grand."

She sounded shocked. "Fifty grand! I'm surprised you have the balls to even ask me for that."

"Sheila, I'm committing to this project, too, OK? The other thing he wanted is a place to stay. This Crash guy is after him, and he's afraid to go home."

"You're bringing this Beto guy into your house? You really are a nut."

"No, no. I'm putting him up in a vacant house I have." Alex saw Del roll his eyes.

"Geez, I didn't know I was teaming up with Donald Trump," Sheila said. "Why don't you pay him the fifty thousand yourself?"

Alex sighed and waved Del out of the room. "Well?" Sheila said.

"Because I'm upside down, Sheila. I've got no cash. I've got five mortgages and no job."

Her tone turned incredulous. "Five mortgages? What other secrets are you keeping? And after all that carrying on in the library about wanting to find the truth—you're broke! Why should I trust you with a pile of cash?"

"I don't know you either. I thought you'd have a good lead for me, given that you used to work at Liberty Industries. But that Ray-bear guy didn't know anything. It's almost like you sent me to the least useful person to talk to." Sheila didn't say anything. Alex would have loved to call her out on her lie about not knowing Beto, but he kept his cool. *Butter her up.* "The bottom line is, we have to trust each other," he said. "Together, we have a chance to do something big here."

"I'm not convinced."

Alex knew why she was playing coy all of a sudden—she wanted Alex to take all the risk and to keep herself—and her cash—out of harm's way. "Sheila, you know Luke would pay to keep this quiet. And I know you want money and, hey, I don't judge, all right?"

"What do *you* want?"

"I'll give you time to do whatever you want with the evidence—"

"Luke would laugh in my face if I told him about this so-called evidence."

"And after Luke pays you off, or whatever, then I get a chance to go to the police. That's all. That's not on you, and Luke can never say you went back on whatever deal you make with him."

"Right," Sheila said. "That is, if the fingerprints haven't been rubbed off the paper by now, if Beto isn't making this whole thing up—how do you propose to find out whether his evidence is any good?"

"I've thought about that, too. We give Beto a taste of his own medicine. I tell him I'll only pay a little up front, with the rest to come once we've verified the evidence. I tell him that if he's scamming us—and I've dealt with this guy before, there's a good chance he is—then I'll tell this Crash character where to find him." Sheila was silent. Alex said, "Beto's scared, Sheila. If we don't move soon, he'll skip town."

"Fine," she said. "I can have some money for you in a couple of days."

"That's wonderful. Thank you."

"I guess I should thank you for finding this guy."

This guy. As if she didn't know who Beto was. Alex looked forward to seeing Sheila again just to see whether, in person, she would betray any more embarrassment over her lie than she did over the phone. "I'll set up a meeting with Beto two days from now."

Sheila didn't say anything.

"Sheila? You said a couple of days. Two days, right?"

"Sure, that's fine. If my lawyer is any good, that'll be fine."

29

Brad's adversary looked nervous. Brad watched him, hunched over counsel's table in the courtroom, as his eyes bobbed from page to page of his notes as if searching desperately for a comma that had slipped off and crawled back to bed. The judge hadn't entered yet. Brad approached his opponent and touched him on the shoulder.

The man flinched but just as quickly regained his composure. He stood confidently and extended his hand. "Jacob Carter," he said. He was Brad's arrogant Harvard classmate, the one who silently sat through the meetings at Boswell & Baker's offices.

"I know," Brad said. "Brad Pitcher. We went to law school together."

Jacob squinted at Brad as if trying to imagine him with eight years' more hair. "HLS?" he said.

"That's the only law school I went to. Look, we have some time before the hearing begins, and there are a couple points on the wrongful termination case I'd like to go over. But does it make sense to wait for Alan?"

"Mr. Matthews won't be attending this hearing," Jacob said. "Plus, I see no need to discuss that case now. Our interaction today will be confined to your motion for interim spousal support."

With that, Jacob maneuvered awkwardly back into his chair. Brad rested his hands on his hips. Brad knew big firm lawyers like Jacob spent more time in the library than in the courtroom. Brad decided to have a little fun with him.

"So, Alan let you go without adult supervision on this one. Good for you. That means he either knows you're going to win or knows you're going to lose. Did he tell you which?"

Jacob screwed his face into a lopsided grimace. "You sound pretty confident for a guy who's gone oh-for-everything on this case."

"Have you argued before Judge Brewster before?"

"Plenty of lawyers in my firm have."

"Have you argued before any judge before?"

Jacob gave Brad a wide-eyed look as if he had been caught relieving himself behind a tree. The bailiff's booming voice filled the courtroom.

"All rise!"

Brad rushed over to the table on the other side of the aisle, and both lawyers stood at attention as the judge entered. Judge Brewster was youngish, in his early forties, with lively eyes and a thick beard that was starting to go gray. He had a fleshy face, and if he had a body to match, that fact was hidden by his black robe. He genially motioned for the lawyers to sit.

"Mr. Carter from . . . Baker & Boswell," the judge said, consulting the briefs in front of him. "Haven't seen you before. Nice suit. Where'd you go to law school?"

Jacob stood up stiffly. "Harvard," he said. "It's Boswell & Baker," he added softly.

The judge rocked his head back. "Harvard . . . I've heard of it. Expensive. Still paying off the tuition?"

"No, Your Honor. I was able to pay my loans off a couple years ago."

"With a Baker & Boswell salary, I believe it. Golden State Law—my illustrious alma mater—isn't quite as expensive as fair Hah-vahd, but I've still got a few years left yet to pay off mine. I should mail in the last check, let's see . . . just about the time I mail the first college tuition check for my oldest. How about you, Mr. Pitcher? Did you go to Harvard, too?"

Brad rose. "I did, Your Honor. As a matter of fact, Mr. Carter and I were classmates there." Brad quickly sat down again.

"No kidding," the judge said. "How about that? Now I feel outclassed in my own courtroom."

Brad rose and said, "You haven't heard us speak yet, Your Honor."

The judge laughed. "I've heard you speak here before, Mr. Pitcher, and I'm glad to see you've lost none of your wit."

From there, the hearing only went further downhill for Jacob Carter. Jacob couldn't give a reason for why Luke had fired Sheila during the divorce proceedings or for why Sheila, now unemployed, shouldn't get alimony. At least, he couldn't give any good reasons. His flimsy arguments annoyed the judge, and his arrogant manner offended the judge, who quickly turned from Gentle Ben to an angry bear.

In the end, Brad had his first little victory, an interim order for Luke to pay Sheila alimony every month until the conclusion of the divorce case. And with a flourish: the judge ordered Jacob to have Luke deliver a cashier's check to Sheila by the end of the day, or else the judge would send a sheriff's deputy to arrest him.

* * *

Brad made a point of walking shoulder-to-shoulder with Jacob as they left the courtroom, though Jacob obviously wanted to get as far away as he could, as fast as he could. When they entered the corridor, Brad said, "Lesson number one for oral arguments—don't be an asshole."

"Very funny," Jacob said.

"Good luck breaking the news to Alan. Maybe he'll let you tell the client on your own, too." With that, Brad walked away before Jacob had a chance to do so himself. He pulled out his cell phone to call Sheila. She would be ecstatic. *Never mind that*, thought Brad, *I'm ecstatic.*

30

At first Sheila wanted to come to Alex's house to give him the money, which made Del happy because he said he wanted to meet her. Del could be so immature. "She's not my girlfriend," Alex said. "Besides, you can't meet her." But then Sheila called and said she was running late, and told Alex to just come by her apartment on his way to meet Beto. Del told him to be careful.

"I'm not scared of Beto," Alex said.

"I meant be careful with Sheila."

Sheila lived in a luxury high-rise apartment on the West Side. She answered the door in a sweater and a dark skirt and wore diamond earrings and a string of pearls. She looked good that way, and Alex noticed that her clothes flattered the shape of her body, but not in the showy way that most of the women he knew dressed. It made him want to watch her more, which he did discreetly as she led him inside.

"I hope you didn't get dressed up on my account," he said. He meant it jocularly, but the words sounded wrong as soon as they left his lips.

"I have a charity event this afternoon," she said over her shoulder.

Inside, she handed him five bound stacks of twenty-dollar bills. That's the way Beto wanted it. It was only one-fifth of the fifty grand Beto asked for.

"You think that'll be enough?" Sheila said.

"I'll persuade him that it is," Alex said. He told Sheila more about the meeting he had set up with Beto—in a public place, neutral ground.

"He'll think you're trying to scam him," she said. "He may get angry."

"I'm not worried about little old Beto Capablanca," Alex said. And he wasn't. Nothing wrong with showing a little justified confidence.

"But he's—he's a criminal. He may get violent."

She didn't know Alex had collared Beto all those years ago, right on the street. "I've seen Beto angry before. I think I can handle it."

"Oh, I forgot—surfers are tough."

"How about 'good luck'?"

"Have you ever walked around with ten thousand dollars on you?"

Ah, Alex thought, *so she's concerned about the* money *staying safe.* "Have you?"

"Every time I step out of the house," she said, and she slipped a manicured finger between her pearl necklace and her collarbone.

"So then what's the big deal?"

"A bag full of cash is a little different than a necklace," Sheila said. "People still respect jewelry."

Alex felt like he should respond but didn't know where to begin, and then she spoke again.

"You'll call me as soon as it's over?"

"I told you, we're meeting at MacArthur Park. There are always hundreds of people around. It'll go fine."

She looked skeptical, then turned away from him. "So you have the money," she said, like she was thinking about more than the money after all, "get out of here before I change my mind."

* * *

MacArthur Park was named after a general, Alex recalled. It was the statue that reminded him. He took a relaxed stroll around the park to look for Beto. Even though it was cool out, there were plenty of people—young lovers wasting time, street vendors, some cops, some kids. The park was in better shape than it used to be. Still, this was a part of town where you didn't flaunt wealth. Alex had the ten grand bundled tightly inside a satchel strapped over his shoulder and across his body. As far as anyone knew, he could have been a bike messenger.

Alex's cell phone rang. "Hello?"

"It's Sheila. Have you found him yet?"

Alex couldn't believe how impatient she was. For a moment, he felt a little for Luke. If she was this annoying with Alex after just meeting him, he didn't want to imagine how high maintenance she must be after years of marriage. "No, Sheila, I just got here. I'll call you when it's over. Goodbye."

Alex found Beto waiting for him on the other side of a fountain. Beto wore a windbreaker and stood hugging his arms, glancing from side to side and generally doing a poor job of looking casual. Alex boxed him playfully on the shoulder by way of greeting, and he jumped. They walked together toward the edge of the park.

"You brought the money?" Beto said.

"Absolutely. And a key to a house where you can stay for a while."

"Let me see the money."

Alex sighed. There were few things less suspicious the two of them could have done right there besides stop and look inside Alex's bag. Plus, Beto might notice that Alex had not brought the full fifty thousand. But Beto had stopped in his tracks like a tired dog, so Alex grudgingly lifted the flap that covered his satchel. Doing so made him feel seedy, but no one around seemed to notice.

Beto started shivering. "That don't look like no fifty grand."

"Keep your voice down," Alex said. "It's a down payment—I'll give you the rest when I know your evidence is the real thing. Let's go somewhere we can talk."

Beto moved flush to Alex's body to obscure the view of those around them and then pulled a gun from the pocket of his windbreaker. Alex didn't know what it was for a moment. It was thin and silver and almost vanished inside Beto's small hand.

"Oh, Beto, put that thing away before someone gets hurt."

Beto had pulled a gun on Alex once before, years ago. It was less shocking the second time—though Alex admitted he liked it better when Beto had pointed the ashtray at him.

"I'm not playing around Alex," Beto said. His wrist quivered alarmingly.

Alex leaned in to him and whispered in his ear. "Del is watching us right now. If you kill me, his next call will be to Crash. You won't leave the ZIP code."

Beto thought about that, then asked, "How do I know you're not lying?"

"Well, you're a gambling man. If you feel lucky, you should just shoot me and see what happens. Or you could use your head for once, and get a lot more money in a couple days. Meantime, you'll be staying in my house. If I stiff you, burn it down."

Beto looked around and then dropped the sleek silver pistol into Alex's bag like it was a rotting fish.

"Jesus, Beto, what'd you do that for? I've got to get you out of daylight."

Alex led Beto to a tiny diner right off the park. They sat down at a booth in the corner. Beto slowly pulled a plastic bag from inside his jacket but shoved it back inside when the waitress clomped over.

"What'll it be?" she said.

Beto scowled at her. "We're not hungry."

The waitress leaned up and back—she was tall—and planted her hands on her hips. "Sweethearts, we're too busy in here to be giving out booths to people who aren't hungry."

Alex went into his bag and peeled out a twenty from one of the bundles. "Give us whatever the last guy had, but don't bring it to us," he said. She put the money in her pocket and left.

Beto pulled the plastic bag out again, his expression full of grave drama. "This is how I got it from Jorge," he said, and he passed it across the table.

It looked the way it was supposed to look—sealed inside a clear plastic bag was a slip of paper, like one from a desktop memo pad, that had a license plate number and a date written on it.

"Now the money," Beto said.

Alex reached into his own bag, felt his way cautiously around Beto's pistol and took out the bundles of cash. He passed them under the table to Beto. "Count them in your lap," Alex said.

Beto glared at him. "I'm not stupid."

Alex's cell phone rang. It was Sheila again. He knew he should ignore it, but he was so annoyed that she was calling again that he couldn't.

"It's Crash," Alex said to Beto. Beto hugged the bundles of money more closely into his belly. "Just kidding," Alex said, "I'll be right back." Before Alex could rise, Beto snatched the plastic bag away from him.

"I'm not done counting," he said.

Alex stood, his satchel still draped over his torso, and looked down at Beto. Beto sat hunched over the plastic bag and the bills that were stacked in his lap.

"You see how much I trust you, Beto? I'm going to leave you here with the money and the goods. I'll be right back with your house key."

Alex moved to the doorway to get away from the clatter of the diner, but all the way there Alex watched Beto, and Beto watched Alex.

"Hi Sheila," Alex said in a hoarse whisper, "I'm still with Beto. I told you—"

At that moment a burly man barreled past Alex and out the door, his arms pumping in a dead sprint. The man brushed Alex as he went by and knocked Alex back on his heels.

A moment later Alex was knocked all the way to the ground by a greater force, an explosion that sent his cell phone flying out into the street and propelled his skull into a wall. The explosion did worse to many others, which Alex saw for himself after he gropingly rose from beneath a blanket of shattered glass. Strangely, he thought, he couldn't hear any screaming. But he couldn't hear anything. He saw agonized faces that he wouldn't soon forget, but he didn't see Beto's. He followed his first impulse and ran out of the diner toward where he thought the burly man had gone.

Alex thought he spotted the man running a half a block ahead of him, but lots of people were running just then, and in all different directions. After a couple of minutes he admitted he had lost the man and stopped running. He tried instead to focus on the last moments at the diner, to recall anything that might be helpful. But once he stopped running, his memories wouldn't fall into sequence. All he could retrieve were unconnected images: A waitress with a pencil stashed in her hair. A child joyfully drumming with a table knife while Alex hissed at Sheila over the phone. The thick arm of the man who raced past him just before the flash—and the man's hand, with a birthmark like wine running over a linoleum floor.

* * *

Crash didn't follow Alex. He stayed in his SUV, watching the diner.

The explosion started a fire, and the firemen came. They put it out quickly, and Crash joined the gathering crowd that drew in around the police line. Some seemed to be looking for loved ones. Others just seemed curious. Crash was tall and he let others stand up front. He watched until they had taken the last of the bodies out, then he got in his car and drove away. Beto was no longer a problem.

31

Alex knocked on Sheila's door and heard her run to it on the other side. She flung the door open, looked at him with surprise, then threw her arms around him. He was too exhausted to react, but wobbled a little in her embrace.

"I saw it on the news," she said.

"Then you know he's dead."

She took him inside and closed the door. For the first time, Alex saw a depth in her eyes that proved she cared about more than just money. He felt himself relax a little.

"When the call went dead, I thought you were gone, too."

"Lost my cell phone," he said.

Sheila gave him a penetrating look. "And the evidence?"

"Gone. The money, too."

"Oh, who cares. I was so worried when I heard about the bomb. To think that I'd sent you to meet Beto, and if something had happened to you—"

"I remember it being my idea," Alex said.

"You know what I mean. I'm just glad you're safe. Did you see it?"

"The slip of paper?"

"Yes."

"Sure, I saw it up close."

"And what do you think?"

"I think Beto was right."

She looked him over, the bruises and the dirty clothes. Her gaze lingered on the backs of his hands, where a constellation of puckering purple cuts had started to scab over.

"From the glass," Alex said. "Luckily, I hit the ground before the windows shattered."

She raised a finger and let it hover over the swollen left side of his forehead. "You've got a bruise." The concern in her voice made Alex feel a little better—he'd stopped thinking about his bruises an hour ago.

"I'll take that over the alternative."

"Let's get you cleaned up," she said.

"I already cleaned up."

"Where?"

"A McDonald's bathroom."

She responded with a crooked smirk that was half amused, half appalled. "Stay here," she said, and she left the room. Alex remained standing.

"Did you see who set off the explosives?" she called from the bathroom. Her disembodied voice echoed through the apartment.

"I think so, for a second," Alex said. "It was a man. A big guy. Does Crash have a birthmark on his hand?"

"Um . . . no. Did you see the man's face?"

"No."

"You talk to the police?"

Alex laughed. "I'm not ready to do that." The police would have asked Alex questions that he didn't want to answer, like what his business was with Beto.

Sheila returned from the bathroom with a tube of ointment and led him into the kitchen. It was brighter there. She propped him up against the refrigerator and unscrewed the cap.

"What's that?" Alex said.

"Just a little medicinal cream. Stand still, it'll stop the bruising."

Alex took hold of her wrist before she could squeeze the cream onto her finger. He welcomed Sheila's new awareness of his welfare, but she'd skipped a step on her way from frosty cooperation to attentive concern. "Why did you lie to me about not knowing Beto?"

"Oh," she said, freezing in place. "That."

"Yeah, that."

He let go of her, they had a little staring contest, and she looked away. "I was embarrassed."

"About what?"

"Beto and I had . . . a relationship."

Alex's eyebrows jumped.

"Not that kind of relationship," she said quickly. "I lied about knowing him because I used him to spy on my husband."

"And you couldn't tell me that?"

"I was ashamed of it, OK?"

"That's hard to believe," Alex said. "You don't try to hide your venom for your husband."

"I didn't want you to think I was . . . seedy."

"I've seen a lot seedier than that. Why did Beto agree to help you?"

"I paid him."

"In cash?"

She rolled her eyes. "No, in chocolate. Of course I paid him in cash."

"How much?"

"Enough to matter to someone like him." Her eyes begged him for a truce. "Why are you asking these questions?"

"I don't like being used."

"You're not being used," she said. Then: "If anything, we're sort of using each other, aren't we?"

"The thing is, if you lie to me about little things like not knowing Beto, it makes me wonder whether you're lying to me about bigger things."

She sighed. "I told you, I was embarrassed about using Beto to spy on Luke. I didn't want you to judge me."

"Too late."

After Sheila had been so stingy and bossy and dishonest, it was satisfying to Alex to make her squirm a little. But she didn't indulge him.

"Fine," she said. "I can play that game. Sure, I told a little lie, but you're not as noble as you pretend to be."

"I never said I was . . ."

"Sure you did. 'I just want the truth.' You want money, pal, and you want it even more badly than I do."

How did she guess that? Alex wondered. Maybe he shouldn't have told her about his five mortgages. He and Sheila were not morally equal. *Just apologize for lying to me*, he wanted to yell. Instead, he said, "Sure, but money's not all I want—unlike you."

"That's not fair," she said. She suddenly looked hurt, like she was going to cry. "You don't know what I've been through. Anyway, I'm sorry."

Alex couldn't tell whether the watering eyes were real or a put-on, but either way her reaction made him feel cruel. It was wrong to continue his attack after she'd raised the white flag.

"I'm sorry, too," he said.

"You have every reason to be angry with me for lying."

"You're damn right I do." Alex knew he shouldn't have cursed at her, but in his mind her remorse hadn't yet caught up with his indignation.

"And I shouldn't judge you, either," she said, "because I don't know all you've been through."

Alex was impressed at how calm she was despite his outburst. "You're right," he said.

"Five mortgages sounds like a lot."

"Too many, it turns out," Alex said sheepishly.

"At least you still have the houses," she said.

"For now," Alex said. Then, thinking of Pamela, he added, "But they've cost me other things." Sheila didn't need to know the details about Pamela—especially since Alex didn't know or trust Sheila well enough yet to reveal his closest secrets—but all the same, he wanted her to know that she wasn't the only one who had suffered.

For her part, Sheila looked puzzled. "Oh," she said finally. "A girl." Alex didn't say anything. He didn't want to confirm her guess, but part of him was relieved that she'd guessed right. He wanted her to understand, without having to tell her.

"Stand still," Sheila said. She squeezed a dab of the cream onto the tip of her finger and lifted it toward Alex's forehead. "Lower your head." He complied, and she began applying the cream in light circles to Alex's forehead.

"I know you think I'm a spoiled brat," she said softly.

Right again, Alex thought. But with her standing inches away and openly discussing her faults, he had lost the urge to strike out at her. "We all have our little entitlements," he said.

"Most people do. But I know you're not really like that." She looked into his eyes, and this close, he could tell why Luke had found her fascinating for so long.

"Well, thanks for trying," she said.

"What do you mean?"

"For trying to help me. The way you put yourself out there with Beto—I thought it was admirable."

"Oh, I'm not done with this case," Alex said.

"Really? I mean, I just assumed that after the explosion . . . someone almost killed you, Alex."

"Now it's personal. I'll never quit."

Sheila took his hand and squeezed it, an encouraging, hopeful squeeze. He squeezed back.

"Luke's dangerous," she said. She rubbed in another dab of ointment but pressed too hard. Alex flinched from the pain, then gave an embarrassed little smile.

"So are you," he said. He gently took her hand and moved it away from his forehead.

Their eyes met, and then their lips did.

32

After hours spent with the full Boswell & Baker team, which seemed to grow with every meeting, Luke now sat alone with Alan in a large conference room. The afternoon had been devoted to strategy regarding Grant Steele's grand jury, which was considering whether to indict Liberty Industries—and Luke. Murder is a state crime, not a federal one, so as a federal prosecutor, Steele couldn't bring an indictment for that. But Steele's theory was that Luke had committed a host of federal crimes—wire fraud and the like—based on the idea that Luke orchestrated the accident in order to kill the employees and get the life insurance money.

Alan swiveled his chair toward his client and looked at him earnestly. "Luke, I know we've strategized about your testimony tomorrow from every angle, but I want to revisit one more time the question of whether you testify at all."

Luke sighed. "Right. Prosecution targets like me supposedly *never* testify in front of a grand jury. But you still haven't given me a good reason why *I* shouldn't."

"I'm happy to go through the reasons one more time."

"I just don't like the whole idea of a secret proceeding of people out to get me."

"Don't think of it as a proceeding. Think of it as a box that Grant Steele needs to check before he can actually prosecute you. And the grand jury process really is almost a formality—Steele puts on all the witnesses, there's no judge, no defense and no cross-examination."

"So, I'll just testify and make the process a little more fair."

"Luke, we don't know what tricks Steele has up his sleeve, or what evidence he has. I can't prepare you like I would for a real trial."

"Then what have we been doing in this conference room all afternoon?"

"It's not the same. It's all guesswork on our side. One wrong step, and you either make Steele's case for him or set yourself up for a perjury charge."

"Give me a break, Alan, I won't perjure myself."

"I know you won't. But any little inconsistency becomes ammunition when he prosecutes you. If you testify, Steele gets to see under your toga but you don't get to see under his. It's a huge disadvantage in the criminal trial."

"This is your whole problem, Alan. You're looking at this like there will actually be a criminal prosecution against me."

"Yes, Luke," Alan said, his tone less polite than usual. "That's what this is all about."

"Wrong." Luke leaned back in his chair and spread his arms wide. "Let me adjust your thinking, Alan. I'm going to testify to ensure there will never be a criminal trial."

"That's your *hope*."

"The problem with you lawyers is you only look at the downside. You're always playing defense. But, Alan, when you're up against a stronger opponent, playing defense just delays the inevitable. I'm going to testify to go on the *offense*." Luke pounded his fist into his palm for emphasis. "If the government's targets *never* testify before grand juries, like you say, then I guarantee Grant Steele won't know what to do with me. He thought he was just going to check a box, but instead, he's got to win a street fight with me before he can even file charges. He's probably more nervous about this than you are."

"Luke, that's . . ." Alan's face slowly grew redder, until it looked like the vein in his forehead might burst. "That's delusional!"

Luke just laughed.

"Luke, you're fooling yourself. You're not negotiating some oil patch deal over martinis here. You're dealing with the federal government. They don't forget, they don't forgive, and they don't run out of money. They can take everything from you, put you in jail. And Steele"—Alan reached out and grasped the hair on Luke's head by its roots—"wants your scalp!" Just as suddenly, Alan let go of Luke's hair and, embarrassed by his outburst, retreated to his chair.

Luke laughed more softly. "Alan, I've known you for years, and before this you've never shown any more emotion than an undertaker."

"Forgive me, I—"

"Forget it; I'm proud of you," Luke said, but Alan looked like he didn't believe it. "Relax, Alan, you've washed your hands of this. You won't get any blame if my little strategy goes wrong."

"It's not about blame—"

Luke held up a hand. "But you won't share the glory when I succeed."

* * *

Someone who ought to have known once told Luke that only drinkers drink on Monday nights. So maybe it was true, or maybe oblivion was just a state of mind. Luke found himself in a hotel bar near Alan's office, and most of those there besides him were jet-lagged businessmen drinking quickly to fall asleep. Crash was there, too, drinking water. Luke had encouraged Crash to have a drink, but in Crash's mind he was always on duty. Luke found Crash's unflagging dedication impressive and, he admitted to himself at times like this, a little intimidating.

He and Crash sat together on stools at a tall table. The bartender brought Luke another gin and tonic and then wordlessly returned behind the bar.

"I dunno why Alan is so down on me testifying. He's a quitter, Crash."

"That's most ungrateful of him," Crash said, as formal as ever.

It was too bad, Luke thought—he would have liked Crash as a friend tonight rather than just a servant. Luke gave Crash a rough pat on the shoulder. "At least I still got you on my side. I'm gonna go in there tomorrow and show everyone Grant Steele is full of bullshit." The word came out like 'bushit.' Luke slumped over his glass. "It's fuggin' bullshit is what it is."

Petra walked in. Luke sat up and lifted his head with surprise and delight. She wore a tight black evening dress, and the clap of her heels on the hardwood floor reset the tempo of everyone's conversation.

Luke roused his gin-thickened tongue to call out a greeting, but stalled when he saw her eyes—two leaping flashes of blue that danced behind her lashes like flames in a gas range.

"You are drinking like woman, that is why you are crying like woman," she said to him. "I get you man's drink." She barked an order in Russian to the bartender, who, whatever his ancestry, understood well enough to respond without hesitation.

Luke staggered to his feet and grabbed Petra by the shoulders. "You look like a million bucks," he said, and she smiled. "But you don't cost a million bucks. You're a much better deal than my wife."

She slapped him. Everyone looked over at them but the bartender. Luke drew her in and embraced her.

"I may go to prison," he said softly.

Petra pushed herself away from him. "And for this you are special? I have two brothers in prison—Russian prison. Do I forget them?"

Luke shook his head. He sat down and mumbled something. Then he said, more clearly, "I'm the biggest fish, honey." Luke illustrated by curling his little finger like a fish hook inside his cheek.

"You are thinking like victim," Petra said. "If you think like victim, you end up like victim." She leaned in slowly, gently bit his earlobe and whispered, "And victims are soooo un-sexy."

Luke stood, and Petra giggled as he swayed on his feet and tried to hold the two of them up. She pressed her body against his, and they swayed together. Crash shifted uncomfortably on his stool.

The bartender brought a tray with two shots of vodka poured into stylish narrow glasses. From his stool, Crash stretched out his thick arm to bar the man's path. Petra casually reached across and took the glasses from the tray. She handed one of them to a beaming Luke.

"Drink for luck," she said. "Drink for love."

Luke stumbled when he tilted his head back to drain the shot glass. Petra took the glass from him and pushed him up under his arms. "You can still stand," she said.

"I think you're right," Luke said. He kissed her neck sloppily, and she giggled.

"I have babysitter all night . . ." she said.

Crash rose and pulled Luke away from her. With an earnest expression on his face he whispered in Luke's ear, "Sir, I think you really need to get some sleep."

Luke looked confused for a moment, and then patted Crash reassuringly on the shoulder. "s'OK . . ." Luke said. "s'OK . . ."

Then Luke launched himself on a staggering path toward the door.

Crash and Petra watched him go, then Petra stepped in toward Crash, close enough for him to smell her perfume. She gave Crash's chin a tight squeeze and said, "Come on and drive us home." Then she quickly caught up to Luke and hustled him in the direction of the exit.

* * *

In the back seat of the car, Luke was all over Petra, and she was loving it, or at least acting like she did, giggling, cooing in a susurrant blend of Russian and English. She caught Crash's eye in the rearview mirror and paused from running her tongue up and down Luke's neck to flash a malevolent grin at Crash and lick the air mockingly.

Luke didn't notice. He was moaning softly in delight. Who wouldn't, with a beautiful nymphomaniac wrapping her lithe body around him? But Luke didn't know the truth about Petra, Crash thought. Crash had protected Luke from knowing that—and, he admitted, in so doing had protected himself.

Luke suddenly roused himself and energetically announced, "I'll kick his ass, P—you just wait."

"Ooh, I know you will, Luke. This Grant Steele is little man with big problem—you."

"You got that right," Luke said loudly. In his drunken fervor he was almost bellowing. "An' you know what I'll do next? I'm gonna adopt Dmitri."

Petra turned serious. "Don't joke, darlink."

"I'm not joking. I know how much it means to you, and I already talked to an adoption lawyer. As soon as the divorce is final, I'm doin' it. And then you and me"—Luke took Petra's hands and kissed them—"are getting married."

Luke and Petra fell into each other and kissed passionately. Crash turned his eyes toward the road. Petra could get herself a husband for all Crash cared, but she couldn't—she wouldn't—get Dmitri a new father. He wouldn't let her.

Luke was insensate by the time Crash pulled up to his mansion, snoring like a twelve-year-old dog.

"You can't let Luke adopt Dmitri," Crash said to Petra.

"Why not?" she said venomously. "Why do you care?"

"You know why I care."

"You're not his father. You're a sperm donor. Plus, you're weird."

Crash glared at her in the mirror. Petra pursed her lips into a sour frown. "Don't piss me off," she said, "or I'll tell Luke where Dmitri really came from." Then her expression changed to a sadistic smile. "I'll tell him you forced yourself on me."

"You—"

"And he'll believe me. You know he will." She unsentimentally slapped Luke across the face to wake him up, which he did with a start, unaware of the violence that had woken him. "Oh, my sleepyhead is awake," Petra cooed. "Let's go inside so I can take care of you."

Luke opened the car door and woozily exited. Before following him, Petra cast another glance toward the rearview mirror and gave Crash a full-pucker air kiss.

33

Luke and Grant Steele faced off in a grand jury room in the federal courthouse. Steele wore an expensive suit, in contrast to the more casual dress of the grand jurors. In the chest pocket of his suit jacket he wore a handkerchief folded so that its four corners poked up in uneven triangles like alligator teeth. He looked at home at the podium.

Luke looked small sitting in the witness box. The grand jury sat in two rows in another wooden box along the side of the room, and the court reporter, motionless except below her wrists, sat to the other side, echoing each question and answer with a flurry of soft tapping on her stenography machine.

Steele's questions started off easy, boring even—preliminaries to establish the factual background. Despite Steele's reputation as a smooth speaker, Luke was surprised to find that in the courtroom Steele wasn't a very polished questioner. He paused frequently to consult notes, and 'um' and 'ah' were sprinkled throughout his speech. Luke kept telling himself not to let his guard down. Any bumbler can be dangerous—when he's trying to indict you.

"You're quite the Wall Street darling, aren't you, Mr. Hubbard?" Steele said.

"I'm not sure what that means," Luke said. He recalled Alan Matthews' advice to keep his responses simple and concrete, not to say more than he needed to.

"What I mean is that in the past two years, you have appeared six times on the covers of these major business magazines," Steele said, hoisting a stack of magazines. "Why do you think that is?"

"I think the interest some business journalists have in me is a reaction to the growth of Liberty Industries and its success over the past two decades." Alan would have been proud of that response, Luke thought.

"Financial success?" Steele said.

"Yes, that's how the financial press measures success," Luke said. Steele scowled, and a young female juror giggled. Steele took a moment to compose himself, then continued.

"Has Liberty's financial success surprised you?"

"I always had faith that, with a little luck, we could succeed."

"Has Liberty's financial success surprised the stock market?"

Luke considered the question, then responded. "I would say so. If everyone expected Liberty to be as successful as it is now, our stock price would have started out where it is now, instead of generally rising up to that level over the years."

"So in the past, analysts expected Liberty to make less money, and now they expect Liberty to make more money, generally speaking."

"Yes, generally speaking."

"And so, over the years, you've often made more money than Wall Street analysts expected?"

"In many cases, yes."

"And that made your stock price go up?"

"Generally speaking, yes, our stock price has risen when we've beaten the analysts' earnings estimates."

"And is the opposite true as well? When you don't meet estimated earnings, your stock price has gone down?"

"That's the basic idea," Luke said.

"Thanks, this is helpful. I'm not a finance guy."

Luke sighed. Steele had been going on like this for an hour.

Steele ostentatiously flipped a page in the notebook he had in front of him on the podium. "Let's talk now about the life insurance policies that Liberty Industries purchased on the employees who were killed in the accident last December 23rd."

"That accident was a tragedy," Luke said gravely.

"That wasn't a question," Steele said sharply. "Here's the question: you didn't buy those life insurance policies knowing those men were going to die, did you?"

"Of course not. The policies were purchased years before, as part of a corporate policy in which we buy life insurance on many employees."

"How much did those policies pay out when those employees died?" Steele said.

Luke responded loudly and clearly. "Two million dollars." He figured there was no need to by shy about innocent facts like this one, especially since Steele was trying to insinuate they were somehow criminal.

"And how much of that money went to the men's families, to their widows?"

"None of it," Luke said. "As you know, the company was the beneficiary on those policies."

"Two million dollars," Steele said, turning toward the grand jury and raising his eyebrows. "Lot of money, isn't it?"

Alan had warned Luke that Steele would resort to grandstanding like this. Luke took a deep breath and forced himself to relax. Then he responded. "Liberty Industries has been fortunate enough to grow its revenues and earnings to the hundreds of millions of dollars per quarter. Two million dollars is a lot of money, to be sure, Mr. Steele. But in the context of an enterprise as large as Liberty, it is not generally significant."

"Is that so?"

"Are you going to ask me every question twice, Mr. Steele?"

Luke knew he shouldn't taunt Steele, but it felt good, and now several of the jurors chuckled. Steele kept his gaze on Luke.

"What were your earnings in the fourth quarter of last year, the quarter that ended on December 31st?"

"You've seen our financials. You know that they were about $205 million."

"Here's a copy of Liberty's quarterly income statement," Steele said. "What does it say Liberty's earnings were for the fourth quarter?"

Luke took the paper from Steele. "Two hundred and six million, one hundred and twenty-three thousand dollars. Like I said, about two hundred and five million dollars."

"And here's a copy of a report from Dow Jones from last December fifteenth. It sets forth the estimate for your fourth quarter earnings by each of the securities analysts that cover Liberty. At the bottom is an average of those estimates. What does it say?"

Steele flapped the paper in front of Luke as he asked the question. Luke impatiently took the paper from him and read off the number at the bottom.

"Two hundred and six million dollars."

"So you met the consensus estimate by how much?"

"A little over a hundred thousand dollars."

"Not a lot of money."

Luke exhaled sharply through his nostrils and gave the grand jury a wry smile. "I doubt many people would agree with that."

Steele stared coldly at Luke. "But not a lot of money in the context of Liberty's operations, right?"

Luke paused and fought an urge to look back at the jurors. "Right."

"So you barely met the analysts' fourth quarter consensus estimate, right?"

"Right," Luke said. His smile had sagged into a frown.

"And without the two million dollars in insurance money, you would have failed to meet the estimate, is that correct?"

Several seconds passed before Luke responded. The court reporter finished typing in Steele's question, and the room was very quiet.

"That's correct," Luke said.

"So by the second half of December, Liberty had an incentive to increase its earnings before the end of the month, didn't it?"

Luke paused, and took another deep breath. He was feeling butterflies in the pit of his stomach. That didn't often happen to him. He knew that success or failure today—and maybe his freedom—hinged on how well he responded to this question. But of all that was at stake, the prospect that haunted him most at that moment was that he would have to slink back to Alan and start following his lawyer's playbook—the defensive, lawyerly playbook. Of course, Alan wouldn't tell Luke "I told you so." He wouldn't have to.

"Mr. Hubbard?" Steele said.

"Yes, Mr. Steele," Luke said. "It's true that my company had an incentive to increase its earnings in December. But I might as well admit, we also had an incentive to increase earnings in November. October, too. And you should also know, it wasn't just last year, but every month of every year since the company was founded. That's what businesses do, Mr. Steele, they try to increase their earnings."

Steele looked at Luke with a smug smile and malevolent eyes. "Mr. Hubbard, please confine your response to the scope of the question." The message was unmistakable—*this is my show.*

Steele moved on. "Mr. Hubbard, I am handing to you a statistical analysis of the effect of a failure to meet earnings estimates on the stock price of companies in your industry over the past ten years. Will you read the average that appears at the bottom of the page?"

"A five percent drop," Luke said. There was nothing he could do but answer the question and wait to see where Steele was headed with this.

"Mr. Hubbard, how much stock do you own in Liberty Industries?"

"Just over two percent of the company's outstanding stock."

"So a five percent drop in Liberty's stock price would reduce the value of the stock you own by how much?"

Luke thought for a moment. "About ten million dollars."

"How much of your net worth does your stock in Liberty represent?"

"Oh, most of it."

"Ten million dollars. That might not be a lot for company as *huge* as Liberty Industries, but it's a lot for you then, is that right?"

"I won't argue with that," Luke said.

"Yes or no."

"Yes."

"So in the second half of December, Liberty was on track to miss Wall Street's consensus earnings estimate. And if that happened, history said that the price of its stock was likely to fall."

Steele paused and looked at the grand jury. Then he stared hard at Luke.

"Is there a question in there?" Luke said.

Steele pulled on the sides of the podium as if he were about to climb over it. "Mr. Hubbard, didn't you have an incentive to increase earnings in whatever way you could, to avoid a drop in your stock price? To avoid losing ten million dollars of your personal wealth? Didn't you have an incentive to kill those employees?"

"Mr. Steele, when we announced earnings in January, the stock price didn't drop."

"Because you met the earnings estimate. But without the two million dollars from those insurance policies, you would have *missed* the estimate. Don't dodge my question. My question is not what happened *after* Liberty received that insurance money. My question is what did you expect to happen before five of your employees conveniently died in an accident that netted your company a seven-figure payday. Mr. Hubbard, my question is this: did you expect the stock price to drop if you missed the earnings estimate?"

The court reporter waited with her fingers curled above her keyboard. Luke took a moment to draw all tension from his face. Then he looked placidly at the grand jury, then at Steele.

"Mr. Steele, if I did expect the stock to drop, and if I cared about that, I still wouldn't have killed anybody. I would have just sold stock before the dip. But I didn't sell any stock in December. I've never sold a share of Liberty stock." Luke turned toward the grand jury and spoke directly to them in a soft, open voice. "I've had a rich life, and I'm happy, but my wife and I didn't have any kids. Liberty is the closest thing I have to a child. When my investors and I bought the company in the mid-nineties, it was nearly bankrupt—that was the only way a guy like me could ever have scrounged the funds to buy it. I nursed the company back to health, then grew it to a size and scope that the rest of the business community never dreamed possible. So, no. I didn't sell any shares of stock in my company. And I certainly didn't profit personally from this tragic accident."

Steele's face turned red and he tugged at his collar. Then, like a dog who's just caught the scent of a squirrel, he turned to his papers on the podium and dug through them furiously until he found the sheet he was looking for.

"Here, here," he said, waving the sheet of paper. "At least three times in the past five years, Liberty has failed to meet quarterly earnings estimates, and on none of those occasions did you sell shares beforehand."

"So . . . that supports my point. I'm a believer in the company long-term. It's important for management to be aware of periodic fluctuations in our stock price—we need to make sure that investors are understanding our story correctly—but those fluctuations will happen from time to time, and it's not something we try to manage. We manage the business for long-term growth."

Steele dug his fingertips into the sides of the podium. The skin around his knuckles turned white from the pressure.

"Mr. Hubbard, all I want from you is a simple answer."

"All I can give you is an accurate one."

Steele pushed himself from the podium in frustration and did a little spin on the sole of his shoe. When he spun back around, his head and arms had slumped like he was an abandoned marionette. The clock on the back wall loudly ticked off several seconds. Steele's next words were barely audible.

"You can go, Mr. Hubbard."

* * *

Luke stood in front of the courthouse, trying in vain to find a cab. For some reason, Crash wasn't waiting here for him and wasn't answering his cell phone. That was a first.

"You made an enemy today."

The voice in Luke's ear was low and menacing. He turned around to see the tense face of Grant Steele glowering at him. Luke laughed. "Hey, Grant. *You* made an enemy when you marched into my building with those G-men and got into my business."

"I'm not joking, Hubbard. I don't joke."

"What's the saying? That a grand jury will indict a ham sandwich? Nice try, though."

"Have no doubt, Hubbard. You've made this personal between us."

"Come on, you came after me and you lost. Take it like a man and move on."

"Oh, I'll move on. This"—Steele gestured to the courthouse behind him— "is not the last stop for me. I'll sit in the governor's mansion someday." Steele lowered his voice again. "And I'll remember you."

Luke stared back at Steele just as grimly. "I believe you—and you can still go to hell."

34

Alex sat with Del in Alex's living room. The lights were out, as usual, but the winter day was bright enough that they could see comfortably.

Alex thought about the night before, in Sheila's apartment after the explosion. Their first time together was electric. With their mutual attraction and the stimulation of Alex's brush with death, they made love with the frenzy of unleashed animals. The second time was more patient, and Alex was surprised that there was no clumsiness between them. It was like each knew where the other was going next. Their bodies fit together. Such a change from Pamela, who, by the end, seemed to approach sex more as a chore than a delight. Alex wasn't sure whether Pamela ever enjoyed it.

Sheila enjoyed it. She'd insisted on seeing him again today.

The fact that they had chemistry didn't mean that Alex trusted her. In fact, he didn't, and that was part of her allure—the danger. Emotional danger in a new relationship was one thing—he'd done that before—but if he was going to hunt down a murderer, he needed to work from a position of complete security. And that position wasn't in bed with Sheila. His mission wasn't worth compromising for a hook-up, exhilarating though it was. So the night with Sheila had to be a one-time thing—God, the realization made his bones ache.

"I've got to break it off with her," Alex said to Del.

"Why?" Del said. "It's been a while for you, right? You should go with it."

"She lied to me, Del, and I don't really trust her. And this case matters more to me than a little fling."

Del looked at Alex like he'd just rationalized his position by reciting a Rudyard Kipling poem. "Whatever, man. If I only slept with chicks I trusted, I'd be married to my right hand. Anyway, I don't know why you're buggin'. Just don't call her back."

"Too late. She's coming here this afternoon. With Beto dead, I need her help to get into Liberty Industries to find who's behind all of this."

Del groaned. "Again with this stupid case. You should forget about it. Someone tried to kill you, Alex. And that someone *did* kill other people."

Alex recalled seeing a young mother at the diner just after the blast, her face starting to drip with blood from cuts on her scalp, screaming at the still body of her child in her arms. He recalled his own guilty feeling of relief that his ears were ringing too loudly to hear the mother's screams. "That's exactly why I can't quit," Alex said.

"That's nuts."

"You wouldn't understand."

"Um, yeah, I would understand. I've had people threatening to break my legs for years. It's very stressful."

* * *

The first thing Sheila asked when she came in was, "Why are all the lights out?" Her tone was crisp, like before. Businesslike. Thank God.

"Long story," Alex said. He introduced her to Del, who was genuinely affable, as he could be when he wanted to. Del excused himself abruptly, saying he had to go visit a friend. He took his skateboard to the door and, before leaving, said to Sheila, "Watch him—I think that bump on his forehead scrambled his brains."

After Del closed the door behind him, Sheila said softly, "Your brother looks a little old to be riding a skateboard."

"That's another long story," Alex said.

They sat down, and Sheila spread out on the coffee table the items she'd brought—a social security card and a California driver's license, both with the name Al Franks. The driver's license had Alex's photograph on it. Alex stood and inspected them by the window, where the light was good. They both looked real.

"Why the name Al Franks, by the way?" she said.

"Same initials as mine, basically the same first name. I figured it would be easier for me to remember."

"I think it's smart," she said, nodding her head thoughtfully. "How'd you pick the home address?"

"It's the address of one of the houses I own. So you really think you can get me a job at Liberty?"

"I basically have. I called the acting head of H.R., a woman who was my protégé and owes me a lot, and told her you were a friend of a friend. You'll have an interview, but it's a formality."

"What department?"

"Security."

"That's ironic."

"I thought you'd be happy about it."

"No, it's perfect," he said. "But won't they be more suspicious about my ID if they hire me in security?"

Sheila waved a hand dismissively. "This is corporate America, Alex. Personal recommendations go a long way."

Alex was excited now—this plan just might work. The résumé he'd put together for Al Franks was the same as Alex's real résumé, but with the name changed. A friend at Rampart Insurance had agreed to serve as a reference for "Al Franks" if anyone called about him. "I really want to thank you, Sheila. This is important to me."

Sheila stood and went to him, and wrapped her arms around his waist. *Uh-oh*, Alex thought. "You don't have to thank me," she said. "It's important for both of us. Are you still sure you want to do this?"

In the past twelve hours, the logic of what Alex was about to do had worn a deep groove in his mind: Luke and Crash worked at Liberty; Beto thought they were behind the accident, and so did Alex; the man with a birthmark on his hand most likely worked there too, and he had killed Beto and almost killed Alex; Alex had to get into Liberty to make them pay for their killings and to stop them from killing anyone else.

"I'm sure," Alex said.

Sheila was looking up into his eyes, waiting for a kiss, expecting it. Things were moving so fast. Too fast.

Alex thought about waiting to break it off with her until after he'd actually gotten the job at Liberty. But they had only spent one night together, and waiting would just make things more complicated. So he'd end it with her, and then she'd either keep helping him or she wouldn't.

"Sheila, don't take this the wrong way."

"Uh-oh," she said.

"Last night was great, but I think we should keep things at a professional level—during the investigation."

She hugged her arms against her torso, like her body was swallowing itself. She'd gone cold again. When she spoke, her voice carried a barely noticeable tremor. "Don't blame it on the investigation. If you're not interested, just say that."

"It's not that."

"I mean, I'd understand. With my divorce and everything, I hadn't been with a man for a while."

"I said it's not that. And me either, by the way." *Was she kidding?* Alex thought. If she was rusty last night, look out when she was back in the groove. Alex took a breath and calmed himself. Sometimes being a man was a pain in the ass. "It's just that this case has gotten a lot more dangerous, and for my own sanity I have to keep things simple."

"So I'm driving you crazy already?" she said shyly.

"That's not it."

She gave an unconvincing try at a smile. "Fine," she said. "No hard feelings. And I'll help you where I can in your investigation, which is what I know you really care about, if"—she held up a finger for emphasis—"if you give me the surfing lesson you promised me."

Right. He'd forgotten about that, more a remark than a promise, muttered while in bed when she'd asked about his surfing and complained that she'd never been, and he'd said, "I'll take you out sometime." He'd been distracted at the time and in his mind's eye had pictured the summer. But now he realized she was offering both of them a graceful way out.

"Sure," he said.

"I brought my bathing suit."

She reached into her handbag and pulled out the kind of fussy designer one-piece that Alex had only ever seen in magazines. He laughed. "You'll freeze your patootie off."

"Oh," she said, clearly disappointed.

"Hold on," Alex said. He went into his garage, looked in a couple of dusty boxes of things he never used, and came back with a rubber bodysuit he'd bought Pamela for Christmas one year and that she'd never tried on. Which shouldn't have been a surprise to Alex, because Pamela had never shown an interest in surfing. Or swimming. Or the ocean. Alex held the suit up next to Sheila.

She cocked her head and regarded the suit skeptically. "You think it'll fit?" she asked.

"It stretches."

"Famous last words," she said with an ambivalent smirk, then took the suit from Alex and headed to the bathroom.

* * *

They took an old longboard Alex had. She was a good student—calm and attentive. She didn't ask a lot of questions, but she asked the right ones. Alex held the tip of the board for her and pulled her out past the waves, then helped launch the board forward for her when the waves came. After half an hour her rides were ending with her balancing upright on the board for a few seconds before falling slowly like a redwood tree to one side or the other. Alex's cheers were louder than the waves.

"Takes a lot of upper body strength," she said, panting, after one run. "Pushing yourself upright."

"You're doing great," Alex said.

"Can I see you ride one?"

Alex took the board out and took the first passable wave that came. He paddled, sprang upright and rode the wave gently toward the shore, feet together and arms at his sides. He steered the board toward Sheila, pretended like he couldn't control it, then smoothly curved away from her at the last moment. She laughed and splashed water at him. He hopped off the board into the water.

"You made it look easy."

He knew she was flattering him, but the way she said it, he didn't mind. Good women were great at that. "I come here almost every morning," he said.

"Can we get out now?"

"It *is* a little cold."

She snorted. "A little."

Alex carried the board out of the water for her. Back at his truck, he gave her a towel. She wrapped it around her hair. "It was right around here that we first met," she said. "You remember that?"

"It was colder that day," Alex said. "Let's get some coffee."

In the truck, she turned on the heater all the way, setting off a loud rattle. Alex turned it down two notches. "What'll you do after the divorce is final?" he said.

She turned the heater up again and raised her voice to be heard over the noise. "What I *want* to do is move away. Start over. I'd really like to get a boat and sail around."

"Sounds nice."

"But I'll need a lot of money for that. I'm sick of all Luke's friends—they're my friends, too—all their gossip." She looked down and frowned, like she'd been told that every time a two-faced socialite slandered a friend, it broke a sparrow's wing somewhere. Alex had a hard time mustering sympathy, but he tried. "Drive," she said. "It'll make the heat come faster." Then a moment later she turned the heat down a bit. "Tell me something. Why do *you* stay?"

"What do you mean?"

"I mean, you lost your job, you've got five houses you can't afford—why not walk away?"

There was no simple answer to that, and Alex didn't like thinking about it—about his father's memory, or his mother's disappointment or his brother's continuing slow slide. "I get asked that a lot. It's just that I've worked so hard trying to get out of the hole I'm in . . ."

"With the houses."

"Five houses, my inheritance." He shook his head. "What was I thinking?"

She laid a gentle hand on his forearm—a welcome gesture. Alex turned the corner onto his street and parked in his driveway. Sheila went on into the house and started the coffee, while Alex stayed in the garage, where he rinsed off the surfboard and put it away. When he got to the kitchen, she was sitting at his breakfast table. He sat across from her, and she handed him a mug of black coffee.

"The coffee's great," he said.

She grabbed hold of his hand and held it. "Forgive yourself," she said.

"What?" He pulled his hand back.

"You made a mistake. You were greedy and naïve, and now you're embarrassed and afraid that people will figure it out."

"Is that what you've figured out?" Alex wasn't so intrigued by her insights anymore, especially when they were right on target.

"Let it go, Alex. You don't owe any loyalty to your mistakes." She took his hand again. "Think about it. Your mistakes aren't loyal to you."

"You've got that right," he said.

"I haven't known you long, but I know that these burdens aren't right for you. You can do so much more than all this."

Alex didn't like her cautious tone. It felt condescending. "What's wrong with *all this*?" Alex said.

"Don't pretend to be offended. You know what I mean. It's honorable that you want to pay back all those mortgages, but I don't think many other people would make the same choice."

Alex set his mug down. "You're probably right."

"I'm sorry. I know it's not my place, but if we're going to sort of go our separate ways, I just wanted to tell you that."

"I get it. Maybe you're right."

"If you'll do me one favor, just think some more about the things holding you back."

"That's pretty much all I think about."

"Fair enough." She sipped her coffee, then made what was an obvious effort to brighten her tone and change the subject—for both of their sakes. "So tell me about your family," she said. "I've obviously met your brother."

Alex didn't feel like sharing any more personal details with her, but she'd agreed to help him and, anyway, he could still be civil. "It's just us and my mom."

"Your father left?"

Alex paused before answering. "Yes, then he passed away."

"I'm sorry," she said.

"I wasn't an orphan or anything. I was in high school."

"I'm still sorry. Were you close to him?"

"Hadn't seen him for a few years when he died. He died in prison."

Her look grazed the ceiling, as if she was trying to make sense of this revelation. "It's funny—sorry, it's not funny—but you don't seem like the son of hardened criminals."

"I'm not. He was a bank president, and a so-called friend lied to save himself. My dad appealed, but . . ." *But*, Alex thought. But nothing came of it. Bad choices, shitty luck and a quixotic search for redemption. Must run in the family. "What about your family?" he said.

"My family? Don't see 'em much . . . Anyway, I've always focused more on the future than the past."

"Guess you won't need a very big boat," he said.

They both laughed a little at that. "Thanks for the surfing lesson," she said.

"Anytime. You know, you're all right."

She stood up, pleased at the compliment. "Mind if I use your bathroom? I'd like to shower before I go."

"Of course. I'll show you where the towels are."

While the shower was running, Alex wondered what the hell that conversation had just been about. Sheila was showing him a way out, a way to shut off the skipping record of self-reproach. Right before she walked away herself. She was a piece of work.

* * *

Del came home late that night. He'd stayed at Alex's house enough nights now that even with a beer buzz he easily found his way in the dark to the couch where he slept. He awoke early the next morning to the smell of coffee coming from the nearby kitchen.

"Well, dude," he called out, "she was pretty hot, but you're better off without her."

Sheila stepped into the living room holding a coffee pot and a mug. She was already dressed. "What do you take in your coffee?"

Del sat up and blinked a couple of times. "How 'bout some Irish whiskey?"

She smirked. "I'll see what I can do."

Alex shuffled into the living room in sweatpants and a rumpled T-shirt. Sheila handed him the mug of coffee and kissed him on the cheek.

"Thanks," he said.

"Alex, can I talk to you?" Del said.

"Oh, don't mind me," Sheila said, and she stepped back into the kitchen. Alex shook his head vigorously at his younger brother. He didn't need Del shooting off his mouth right now.

Del spoke in a softer voice, "Alex, I really need to talk to you."

Sheila instantly returned to the living room with her eyes narrowed in a steely squint. "And what will you tell him? That I'm no good? That he can't trust me?" She turned to Alex. "I've got to go."

"Sheila—"

"No, I'm leaving." She took her purse from the kitchen and left by the front door.

Alex watched her go. If anything, the second night with her had been more pyrotechnic than the first. They'd been more relaxed, and better rested, and better acquainted. And now Del had driven her away before breakfast. "Del, what did you do?" he said.

"Me?"

"Couldn't you even wait until after coffee to insult her?"

Del stood up, looking offended, even though Alex knew him too well to take him seriously. "She's right," Del said. "I don't trust her."

"You don't even know her."

"Neither do you."

Del always had strong opinions about Alex's girlfriends, even while he jealously defended his own prerogatives for seeking debauchery and indebtedness in Vegas or anywhere else someone was willing to take his money. But Alex didn't feel like another schoolyard debate with his brother. "I think it's time you found someplace else to stay."

Del blinked a couple of times. Then, without a word, he took his suitcase out of the closet, collected his toiletries from the bathroom in a matter of seconds and swept back into the living room. He looked around the room, found Alex's keychain, and removed one of the keys.

"What are you doing?" Alex said.

"I'm moving into the vacant house. You know, the one I helped you buy."

"Then you can start paying me rent."

Del gave Alex a look of disgust, shook his head and left, slamming the door behind him.

As soon as the door closed, Alex wished he could take it all back. Del's heart was in the right place, and with all Del's personal problems, what he needed from Alex was to keep him grounded, not drive him away. What Del needed was a big brother, and those were in short supply about now. Alex sat in the kitchen with his head in his hands, the mug of coffee by his elbow. A minute later, there was a loud knock on the door.

"Come in, you idiot."

Another knock. Alex went to the door and threw it open. There he found a large man who slapped a sheaf of papers against his chest.

"Alex Fogarty, you've been served."

Alex scanned the top lines of the papers. They were for the loan on his truck, the one that Del had reported stolen.

The process server cocked a finger up toward the porch light, which Alex hadn't turned on in weeks. "Your light's burned out," he said. Then he walked away.

After weeks of hiding, Alex finally had his ruse exposed. He decided to give Sheila and Del equal blame for that. And now that this guy had found him, Alex knew that collectors for his other debts would soon be knocking on his door—literally. *That's great*, Alex thought, *just great.*

Then, pleased with his sudden ingenuity and excited to have an excuse to call her, he thought, *Maybe I can crash at Sheila's place for a few days.*

35

The morning Luke testified before the grand jury, Crash dutifully arrived at Luke's house to pick him up. When Luke and Petra had emerged bleary-eyed from the house half an hour after they were supposed to, they found Crash waiting patiently for them in the SUV. Petra tried to gauge Crash's mood. If Crash still harbored resentment for Petra's interference the night before, he didn't show it. They entered the car to find that the cup holders for the back seats held their favorite coffee drinks.

When they arrived at the courthouse, Luke resisted Petra's offer to accompany him.

"I need to focus," he said. Standing in daylight by the open car door, he leaned into the dark cabin and gave Petra a chaste kiss goodbye. They were both tired. He promised to call her when it was over, and she nodded.

Luke shut the heavy car door, and the car became a dark cave again. With the tinted windows, all that Petra could see of Crash in the rearview mirror were the glossy sparkles of his eyes looking back at her.

"What?" she said defensively.

"You can't let Luke adopt Dmitri," Crash said.

"That again? Look, you want to stop the adoption, you talk to Luke yourself. But it won't do you any good. He'll believe *me*. You know he will. Now take me to Beverly Hills. I want to go shopping." With that, Petra pulled out her cell phone and began texting friends.

When she next looked up, instead of palm trees she saw planes landing. They had come to a stop near a runway at LAX.

"Crash, you idiot, where are we?"

Crash didn't turn around, but his eyes found Petra's in the mirror. His face looked perfectly serene. "You won't lie to Luke about me. You won't lie to anyone ever again."

Petra's eyes widened and her face went slack, then she gasped—a sharp, shallow inhalation—and threw open the car door just an instant before she heard Crash flip a switch to lock the car up. She took her high heeled shoes in her hands and fled in bare feet.

Outside, she found that Crash had parked the SUV on an isolated gravel road. The road ran through an empty field that lay between the airport and the sea.

Crash chased her through the tall, brown winter grass. The sky overhead churned with white and gray clouds tumbling in from the ocean. They ran against the wind.

There was no path to follow, only pebbles and sharp stones that came too fast to avoid. Up ahead Petra saw the beach, a thin beige band that, with each pounding step she took, bobbed teasingly above the brittle grass and bushes before her. Even if she could reach the sand, on a cold day like this would there be anyone there to save her? Petra cursed herself for running into the field instead of back down the gravel road, and then she felt Crash's thick fingers paw her shoulder.

Just three of his fingers catching the edge of her shoulder were enough to spin her around, and she let herself be spun. She let the momentum swing her outstretched arm like a hammer, and she aimed the heel of the shoe in her hand at his large white head.

The heel punctured his cheek, and he grunted. As Petra fell to the ground she saw him stagger. Then the back of her head hit the ground hard, and she lost a moment. The next thing she knew, Crash was balanced on both feet and looming over her, moving in with those big hands. She snapped her body up from the shoulders like a mousetrap and landed both feet on his chest, which knocked him backward and left a narrow bloody footprint on each lapel.

The move got her a moment back, but it wasn't enough. She scrambled to her feet, but three steps later he was upon her again with his arms around her chest, and he smothered her into the rocky ground. She couldn't see his face, but she could feel his breath on her neck. They were panting like dogs.

"Don't kill me. I'll leave if you want, I'll run away."

Crash turned her onto her back and sat up on top of her legs. "If you really loved him, you wouldn't want to leave."

Petra started crying softly.

Crash took a large rock from the ground. He raised it overhead.

From the ground, Petra waved her hands in front of his face as if trying to flag down a speeding car from a crosswalk.

"Wait!" she shouted. "Our son—promise you'll take care of Dmitri."

A troubled look passed over Crash's face, and his hands sagged just an inch with the weight of the rock. From the sea, the sound of a jet airplane coming in to land split every atom into two.

"Promise!" Petra strained every muscle to be heard over the jet engine.

She saw Crash's mouth form the words, "I promise." Crash looked like he was shouting, too.

She saw the airplane pass like a surfacing whale over Crash's shoulder, close enough to touch if it had gone a little slower.

She shut her eyes.

36

Alex waited several hours to call Sheila, and led off by apologizing for how Del behaved. She was gracious about it. Toward the end of the conversation, he mentioned the process server, as in "what another rotten piece of luck." Sheila took the cue and offered him a place to stay for a few days if he needed to get away from his own house and the bill collectors lurking around it. After some token resistance, Alex agreed.

She and Alex spent the next couple of days together—working. There was a conspiratorial energy to their long conversations. Alex wasn't sure if his excitement was about her or the mission. Probably both. Hopefully both. He was sure about the mission, in any case.

She was excited about the mission, too, which was striking when compared with her prior ambivalence. For Alex's investigation from the inside to be effective, he had to know in advance as much about Liberty's inner workings as possible, and Sheila educated Alex about the procedures and all the internal politics at Liberty as only a former head of H.R. could do.

There was time for sex, too. If anything, their shared anticipation for Alex's undercover foray made the sex more intense than before. But the job was more of the focus—for both of them.

During their conversations Alex asked for, and Sheila gave, grudgingly at first, more background on Luke and the ongoing divorce. She told him about

Brad Pitcher's blunder in asserting that Luke was Dmitri's father, and about Luke's bluff in proposing to adopt Dmitri.

She spoke with bitterness about Luke's attempt to "starve her out," as she called it, by refusing to pay her any alimony, and how her numbskull lawyer had finally done something right and gotten her alimony to pay her living expenses until final disposition of the case. Looking around Sheila's luxury high-rise apartment, Alex didn't think she was anywhere near starving, but he didn't argue the point. She expressed her hope that Luke's upcoming deposition would turn the case around for her, and that Brad was finally hitting his stride.

They saw stories about Petra P's murder on the news. The police didn't suspect Luke or, if they did, they weren't revealing that to the press. Alex wondered if Petra had become inconvenient to Luke. What if Luke really was the kid's father, and he had to get rid of Petra to avoid paying child support? Alex was intrigued by the idea that Luke killed Petra, but it didn't square with the fact that Luke was now looking after the child, and had previously said he wanted to adopt him.

"Do you think it was Luke?" Alex asked Sheila.

"I don't know," she said. "I hope not." She noticed the concern on Alex's face and said, "Why so glum? You already thought Luke was a murderer, didn't you?"

"Sure," Alex said, without much conviction. He still believed Luke had orchestrated the accident—but that sort of crime, setting up a van to explode in an accident, was almost an academic exercise compared to bashing Petra's head in with a jagged rock.

"Murderers murder people, Alex. You should know what you're going up against."

"But you don't think Luke killed her."

"I don't know who killed her," Sheila said. "But I sorta wish it had been me."

"Sheila!"

"Sorry," she said. "Bad joke."

* * *

On his first day at Liberty Industries, Alex, as Al Franks, was sent to a room for orientation along with a half dozen other new and recent hires. He signed some papers and ignored a series of speeches by H.R. and other supervisors. After an hour, he was sent to the daily morning meeting of Liberty's security department.

The room was on the first floor of an older building, with a row of large wood-framed windows that looked out onto the company parking lot. Alex found a dozen or so security employees there, tall and short, but all with weight room physiques. They bantered with each other about sports and women while they waited for the boss to show up. The boss was Alvin "Crash" Bailey. Alex took a seat and stretched his legs out and waited.

After hearing so much about Crash, Alex couldn't wait to meet him—especially because Alex suspected that Crash and Luke were in cahoots with the man with the birthmark on his hand. Alex thought about Beto's trembling fear of Crash and about Sheila's description of him. Violent, decisive, yet faultlessly polite and almost deferential to the company executives—it was hard to imagine everything he had heard applying to a single person.

A man in a business suit entered the room and everyone else ambled to their seats. He was a young, thin man with dark hair. His stiff manner and serious expression poorly masked his nervousness. Alex whispered to the man sitting next to him, "Is that the famous Crash Bailey?"

"Hell, no," the man whispered. "Crash has been AWOL for the last two days."

The boss called out Alex's alias in a tremulous voice. "Is Al Franks here?"

"Here," Alex said, and he raised his hand.

The man nodded and began reciting Al Franks' duties for the day. The other men drifted into conversations among themselves, until one of them called out, "Dude, someone's trying to steal that truck."

Alex rushed with the men to the windows, where he saw a man inside the cabin of a pickup truck—his uncle Hugh's truck. The man's hands were beneath the dashboard, but his shoulders and elbows were a whirl of motion above it.

"I can't believe it," Alex said.

"I saw him jimmy the door open," one of the men said.

"He's stealing my truck!" Alex said. His new coworkers looked at him in disbelief. Then Alex heard the ignition engage, trying to turn the engine over. The thief sitting inside his uncle Hugh's truck pumped a fist with delight. The security crew around Alex groaned. He couldn't let himself be the second Fogarty brother to have a truck stolen out from under him.

"You just lost your truck," one of them said.

Another said, "Just give me your tag number and we'll call it in."

Alex imagined them making that call, and then imagined having to explain to his coworkers why the truck that he claimed to own was registered to someone named Hugh Fogarty rather than Al Franks.

"The hell I've lost it," Alex said. He took the heavy wooden frame of the window in both hands and heaved it upward. A coat of paint that held it down let go with a sharp crack. To the cheers and hollers of his new coworkers, he sprinted across the parking lot.

Alex reached his truck just as the thief had got the engine running and put the transmission into reverse. Alex managed to grasp the driver's side door handle. Chasing the truck backward, he hurried his feet as if he had been dropped onto a treadmill. The truck backed out of the parking space and then stopped suddenly—and Alex's momentum threw him to the ground. From there he looked up helplessly at the truck's tailpipe.

Alex instantly scrambled onto his hands and feet and grabbed hold of the truck's rear bumper—it was a rash gesture and should have brought him injury. But the thief struggled to put the truck into drive, and Alex had time to clamber over the tailgate and into the pickup bed. There he rose into a low wrestler's crouch. The truck lurched forward. Alex's feet went out from under him and he found himself hanging over the tailgate and staring once again at the tailpipe.

Working against the momentum of the accelerating truck, Alex crept forward again. It was like trying to run in a swimming pool. When he finally reached the cabin, he gathered his weight and slammed his elbow into the rear window—his left elbow. Alex wanted to save his right arm to beat the thief senseless.

The window didn't break. The thief, startled, hit the brakes. That launched Alex into a cartwheel over the roof of the truck—a sky with puffy white clouds wheeled across his field of vision. He landed on the hood with a belly flop that knocked the wind out of him. Alex felt himself begin to slide forward, his legs dangled alarmingly over the grille, and he flung his arms toward the windshield in desperation.

Almost by accident his left hand touched one of the windshield wipers, and Alex held on tight. The thief steered the truck erratically down one row of parked cars, then another. All the while Alex gripped the wiper rod, while his right arm waved free, jerking spasmodically with the truck's movement the way a flag snaps in the wind. Alex now faced the windshield and saw the thief's face for the first time—he was a white guy, probably a teenager, and looked as scared as Alex felt. How would their tango end? Alex figured the kid wouldn't have the sense to slow gently to a stop and flee on foot.

Alex was right. The thief turned on the wipers, and the motion flung Alex across the hood—now his feet dangled over the front left headlight. How fast were they going? Alex couldn't tell. But even at twenty miles an hour, falling off could be deadly, and Alex knew they were going faster than that.

The truck tumbled over a speed bump—hard—and the wiper rod snapped off in Alex's hand. The force of the bump launched Alex over the side of the hood. His heels hit the asphalt off to the side of the truck, and he backpedaled furiously to keep his balance until he fell sprawling onto the hood of a parked car. There he lay, stunned and motionless, like a frog on a dissecting table.

From that vantage point Alex watched the truck squeal to a stop in front of two Liberty security cars that blocked its passage. Alex rolled out of the dent he had made and, waving the windshield wiper overhead like a lasso, ran yelping toward the action. There a knot of his coworkers surrounded the thief. They shouted conflicting commands and tossed him to and fro like a medicine ball.

With another agenda in mind, Alex ran past them and jumped into the cabin of his truck. He swiftly grabbed anything with his name or his uncle's out of the glove compartment and threw it under the seat.

* * *

When the cops finally came and took the kid, he looked relieved to be out of the custody of the Liberty security team. The whole team was pumped all day, and they took Alex to their favorite bar after work, where Alex felt compelled to buy them a round. His new friends then reciprocated with rounds of ever more exotic and vile liquors, and by the time Alex returned to Sheila's apartment he was in bad shape. She wanted to know all about Alex's first day at Liberty, but Alex couldn't string two sentences together. She stormed off to her bedroom, offended that Alex had gotten so drunk. Alex followed to try to explain that he had to drink in order to ingratiate himself with the rest of the security team, but in his liquored state he couldn't say "ingratiate." At that, Sheila rolled on the bed in laughter, and Alex knew she was all right. The last thing he remembered was kissing her neck, which tickled her and made her laugh even more. He woke up still wearing his clothes. Over coffee and eggs, he told her all that had happened the first day. She thought it was a good start. Alex did, too.

At the office, the nervous fill-in supervisor pulled Alex aside before roll call.

"The chief wants to see you."

Alex's heart leapt. "You mean Crash?"

"No," the supervisor said. "Mr. Hubbard."

* * *

The windows of Luke Hubbard's personal office were framed by heavy ballroom curtains that were drawn almost fully closed. The shadows and dark wood made Alex feel like he had stepped out of a bustling office and into an old fashioned social club.

Alex had no inkling why he had been summoned. He hoped that it wasn't because someone at Liberty had figured out that Al Franks was a fake identity.

Alex stepped stiffly into the office, keeping his weight off an ankle he'd twisted a little when falling off the truck. Luke asked if his ankle was hurting him. Without booze, it hurt like hell, but Alex said he was managing fine and, to Luke's evident surprise, Alex immediately accepted Luke's invitation to prop his ailing limb on a coffee table. The tabletop was fashioned from a single cut of teak.

"I heard about your adventure yesterday and I wanted to meet you," Luke said.

"Thank you, Mr. Hubbard."

Luke told Alex to call him by his first name. It felt more like an instruction than an invitation. Luke sat down across from Alex and asked him a little about his background. Alex told the truth, just with the names changed. Alex found Luke simultaneously charming and aloof. Luke struck Alex as a stereotypical businessman—focused, practical, social, not given to uncompelled self-reflection. But would planning the murder of the employees in the van have been possible at all without some reflection during the process? Alex wondered how this man with perfect hair and manicured nails would have rationalized that bloody business to himself.

As they spoke, Alex got the sense that Luke was sizing him up, too. "About yesterday," Luke said after a while. "Is it true what I hear, that you're not going to press charges against that boy?"

"That's right."

"But—just put aside the theft—the way he drove, I hear you could have been killed."

Alex shrugged. He obviously wouldn't be revealing to Luke why he needed to prevent discovery of whose name the truck was registered in. "Sure, I could've been killed," Alex said. "But I wasn't, and chasing after him was my choice anyway, and not a particularly rational one."

Luke chuckled. Alex could see that Luke was responding well to his understated approach.

"Anyway," Alex said, "he's just a kid, and I know the whole thing got him scared shitless—excuse my language—no need to ruin his life over it."

"You're surprisingly philosophical for a security guard," Luke said.

"Yeah, the guys are ribbing me about it, but I don't care."

Luke nodded sagely. "Al," he said, "I called you up here because I had a feeling you might be the right man for a special project and, after speaking with you, I now believe that you are."

Alex waited for him to continue, and he did.

"What do you know about Alvin Bailey?" Luke said.

"Crash? I've only heard of him. Seems like sort of a legend around here."

"He is, and deservedly so. The energy business is very competitive. The need for security is great. And Crash has always protected Liberty from its enemies, both external and internal."

Enemies. Alex thought that was a revealing choice of words, and Luke's voice had now taken on a more formal tone as he extolled Crash—a tone of admiration and almost of reverence. Alex felt like he wouldn't want to become one of Luke and Crash's enemies. "People around here seem a little scared of Crash, to tell you the truth," Alex said.

Luke raised an eyebrow. "If so, that's fine with me—a reputation can be just as effective as reality. But in reality Crash has a gentle heart."

Alex nodded, but he had trouble squaring that assessment with some of the stories he had heard. At the bar last night, Alex's coworkers had given him a lot more stories.

Luke continued. "I know this about Crash because I know him better than anyone else. I suppose his size and build can intimidate people—he got his nickname playing football. But he's a complex man . . . loyal, scrupulously principled, by his own lights, at least. But at the same time he's clever and practical, very grounded."

Luke's gaze drifted past Alex, and his mind seemed to have drifted as well. Alex wondered where Luke was going with this.

"Crash is in some trouble."

Now we're getting somewhere, Alex thought.

"The police suspect he's killed someone, a woman I loved very much."

Petra P, Alex thought, remembering the stories in the paper.

"And you want me to help clear his name?" Alex said.

"No," Luke said. "Between you and me, I'm quite sure he did it. I want you to find Crash before the police do."

Luke's tone suggested he believed Alex's obedience would be immediate and unquestioning. Alex slid his ankle off the table and started to stand up. "I'm not a hit man," he said flatly.

Luke shook his head and motioned for Alex to sit.

"I don't want you to kill him," Luke said. "Just the opposite, I want you to bring him to me so that I can get him legal counsel and negotiate his surrender to the police."

That was an answer Alex didn't expect. "Luke, I don't know you, but I've got to ask—you said you loved this woman?"

"I loved her very much," Luke said. He spoke in a monotone, as if reciting a mantra. "I love her son, too, like he's my own. Little Dmitri is with me now."

"I don't get it. Why not let the cops handle this? Getting involved will only make them suspect you."

Alex threw in the bit about the cops to see if it rattled him—he wondered if Luke had a hand in Petra's death—but Luke didn't look offended or surprised by the suggestion.

"I've been through that," Luke said. "My fear is that if the police get to Crash first they'll hurt him or kill him—or the other way around—and I don't want that."

"Now you're the one being philosophical," Alex said. "If I were you, I'd want revenge, friend or no friend."

"Mm. The urge for revenge is natural. But reverse the roles, and I know Crash would be thinking about how to protect me. He's always put my interests above his own."

"You make him sound like sort of a sucker." Alex thought Luke must take *Al Franks* for a sucker. To Alex, the most likely explanation was that Luke had Crash kill Petra—for whatever reason—and now wanted Alex to find Crash so that Luke could stop Crash from snitching—permanently. And at that point, of course, Luke would need to stop *Alex* from snitching. This game was getting complicated fast.

"Crash is definitely not a sucker. More like . . . a son. You see, he didn't have a real family, was mostly in foster homes as a kid. Took out all his rage on the football field, and managed to get recruited to 'SC. That was about ten years after I graduated. Anyway, his junior year he finally wins the starting fullback spot, wreaks all kinds of havoc on the field, until one day he blows his knee out. Football was all he had. Next, he's flunking out of school—and he's no dumb jock, by the way—and then late one night he beats a convenience store clerk into a coma because the guy couldn't make change right." Luke shook his head at the memory. "Football players get away with a lot at 'SC, but this was off campus. Coach wanted to help but didn't know how, so he called me." Luke gave a little shrug as if that explained the rest of the story.

"And?" Alex said.

"The clerk came out of his coma, and I got some boosters to throw a little money his way not to press charges. I had Crash come work for me, first as a personal assistant, later as part of the security team, and pretty quickly after that as head of security. I took him under my wing, and I think sort of took over for Coach as a father figure. And as a result he's been unfailingly loyal—"

"Killing your mistress is loyal?"

"My fiancée," he corrected. "What I suspect is that Crash, somehow, did think he was serving me by . . . hurting her. Maybe he got a little confused. I've seen more of that lately . . . maybe concussions from his football days . . . but we are where we are. Don't the Christians say 'turn the other cheek'?"

Alex was too stunned to say anything. Luke seemed not to notice.

"So you'll help me?"

Alex wanted to decline, to get away from Luke as fast as he could and forget the name Al Franks. Either Luke was deluded or else this was a trap—and either way was dangerous. But Alex knew that this stroke of good luck was his best chance, probably his only chance, to get close to Luke and Crash and get the information that he needed—assuming he could then get away before he found himself in Luke's crosshairs.

"You just want me to find him?"

Luke nodded. "And bring him to me."

"I guess I can do that."

Luke's face opened up in delight, relaxing for the first time in their conversation. "I knew you would, once you understood things. The baboons who took you drinking last night—no offense, but that's what they are—are capable of thinking only with their biceps. This job requires a philosophical perspective."

"I hope you're right."

Luke smiled and pressed his hands together. "Now then, let's discuss logistics. Do you own a gun?"

37

The pistol Luke gave Alex was for self-defense. That's what Luke told Alex and what Alex told himself. Self-defense against Crash? Against the police who pursued him? Alex sure as hell wasn't going to draw a gun on a cop. He acknowledged he probably couldn't draw a gun on anyone. Luke didn't elaborate on the dangers he was sending Alex to face, and Alex didn't ask him to. As far as Alex was concerned, he was on his own errand, not on Luke's.

And the target of Alex's errand was Luke. Alex discussed it with Sheila after he left Luke's office, and he intended to do just enough work to win Luke's confidence and then get information on the accident. All the same, if Alex was going to be looking for Crash, he felt better having the pistol holstered under his jacket.

But it felt downright weird to have the gun with him now, driving around town to check in on his investment properties. He pulled his truck into the driveway of one of his houses—the vacant house that Del had left to go stay in—and saw right away that the doorway was too dark. When Alex exited the truck, he confirmed that the reason was the front door was open.

He silently cursed Del. How could his brother be so irresponsible as to not close the front door?

As Alex got closer, he wondered whether he'd had a break-in. He'd had break-ins before—one time, by some teenagers who left some empty beer bottles and wrote the word 'weed' in feces on the living room wall; another time, by some drug addicts who left behind used needles but no written record of what the needles contained. It was likely that his dark doorway meant uninvited guests.

The gun felt all right now. Alex put a hand under his jacket, so that he could reach the pistol if he needed to, and with the side of his foot eased the front door all the way open. Nothing jumped out at him from the living room, or the kitchen. When he entered the bedroom, he recoiled. A man lay curled up on the floor, bleeding onto the carpet. His face was bruised and one eye was swollen shut. He was groaning. Alex kneeled down by him.

"Del," he said. Who had done this to Del, to his little brother?

"Alex?" Del's good eye searched the shadows until it found Alex's face. "He was breaking in. I tried to jump him, but that didn't really work out."

"Did you see who did it?" Alex said.

"No. He was big, though. And one of his hands was darker than the other."

Alex thought for a moment. "Like from a birthmark?"

"Maybe. His hands were flying pretty fast. He kept asking about some guy named Al Franks."

Alex felt his stomach drop to the floor. Alex regretted thinking Del had left without closing the door and, for that matter, regretted kicking Del out in the first place. Brothers were supposed to have each other's backs, and when Del had been beaten in Alex's own house, Alex hadn't been around.

"Oh, Del, I'm so sorry."

"Nothin' you could do. It was a random nut."

"No. The man was looking for me."

Del opened his mouth in surprise, and Alex saw that the man had chipped one of Del's teeth. "Oh," Del said. "I told him my brother owned the house. Was that bad?"

It's not good, Alex thought, but he didn't reply because he didn't want to make Del feel more guilty than he already did. It was Alex who had put his brother in danger, not the other way around. "I'm taking you to the hospital."

"Don't tell Mom, all right?"

Alex lifted Del under the arm and gently pulled him upright.

Taking a gun into an emergency room would have been bad, so before Alex helped his brother out of the truck and into the emergency room, he slipped the gun under his seat. Del was too out of it to notice. Before Alex let go of the gun, he let his fingertip linger on the crosshatching on the grip, and he thought about the man with the birthmark on his hand.

Alex realized that whoever beat up Del must have been from Liberty, because he asked Del about Al Franks, not Alex Fogarty. But the man with the birthmark couldn't have been sent by Crash, because Crash had fled. And now that Luke had decided Al Franks was a stand-up guy, Luke also had no reason to send a goon out to Al Franks' house. So somehow Al Franks had made his way onto someone else's enemies list.

* * *

"Do you have to leave?" Sheila said in a whisper. They were in bed. In the shadows, Alex could make out clearly her shoulder and the strap of her nightgown that had slipped off it. Seeing the line of her body made him want to stay.

"I have a meeting with your husband," Alex said.

"Don't call him that." Her voice told him not to be cute.

"Sorry," he said.

It was a few minutes before daybreak, and just enough light came through the blinds for each of them to track the glistening action of the other's eyes atop the pillows.

"Are you angry with me?" she said.

"No," he said.

"If you're having second thoughts about our little project, I hope you'd tell me."

"I'm not," he said. Then, still in a whisper, he said, "How do you think you and your—how did you and Luke go wrong?"

"Ah . . . so that's it." She pulled the sheet higher over her body. "You've met him now; he's a charmer. When people first meet him, they come away thinking he's a saint. He's hard to get to know, really, and when you do, he's very needy, very narcissistic."

Alex didn't say anything. It was heartening to hear a little about Luke's faults—especially from Sheila's lips—because Luke had been so impressive in person. Luke came off as so polished, so confident, so successful—Alex didn't know whether to shake his hand or break his nose.

"I'm not saying I'm perfect," Sheila continued, "but the affairs . . . eventually I reached my end. People are just a means to an end for him, and that includes me." After a pause, she added, "And you."

Alex remembered Beto's claim that Luke liked to sleep with teenage girls. "Were there a lot of affairs?"

Sheila lifted herself up onto an elbow and turned toward him. She firmly set back in place the lacy strap that had looked so inviting as it hung loose a moment before. "This is some pillow talk," she said. She said it in a daytime voice that felt like it was breaking a truce.

Alex looked up at her from the mattress and responded in a quieter voice than hers. "It's really none of my business. Meeting Luke just got me thinking."

Alex saw her eyes searching the shadows for his face. Finally, she spoke into the shadows. "Alex, don't tell me whether you love me. But I'd like to know that you trust me."

Sheila's mention of the word "love" sent a nervous twinge through Alex's gut, and he was relieved to immediately be let off the hook. "I'd like to trust you," he said.

"I trust you," she said softly. Then she drew her body against his, from his knee to his chest to his shoulder, and whispered in his ear. "I need to trust someone." He held her until she fell asleep again.

* * *

Sheila woke up a little while later, when the day had brightened just enough to fill her bedroom with a cool, ambient glow.

Alex was crouching next to the bed, stroking her hair. She smiled. He had gotten dressed. She mouthed the word "hi."

"I wish I could stay with you," he said.

"Me too."

"I have something I want to give you."

Sheila's eyes brightened, and she lifted her head off the pillow.

Alex lifted his hand to show her what he had, and in the dim dawn light, without the benefit of any hints, it took her a moment to recognize it as a small silver pistol.

"Don't freak out," he said.

"Too late." Her eyes remained fixed on the gun.

"Have you ever used one?"

"I don't think I need one," she said, her voice trembling.

"I don't think so either, but just in case."

"Just in case what?" She looked at him with both skepticism and alarm.

"I finally met Luke and I've learned more about Crash. Frankly, I think they're both nuts. And we already know they're violent."

Her face softened and she sighed in resignation. "Some men just buy women jewelry . . ."

"I didn't buy it. Beto gave it to me."

Sheila's eyes widened.

"Don't ask," Alex said.

Sheila sat up in bed, pulling up the sheet to cover herself. "We hunted a little growing up, but with rifles, and I haven't touched a gun in years," she said.

She took a longer look at it. It had a slim profile and rounded edges. It looked like a ladies' gun. "Doesn't it look a little underpowered?"

"Hopefully you'll never use it."

"But you're the one looking for Crash. Shouldn't you keep it?"

"I've got one of my own now," Alex said. He laid Beto's pistol on the nightstand and kissed her on the forehead.

She laughed roughly and dropped back onto the bed. "I would have settled for flowers."

38

The head coach of the USC Trojans football team was a hard man to get to see. His secretary insisted that she didn't know where he was and that he didn't have any openings for interviews for the next three weeks.

"I don't want an interview," Alex said over the telephone. "I just want to speak with him."

"And what may I tell him this is about?"

"Never mind."

Alex drove downtown to USC's campus, which had once been in a decent part of town, but was now an island of cultivation and promise in an otherwise dreary urban expanse.

Alex had asked himself, what was the closest thing to a home that Crash knew before he went to Liberty? The Trojans football team. And who was his protector there? The head coach. Alex had to see him. Alex was pretty sure Crash would come back to campus eventually, if he hadn't already.

The coach wasn't in his office, the woman at the field house told him. Then she said, "You're the one who called before, aren't you?"

"When will he be back?" Alex said.

"After practice," she said, "but like I told you, he doesn't have any time." Alex turned to leave. "It won't do you any good to go down there," the woman called out after him. "It's a closed practice."

She was right. Alex could see that practice was closed well before he got to the field. A big guy at the gate was checking the IDs of those who tried to enter—a football practice bouncer, of all things. Alex went back to the field house and, trying to look casual but feeling like he didn't, took a stroll around the perimeter until he found something he could use as a prop. He found a stack of folded and laundered towels lying on a maintenance cart, which he decided would do the job. A bag of footballs would have been ideal, but the towels were better than nothing. He held the stack of towels under one arm and headed toward the entrance to the practice field.

"Coach asked for some more towels," he told the guy who barred the way in.

The man just laughed. "Coach did?" he asked skeptically. "That's a new one. No agents." Alex wanted to protest, but saw that he was getting nowhere with this guy. He shrugged, put the towels down and waited.

Waiting along with him were a few of the players' girlfriends, some with infants. After a minute one of them approached and started to tell Alex about her man who was a star on special teams. Alex waited until she took a breath and then leaned in and whispered, "I'm not really an agent." She gave him a look of outraged disgust, like he had been conning her, and returned to the little group of girlfriends.

Practice lasted another hour. Through the gates, Alex could see the players from afar, running drills, collecting into groups and breaking up, all in response to whistles and yells from the assistant coaches that Alex could hear clearly even at a distance. The head coach never yelled—not that Alex could hear, at least—and the coach's face was invisible in the shade cast by his cap. He would watch, and approach, then withdraw, and the players would move or gather or split up again without hesitation.

When practice was over, the team emerged from the gates like a herd of steer. Up close, they were that big. Their rubber cleats tapped the asphalt like a hailstorm. Players, coaches and assistants—probably close to a hundred of them on the move, jogging in a loose column toward the field house and the showers. Alex picked up his towels and fell in near the back.

The woman at the desk, the one who said the coach was too busy, didn't see Alex enter the field house among the players and support staff. Alex went with the flow, until he found himself standing near the showers, still holding the stack of towels. A crusty old assistant coach told him to take the towels somewhere. Alex nodded and turned down a corridor.

"The other way," the coach said.

The other way led to a supply closet, which had lots more towels, and beyond that, Alex found after a minute of walking, a suite of offices. The head coach's office was there, too, according to a nameplate on the door. The offices were all empty. Alex opened the door to the head coach's office, entered and shut the door behind him. Inside, the walls were bare of decoration, except for a faded photograph of a sunset over the ocean, which told Alex the coach had taken at least one vacation in his life. Alex sat in the coach's chair, swiveled a little, then kicked his feet up on the desk.

"Who the hell are you?"

Alex stood up.

"Well?" the coach said. He was smaller than any of his players, but more menacing. The room felt smaller with him in it.

"I'm—" Alex said. "I'm here about Crash Bailey."

The coach responded with a squint and a barely audible snort. He circled around to the back of the desk while Alex circled around to the front of it. The coach sat down and motioned for Alex to sit in one of the guest chairs. "How do you know Crash?" the coach asked.

"I know Luke Hubbard. Luke asked me to find Crash."

"To turn him in?"

"To save him."

The coach exhaled softly. "I'd like to think that's possible," he said after a moment. "But I'm not sure it is."

The coach looked like he had more to say. "What do you mean?" Alex said.

"Crash came here. Couple nights ago, when everyone else was gone. Hadn't seen Crash in probably . . . eight years."

"And?"

"I didn't ask him about what happened. When players come back to me, I never ask."

"But he told you."

The coach nodded.

"About Petra," Alex said.

"About a lot of things, in a roundabout way." The coach tipped up his cap and scratched his forehead. "I've always believed that football tells you all you need to know about a man. I saw Crash play, and I thought I knew him."

"That's why you called Luke, back when Crash got in trouble in college."

The coach nodded glumly. "I don't know Crash anymore."

"What did he say?"

"He didn't make any damn sense," the coach said. "The only coherent thing he said is that he wanted to get someone named Dmitri. Said he was his son. I couldn't figure out what the hell he was talking about. I sat him down and said, son, you need some help. The man thought I was offering to team up with him in some sort of shoot out. No, I said, professional help. That's when he got offended. Accused me of wanting to turn him into the cops." The coach shook his head. "Of course not, but he wasn't hearing it. That's when he left, yelling about making me pay." The coach pulled a key from his pocket and unlocked a drawer in his desk. "The next day I bought this." The coach took a polished steel revolver out of the drawer and set it on the desk. To Alex, the gun looked comically large, but the coach wasn't smiling.

"Did you tell the police?" Alex said.

The coach just scowled at Alex in a way that told Alex his question had been terribly rude. "Sorry," Alex said, but the coach didn't acknowledge the apology.

Instead, he tossed his cap wearily onto his desk, revealing a matted head of salt-and-pepper hair. "You win a bunch of goddamn football games, and everyone thinks you're a winner." Alex waited for him to elaborate, but he didn't. "Does Luke know how bad off Crash is?" the coach asked. Alex shook his head. "He should," the coach said.

"I'll tell him," Alex said.

"I sent my wife and kids out of state."

Alex thought of Sheila and was glad he had given her the pistol. "Luke's getting divorced," Alex said.

"Right."

Neither said anything for a moment.

"Well, I've got work to do," the coach said, and so Alex nodded and stood.

Alex looked back at the coach before he closed the door. The gun was on the desk.

* * *

Alex called Luke straightaway and told him about the meeting with the coach. For the first time, Alex heard worry in Luke's voice—not so much for himself, it seemed, but for Crash. Alex thought Luke was in denial. He suggested that Luke get out of town for a while, like the coach's family, or add a personal security detail, but Luke was unperturbed. "Crash needs my help, not my fear," Luke said.

They talked about what Alex would do next. Alex's plan was to take some of the Liberty security crew out for drinks. Some of them were friendly with Crash, and so Alex figured maybe—knowingly or not—they would have something useful to tell Alex about where Crash was hiding.

Luke was cool to that idea. "Tell you what," he said. "Why don't you go see Les Frees instead? He and Crash are pretty close, as I recall. If anyone knows where he is, Les might."

39

Brad stood before the mirror that hung from the back of his office door. Quietly, he cleared his throat. He flashed himself a smile, didn't believe it, and shut his mouth. Now that Sheila had money to pay Brad's past due bills, he'd gone out and bought a new tie. He liked it. He thought Cindy would like it. He straightened his tie, and straightened the mirror. Then, with a sweeping, unstoppable motion, he threw open the door.

Cindy sat in the reception area typing on a keyboard. The rush of air from the door startled her, and she emitted a chirp like a small bird. "Oh, sorry, Brad, you surprised me there. Got something for me?"

"Yes," Brad said. Then, almost as an afterthought, he stiffly handed her a short stack of signed checks. "These should go out today."

Cindy flipped through them. "Ted's Speedee Copies . . . I sure won't miss the collection calls from ol' Ted. Nice tie, by the way."

"Thanks. Yeah, now that I've got this case under control, I actually have time to go out for a real lunch . . ." Brad cast a glance toward the closed doors of the other offices in his suite. Walt Peters and the others were either away or in meetings. "Have you had lunch yet?"

"No, I'm meeting a friend."

"Walt?" Brad's voice broke a little.

"No," she said. Then she added in a whisper, "Does that guy *have* any friends?"

Brad smiled at her. "Tons—just ask him."

Cindy giggled.

"If not lunch, how about dinner?" Brad said.

Cindy narrowed her eyes. "Are you asking me out on a date?"

Brad blushed and stammered. Cindy laughed. "Is this how you answer questions in court?" she said.

"If we were actually in court, now is when I would make an objection—harassing the witness."

Her eyes sparkled at his little joke. "Well, I don't object to dinner," she said.

"Great, how about tomorrow? I mean, whenever you're free."

"Tomorrow's fine."

"You like French? How about Le Chat Riant?"

"How about somewhere I can see you without a tie on? A good burger and a cheesy movie would be great."

"Or a cheesy burger and a good movie?"

"You pick. But nothing with subtitles, all right, Mr. Harvard?"

"Are you kidding? I've got enough trouble with English."

She laughed again, this time with a silvery tinkle in her voice. "You've got that right."

* * *

Cindy's musical laughter echoed through the empty street. The street was quiet, except for the voices of Brad and Cindy, who slowly followed the gentle rise of the sidewalk to her apartment building. The night was pleasant. It was nice to get out for a few hours and think about something other than his case, and the deposition of Luke that was only two days away. It was especially nice to spend a few hours with Cindy.

What Brad liked about Cindy wasn't innocence so much—she was nobody's fool. It was that she gave people the benefit of the doubt. She assumed you were a good guy until you proved otherwise. It was so different than most lawyers that Brad knew—hell, even different than Brad himself. When he was with Cindy, he could imagine himself as the lawyer and man he came out of law school wanting to be, because she assumed he already was that man.

Her street was in an older but well maintained part of town, with lamp posts that alternated with palm trees along the sidewalk. The lamp posts were attractively styled and bore acorn-shaped bulbs on top that radiated a soft white light.

On the sidewalk each lamppost was the center of a glowing circle with edges that bled slowly into the darkness. Each time they came into the light Brad could see Cindy smile, and each time they left the light he could see her eyes sparkle in reflection of the next light to come. He didn't mind if the evening ended early. It had been a good beginning.

"It's good to finally get you out of the office," she said. "And I like the suit without the tie."

"Did you notice the actor in the movie?" Brad said. "The leading man? Sure enough, suit with no tie."

"See, you could be an international spy."

Brad laughed. "I think I need more hair for that," he said. "Actually, I feel more like Ahmadinejad," he added, referring to the Iranian leader who favored the same attire.

Brad suddenly worried that she might not get the reference and he hoped she wouldn't feel embarrassed if she didn't, but she laughed warmly.

"I know," she said. "Why can't that guy put on a tie?"

"Because he rejects all decadent Western practices. Like secular democracy."

She laughed again.

They reached the steps of her apartment building and spoke over each other with friendly farewells, each watching the other's eyes more than they listened to each other's words. He kissed her. It was short but nice—it sent warmth through his body—and then they said good night. Cindy walked the steps up to the front door of her apartment building, looked back and smiled.

Brad stood on the sidewalk and watched her open the front door and go in, and waited until he saw the light go on behind the curtained window to her second-floor apartment.

He was still smiling when he turned away.

The man who stood facing him was not smiling. He wore a windbreaker and stepped out from behind the shadow of a palm tree. His face was obscured by a baseball cap pulled down low.

"Hey Brad," the man said.

"Who are you?" Brad said.

"You know me." The man stepped into the light.

"Jeff Smiley," Brad said coldly. "What happened to the fedora?"

"For crying out loud, don't say my name. I need to speak with you."

"Were you . . . following us?"

"In private."

Once again, Brad thought, this guy seemed incapable of actually answering questions. Brad looked around. There was no one else to be seen. "I'm comfortable here."

The man rushed toward Brad and hooked him by the arm, hustling him off balance and into the shadows on the far side of Cindy's apartment building. Up close, it was clear that Smiley was nervous.

"I've got the solution for your case," Smiley said.

"What are you talking about?" Brad said.

"Luke's not just a jerk, Brad, he's a murderer. And I'm going to give you the chance to prove it." Smiley pulled a manila envelope from inside his jacket and pressed it into Brad's chest. "Take it," Smiley said.

"What is it?"

"A transcript."

"Of what?"

"Luke's testimony before a grand jury."

"Why give it to me?" Brad said.

Smiley leaned in and whispered. He whispered so hoarsely that spittle kept flecking his lips, and he kept wiping it off. "You know I work for Grant Steele. We had a federal grand jury convened and were ready to indict Luke—until Luke testified and threw up a bunch of smoke and mirrors and the grand jury fell for his smooth B.S. and refused to indict. But we"—Smiley caught himself—"*I* know that Luke is one bad dude, and I know you know that, too. We"—he caught himself again—"*I* want you to run with this information from Luke's testimony and use it your divorce case, then tell me what you learn."

"Why all the cloak and dagger stuff?" Brad whispered.

"The transcript's under seal."

"Then I don't want it," Brad said out loud. Brad tried to give the envelope back, but Smiley pushed it back.

"Read first, then decide," Smiley said.

"I'm an officer of the court, I could be disbarred. You know that."

The man shoved his hands into the pockets of his jacket and laughed bitterly. "Tell me about it, pal."

With that, Smiley turned and walked back toward the sidewalk, his short legs ferrying him along with surprising speed. Smiley didn't look back. "Think about it . . ." he called out in a singsong voice.

Brad stood on the sidewalk with the envelope in his hand and watched the little man go. Finally Brad turned around to leave and noticed the light still on in Cindy's window. There, a corner of the curtain that had been lifted up now floated back down into place.

40

Luke wanted Alex to speak with Les Frees, the head of Liberty's motor pool, because Les might have a way to track the company SUV that Crash absconded with—and because Les was close with Crash. Apart from the search for Crash, Alex was very interested to speak with him because Jorge Ramirez had also worked in the motor pool before he died. Alex went to Les's office first thing in the morning on the day after he'd met with the USC football coach.

Alex entered the cavernous garage that housed Liberty's motor pool and ascended a staircase made of unfinished wood near the back. Les's office overlooked the interior of the garage. Alex saw an open padlock hanging on a nail by the office door. *I guess Liberty's standard locks aren't good enough for Mr. Frees,* Alex thought. *What's he hiding?*

Les was a gruff, burly redhead with freckles that might almost have joined into a nice tan during summer. In late winter they remained apart, spread thickly across his face like a photographic negative of the Milky Way. Alex had to concentrate to keep from staring at the freckles. Alex asked Les if he'd given the police any information about Crash's missing SUV.

"Cops haven't called me," Les said. "And I haven't called them either."

"Do you put a transponder on your vehicles? Something to track them if they get stolen?"

"Oh sure," Les said.

Alex's cell phone rang loudly. He apologized and pulled it from his jacket, moving his arm slowly so not to reveal the holster underneath his left arm. It was his brother calling, probably calling because he had gotten bored again lying in the hospital. Alex didn't answer it.

"Have you used this transponder to find where Crash's SUV is?" Alex asked.

"No, I'd have to call the vendor to do that," Les said flatly. Alex couldn't tell whether Les was stubborn or just dense.

"Wouldn't that be normal procedure when a vehicle is stolen?"

"No one's told me that Crash's SUV has been stolen."

"OK, I'm telling you," Alex said, getting tired of this game. "So you'll call the vendor?"

"Sure, I'll call them," Les said, but he didn't move. They stared at each other. Les had the powerful but unlovely physique of a football lineman and he seemed offended by Alex's brusqueness with him. Les had at least fifty pounds on Alex. They both knew Les would win a fistfight, but Alex had a secret. It was silly, but with the weighted holster under his arm, Alex had less patience with bad attitudes.

"Why don't you call the vendor now," Alex said, but not like a question.

Les grunted tersely and picked up the phone on his desk. Alex paced around the man's office, scanning the photographs that hung on the walls. He looked back at Les impatiently.

Les held the telephone pinched between his ear and his neck. "On hold," he said.

Alex nodded. He found a photograph of Les and two other men, all dressed in tuxedos in front of a church. One of the other men was Crash; Alex recognized Crash from some photos that Luke had given him. Alex cocked a thumb at the photo and said, "Who's getting married?"

"Me."

"Where's the wife?"

Les gave Alex a hostile stare. "She's not in the picture, all right?"

"Crash was your best man?"

"One of the groomsmen," Les said. "You know Crash?"

Alex ignored the question. "Is that why you didn't report the SUV as stolen?"

Les didn't answer. Instead, to Alex's surprise, he replaced the telephone roughly in the receiver. "All right, I've got a question for you," he said. "Alex Fogarty."

Alex waited for Les to say more, but he didn't. Everyone at Liberty Industries knew Alex by his alias, Al Franks. Alex had never met Les before. How had Les heard Alex's real name?

Les patiently looked Alex up and down as if waiting for Alex to betray himself with a twitch or nervous smile. Alex decided to assume Les didn't know his secret identity, and so he bluffed. "Alex is a cousin of mine. You know him?"

Les rested his hands on his flimsy desktop and pushed himself up to standing. As he did so, Alex saw that a burgundy birthmark covered his left hand—just like the hand of the man he pursued from the diner after Beto was blown up. Alex felt his entire body stiffen. The man who just uttered Alex's real name was the same man who nearly killed Alex, the same man who beat his brother bloody.

Les lumbered around to the front of his desk and planted himself in front of Alex, close to him, like they were two boxers facing off. He was three inches taller than Alex and much bigger. Alex didn't move a muscle.

"Do I know Alex Fogarty?" Les said. "Not really. But I went to his house once."

Alex smiled tightly. "Will you make that call to track the SUV now?"

"Another thing I found out . . . used to be an Alex Fogarty who worked for Rampart Insurance, left about the time you did. Is that your cousin, too?"

"So what? He didn't like it there."

"Same job . . . same initials . . ."

Alex felt sweat start to bead at his temples. The man who had tried to kill him stood inches away from him, teasing him about his fake identity. Alex's body was still, but his mind screamed "danger." Against his will, Alex's thoughts crept to the gun holstered under his arm. The urge felt like lust, he couldn't ignore it.

"Am I making you nervous?" Les said.

Alex's right hand moved tentatively across his body, toward the pistol. To maintain control he pressed both hands straight down the seams of his pant legs like he was a tin soldier.

"It'd be better if you didn't," Alex said quietly.

Les guffawed, then jabbed a meaty finger into Alex's breastbone. "Stay away from Crash."

Alex concentrated very hard and forced himself to smile. "Will you give me the number for the transponder company, then? Luke Hubbard told me to find the SUV, so I've got to find the SUV." Alex figured dropping the CEO's name couldn't hurt.

Les wiggled his hands in mock horror at the mention of Luke's name, then, walked slowly back around to his own side of the desk, checked his computer screen and wrote out a telephone number on a scratch pad. He silently extended his hand for Alex to take the paper.

"Thanks," Alex said, "so sorry to interrupt your morning." He turned to leave. When he'd gone as far as Les's wedding photo on the wall, Alex stopped. "One more thing," Alex said over his shoulder. He lifted his arm and hammered his elbow into the center of the photograph. The glass that covered it shattered and fell in shards to the floor. "You should stay away from Alex Fogarty."

41

When Brad arrived at his office, Cindy handed him a stack of envelopes she had slit open for him. She smiled at him. "Sleep well?"

"Very. And you?" He smiled back.

"I did."

"Look at this," he said. He eagerly removed the contents of one of the envelopes and displayed them for Cindy. "Did you see this one?" he said.

She shook her head vigorously. "Oh, no, I never look inside."

"Those lowlifes at Boswell & Baker slapped a defamation suit on me, just because I raised the possibility that Luke Hubbard fathered a love child with his mistress."

"What jerks," she said. Then, leaning toward Brad, she said, "Did he do it?"

"All I know is that this notice says he's adopting the little bastard. Naturally, that means they're dropping this ridiculous lawsuit."

Cindy giggled. She looked at the papers Brad showed her and said, "Dismissal with prejudice, what does that mean?"

"It means they can go to hell," Brad said. Cindy smiled and looked up at him admiringly. "But now I've got a decision to make," he said, "and that's whether to ask the court to sanction them for filing a frivolous lawsuit against me."

"Why in the world wouldn't you?"

"Easy, there. I've got to think long term. The legal community is actually pretty small. No need antagonizing people once you've got what you want."

Cindy looked disappointed.

"But it'd be fun to make them squirm a little, wouldn't it?" Brad said. He continued flipping through the mail, until he came to a letter from the state bar association.

Another bill, Brad thought when he saw the envelope, but the page inside bore the letterhead of the bar Disciplinary Committee. Brad read the letter, shook his head like he was trying to clear a bad dream, then read the letter again.

"What's wrong?" Cindy said.

"Nothing," he said. "It's nothing." *Just the other shoe dropping*, Brad thought with despair. He took the letter and shuffled like a sleepwalker into his office.

Those bastards at Boswell & Baker had done it to him again. Give with one hand and take with the other. They had lodged an ethics complaint alleging that Luke's defamation lawsuit gave Brad an unwaivable conflict of interest with respect to Sheila, his client. It was unusual for the bar to investigate conflicts of interest without a complaint from the client, but clearly they were willing to make an exception—Boswell & Baker always got its share of exceptions. And if the bar agreed with Boswell & Baker's analysis, it wouldn't matter that Sheila had agreed to keep Brad as her lawyer.

Shit, he thought. *Shit, shit, shit.* They wouldn't disbar him. No, not for a first offense, not without a complaint from Sheila. But they could reprimand him, or suspend him.

Brad pressed his hands to his temples. He couldn't afford to be suspended now. He'd finally gotten current in his bills. Either result, reprimand or suspension, would follow him the rest of his career. And he definitely did not need this headache the day before he took Luke's deposition. He was being railroaded, no doubt about it, but those who understood that wouldn't care, and those who cared wouldn't understand.

. . . Cindy wouldn't understand.

Brad dropped himself into his office chair. Sanctioned by the bar . . . what a disaster. *I'm finally first in my class in something*, he thought.

There could be no negotiation with Boswell & Baker over this, there could be no bargain they had in mind. They had taken their complaint straight to the bar, and now it was in the bar's hands. This was just Boswell & Baker's attempt to get rid of Brad. So why did they want to get rid of him? It couldn't be because they feared Brad as an adversary—they didn't even consider him a peer. Brad knew that from reading the face of his old classmate Jacob Carter when they met in court—as arrogant when he lost as when he won. No, there must be another reason. *What are they afraid that I'll discover?* Brad wondered.

Brad drummed his fingers on his desk.

Luke was in the news a lot. Life insurance scams, murdering employees, murdering his mistress—the rumors never stopped, but nothing ever came of them, and Brad had always assumed they were baseless. But what if they weren't? Maybe they feared Brad was already close to the truth . . .

. . . or that the truth was close to Brad.

Brad shifted his hand from the desktop to his desk drawer and opened it. Inside lay the unopened envelope that Jeff Smiley had given him outside Cindy's apartment, the envelope that supposedly contained Luke's sealed grand jury testimony. Brad laid the envelope on his desk.

Brad couldn't imagine what value Smiley's transcript had. After all, if the prosecutors had found real evidence against Luke, wouldn't the grand jury have indicted him?

Brad was a lawyer—for him to read a transcript that was under court seal, even just to have it in his desk, was an ethical violation. Another ethical violation. What harm could come from one more? No one would have to know, except that Jeff Smiley guy, and he'd never tell because he was in as deep as Brad with the purloined transcript. Even if Brad didn't read the transcript, he was in trouble with the state bar already. And if the alternative to reading the transcript was disciplinary action *and* losing his case . . .

Brad's hand found a letter opener. The letter opener idly tapped the top of his desk. The sound was like a faucet with a slow drip, a drip that fooled you into thinking it had stopped.

Cindy wouldn't understand . . .

* * *

Cindy came into Brad's office a couple of times during the afternoon and tried to initiate a new round of their usual amusing banter. She wanted to find out what bothered him so much about that letter. But he didn't respond—not really, anyway—and he didn't look bothered anymore. He was focused, absorbed, obsessed—printing documents and reading, printing and reading. She had become invisible. After three hours of being ignored, she collected herself and brought him a hot cup of coffee. The coffee got his attention, and he even thanked her for it.

"What're you up to?" she said. She tried to sound casual.

"What I'm best at." Brad smiled and pushed his glasses up the bridge of his nose. "Homework."

42

After leaving Les Frees' office, the loyal thing for Alex to do would have been to call Luke, to report that Les was very defensive about Crash, and so might know where Crash was hiding. Instead, Alex called Sheila.

"I found the man with the birthmark."

"Really?" she said.

"He's head of the motor pool at Liberty."

She gasped. "Are you sure it's him?"

"I'm sure. I'm also sure he's the one who beat up Del."

"Did he say so?"

"He said enough. I think he also knows where Crash is. It's all starting to come together."

"Have you told Luke?"

Who's running this show? Alex asked himself, annoyed at her nosiness. "Not yet. I don't want to officially 'find' Crash until I've got the evidence I need from Frees about the accident."

"You need your search for Crash as an excuse to snoop around Liberty."

"Exactly, and I don't have a lot of time. Frees suspects my fake identity, and Luke has already asked me for a status report on finding Crash."

"Be careful, Alex."

"Don't worry. I've got a plan."

Alex's plan required a skill that Alex didn't have. Despite all his brother's faults, Del was the person he trusted the most for the stunt he had in mind. But Del was in no shape to participate, so Alex reluctantly called Zeke.

"Zeke, I've got a scoop for you."

"I'm all ears."

Sure, Alex thought, *Zeke's always ready to help when there's something in it for him.* "I need your help with a little errand, and then I'll explain everything."

"What's the errand?"

"It shouldn't take more than an hour. I'll pick you up tomorrow at seven a.m."

"What? Where's the scoop?"

"Be ready. And bring your lock pick." Alex hung up before Zeke could protest—or probe—any further.

Sheila had social plans that evening and didn't come home until after Alex was asleep. Alex instead spent the evening with Del, who was now patched up and, except for a few cuts and yellowing bruises, well on the way to recovery. They went to a bar, had a couple of beers and watched a basketball game. Alex paid, even though he couldn't afford it. Del could afford it even less. Del said he was thinking of leaving L.A. Alex told him that could be a good idea. Or a bad one. Del said he was still thinking it through.

The next morning, Alex got out of bed without waking Sheila, strapped the holster and pistol beneath his sport coat and drove to Zeke's house. Zeke was grumpy but ready to go. "This better be good," he said.

Alex parked in the Liberty lot. It was all but empty at this hour. Alex led Zeke across the quiet facility until they got to the large garage that housed the motor pool. The garage was closed and dark.

"How are we going to get in?" Zeke said.

"I work here," Alex said. He handed Zeke a pair of leather gloves. "Put these on," he said.

"What do I need gloves for?"

"Cold morning," Alex said brusquely.

"No, it isn't," Zeke said. "And since when do you work here?"

Alex ignored him. Alex was also wearing gloves, a thinner wool pair. He pulled a keychain from his pocket and unlocked a side door to the main garage.

"If you work here, then why are you wearing gloves?" Zeke said, but Alex ignored that, too. He just made sure Zeke put on the gloves.

Inside, the sound of their footsteps on the concrete floor made a lonely echo off the walls. Alex took Zeke to the staircase that led up to Les Frees' office.

"Where are we?" Zeke said.

Alex put one of his keys up to the lock above the door, but it wouldn't fit. "He's installed his own lock," Alex said. "Did you bring your tools?"

"Just like you asked," Zeke said. "Whose office is this, anyway?" Alex didn't answer. Zeke shrugged and hunched over the lock. He probed it tentatively with a thin, flat needle. Then he looked up and said, "If we get caught, I'll rat you out."

"I know you will," Alex said. "Quit stalling."

"This lock is a little more complicated than *The Chronicle*'s liquor cabinet," Zeke said.

Zeke scratched at the lock for a couple of minutes that passed as slowly as if a dentist were scratching at Alex's teeth. Then the lock turned, and Zeke stood up straight and wiped his forehead with the back of his hand. "After you."

Inside, Les Frees' office was just as Alex recalled it, except the broken glass from the picture frame had been swept off the floor.

"What are we looking for?" Zeke said.

"This is the office of Les Frees, who planted the bomb in MacArthur Park that almost killed me."

"Wait. Slow down. You were there?"

"Yes, I was there trying to buy some evidence that Luke Hubbard was responsible for the accident over Christmas." Alex took Zeke over to the wall and showed him what was left of the photograph of Les and Crash at Les's wedding.

"Frees is also tight with Crash Bailey," Alex said. "Crash killed Luke's mistress. Luke Hubbard asked me to find Crash. When I came here yesterday to speak with Frees, he was very protective of Crash, and he correctly suspects that I'm using an alias here. I just need to pin the bombing on Les before he finds proof of my real identity."

Zeke looked stunned. "Talk about a scoop. You've been holding out on me."

"I wonder why."

Alex spent several minutes swiftly but methodically searching the papers on and around Les's desk, a task the gloves made harder. Meanwhile, Zeke shifted nervously from one foot to the other, like someone waiting in line for the bathroom.

"Hurry up, Alex. This is freaking me out."

Alex stopped his search and sighed. "Just what I was afraid of. No obvious paper trail. So much for the easy way."

Alex dropped onto a decrepit old couch pushed against one wall of the office. At that, Zeke threw up his hands, and spoke with obvious strain in his voice. "This guy Frees could show up at any minute."

"I certainly hope so," Alex said.

"Then why the hell are you sitting on his couch?" Zeke asked with a tremor of panic.

"I'm waiting for him. I want to talk with him."

"What makes you think he'll want to talk with you?"

Alex casually lifted the lapel of his sport coat so Zeke could see the pistol.

Zeke emitted a sharp sound between a cough and a squeak. "What the hell is that?"

"Zeke, this guy tried to kill me. You wouldn't understand."

"You've got that right."

"You can leave if you want," Alex said, and he meant it. Zeke had gotten Alex into Les's office; Alex didn't need Zeke's bad mojo making the next phase even harder.

Zeke looked vacantly at Alex as if trying to work out a crossword puzzle in his head. "What if he calls out for help, Alex? Will you shoot him? You'll go to jail."

Alex furrowed his brow as he considered this, then he realized that, for once, Zeke was right. He bolted up from the couch. "I'm glad I brought you along," he said. "Let's get out of here."

Before they could leave, they heard the steady, assured footsteps of someone ascending the wooden staircase. The footsteps of a man.

Alex motioned for Zeke to find a place behind the open door, out of sight of anyone entering the office. Alex himself rose and pivoted feverishly back and forth, searching for a hiding place. The footsteps on the stairway outside kept their own time, indifferent to the bustling inside the office. Alex found nowhere to hide and so dropped back down on the couch. There he put his hand on the handle of his pistol inside his jacket and tried his best to look menacing. Out of the corner of his eye, Alex saw that Zeke had hunched his shoulders and shut his eyes tight against whatever was to come.

The man ascending the stairs looked into the open doorway. "Al?" he said.

Alex felt a wave of relief like a sudden shower of warm water. At the top of the stairs stood a coworker from the security department. "It's Jerry, right?" Alex said, trying to keep his voice steady. Inside his jacket, Alex moved his hand from the pistol to a handkerchief, which he pretended to wipe his nose with. Zeke retreated farther into the shadows behind the door.

"So you've heard the news," Jerry said.

"That's why I'm here," Alex said blandly.

"News travels fast." As Jerry shook his head, Alex wondered what in the world was going on. "What a shame," Jerry said. "He'd worked here almost twenty years."

So Frees was fired, Alex thought. *That was sudden.* "What's the protocol here?" Alex asked. "Same as with any termination?"

"Right," Jerry said. "Termination—I never thought of the word that way."

"So have IT take the computer, forward his personal effects?"

"Right. I already called IT. They'll be here any minute."

"Great. I've got this one, Jerry. You can head out."

"You don't mind? I knew him pretty well, and I'd rather not go through his things, you know?"

Jerry turned as if to go, then paused. He looked back at Alex.

"Did you know Les at all?"

"Not really."

"He was a great guy. I can't believe he's really dead."

43

Brad insisted on holding Luke's deposition in his own office, rather than the comfortable, modern skyscraper where Boswell & Baker did business. Brad was used to suffering for hours at a stretch in the windowless, low-ceilinged chamber that served as his conference room. He knew Luke and Alan Matthews were not.

Brad had been talking up Luke's deposition to Cindy, and she asked Brad to contrive a way for her to watch. Could she pretend to be his paralegal? Brad kept putting her off. But once the legal stenographer arrived with her equipment, there wasn't space for any spectators in the little room anyway. And after Luke greeted Cindy by barking a demand for coffee, she no longer seemed as keen to join the proceedings.

The judge decreed that Brad could depose Luke for eight hours. After seven and a half hours, Luke and Alan both looked worn. With the two of them, the stenographer and Brad gathered close around a small table, the room had grown warm and uncomfortable, but neither Luke nor Alan would give Brad the satisfaction of loosening their ties. Brad felt stifled, too, but was willing to suffer for the cause.

"Mr. Hubbard, last December, didn't you have a motivation to increase Liberty's earnings?" Brad said. He had spent the last ten minutes effectively asking the same question in different forms, covering the same ground that Grant Steele had questioned Luke about in the secret grand jury transcript.

"What does any of this have to do with the divorce?" Luke said. "Wake up, Alan."

Alan twisted his head lethargically toward Brad. "Objection as to relevance."

"Answer the question please, Mr. Hubbard," Brad said.

"My attorney has just objected. I'm not going to answer."

"Off the record," Brad said to the stenographer, and she stopped typing. "Fine," Brad said to Luke and Alan, "in that case, I'll have the court compel you to answer and we'll meet back here another day and do this all over again."

Alan rose and squirmed between the wall and the table to get to where Brad sat. He motioned for Brad to join him outside, and the two of them stepped out into the hall.

"What the hell's going on here?" Alan said. "Are you litigating a divorce case or auditioning for district attorney?"

"It's all relevant, Alan. It goes to the value of his Liberty stock."

"Isn't that why we have a stock market?"

"But the market price fluctuates every day. What does *Luke* think the stock's worth?" Brad knew his rationale didn't really make sense, but being a lawyer sometimes meant arguing the point.

Alan scrutinized Brad's face, looking for a tell. Finally he shrugged. "You want to waste your last few minutes with Luke going down a rabbit hole, that's fine with me."

Brad swept back into the little conference room with Alan in tow. "Back on the record," Brad said to the stenographer. Brad asked his next question immediately, even before he was fully seated. "Mr. Hubbard, last December, didn't you have a motivation to increase Liberty's earnings to meet analysts' expectations and keep Liberty's stock price from plunging?"

Luke cast a disgusted look toward Alan. "These questions are all silly," he said. "But since you won't let it go, the answer is no. I hold my stock in Liberty for the long term, so the periodic rises and falls aren't important to my personal calculations."

"Not at all?"

"Look, if I worried about short-term fluctuations, I would sell the stock whenever I thought the price was high."

"So, if you had been worried in late December about missing the analysts' earnings estimates and a drop in your stock price, you would have sold stock then?"

"Exactly."

That was how Luke had answered the same question before the grand jury. That was how Brad was hoping Luke would answer now. Brad opened one of several file folders he had laid out on the table in front of him and pulled out a several-page document.

"Mr. Hubbard, I'm looking at Liberty Industries' stock trading policy for its executives. Pretty standard policy for a public company, as I understand it, to make sure executives aren't trading on inside information. According to this, the company prohibits executives like you from selling Liberty stock during the last month of any fiscal quarter. So wouldn't that policy prevent you from selling stock during December?"

"I guess so."

"You guess? Are you unfamiliar with your company's own trading policy?"

"I'm familiar with it. I just don't spend much time thinking about it, because—if I have to tell you twenty times, I'll tell you twenty times—I don't sell just because the stock price is high. I've never sold a share."

"Let's move this along, Mr. Pitcher," Alan said. "He didn't sell, and he's told you why."

"Fine," Brad said to Alan. Turning back to Luke, he said, "You have an expensive lifestyle, don't you?"

Luke looked at his watch. The deposition was almost over. "Compared to most people, I'm sure that's true."

"How much did you spend last year?"

"I'd have to check with my accountant."

"Surely you have a rough idea. Was it more than a million dollars?"

"Certainly," Luke said.

"More than two million?"

"I don't know, maybe. A lot of that spending is Sheila's, y'know . . . clothing, jewelry, spa dates, who knows?"

"And a lot is for your mistress, as well?"

Alan's lurched from his seat and coughed out a vehement objection. Brad and Luke stared at each other coolly, oblivious to Alan.

"Less for her than for Sheila," Luke said.

"And what was your salary last year?" Brad said.

"One million dollars exactly, just as it's been for several years."

"Not enough to pay for your lifestyle, then, especially after taking out taxes."

"Is that a question?"

"Here's the question," Brad said. He leaned forward and stared straight into Luke's eyes. "How do you fund your lifestyle?"

* * *

After leaving Les Frees' office, Alex returned to the security department, which was abuzz with rumors about what had happened to Frees. Depending on who was doing the talking, Frees either had been stealing from the company or had been plotting some sort of home-grown terrorist act or had found dangerous information about Luke Hubbard. Whatever the cause, he had run. They found him with a suitcase full of disguises. Or maybe they didn't. He was diabetic and died in a motel room in Santa Monica from an adverse insulin reaction—that was the only hard fact. Somebody's brother who was a doctor said accidental overdoses sometimes happen in unfamiliar environments. In a way, they said, Les had won. Whoever was chasing him wouldn't have the satisfaction of catching him. Imagine what the poor motel cleaning lady must have thought, someone mused, though in her line of work she may have seen worse. At least he didn't leave a mess, another said. Les could piss people off, but he was a good guy, everyone agreed. People were meeting up after work to have a few drinks in his memory—no wife, no kids, that left his friends to do the honors.

Alex listened to all this with wide-eyed attention, but after hearing what his colleagues had to say, he was more curious than before. One thing the rumors didn't explain was why Les Frees would want to kill himself or, in the alternative, why he would be so careless in administering an insulin injection that he did every day. But more important, why had Frees been in a motel at all?

Had Frees been running from Alex? That was unlikely, given the way Frees tried to intimidate Alex in his office. Alex listened to his coworkers and asked some questions, but tried not to seem like he cared about the answers too much. After an hour, he knew where he had to go for real answers.

44

In the cramped conference room, Brad pressed on.

"Mr. Hubbard, you spend more than a million dollars a year, but have a salary of only one million dollars. If you don't sell stock, how do you fund your lifestyle—the house in the hills, the cars, all the rest of it?"

"Liberty pays me other compensation."

"How much other compensation did Liberty pay you last year?"

"I'd have to check," Luke said.

Brad opened another of his folders and passed the papers from inside to Luke. "Here is Liberty's most recent shareholder proxy statement," he said. "This lists how much you and the other top executives got paid last year. What does it list as your total compensation last year?"

"Just over twenty million dollars."

"Is that number accurate?"

"If that's what the proxy says, I believe it," Luke said.

"Personally, twenty million is a number that I would have remembered," Brad said with a smile.

"Objection," Alan said.

"And of that twenty million, one million was salary. Where did the other nineteen million come from?"

Luke again checked the proxy statement Brad had given him. "Eighteen million from my bonus plan, the rest is attributable to various perks and accounting charges."

"Did anyone else get bonuses under this plan?"

"No, it's just for me. It was put in as part of the last employment agreement I negotiated with the company."

Brad took the proxy statement away and pulled another document from yet another folder. Alan craned his neck to see what it was.

"Is this a copy of your bonus plan?" Brad said.

"Where did you get this?" Luke said.

"This was filed by Liberty Industries with the Securities and Exchange Commission."

"Alan, do we file this with the SEC?" Luke said.

"Mr. Hubbard's question is off the record," Alan said. He took a look at the document and nodded in the affirmative.

"Yes, this is the bonus plan," Luke said.

"How was your bonus for last year calculated under the plan?" Brad said.

"Well, it wasn't just for last year. The plan has been in place for three years, but didn't pay anything out until this year."

"Fine, a bonus for three years," Brad said. "How was it calculated?"

"The size of the bonus depended on Liberty's cumulative earnings over that three-year period."

"The three-year period ending last December?"

"Correct. Earnings had to be at least three billion dollars over that period."

"They had to be at least three billion, or else what?"

Luke looked at Brad scornfully, like he thought Brad was feigning stupidity just to annoy him. "Or else I wouldn't get a bonus under the plan," Luke said.

"Nothing at all? Not a smaller bonus?"

"Nothing. The bonus was either-or."

Brad handed Luke some additional documents. A small pile of paper was now gathered in front of the CEO.

"Here are copies of Liberty's annual reports for those three years," Brad said. "I've circled their earnings for each year. I added up all three years and got three billion, fifty-three thousand dollars. Do you agree with that calculation?"

Luke looked the pages over quickly. "Yup."

"So in percentage terms," Brad said, "Liberty met the bonus threshold by just .002%. You just barely earned that twenty million dollar bonus, didn't you?"

"That's right. And it was eighteen million, not twenty."

"So in late December, you must have been pretty nervous about whether you would earn that big bonus, isn't that right?"

"Not really."

"Not really? An eighteen million dollar payday wasn't on your radar screen? Whether or not you earn a bonus that you need to fund your lavish lifestyle is beneath your notice? I remind you that your testimony today is under oath."

"No need to remind me, Mr. Pitcher. Like I've said, my focus is on the long-term health of the business. If the business does well, I'll do well."

"You'll do well. I see. So if you hadn't earned that bonus last year, you would have had another chance to earn it?"

Luke looked surprised at the question. "No, the bonus plan ended last year."

"So you have another bonus plan in place for this year?"

"Um, no, the board hasn't approved another bonus plan."

"Why not?"

"That wasn't in the terms of my employment agreement."

"Do you expect the board to approve another bonus plan for you like this one?"

"I have no idea what the board will do," Luke said, having recovered his accustomed polish.

"My question is about your *expectation*," Alex said. "Do you *expect* the board to renew the bonus plan?"

"Same answer: I have no idea."

"OK, has anyone on the board proposed renewing the bonus plan?"

"Not to me."

"Have *you* discussed renewing the bonus plan with anyone on the board?"

"We talk about compensation in general terms from time to time, so it may have come up, but there was never a proposal."

"What was the board's response to the possibility of renewing the bonus plan?"

Luke sighed in frustration at Brad's persistence. "They said it would depend on what the compensation consultants say."

"Why is that?"

"The board hires a compensation consulting firm to look at executive pay at similar companies and make sure Liberty's pay is in line with its peers'. It's standard procedure."

"And did the compensation consultant find that your peer companies have bonus plans like the bonus plan of yours that just expired?"

"No."

"Why not?"

"Bonus plans like that have sort of gone out of fashion."

"I see. So to sum up, you had a special bonus plan, it wasn't likely to be renewed and so last year was really your one-time shot at an eighteen million dollar windfall, wasn't it?"

"I wouldn't call it a windfall."

"Just answer yes or n—"

"Yes, yes, already."

"So, it was pretty convenient for you personally the way things turned out, wasn't it?" Brad said.

"I'm not sure what you mean," Luke said.

"I mean the way five of your employees died barely a week before year end and the life insurance proceeds enabled you to get the bonus."

As soon as the word "died" left Brad's lips, Alan lurched out of seat, hurling a stream of profane invective that the stenographer either couldn't keep up with or refused to transcribe. At the end of it, Alan stood panting and hunched, glaring at Brad.

"Off the record?" the stenographer said.

Alan nodded dourly, and Brad and the stenographer both stood and left Luke and Alan alone in the room.

* * *

"We need to stop this," Alan said to Luke once the door closed. "*I* know you didn't kill anybody; I've known you for twenty years. But the coincidence— your bonus and the accident—it looks really bad. What if this little shit Pitcher helps the media connect the dots on the bonus plan? What if he clues in Grant Steele?"

Luke's eyes were like burning embers and his voice was calm but firm. "Alan, my view is that you let Pitcher lay a trap. He played you." Luke stared stonily at his lawyer for several painful seconds. "But we are where we are," he said. "How do you suggest we fix this?"

"We settle this divorce. We get Sheila to drop the wrongful termination case, and we get a strong confidentiality clause that keeps her and Pitcher quiet."

Luke's eyes narrowed. "So, give up. That's your solution."

"Luke, when something looks this bad, people have to react. And they *will* react to this. The papers will, Grant Steele sure will. Oh, and your board of directors has about lost patience with all your recent legal troubles. Don't pretend for a second that they wouldn't fire you if Liberty had another round of bad press."

"Come on, they can't fire me."

"Oh yes they can. Even you. Even though firing you would be the worst thing they could do to the company."

Luke sighed and stared at the ceiling. "Losing is bad enough, but like this . . ."

"How much pain has Sheila caused you?" Alan said after a moment. Luke didn't say anything. "Look at it this way," Alan said. "Finalizing this divorce will be like removing a cancer . . . and cutting out a tumor is something to celebrate." Alan smiled weakly at Luke. *Doesn't that make sense?* his smile asked.

Luke looked around the room, at the table, at the door, at the clock. "Ten more minutes, and I would have been fine," he said.

"Luke, you *are* fine. You've got a dream job. You've now got the son you always wanted. And once we settle this, you'll be rid of Sheila."

Luke continued staring blankly at the wall, and Alan said, "When I got divorced—both times—the day I signed the papers I just felt an overwhelming sense of relief—and even more, of freedom, like I'd turned off a narrow country road onto a ten-lane freeway. But this? This moment here"—Alan pointed at the table where they sat—"I know what it feels like. It's the worst."

Luke gave a weak smile himself. It was the baseless, undirected smile that he used when meeting strangers. Twenty years' worth of memories and emotions churned in Luke's mind, but that mask kept them private.

Finally, he nodded to Alan. Alan rose and placed a steady hand on his shoulder, then opened the door and called for Brad, who stood with the stenographer a respectful distance away. Cindy peered eagerly over Brad's shoulder.

Pointing at the stenographer, Alan said, "You can take her off the clock now."

"You know damn well I've got ten more minutes," Brad said.

"Brad, I mean the deposition is over. We're ready to talk about a settlement."

It took a second for the momentous news to sink in, then Cindy clapped her hands and then reached around Brad's neck and hugged him joyously. Tentatively at first, Brad's mouth widened into a triumphant smile.

45

The guy at the front desk of the motel reacted like he was used to people coming by to ask questions. He must have thought that Alex was a police detective, because as soon as Alex mentioned Frees' name, the man began complaining loudly about how he couldn't rent out the room where Frees died because "you"—he pointed an accusatory finger at Alex—"still have it sealed off." Alex said he would see what he could do about that, which calmed the man down. The man's own information was not much more precise than what Alex heard from his coworkers, but Alex did learn from the man that Frees checked in alone in the afternoon of the day before his body was found. Did Frees leave his room after checking in? The man didn't know, because the doors to the rooms opened directly onto the parking lot.

So much for the direct approach, Alex thought. He thanked the motel attendant, left the office and took a stroll around the building. Sure enough, yellow police tape still festooned the door to one of the rooms.

The door was locked. Alex tried to peek under the door but saw nothing. Then he noticed a cleaning lady eyeing him suspiciously from several doors down, where she struggled to lift a vacuum cleaner from her cleaning cart. Alex stood, smiled and waved. She waved back, tentatively.

Alex looked around to see if anyone else had noticed him, but he saw no one. Then the vacuum cleaner started to whir loudly, and Alex got an idea. He walked casually over to the cleaning cart that stood outside the empty room. As he expected, its supplies included a box of rubber gloves. If the police still had the room sealed off for investigation, Alex didn't want to leave fingerprints. Protected by the din of the vacuum cleaner, he took two gloves from the cart, put them on and took the cleaning lady's keychain that hung from the cart. In a few moments he was back at the door to Frees' room, testing the keys to find the one that turned the lock.

Soon he was inside the room, a musty little den furnished in earth tones and with thin, worn carpet. In a flurry of motion he opened every drawer and looked under every piece of furniture. His heart pounded from the danger of being found inside. He threw open drawers and threw them closed again. He wondered why he was doing this. Curiosity? For what—to find out why a dead man had tried to kill him? It was foolish—Alex didn't have a stake in stopping Frees anymore. But at the nightstand table Alex met with unexpected delight. When Alex flung the drawer open, a cell phone and a set of keys hurtled out from behind the Bible like dice falling onto a craps table. Not knowing what else to do with this booty, Alex dropped the items in his jacket pocket and quickly left the motel room.

His heart still pounding, Alex discreetly dropped the cleaning lady's keys back on to her cart as he walked by her open door. The vacuum cleaner was silent now, and she had moved on to the bathroom.

Alex felt the weight of the cell phone and keys in his pocket. He had them now, and couldn't well give them back. He would keep them as souvenirs.

***

That night, Cindy went with Brad to the fancy French restaurant he was always talking about. Sheila had come as well, with Alex as her date.

The dinner was a victory celebration for Sheila's divorce settlement. And it sounded like the settlement was a good one, though in the car on the way over Brad clammed up when Cindy asked him how much money Sheila had gotten.

Cindy couldn't help feeling embarrassed at how much everything cost. The cheapest thing on the menu was a simple salad, but even that cost as much as she was used to paying for a whole meal at a restaurant.

The others ostentatiously deliberated over which extravagant dish to order. Cindy quietly told the waiter just the salad would be fine. She didn't say it quietly enough, because Brad asked her if she was feeling all right. Sheila just gave Cindy an impatient look like she thought Cindy was one of *those* girls.

This dinner was the first time Cindy had ever said more than two words to Sheila face to face. Cindy liked Sheila even less in person than on the phone. Sheila smiled and acted friendly, but Cindy kept thinking about the times over the past weeks she'd been brought almost to tears by Sheila's snotty attitude, and about how Sheila so often yelled at Brad for no reason.

Cindy picked at her salad as Sheila told a rambling story. Sheila had already put away two cocktails and a glass of wine, but it was her party, so Brad was making sure to laugh at the right times. Cindy could tell he was being insincere and wanted to turn away from the demeaning spectacle.

"Don't you like the wine, dear?" Sheila asked her.

Cindy looked at the still-full wine glass in front of her. "Oh, It's great," she said. "It tastes very . . . expensive."

"I can see how it might overpower the salad," Sheila said dryly.

"Well, that just leaves more wine for you." Cindy tried to suppress a mischievous grin—in vain.

Brad gave her a concerned look. Brad had gotten the lobster, and the melted butter lay in a glistening halo around his lips. Cindy wished she and Brad could just sneak away for some burritos. She felt hungry.

Sheila turned to Alex. "So," she said, "what do you think—Switzerland or Tahiti?"

"Why not both?" Alex said with a smile.

"Ah, decisions, decisions," Sheila said airily. "It's not easy to figure out how to spend ninety million dollars."

Cindy dropped her fork. It hit the plate with a sound like a muffled bell.

"Quickly," Alex said, smiling, though he looked distracted.

Brad leaned over toward Sheila and whispered something about a confidentiality clause in the settlement.

"Oh, lighten up," Sheila said. "You know . . . if we had broken nine figures, I was planning to give you a bonus."

Brad chuckled nervously and glanced at Cindy.

"Oh, just kidding," Sheila said. "I'll give you a bonus anyway. Besides, the confidentiality clause isn't really about the amount of money he's paying me, it's about him paying to keep you and me quiet about his deposition." She let out a laugh that was more like a snort.

A waiter walked by, and Sheila stopped him by grabbing a fistful of the back of his jacket.

"Excuse me," she said. "Can we have another bottle of wine here?"

* * *

Alex had decided to leave with Sheila. Switzerland? Tahiti? It could have been Antarctica, as far as he was concerned, because he was ready to leave L.A. Sheila offered to repay his mortgages if that's what it took to get him to come with her, and Alex figured, why not? That way he wouldn't be leaving town as a deadbeat, which he refused to do. Sheila understood that paying back the mortgages was a matter of principle for him and floated her offer of assistance in a gentle way that respected how serious the matter was to him. He'd liked that. Who knew where his relationship with Sheila would lead, but a change of scenery would give him a new start, if nothing else.

Alex resolved to quit his fake job under his fake name at Liberty. He hadn't figured out exactly how. Maybe by postcard. If quitting suddenly meant that Al Franks' name was blacklisted, who cared? Al Franks didn't exist.

Alex was rifling through a drawer, looking for his passport to check the expiration date, when his cell phone rang. With one hand still in the drawer, and without looking at the number, Alex answered the phone. Zeke's voice greeted him on the other end of the line. *Shit*, Alex thought. "You gave me a journalistic equivalent of blue balls," Zeke said, omitting any conventional greeting.

"What are you talking about?" Alex asked innocently.

"You know damn well what I'm talking about, which I'm sure is why you've been dodging my calls. I mean that scoop. You have me break into an office for you, you tell me all sorts of juicy rumors about the MacArthur Park bombing, we learn your alleged bomber has died, and then you just hustle me out of the office? I need quotes, Alex. I need other witnesses I can talk to. I need something definitive that I can actually, you know, print in the paper."

"Well, Zeke, sorry I can't help you there." Alex found the passport, flipped open the cover and confirmed that the passport was good for another two years. "But my investigation has just about reached its end."

"You found out who was behind the accident? Was it Frees after all?"

"Frees was definitely part of it. Luke Hubbard too, maybe."

"Maybe? You're ending your investigation with 'maybe'?"

"I'm leaving," Alex said. "With a friend. For a while, at least."

"A friend," Zeke said skeptically. "A new girlfriend? But where will you go? You have no money."

"She does," Alex said.

"Well, congratulations," Zeke said. "If that's what you want . . ."

"What does that mean?" Alex said roughly.

"What I mean is, you uncovered the corporate scandal of the year—of the decade—and you just drop it all once you find a sugar mama."

"Don't call her that," Alex said. "You don't know her." *Where does he get off?* Alex thought.

"Ooh, didn't mean to offend your tender sensibilities."

"Yes, you did."

"Fine, I did. And what about Roberta Cummings? Sure, Rampart reinstated her insurance, but she doesn't make enough to pay her mortgage."

For a guy who blindsided Alex with a newspaper story that cost him his job, and who helped Alex break into a locked office, Zeke sure had gotten scrupulous all of a sudden; and Alex didn't like change—especially Zeke's new self-righteousness. "It really sucks that Roberta Cummings is poor," Alex snapped, "but it's not my problem."

"She'll probably lose her house."

"No one likes a self-righteous prick, Zeke. I never should have answered the phone."

"Self-righteous? You know who told me she'd lose her house? You did, pal. Remember?"

Yes, Alex remembered. And he didn't like being reminded about it. "You want to give her a house?" Alex yelled into the phone. "I've got four extra. I'll send you the paperwork. You can sign my name on whatever you need to while I sit on a beach somewhere they don't speak English."

"This isn't the Alex I know," Zeke said softly.

Alex was still hot when he replied. "Yeah, well maybe you don't know me that well."

Alex hung up before Zeke could. *Throwing my own words back at me like that*, Alex thought. *When did I ever ask for his opinion?*

Alex looked down and saw the passport lying on top of his folded socks. He snatched it up and flung it against the wall like a Frisbee. *Fucking Roberta Cummings.*

46

"**D**o you remember me?" Jeff Smiley said.

"You've got the fedora again," Brad said. "It really doesn't suit you."

They were sitting across from each other in Brad's office. Neither man seemed eager to make eye contact.

"Do you remember the package I gave you?" Smiley asked.

"Of course," Brad said. He thought back to his first date with Cindy, when the man who now sat across from him stepped out of the shadows and gave him the leads he used to ambush Luke in his deposition. This guy was like gum stuck to the bottom of Brad's shoe. Brad really, really wanted to move on with his life.

"I see my little package has been very valuable to you," Smiley said through pursed lips. "Now I'd like you to return the favor."

Brad didn't respond.

"I know you've settled the divorce, and for a lot of money," Smiley said. "I'd love to see what Hubbard had to say in his deposition."

"I'm not sure what you mean," Brad said.

"Don't make me spell it out." Smiley looked around Brad's office as if he worried someone might be listening.

"I'm not important enough for anyone to bug my office," Brad said, annoyed at Smiley's melodrama.

"What I mean is a quid pro quo," Smiley said. "I gave you *my* transcript, now you give me *your* transcript." When Brad didn't respond right away, Smiley said, "I told you what I wanted when I gave you the grand jury transcript."

"I never agreed to any deal."

"But you used my transcript—no, don't tell me you didn't—and that's agreement enough for me."

"Really, I just can't do it," Brad said. "The divorce settlement includes a confidentiality clause."

Smiley grimaced and pressed his hands down his thighs as if trying to iron his slacks with his palms. "Mr. Pitcher, the transcript I gave you was under court seal. It was bad for me to give it . . . and bad for you to receive it. But that's just what you and I did."

"That doesn't mean we should do it again."

"Did you tell anyone about what I gave you?"

"No—of course not."

"So . . . you've kept it confidential," Smiley said. "Just like I'll keep the deposition transcript confidential."

"But you'll use the information for . . . whatever it is you're doing."

"Don't worry, I'll cover my tracks," Smiley said. "Otherwise we're both in trouble."

"I wish I could help you," Brad said. "But the thing is, I'm already on thin ice with the state bar. They've started disciplinary proceedings on something else. It could mean losing my license."

Brad searched his visitor's face for some trace of sympathy. Instead he saw only contempt.

"I trusted you, Mr. Pitcher," Smiley said. "I trusted you without knowing you—and now you won't trust me."

"I'm sorry, I . . ." Brad struggled with how to explain himself to this strange little man. Brad wasn't sorry. Brad wanted to take the fedora and shove it down the man's throat. "I'm just sorry."

* * *

As Alex thought about his conversation with Zeke, Zeke's criticism really got to Alex. Zeke was right—Alex was acting like a jerk, a selfish jerk. Alex had found an easy way out of his financial straits and was ready to take it, never mind helping Roberta Cummings and bringing a killer to justice—the causes that motivated Alex to risk so much in the first place. Alex figured that there was little he could do now to go back and fight for those causes.

Though as Alex thought about this, he did remember something Sheila had said at the celebration dinner with Brad the night before. She'd said something like Luke was paying to keep his deposition quiet. Why? And did the reason have something to do with why had Luke had gone from a scorched earth campaign against Sheila one day to unconditional surrender the next? Alex figured Brad must have uncovered something in the deposition, gotten Luke to admit something, that changed the whole case. Did that something relate to the car accident? Probably not. But there was only one way to find out. And it was worth a shot, given the way Alex had let Roberta Cummings down.

Alex drove to Sheila's apartment.

Sheila wasn't home, which was what Alex hoped for. Alex let himself in with a key she'd given him. "Another one for your collection," she'd said.

Sheila had gotten copies of all the filings and transcripts from her divorce proceedings. If it were Alex, he would have been happy with just two pieces of paper—the final divorce decree and the settlement check. Maybe Sheila was just cautious, or maybe she was more sentimental than she seemed.

Alex felt bad about leafing through Sheila's legal documents and reading the transcript of Luke's deposition, but he did it anyway. If Sheila and Brad's secret related to the accident, Alex had to know.

He skimmed most of the document until he got to the last few pages, which were gripping reading—Brad's last series of questions to Luke was sharp and unrelenting, and Luke's answers showed that Brad had trapped him. To Alex, after reading the transcript it seemed all but certain that Luke had orchestrated the accident in order to juice Liberty's financial results and trigger a bonus payout. Alex couldn't believe that Sheila had hidden this from him. The one thing Alex wanted was to find the truth about the accident, and Sheila decided to trade this dynamite lead for her windfall payout.

Alex couldn't believe how stupid he'd been. He should have known he couldn't trust Sheila after she lied to him about knowing Beto in the first conversation they ever had. Now Sheila had lied to him a second time.

Right now Alex didn't feel so bad about removing the transcript, and that's what he did. After stopping to make a photocopy and buy a large envelope and a bouquet of flowers, he drove a few miles into a neighborhood of modest single family homes.

The little stucco Cummings house looked like he remembered it, except that occasional drizzles had brightened the unkempt lawn from a dead winter brown to a hopeful green. Roberta Cummings still hadn't found anyone to help her look after the place. On the lawn near the sidewalk, the thick grass held up a discarded fast food cup on the tips of its blades. Didn't any of her neighbors care?

Farther back on the lawn, Alex saw a real estate sign posted in the earth, with a placard on top that said "REO"—real estate owned, in realtor jargon; foreclosure, in plain English. Alex hoped it wasn't too late for a different answer.

Alex put on dark sunglasses and a baseball cap. Weeks had passed since Roberta Cummings slapped Alex in the face and broke down at Rampart's offices, but Alex still wanted to minimize the risk that she would recognize him. He knocked on the door and held the bouquet of flowers in front of him and smiled so that she would open the door for a stranger. She did, and she smiled when she looked at the flowers.

"Who are *these* from?" she said. She looked in vain for a card attached to the bouquet.

"From a friend—an anonymous friend," Alex said, keeping his head down so she wouldn't recognize him.

She squinted and studied Alex's face, as if searching her memory for when she had seen him before. "Who are you?"

"Someone who wants you to get what you're entitled to," he said. He handed her the envelope. "Take this to a lawyer, and do it today—you need to sue Luke Hubbard to save your house."

She was too confused to reply, and Alex didn't wait for her to. He left her standing in the doorway and hurried away.

"Take that, confidentiality agreement," Alex said to himself as he drove away. Sheila and Brad wouldn't show Luke for the murderer he was, but Alex was sure plenty of clever and greedy L.A. lawyers would be eager to help Roberta Cummings do so.

Once on the road, Alex called Sheila. He got her voicemail, which made him even angrier. He didn't want to leave her a message; he wanted to bellow curses in her pretty face and make her cry. He hung up the phone and did the next best thing, a break-up by text message: "TAKE YOUR $ TO SWITZERLAND W/O ME. GOODBYE LIAR."

47

Three days later: It was morning, and Luke had just finished giving a presentation on the energy industry to a conference of analysts and investors. He stepped down from the stage and took questions from a polite huddle of friendly audience members. The little crowd was laughing softly at a joke Luke made when a man bouncing on the balls of his feet at the periphery of the group called out, "Are you Luke Hubbard?"

"Was it the banner above the stage that gave it away?" Luke said.

The crowd gamely laughed again, and the man tossed a thick, stapled sheaf of papers like a grenade over the heads of the other people. The papers landed at Luke's feet. "I'll bet he's got a mean forehand," Luke said to an assistant standing next to him.

"You've been served," the man said loudly. Luke's audience turned its attention to the man, but he quickly walked away.

Luke picked up the papers and scanned the first page. He and Liberty were being sued again. Luke had never heard of Roberta Cummings. He handed the papers to his assistant and said, "Call Alan Matthews now." Then he looked up and smiled at the people still waiting to speak to him. "Who was that masked man?"

* * *

It was after lunch, and Sheila was monopolizing the time of a hopeful young jewelry salesgirl whose annual salary, even with commissions, wouldn't cover any of the pieces Sheila was considering. In the girl's favor, she was thin and pretty, but so was Sheila.

Sheila was taking her time. She could afford anything in this store now, but wanted to choose the right piece to mark the occasion—the successful closing of one chapter of her life and the auspicious start of a new one. She wanted something to dazzle, something that both men and women would notice.

Finally, from among the array of costly necklaces, she chose a platinum strand studded with diamonds. Laid over her collarbone, it looked like a thread of spider's silk lined with dewdrops.

Sheila handed the sales clerk her debit card and, as she waited, she twisted her torso by millimeters to watch the diamonds sparkle in the mirror.

Finally, the clerk returned wearing a sheepish expression. "For some reason it's not taking the card," she said, and she presented the offending slip of plastic to Sheila.

"That's impossible," Sheila said. "I know for a fact that the funds are there."

"I'm sure they are, ma'am," the clerk said. "It's probably just a glitch on our side. Would you like to call the bank? Or maybe try another card?"

The settlement money wired by Luke *was* there, Sheila knew. The funds had cleared yesterday and should have still been there. Something must have gone wrong. Sheila felt her guts knot up. She forced a smile and removed the necklace. "Hold this, please," she told the sales clerk. Then she picked up her purse and walked quickly from the store.

It was late afternoon on what had been a quiet day, and Cindy was in Brad's office. His office was much cleaner now that the divorce case had settled.

Cindy was pressing him about why the settlement was so hush-hush. Brad explained that confidentiality clauses, applying to both parties, were common in high-profile divorces, and went on and on about other examples he had seen.

"I know what you're doing," she said with a smirk.

Brad smiled back at her. "Just complying with my confidentiality obligations."

"Sheila already said at that awful dinner how much money she got."

"I'm not going to confirm or deny that," Brad said with a grin.

"Brad, you've gotta give me something. How did you win in the end? At least tell me that."

Brad thought for a moment, then said, "Well, there were some details—tactical things about how I wound up the case—it's sort of inside baseball, though, you'd probably be bored."

"Spill it," she said.

"Well, I guess we have . . ." Brad's hands shuttled back and forth over his desktop as if the gesture would generate the words. "There's . . . implied confidentiality between us."

"Does that mean you're asking me to marry you?" Cindy said wryly.

Brad blushed for just a moment, then proceeded to recount, with strenuously understated pride, how he had baited Luke in his deposition to admit a motive to kill his employees, get the insurance money and earn a large bonus. At the end of the tale, he looked at her with a restrained smile, but Cindy wore a look of disgust.

"So . . . do you think Luke Hubbard actually killed those poor people?"

"Sure. I mean, probably."

"If you really think that, then why don't you turn him into the police?" Cindy said.

"Well, my job is to advance my client's interest, and—oh, who knows anyway? I mean, no one really knows if Luke did it or not—and no one will know, because the police didn't really investigate, and the evidence is stale, and . . . all the rest."

Cindy's expression hadn't changed.

"And anyway," Brad said, "I'm bound by the confidentiality clause."

Cindy looked at Brad with eyes as dark as ink. "Some confidentiality clause—you just told me, didn't you?"

Brad laughed nervously. "You ask questions like a lawyer."

"I wish you wouldn't answer them like a lawyer."

Brad was stuttering a lame response when the door to the office burst open. A scruffy bike messenger leaned in just far enough to snap a manila envelope like a Frisbee toward Brad's head. He dodged the missile and avoided a bruise to his neck. The intruder disappeared before Brad had a chance to protest. After he had gone, a woman they had hired part-time to do administrative work rushed to the doorway.

"I tried to stop him, Mr. Pitcher, but he just ran right in," she said.

"It's all right, Estelle," Brad said, waving her away.

"What is it?" Cindy said.

Brad smiled at her as he opened the package beneath his desk with shaking hands. Inside was a single page, a heavy watermarked sheet of paper with the Boswell & Baker letterhead. Brad quickly scanned the letter, and when his eyes reached the bottom, his face went white.

"But I didn't give anyone anything . . . they can't do this," Brad said.

"Can't do what?" Cindy said.

Brad looked up from the letter with wide, frightened eyes. "Hubbard says we breached the confidentiality clause. He says we gave information from Luke's deposition to the widow of the guy who drove the sports car in that accident."

Cindy smiled at Brad as if she understood, then said, "What does that mean?"

"It means Luke's cancelling the settlement. He says he won't pay a dime."

48

The day was almost over. It was the third day that Alex had ignored Sheila's voicemails and text messages, and he would be happy to do so forever. It was cruel, but he enjoyed listening to the pain in her voice. Alex had called Del, now that he was out of the hospital, to offer him a place to stay if he still needed one, but Del hadn't responded. Whatever.

Armed with his new knowledge from the deposition transcript, Alex had restarted in earnest his hunt for Crash and his mission to ingratiate himself to Luke. Alex now knew Luke's reason for killing the employees in the van, and he wouldn't rest until he found evidence that proved Luke's guilt.

Yet his conversations with Crash's friends and acquaintances had not been productive. None of them knew Crash well enough to give any details of his personal life—or, at least, none of them would share with Alex anything personal about Crash. From all they had to say, one would think that Crash had never had a girlfriend and didn't have any outside interests besides exercise and rooting for the Trojans. Alex was hoping that at least one of them would be closer with Crash than that—like Les Frees. But as Alex drove home after a third day of taking various security guys out for beers, he realized he had nothing to show for his work but detailed insight into Crash's exercise routine and football betting pool strategy. Alex had one idea left: Les Frees' funeral was the next day, and Alex figured that Crash, one of Les's groomsmen, would feel duty bound to make an appearance. But even if Alex was wrong, Alex needed to put in the effort to make Luke see him as hard working and trustworthy.

Alex got home as the sun was starting to go down. He sat in his living room, lights out, as the room grew dimmer with the evening. He thought about Sheila, and Pamela, and how they had seemed so different from each other when Alex first met Sheila, but how they had both ended up being the same. Users. Liars. Why did women keep pegging him as a sucker? *Maybe because I'm the kind of guy who sits in a room with the lights off feeling sorry for himself,* he thought.

He stood up. He wanted fresh air. There was a knock at the door. Alex cautiously went to the front door and opened it, expecting another bill collector. He found no one outside. He heard another knock, and realized it was coming from the back. He hoped it was Del, rather than a bill collector.

When Alex opened the back door, he found Sheila holding a bouquet of flowers and smiling sheepishly. "I remembered to come from behind this time," she said.

Alex didn't smile back. After stewing in his own bitter juices, seeing her now only made him feel meaner. "We're through, Sheila."

"Can I at least come in?"

Alex figured he could at least be civil. Anyway, he already knew what his response would be. He swiveled his body to let her pass into the kitchen. She laid the flowers on the counter.

"Let me explain," she said. "You found out what happened at the deposition?" When Alex didn't respond, she continued. "I'm so sorry I didn't tell you about what Brad found. But I knew you wouldn't stop until you found Crash and busted Luke, and I know how the two of them are—how dangerous they are. I was afraid you would keep after them and that you would get hurt."

Alex didn't trust the meek look on her face for one second. When had she ever been meek? "Ah, so you lied to me for my own good—how can you even say that with a straight face?"

Sheila took his two hands in hers and led him to the breakfast table, where they sat. "No, Alex. I kept the transcript from you because I didn't want to lose you. I can't imagine losing you. We haven't known each other long, but I know we have something special." She laughed a little to herself. "When I first met you, I thought you were just a typical slacker." Alex was a little offended by that, and it must have showed, because Sheila smiled. "A cute slacker, but see how ridiculous that seems now? A relationship doesn't just happen, Alex—two people create it. And the strongest relationships are created in hard times."

She was smooth, all right, but Alex wouldn't let himself be duped yet again. "So we had a wartime fling," he said. "So what? The war's over and now it's time to go back to our real lives."

She squeezed his hands. "I know I have to earn your trust. I'm ready to do that. This divorce has been stressful for me, really the most stressful thing I've ever been through. You don't know what it's like when you're forced to question everything you took for granted." Alex thought of his father's insider trading arrest, and how their respectable, affluent family had become downscale and shunned almost overnight. Sheila must have remembered their conversation about that, because she said, "Sorry, of course you do."

"Thanks," Alex said begrudgingly. To her credit, Alex thought, Sheila really was perceptive. She understood him well enough to guess his thoughts and feelings—but that may also have explained why she was so good at deceiving him.

"What was hardest is that when the divorce started, I realized I'd been lying to myself—about Luke, about my marriage—for years. And I know I've handled it poorly, I've been immature. Oh, I wish you could have met me some other time. I feel like this court battle has aged me, Alex."

"That was never the issue," Alex said.

"I don't judge you for your own mistakes, Alex." She said this sympathetically. "I know what it's like. That's what makes us such a match."

"So now we just run away from our mistakes together," Alex said. "That's not love, Sheila. That's a little girl's fairy tale."

She shook her head. "Not run away. Start over. We have a chance to do that together. It's not the money. Luke's going to take that away." That was a surprise to Alex. "Oh, yes," Sheila said. "That widow is suing him; someone gave her the transcript of Luke's deposition."

"Sheila, I was upset."

"Don't say anything. I knew it had to be you who gave it to her. I know why you did it and I've already forgiven you."

For the past year, ever since Pamela had left him, Alex had acted like he was owed some payback. Now Alex suddenly felt like he'd overreacted in going behind Sheila's back and reading the transcript, like he'd punished Sheila for

Pamela's lies. He felt awful. Sheila's head drooped toward the table, and her hair fell over her eyes.

"I don't like to beg," she said. "It makes me feel weak, but I don't care—I'm begging you."

She began weeping in soft sobs that she tried to hold in and that came out like a kitten's hiccups. Alex lifted her chin.

"I don't think you're weak," he said. "Anyway, you're no weaker than me."

He leaned forward and kissed her. Her lips were warm and swollen from crying.

* * *

Alex and Sheila made love slowly as night fell. For Alex, it felt like the first honest act they'd done together. There was no lingering prospect of advantage between them. They were past lust. There was no more excitement about the settlement money, or about nailing Luke together. It was just the two of them, with all their faults finally out in the open.

Lying in bed, they listened to the ocean waves rolling onto the sand two blocks away.

"I've still got to bust Luke," Alex said.

"I know," Sheila said.

"I could try to blackmail him for you, maybe get some of your money back."

Sheila sighed. "No," she said. "You couldn't live with yourself if you didn't actually send him to jail."

A couple of waves rolled in.

"Les Frees' funeral is tomorrow. I'll show up, see if Crash shows up. After that, I figure I'll have done enough legwork that I should be in with Luke, have his trust. And at that point, enough chasing after Crash; I'll start setting up my sting against Luke."

"OK," Sheila said flatly. After a moment, she added, "Just don't let tomorrow be your funeral, too."

49

The next morning, Alex strapped on his gun beneath his jacket and drove to the church.

Alex arrived well in advance of the starting time for the funeral; he didn't want to miss Crash's arrival, assuming he came. A small old woman entered the sanctuary just ahead of him and crossed herself before taking a seat near the front to pray. Alex self-consciously tried to mimic the gesture and then quickly found a seat in back, in a shadow between two of the kaleidoscopic beams of sunlight that shone down through the church's stained glass windows. After a while, the old woman left. A while after that, two young men brought in a coffin on a wheeled table. Flowers were already set up near the front of the sanctuary. Off to the side were confessional booths—of no further use to Les Frees, Alex thought.

Alex had never understood the concept of confession. Why tell all your personal problems to someone else, particularly a man who didn't have sex? How could someone living a lifestyle from the Middle Ages possibly tell you how to live your life in this world?

A priest escorted an older couple in through a side door—Les's parents, Alex figured. They spoke quietly to each other. A little while after that, Alex noticed a pair of large men in suits enter from the back of the sanctuary and sit down a couple of rows behind Alex and across the aisle from him. Les's parents kept looking their way, waiting for them to introduce themselves and give their condolences. They never did. *Cops*, Alex thought. Alex buttoned his jacket to make sure the gun under his arm wasn't visible. What if the cops spotted Crash first? What if they—or Crash—started shooting? *This could get complicated*, Alex thought.

A few minutes later, Les's friends and other family members arrived. There were a few guys that Alex knew from Liberty. Alex averted his head and pretended to read a Bible that he took from the pew. Having someone recognize him or sit with him would make his job harder.

The mourners all sat together in the front. They only took up the first few rows of pews. The sparse attendance made Alex happy, in a vindictive way. The priest started the service. Still no Crash.

The priest, a younger man, was somber but not sad—Alex figured he must not have known Les. The words he said could have been spoken at just about anyone's funeral, but Les's parents looked moved. Les's cousin gave a eulogy, then a high school friend did, then his father did. And then it was over. The cops left first, then the mourners left in a group up the aisle. As they did, Alex tiptoed off to the side of the sanctuary and stood behind a column so he wouldn't be recognized.

Alex couldn't believe it. He had been sure Crash would come to his friend's funeral. When the mourners were gone, Alex took a stroll around the sanctuary. Could Crash have been hiding behind one of the other columns? By a doorway? Under a pew? No, that was ridiculous. An older priest coming in from a side door encountered Alex at the front of the sanctuary as Alex stood up from looking under the pews.

"Are you here for confession?" the priest asked. His bushy eyebrows were unkempt, and there was hair growing out of his ears. He looked like he could have just returned from a hermitage high in the mountains.

"No," Alex said, "I was just leaving."

The priest searched Alex's face for some deeper meaning. "Well, we're always here," he said.

Great, Alex thought, *now he thinks I'm keeping some deep secret*. He started walking toward the front of the church to leave. Behind him, he heard the priest open the door of the confessional.

"I'm sorry," the priest said, surprised. "I didn't know anyone was in here. Are you here for confession?"

This priest is like a broken record, Alex thought.

"No," came the reply, in a deep baritone. "I'm just leaving."

Alex turned around on hearing the voice. Next to the priest he saw a tall, muscular man in a dark hoodie with short silver hair. Crash had been in the church all along, just hiding.

"Stay, my child," the priest said. "I can see your soul is burdened . . ."

Crash didn't respond to the priest. Crash was staring at Alex. Without thinking, Alex reached a hand under his jacket, where his pistol lay nestled in its holster. The colored light from one of the windows momentarily blinded Alex, so he stepped out of the aisle to see. Too late, he saw Crash race through a side door and outside. Before Alex followed, he reflexively caught the eye of the priest. In an instant the priest's gaze traced a crooked line from Alex's eyes to his shoulder, his shoulder to his arm, his arm to his hand. Alex's hand was in his jacket.

Their eyes met again, and the priest transfixed Alex with a look of recognition. It was the look of a man who understood cause and effect, of a man who recognized sin.

* * *

Outside the church, the hearse and the mourners were long gone. Alex was too far behind Crash to stop him from climbing into a parked sedan and driving off. Finding Crash and then losing him was more pathetic than not finding him at all.

Alex called Luke. To Alex's surprise, Luke took the news calmly, though he probed every detail of what Crash had said and done. When Alex finished, Luke said, "And I have some news for you." Luke explained that the night before, the security cameras at his house had captured a man lurking around the gate outside. Luke had looked at the footage himself and was sure the man was Crash.

"I'd like you to come to my house tonight, because I think Crash will come to find me. I could use your help."

On the one hand, Alex thought, helping Luke meant putting himself in harm's way if Crash showed up. On the other hand, what better way for Alex to entrench himself once and for all in Luke's inner circle? Alex said yes. Then he called Sheila and told her about finding Crash and Luke's request. She begged him not to go to Luke's house. Alex told her he could take care of himself and asked her if she still had Beto's pistol. She did. "Hold onto it," he said.

50

Luke lived in a mansion, but he answered the door himself. It was grand for L.A., like a poor man's Versailles hidden behind high walls and hedges. Alex felt like he should say something admiring about the property, so he did, but Luke's reaction was muted.

"This was all Sheila's thing," he said, gesturing toward the gardens. "I'll probably just sell the place with the divorce."

Luke looked tired. He explained to Alex the layout of the property and what he wanted Alex to do, which was stay during the afternoon and night, keep an eye out for Crash and prevent him from entering the house. The cries of a young child echoing from another room interrupted them. Luke excused himself. "Petra's son," he said, "now my son."

Luke motioned for Alex to follow, and led Alex to the child's room, where a nanny was comforting the boy. "Dmitri, say hello to Mr. Franks," Luke said. Dmitri looked blankly at Alex. Luke stayed with Dmitri and had a servant show Alex the rest of the house.

In the kitchen, a cook asked Alex if he was hungry, and Alex had her make him a couple of sandwiches to last him through the evening. Alex took the sandwiches and went outside.

He walked around the property all afternoon and became familiar with it. Eventually the sun began to set, and tall cypress trees that ringed the expansive property cast long shadows across the gardens. The outdoor lights came on. Alex made several easy circuits around the grounds, staying out of the light so as not to be seen by Crash if he tried to sneak in.

Close to midnight, Alex was tracing the dark perimeter behind the house when he noticed movement in the shadows on the other side of the gardens. He pressed himself into the hedges near the wall and watched.

For a while he wondered if he had seen nothing. It could have been a bird, it could have been the wind. Alex was about to give up and keep walking when he saw it again—movement against the far wall, a large shadowed figure. It stopped just as suddenly as it started, like the person on the other side was pausing after each few steps to see if he had been spotted. Alex stayed where he was and watched without following. After another long interval the figure moved again, only now he moved continuously toward the house.

Alex figured that meant the man wasn't looking behind him anymore, so Alex, keeping against the hedge, moved toward the house as well. The gardens ended a few yards before the house, and Alex saw the man dash over that last, exposed territory. The man was big enough to be, he could only be, Crash. In the shadows of the house, the man quickly opened a side door and disappeared inside.

Alex sprinted across the gardens, indifferent to the artificial light that shone there, awkwardly hurdling waves of shrubbery, until he reached the same door. It was unlocked, and he opened it and stepped inside. Crash was gone. A console on the wall began beeping. It was the alarm system, giving Alex a chance to prove he belonged there by punching in a code that would prevent the alarm from sounding.

Alex of course didn't know the code, so he just kept on, running upstairs to where Luke's room was. After about a minute the alarm sounded, and a few seconds after that, footsteps sounded from throughout the house, all going at once, as if a giant centipede had gotten itself tangled up in the mansion's halls and stairways. Alex was running so fast he nearly knocked over Luke, who was hurrying down the hallway in his pajamas.

"Crash is in the house," Alex said.

"I know," Luke said, shouting over the din of the alarm. "Take Dmitri away."

Alex ran down the hall, trying to remember which was the boy's room. He heard a small voice wailing from behind one door and opened it to find Dmitri standing up in bed and crying. "Your father asked me to take you away," Alex said.

"No!" cried the boy.

Alex heard a large, deep voice from down the hall shout Dmitri's name, followed by the sound of heavy footsteps running toward them, and Alex decided it wasn't safe for him and Dmitri to leave by the door. He looked out the window and saw that it opened onto a sloped roof covering a portion of the first floor. Alex threw open the window, gathered Dmitri under his left arm and stepped up and into the open window frame.

"Stop." The voice was Crash's, loud but calm and commanding. He loomed as a menacing silhouette in the doorway of Dmitri's room. Alex froze in the window frame. Then he reached into his jacket and pulled his gun. He pointed it at Crash. Alex's wrist wobbled with the heavy gun as if it were a divining rod. Alex had never pointed a gun at anyone before.

Slowly, as if he understood he shouldn't spook Alex, Crash drew his own pistol from his waist and pointed it steadily at Alex. "Put the gun down. Give me my son."

Your son? Alex thought. "OK," he said. "Gun down. Right." Slowly, Alex lowered the gun and set it on a nearby toy chest. He raised his right arm in the air as if in surrender. In his left arm, he still held Dmitri.

"Now give me the boy," Crash said.

Alex squeezed Dmitri a little tighter and, without a backward glance, rolled his body out of the window and onto the sloping roof. He heard a gunshot and the window pane shattering above him. Their rolling accelerated. Alex threw a leg out sideways to slow them down, but they kept tumbling.

* * *

Luke heard the gunshot and sprinted back to Dmitri's room. He found Crash standing by the open window, aiming his gun outward toward the roof outside.

"Crash!"

Crash swiveled and pointed the gun at Luke. Luke raised his palms.

"Crash, what are you doing?"

"Keeping a promise," Crash said.

"To whom?"

"To a woman I hurt."

Crash's responses came quickly, and Luke's came more slowly, as if he'd arrived late to a party and was trying to catch up with the conversation. Luke stepped cautiously up to Crash. With steady hands, he lowered Crash's gun. "I can help you. You don't have to run."

"I can't let you take Dmitri from me."

Luke gave a pained smile. "Dmitri's . . . your son?" Crash didn't answer. "H-how?" Luke asked.

"You remember when I rescued her from . . . where she was," Crash said.

"Petra," Luke said.

"When we were running from the gangsters who were after her, we were together for a few hours. And it happened."

"Crash, I trusted you." Luke stood with his hands at his sides and regarded Crash thoughtfully. His eyes were filling with tears. "Why'd you kill her?"

That was a question Crash had to think about a moment. "She wanted to take Dmitri away from me, too."

Luke nodded, but looked confused. Then, almost bashfully, he said, "How many others?"

Crash didn't answer. Police sirens now rang out in the distance. Crash noticed the sound, cast a final glance out the window, then fled past Luke into the hall. Luke went to the doorway and watched as Crash left him.

* * *

As Alex felt the end of the roof pass under his backside, his thoughts raced for ways to protect Dmitri from the fall. *Don't crush him. Get my legs under me. Roll with it. But don't crush him.* Turf would be better than concrete. They landed in a hedge, which was a blessing but which terrified Alex because the sensation of a thousand twigs pricking him all over came as a surprise. Alex didn't crush Dmitri. Alex sprang up immediately from the ground and, with Dmitri tossed over a shoulder, ran to where he had left his truck. About halfway there, he realized that he hadn't broken any bones. He also realized he'd left his gun in the boy's room.

51

Alex heard the sirens in the distance but kept running. He put Dmitri down and, with trembling hands, unlocked the door to his truck. Little Dmitri was too much in shock to run away. Alex lifted the boy into the truck and accelerated around Luke's circular driveway and out the front gate. Luke's property was deep in the hills, where the streets were largely unlit. As Alex sped away in the dark, three police cars passed him on their way to the mansion.

After a minute, Alex's heart rate slowed enough that he could think again. Dmitri was huddled into a ball in the seat next to him, sniveling. "Don't worry. You'll see Luke soon." Alex called Luke on his cell phone. "I've got Dmitri, we're safe," Alex said.

"Al, thank God. Where are you?"

"In my truck. Driving away. Is it safe to come back?"

"Not yet. The police just got here. They're searching the property."

"I'll keep driving arou—"

Alex lurched forward in his seat. Someone had rear-ended them—hard. Dmitri screamed. Alex glanced in his mirror and in the dark saw the shape of a car, its headlights off, speeding up to ram him again. Alex hit the gas and pulled away. The car stayed with him. Luke's tinny voice sounded from Alex's cell phone, which he'd dropped between the seats. "Al? Al?"

"It's Crash! Crash is chasing us! Tell the police!"

"Where are you?" Luke said.

Hell if I know, Alex thought. The roads were all dark, narrow side streets. Alex hung a quick right turn and gunned the truck uphill on another street. Crash was slow to react—his brakes squealed, and he had to go into reverse before he could follow them. Alex felt grateful for the few extra seconds. The truck had a lot of power, but so did Crash's car.

The street leveled out, and Alex saw a streetlight ahead. *Civilization*, he thought. Seconds later, he saw that the streetlight stood alone. In a cul-de-sac.

The street ended in a wide circle of asphalt. *Don't let this be the end*, Alex thought. He bellied right as he got to the cul-de-sac and then turned the steering wheel sharply to the left. The truck reeled around to face the opposite direction. Dmitri was thrown against the door. He screamed again.

Alex saw Crash's car stopped in the middle of the narrow street ahead of him. He saw Crash step out of the car. He saw Crash point a gun. Instantly, Alex flipped on his brights and hit the gas. He pushed Dmitri's head down, kept one eye above the dashboard and aimed the truck at Crash's open car door. No—at Crash himself, standing behind it.

The door came off like it was fastened with masking tape. Alex's front bumper launched it into the air, where it fluttered and spun until it landed somewhere else. Alex didn't look back. Downhill was the smart direction to go, and after a minute or two Alex reached a two-lane road with streetlights. A couple minutes after that, he was back in the city. At this hour, the streets were empty. He didn't see anyone following him. He kept driving, though, just to be sure. He looked over at Dmitri, who had withdrawn into a ball. Alex placed a hand on his head, and the boy flinched.

"That man is gone, Dmitri. He can't hurt you anymore. I'm taking you back to Luke now, OK?" Dmitri didn't react. Alex pulled onto a side street and called Luke.

"It's Al. We escaped. I think he's dead."

"Thank God," Luke said. "Is Dmitri all right?"

"He's pretty scared."

"I'm here with the police. Come back as soon as you can."

"We're on our way."

Alex squeezed Dmitri's shoulder and drove toward Luke's house. Alex felt sad for the boy that there wasn't a cure for nightmares. The cell phone rang again. Alex took the phone and started speaking. "We're at San Vicente and Bundy," Alex said. "We'll be there in ten minutes."

The voice that responded was low and hoarse. "You missed me."

Alex yelled into the phone. "Crash—I'll run you over again, you bastard."

"No, you won't. You'll bring the boy to me."

"Why don't you meet me at Luke's house and we can talk it over?"

"No. We'll discuss it at Sheila's apartment."

Alex was so surprised he almost dropped the phone. "What?"

"Yes, Alex Fogarty. Les Frees warned me about you. And after he died, I figured that you and Sheila were working together. Then I followed her and proved it. Bye now. I'm stepping into her elevator."

The line went dead. In a panic, Alex pulled over and punched Sheila's cell phone number into his cell. The call connected, then dropped. Alex dialed again, and this time went straight to voicemail. "Wake up," he screamed into the phone. He dialed her home phone number. The phone rang on the other end. Once. Then again. "Pick up, goddammit!" Alex's yelling made Dmitri cry again, and Alex wanted to slap him. Alex heard the phone pick up. "Sheila, get out of the apartment! Get out now!"

"I'm afraid you're too late," said Crash.

"I swear if you touch a hair on her head—"

"A trade," Crash said. "Sheila for Dmitri. You come alone. Simple as that." Then he hung up.

Alex threw his cell phone onto his dashboard. He saw that Dmitri was shivering. "I'm so sorry," he said to the boy. He called Luke. "Change of plan," he said when Luke answered.

"What?"

"Crash is alive. He's in Sheila's apartment."

"Who? My ex-wife?"

"He's going to kill her unless I give him Dmitri. Meet me at her building with the police."

"Wow. He's really gone off the deep end. She lives at—"

"I know where she lives," Alex said, and he hung up.

52

In front of Sheila's apartment building, before he said anything to anyone, Luke ran to where Alex sat, pulled the boy away and hugged him tight.

"No one will ever take you from me again, understand? Never again."

The police had driven in with Luke, and an officer with an air of authority walked up behind him. "You say this Crash Bailey is in Ms. Hubbard's apartment?" he asked Alex.

"That's right. He answered the phone there and threatened to kill her."

"And your relationship to her?"

"We're dating," Alex said. Luke gave Alex a bewildered look. Alex just shrugged.

"And your name is?" the officer said.

"Alex Fogarty."

Luke's look now was penetrating and unforgiving. Alex gave him the same look back. *How do you like not being in control, for once?* Alex thought.

"We've got this covered," the officer said. "We've evacuated the other apartments and shut off the elevators. We have a SWAT team ready to rappel into the apartment from a higher floor and incapacitate the suspect with flash grenades and tear gas—"

"No," Luke said. "It's too dangerous. I'll go up and speak to Crash. I'm the only one he trusts."

"Mr. Hubbard, we can't let you go up there," the officer said. He cast a wary look at Alex. "Or any other civilians. The suspect is too unstable."

Luke was about to protest when Alex's cell phone rang. Alex answered it immediately.

"I'm waiting," said Crash.

"It's him," Alex whispered to the others.

Luke grabbed the phone from Alex's hand. "Crash, it's me. I'm going to get you out of this."

"I need Dmitri," Crash said.

"I know you do. Sit tight. I'm coming up." Luke ended the call and gave the phone back to Alex.

"What the hell was that?" Alex said.

"That was some tough love. Now excuse me." Luke started to leave, but the officer stopped him with a palm to his chest.

"Sir, you need to let us do our job."

Luke got in the officer's face. "Which is what? Shoot him? Maybe shoot her in the bargain? You need someone he trusts up there."

"Sir, we don't do this by committee." The officer's voice was even, but he was fuming.

"Get the chief of police on the phone," Luke said.

The policeman drew back in shock. "I beg your pardon?"

"Fine, don't," Luke said. "I'll call him myself. Did I mention that Joe and I play golf together?" Luke pulled a cell phone from his pocket and began scrolling through the contacts.

The officer hastily said, "Put your phone away. I'm not waking the chief. Look, we'll put you and Crash on the phone with one of our hostage negotiators, OK?"

"Very good," Luke said. "And I want this joker locked up." Luke turned to where Alex had been standing, but Alex was gone. "Where? Son of a—"

The officer spoke into a mouthpiece fastened to his chest. "We've got a civilian that just entered the building. Repeat: civilian in the building. Do not shoot." To no one in particular, the officer grumbled, "I'm gonna kill that guy."

"Don't you have officers inside who can stop him?" Luke said.

"I'm not going to take them away from their positions. Protecting the hostage comes first." After thinking a moment, the officer added, "I'm just gonna have to send in the SWAT team now, before your friend makes it to her apartment." He reached for his mouthpiece to give the order.

Luke grabbed the officer's wrist. "Wait," he said. "Now you really do need me."

53

After slipping away while Luke and the police officer argued, Alex used the keys Sheila had given him to open an exterior door to the building's staircase. Seeing Crash so unhinged made Alex consider whether Crash alone was behind the car accident. Alex only had circumstantial evidence of Luke's involvement. But what about Crash? Crash had killed Petra. And he was tight with Frees.

But if Crash orchestrated the accident without Luke's knowledge, what was his motive? Who knew?—Crash was nuts, after all. As Alex raced up the staircase, he considered that he still needed hard evidence to link either Luke or Crash to the crime.

Then Alex realized that he might already have the evidence he was looking for—if he was lucky. He stopped in his tracks. He figured he had a few moments to spare before the cops outside realized he was in the building, and Alex preferred to know just how guilty Crash was before confronting him upstairs. Alex slapped the different pockets in his jacket until he found the cell phone that he had taken from Les Frees' motel room. He had forgotten all about it. Wouldn't it be interesting to see if Frees had conferred with anyone— like Luke or Crash—around the time he planted the bomb that killed Beto? Alex navigated the phone's glowing menu in the darkness of the stairwell.

The phone's log of calls made and received didn't go back in time as far as the MacArthur Park bombing, but it did cover more recent calls. The call log was organized with the most recent calls first. The log started off in a heartbreaking way with a call from a contact identified as "Mom" early on the morning that Frees' body was found. Alex remembered seeing Frees' sorrowful mother at the funeral. *Even murderers have mothers*, he thought. Alex kept scrolling through the recent calls.

The day before that, the day Frees died, there were three separate calls to and from a local number, a phone number that Alex recognized. Alex stared at the little screen on the phone. He felt confused, then vaguely uncomfortable, and then everything became clear—what happened to Les Frees, what happened in the car accident.

Sheila's apartment was ten flights up, but Alex felt a new surge of adrenaline that carried him quickly up the floors, three steps at a time. He knew that Crash was armed. He knew that his own gun was back in Dmitri's bedroom. Yet now he also knew the key to the entire puzzle.

To put the pieces together, he needed to get to Sheila's apartment before the SWAT team stormed the place and turned it into a slaughterhouse. What the hell would Alex actually do once he was in the apartment? He'd figure out the details when he got there, if he could still stand up straight. *Boy*, he thought, *an elevator would have been nice.*

* * *

In the elevator, Luke wouldn't stop talking.

"Think about it, Clancy. You go in there with me, and Crash sees you with your helmet and your body armor and your black rifle? He'll start shooting."

The cop stared straight ahead at the digital display on the wall in front of him, refusing to react. *Fourth floor, fifth floor.*

"And when Crash starts shooting, you'll start shooting," Luke said. "Your brother officers coming through the windows and they'll start shooting. And then? Then people will get shot. You'll be fine—probably—you've got the vest." Luke patted the Kevlar vest covering Clancy's chest. "But Sheila? That nut who's running up the stairs right now to the apartment? Me? Who knows. Can you live with that?"

. . . seventh floor . . .

"We got our procedures," the officer said. "I gotta call the lieutenant on this one."

"There's no time to check in with teacher, Clancy. This one is all you. You've got to make the call, and—you know this—there's only one call to make. And you don't have time to ask for permission, so you'll just have to ask forgiveness."

"I don't know . . ."

"Clancy, here's all you need to know: if you let me go in alone, Crash and Sheila and I have a chance of making it out alive; if you insist on coming in with me? Bloodbath."

A light above the doors flashed on. *Ding.*

Clancy shook his head in resignation. "It's your life, Mr. Big Shot."

54

At the tenth-floor landing, Alex cautiously opened the door to the interior hallway. His lungs felt like he'd inhaled burning smoke, and his thighs felt like clay. He panted while he walked toward Sheila's apartment, trying to recover his breath. As he neared the middle of the hallway, the light above the elevator doors lit up and a bell chimed. The doors opened, and Alex was shocked to see Luke, standing in front of a cop in body armor and a helmet.

Luke was as blasé as ever. "You should really try the elevator on the way down," he said to Alex.

"How did you—"

Luke and the cop stepped out of the elevator. "When we spotted you entering the building, I made the lieutenant see that the only way to stop you from making a mess of things was to send me up to talk with Crash. So, thank you, I guess." Luke turned to the cop. "See you soon." Then Luke walked quickly toward Sheila's apartment.

Alex muscled his way even with Luke, which Luke seemed to expect, and they walked as a pair to the apartment door.

"By the way," Luke said, "how long have you been screwing my wife?"

"Not as long as you've cheated on her."

That made Luke laugh. At Sheila's door, Luke knocked loudly. "Crash, it's me," he called. "I've got Sheila's boyfriend with me. We're coming in."

Luke opened the door slowly, and they both entered. The lights were off inside the apartment, but the sun was beginning to rise and everything was visible in grays that were starting to warm into color. Alex saw Crash standing in the living room. Sheila sat on the couch in her pajamas. She wasn't tied up. Crash was relying on fear to keep her in place. She sure looked afraid.

"Crash," Luke said. "I can get you out of this, but you've got to listen to me."

"I want my son," Crash said.

Sheila unexpectedly began crying, and the others turned to watch her. "You see this, Luke?" she said between sobs. "This is all your fault."

"My fault?"

"Yes, take responsibility for once, will you? If you hadn't gone back on the settlement I'd be"—she sniffled loudly—"in Switzerland by now."

"Christ, Sheila, that was your choice. Don't put that on me."

Alex watched Luke and Sheila with wonder and mild embarrassment at the spectacle of them squabbling at a moment like this.

"Oh, you're impossible," Sheila said, sniffling again. "Crash, hand me my purse, will you? I've got some tissues in there."

Crash brought her the purse from across the room. Sheila dug through it, pulled out a tissue and blew her nose loudly. "That's better," she said. Then she turned to Luke. "So how are you going to get us out of this one, genius?"

Luke ignored her and looked at his friend. "Crash, ever since Petra died, I've been trying to find you, so I can protect you from the police. I've talked to lawyers, Crash, the best in the business, and you've got a great basis for an insanity plea."

Crash's eyes flashed with anger. "I'm not crazy."

"Be practical, Crash. You can't be with Dmitri if you're in jail for the rest of your life. And that's where you're headed, unless you listen to me."

Crash put his hand on the pistol lying in a holster at his waist. "You're trying to trick me."

Luke lifted his palms in innocence. "No, I'm not. That's why I hired Al Franks"—Luke cocked his head toward Alex—"to try to find you."

"You mean Alex Fogarty?"

"Right," Luke said. "Him."

"You're lying to me. You don't even know his name." Crash drew his pistol and pointed it at Luke.

"S-stop," said Luke. "Think about Dmitri. If we're both gone, who will take care of him?"

"I won't let my son be raised by you."

"He's telling the truth," Alex heard himself say. Crash looked at him, and the pistol dropped a few inches. "Crash, you know my real name. I lied to Luke because I thought he'd committed a crime and I was trying to find the evidence to take him down. But Luke thought I was a regular employee. He was always trying to help you—he told me so." Alex's heartbeat felt like a skipping CD. By speaking, he had delayed the slaughter—and he hoped it was for more than a few seconds.

Crash's eyes narrowed. "You're lying, too," he said. "All I know is, Les Frees talked with you and a few days later he was dead. I can't prove you killed him. But I don't need to."

Crash's gun was pointed at Alex now. From the corner of his eye Alex saw Sheila pull something small and silver from her purse—Beto's gun. She squeezed her eyes shut and fired at Crash. The sound from the little gun was like a balloon popping, and off to the side a window blew into bits. Crash's eyes widened with rage, and he swiveled toward Sheila.

Alex saw what was coming next and without a moment's thought reached for his back pocket and pulled out his wallet, which he pointed at Crash like a gun. "Crash!" he yelled. Crash's head turned toward Alex, and the pistol followed. Alex saw the gun pointing at him, the dark hole of the barrel staring at him like a dead eye. He saw Crash's finger on the trigger, moving.

Sheila fired an instant before Crash did. Her bullet hit Crash's shoulder just before Crash's own gun went off. Alex's left leg flew out from under him and he fell down sideways onto the floor. Only after reaching the floor did he start to feel the pain from the gunshot wound in his thigh.

The SWAT team was already breaking in through the windows, men in black armor with black guns, ready to shoot. Alex saw Luke race across the room and tackle Crash to the ground. The cops put their guns down and swarmed the two, pulling Luke away from Crash and beating Crash into submission.

Alex tried to stand up but couldn't. He saw he was bleeding a lot. He thought he should do something about that, but couldn't think of what. As he felt himself pass out, he looked up and saw Sheila's face above his. She was stroking his hair. "You'll be all right," she said. "In spite of yourself."

55

Mealtime again. The nurse was different than the one at breakfast, but her manner was the same. Hurried and brusque, she made "good morning" sound like an insult. Alex hated hospitals. He picked indifferently at the food, and then the nurse returned. "I'm not finished yet," Alex said.

The nurse eyed him wearily and uttered one word before retreating: "Visitor."

Zeke entered, slowly and quietly, as if he were approaching a sleeping bear.

"Zeke?"

"Hi, Alex. You look upset."

"No, I was just expecting someone else. Come on in. Gunshot wounds aren't contagious."

Zeke smiled at that. "You warm enough?"

Alex said that he was, and Zeke sat down.

"Well?" Alex said.

"I'm sorry."

Zeke said he was sorry about everything that had happened to Alex, from losing his job at Rampart to—Zeke just pointed at Alex's injured leg to indicate the end of the story.

"If I hadn't gotten you fired, all the rest of it probably wouldn't have happened," Zeke said.

You don't know the half of it, Alex thought.

"Look," Zeke said. "When I wrote that story about you and Rampart, I was stuck writing feature articles and I knew my job was in jeopardy. And then, after all that, this week I finally got laid off, if you can believe that."

"I believe it."

"I was just trying to write something with zing, maybe get another chance to do investigative work. I didn't mean to ruin your life."

"I'm gonna live, you know," Alex said. "You don't need to get sappy."

"About that . . ." Zeke said.

"Getting sappy?"

"No—living. Have you thought about what you'll do when you get out of here?"

"I'm still thinking about that." When Alex thought about his future, he saw more uncertainty than anything else. He had no job and, after burning bridges at Rampart, no great prospects of getting an investigator's job at another insurance company. So in a way, he had wide course ahead of him, though no map. The only certainty was his five houses, and five mortgages.

"You're not going back to Rampart Insurance, are you?"

"No way."

"Not going to work for your uncle's—what is it, an accounting firm?"

"Not in a million years."

Zeke's face slipped into a grin, then he forced his features back into a more serious expression. "Here's the thing," he said. "I'm out of a job, right? And so I thought, why not keep doing what I do best, but just become my own boss?"

Alex was mystified. "Did you buy a printing press?"

Zeke let himself grin again. "No. I've been kicking around this new idea—private journalism."

"What's that?"

"It's simple. If someone wants to know something—they need an investigation or whatever—they hire me, and I find the answer and tell them."

"It sounds like being a private detective," Alex said. "Where's the journalism?"

"Ah, that's my special twist," Zeke said, wagging his finger eagerly. "I'll do the investigations, but I'll also have a blog where I write about them."

"Huh," Alex said. The idea sounded half-baked—people who needed private detectives generally also wanted privacy. "Private detective plus public blog. Sounds like it could get complicated."

Zeke waved a hand in front of his face as if shooing a fly. "I'm still working out the details," he said. "Anyway, you interested?"

"In becoming a private journalist?"

"In becoming my partner," Zeke said. "In the investigations."

Alex considered the idea. As he'd thought in the past, working for himself would certainly be more appealing than working for another bureaucratic company. And having a partner could be an advantage. "Are you flexible on the blog aspect?"

Before Zeke could answer, the nurse poked her head in the room again and announced, in the same tone as announcing a change of his bedpan, "A woman's here to see you. Says her name is Sheila."

Alex nodded at the nurse. "Zeke, I've got to see her."

Zeke stood up to leave. "Like I said, I'm still working out the details, but think about it, OK?"

Sheila swept into the room, ignoring Zeke and the nurse and walking straight to Alex's bed, where she wrapped her arms around his neck and squeezed him tightly. "I tried and tried to get in before, but they said family only for the first two days." She released the tightness of her embrace and sat down next to his bed, with her arms still draped around his neck.

"That's all right," Alex said breezily. "I hardly remember the first two days. Thanks for the flowers."

He could tell from her bearing that she was back to being the peremptory Sheila—simply assuming that the world was as she wished it to be. And after Alex had drawn gunfire from Crash in order to save her, it was natural for her to assume that Alex loved her. That's what Alex expected her to think. That's what he wanted her to think.

"Oh, I wanted to see you in person," she said. "After the paramedics took you, I drove straight here, to the hospital, and waited for word. They wouldn't tell me anything because I'm not family. Finally, yesterday, one of the nurses took pity on me and told me you came through surgery all right. They say you'll heal well?"

"I'll limp for a while, but hopefully, yeah."

"I'm just so glad you're alive." Sheila turned to the large vase of flowers by the bed and rearranged them. "I've been thinking that some good will come out of all this. For us, I mean."

"Oh?"

She didn't seem to notice his wry tone, and continued in earnest. "We started off wrong, Alex, and there wasn't a lot of trust. I wondered if you loved me, and I even wondered if I loved you. But in the apartment with Crash, you took a bullet for me—that was quick thinking, pulling out your wallet like a gun."

"I didn't really think about it, I just did it."

"See? That's what I mean. It showed your true feelings."

"Yes," Alex said.

"That you love me."

"I do, Sheila," he allowed. That was true. But it didn't change what Alex had to do. "I know I've fought that, but I do. And you fired at Crash first, to save me."

"Sorry I missed."

"You got him the second time, and I'm still alive, so that's all that counts," Alex said. Seeing her so emotionally open and vulnerable was torturing him, knowing what was coming next. So that he wouldn't lose his nerve, he leaned forward. "I've got something for you," he said. Sheila's eyes brightened with curiosity. "I was thinking about Les Frees, dying in that motel room. You know, I just couldn't figure out why he was spending the night in a motel in his own town. So after he died, I went there, to his motel room. I found this." Alex took Frees' cell phone from the table next to his hospital bed and held it up for Sheila.

"It shows all the phone numbers Frees had contact with on the day he died," Alex said. "Including all the calls to and from your cell phone."

"I don't know what to say," she said. Her expression showed that she was touched, that she thought this was Alex looking out for her again.

"I figured it was better for you to have it than for the police to find it. Though I'm surprised that you left it in the motel room—I mean, I assume it was you."

She nodded her head uncertainly.

"Just for me, just so I know, was it really an overdose?"

She sighed, then came back to his side and squeezed his hand. "He was going to hurt you, Alex. He figured out who you were and that you could identify him as Beto's killer. I knew he was diabetic, and I had him get a motel room where we could talk and no one would spy on us. I put something in his drink and then injected him. I had to stop him."

"That's what I figured."

She shook her head as if trying to banish the memory. "It's so ugly, Alex. How long have you known?"

"Since the night Crash came to your apartment. I looked at the phone when I was in the stairwell, and I recognized your phone number in Frees' call log. I figured the only way it made sense for a grease monkey like Frees to be calling you was if you and Frees were the ones who killed Beto. And the only reason to kill Beto was if Beto really did have evidence of who caused the van to explode. Tell me, Beto's little slip of paper with the instructions to Jorge Ramirez, the paper I tried to buy from him—it had your handwriting on it, didn't it?"

"Let's not speak about it." She squeezed his hand harder. "Let's never speak about it."

"I'd rather not," he said with a little half smile. "But before I limp off into the sunset with you, I want to know why you did it. The van, I mean."

"Oh, Alex, it doesn't matter anymore. And, anyway, it was Frees who actually planted the explosives in the van."

"But Frees didn't have the brains to invent a scheme like this. No, the only reason I can see for you to blow up the van and the five employees in it is the same reason your lawyer figured out in Luke's deposition—the eighteen million dollar bonus, which you and Luke would have kissed goodbye without the life insurance proceeds from the accident." Alex noticed his voice rising. He quelled his anger. He wasn't finished. "You needed Luke to earn that bonus so that you could take your share when you divorced."

Her eyes were filling with tears. "Why are you doing this? Stop this."

"I just need to know two more things, and then that's it."

"OK," she said. She took a deep breath as if preparing to dive underwater.

"Two little things. First, I need to know there aren't any other loose ends out there."

"Loose ends?"

"Like Frees, or Beto. I don't want us to be looking over our shoulders the rest of our lives. Is there anyone else who was involved in the accident?"

"No," she said, shaking her head emphatically. "Jorge Ramirez was the only other one, and he's gone, of course, which was always the plan."

"OK," Alex said. "So that gets to the second thing, and after this, we'll never discuss it again." Sheila looked at Alex with a mix of hope and fear. The answer to Alex's first question was enough, legally speaking, and in later years Alex often thought that what he next said to her, and let her say in response, was the most vindictive thing he ever did. Alex gazed into Sheila's eyes with the most soulful, entreating look he could muster. "Sheila, can you be happy with me now that Luke's money is gone?"

"Yes." She responded without hesitation.

"Even though I'm the one who lost it for you."

"Yes, Alex, I don't care."

"Really? Don't just think about today, how will you feel years from now? After all"—Alex lowered his voice—"you were willing to kill for money."

"I didn't kill Jorge and the others. Frees did that."

"And now the money's gone. All gone. And take a look at me, Sheila, I'm not the guy who can get that back for you."

"Oh, Alex, I only did all that because I was focused on Luke, on getting everything I deserved for all the years of his crap that I put up with. But now I don't care about Luke. I don't care if he's rich or poor, or dead or alive." She leaned toward him and stroked his hair. "I care about you. I'm ready to start over with you." Tears rolled off her cheeks onto the sheet of Alex's bed. She gave a little hopeful smile. "So those were your two things?"

"I just thought of another."

She stood. "Alex, please. This is killing me."

"When I met with Beto in the park, I almost died too. You sent me to meet Beto knowing that Frees was going to plant a bomb. You sent me into a trap."

Sheila's face became sad and tired and pained. "Oh Alex, I hoped you would make it. I hoped and hoped." She grasped Alex's wrist. "And I called you, remember? I called you right after I called Frees, to tell you to leave, to save you, and that was before I even loved you. Now the thought of us being apart is—it's unbearable, Alex."

Three men entered the hospital room—a middle-aged detective in a sport coat followed by two uniformed police officers. The detective said, "Sheila Hubbard, you're under arrest for murder."

"What?"

"Ma'am, do not resist."

"Alex, stop them. Do something, Alex." She looked pleadingly at Alex as one of the officers cuffed her wrists. Then her expression changed. "You lied to me!" she yelled.

"I told you the truth," Alex yelled back. "I told you I'd solve this case. I told you."

"But you love me!"

"Some things matter more," Alex said, softly but firmly. She snapped her gaze away from him—cold once more, cold now forever—and let the two officers lead her from the room. Alex let his head drop to his chest. The detective stepped over to Alex's bed and removed the small microphone that was taped to his chest underneath the hospital gown. Before leaving, the detective squeezed Alex's shoulder. "Feel better," he said.

56

Brad Pitcher sat in the late afternoon haze on a plastic bench covered with graffiti, resting his forearms on his knees as he tried to concentrate on a newspaper.

Sheila was in jail and would certainly never pay the rest of his bill. And the bus was late again—that mattered because Brad had sold the BMW for cash to keep his practice going.

All the newspapers portrayed him as the foolish lawyer who got bamboozled by a murderer. "No comment" was his stock response whenever the reporters called. They were about the only ones who called his office these days. With business at a lull, Brad spent most of his time tending to his disciplinary proceedings with the bar association. It was all too painful to think about. He wondered whether he should just screw it all and move to Hawaii to become a beach bum. *Nah*, he thought, *I'd be bored after an hour.*

Brad heard the steady clap of high heels on the sidewalk nearby. He looked up and saw Cindy approaching. She looked lovely. He sat up straight and smiled at her, hoping they might ride the bus together, but she ignored him as she walked by.

Brad craned his neck to watch her as she walked away. The scent of her perfume followed her, and she looked like she had put on makeup before leaving the office. Then he put it all together: she had a date.

* * *

Alex looked around the living room of his vacant house. Not only had it been cleaned of the mess that Del left, Alex had given it a fresh coat of paint. It looked great in the morning light. Great for a little family. Alex locked the front door and limped to his truck. His leg was feeling better each week.

This house was paid off now. A few weeks before, Alex wouldn't have believed that was possible, but a local television station paid him a handsome sum for exclusive rights to his story. After Sheila's arrest, the public became fascinated by the story of how she orchestrated the car crash, set up her husband to take the blame, and killed Beto and Les Frees to cover her tracks.

The TV station's fee enabled Alex to pay off the mortgage—and just in time to save the house from foreclosure. Alex looked at the little house one last time before stepping into the truck. *One down, four to go*, he thought. He got in the truck and started driving.

Sheila took a plea bargain. With her hospital room confession on tape, she didn't have much choice. She got thirty years—but no needle, so in that way she got off easier than Beto or the unlamentable Les Frees. Alex was happy he wouldn't have to testify against her. He knew he'd be even happier when he didn't think about her anymore.

He'd been thinking a lot about Del. First, wondering where he'd been. Then, after receiving a letter from him, wondering how to respond. Alex had been carrying around a nearly finished letter to Del for days now.

Del was in Alaska, on a fishing boat. "Didn't you know bookies get seasick?" was how Del explained the move. Alex was happy for Del, happy that he'd left L.A. It was such a dramatic change for Del that Alex had trouble believing at first believing the letter was genuine, until he got to the letter's postscript, which showed his brother's quirky humor: "These fishermen can't play cards worth a damn—kidding." The second postscript had another surprise: "I forgive you." Del had the courtesy not to say for what. Reading that, Alex felt ashamed. Alex had never really admitted to himself how he'd done wrong by Del. Maybe Alex could forgive Del, too; Alex couldn't get shown up by his younger brother. Besides, forgiving Del was a lot easier now that Del was two thousand miles away.

Luke Hubbard, of all people, also showed a surprising capacity for forgiveness—or more likely for expedience. He had called Alex out of the blue a few days earlier to ask Alex, of all things, whether he wanted a job at Liberty as head of security. "Why me?" Alex asked. "Because Crash is in prison, and I've seen how effective you are in action," Luke said. "Besides, we have something in common—we were both fooled by Sheila." The number Luke threw out was more than triple Alex's salary at Rampart; "plus stock options," Luke emphasized. Good pay, responsibility, a company whose environmental mission Alex admired—the job had everything he could have wanted. Plus, it turned out Luke wasn't the quite devil that Alex initially thought he was.

Luke had been humbled, if only slightly. He was still CEO of Liberty Industries, but the board of directors had taken away his title as chairman of the board and given it to another director to provide more oversight. After Sheila's guilty plea, when it was clear that Luke wasn't responsible for the car crash, Luke's lawyers at Boswell & Baker got the lawsuit by Roberta Cummings dismissed. A bright note for Luke, but not for Roberta Cummings, because it meant she lost her last hope to stop the foreclosure of her home.

But it turns out that wasn't so bad.

Alex parked his truck in front of Roberta Cummings' house. The door was open, and inside Alex could see a living room filled with moving boxes and Mrs. Cummings taping one of them shut.

"Knock, knock," Alex said.

Mrs. Cummings came to him and greeted him with a smile. "We're just about ready here," she said.

Alex pulled the keys to the vacant house from his pocket and gave them to her. "Now you're completely ready," he said. Her eyes started to tear up, and Alex let her hug him.

"I don't know how to thank you, Alex," she said.

"Don't thank me. Just make sure that kid of yours mows the lawn when he gets older."

She looked at her young son, busy in the house playing among the boxes like they were a fort. "We'll see about that," she said.

"I'm not great with goodbyes, so . . ." Alex turned to leave.

"Alex, before you go: I want you to know I'm sorry I slapped you that time."

Alex laughed. He'd almost forgotten about that. In a moment he recalled all that had followed from Mrs. Cummings' confronting him. "I'm glad you did it," Alex said. Alex smiled, then turned again and walked toward the street.

"I hope you don't go back to Rampart," she called out. "I don't like those guys."

Me either, Alex thought.

A few months ago, Alex would have accepted Luke's job offer in a heartbeat. On balance, Alex figured, Luke probably did more good for the world than bad. But Alex had seen what happened to those who were close to Luke and had decided that Luke was the kind of big man who makes the people around him smaller. Luke sounded quite surprised when Alex responded that he didn't need to sleep on Luke's offer and that the answer was no.

Alex drove home, parked the truck on the next block and snuck into his own house through the back—the money from the TV station hadn't covered all his bills. The house felt empty. Alex pulled the unfinished letter to Del from his pocket and without hesitation wrote the postscript he'd been searching for: "Anytime you're in L.A., you're welcome to crash at my place." He sealed the letter in an envelope and put on a postage stamp. He left the house and walked toward the post office.

It was a warm spring day, and the coastal haze was just starting to burn off. Alex took out his cell phone and dialed Zeke's number.

"Zeke, it's Alex."

"Can't talk now, Alex. Too busy."

"Yeah? You sound pretty wound up. How many cigarettes have you smoked this morning?"

"Too many. Oh boy, I thought this private journalism thing would be simple—no way. I've had to rent office space, plan a marketing campaign, buy accounting software—like I know anything about accounting. Ooh—I got these totally great spy toys. Mini cameras, microphones . . . They just keep making 'em smaller. Best part—the website goes live next week. I'm just hoping I don't die from a nicotine overdose before then. You have no idea how much work goes into starting a business."

"I probably don't," Alex said with a smile. "Are you still looking for a partner?"

***

ACKNOWLEDGEMENTS

I thank the many people who helped in the completion of this book. Independent editor John Paine's advice was always apt and practical. My father, Alex Neymark and Joe Weber encouraged me, read multiple drafts and provided thoughtful comments that showed me both flaws and opportunities I would otherwise have missed. The time they spent reading and discussing the story illustrates generosity and friendship. Rebekah Webb gave valuable advice on publishing and other matters. Also essential to this effort was the support of my family, most of all my wife, who read more drafts, indulged more undirected brainstorming and endured more hours alone as part of this project than anyone could who was not motivated by love.

ABOUT THE AUTHOR

Dan Webb lives in California with his family and an aging but energetic Labrador retriever. This is his first book. His website address is www.danwebbsite.com.

www.ingramcontent.com/pod-product-compliance
Lightning Source LLC
Chambersburg PA
CBHW070210260626
47160CB00002B/507